INTO THE RAIN

Suzanne Cass

S C
STORM CLOUD
PRESS

Into the Rain

Storm Cloud Press, Perth Australia

Copyright © 2023 by Suzanne Cass

Edits by Evermore Editing

Cover by Vikncharlie

All rights reserved.

To all the daughters of narcissistic mother's.
Remember, you are good enough.

CHAPTER ONE

Lacey let out a frustrated grunt. "Stupid freaking thing. Why can't you have the engine in the front like every other car?" She straightened from where she'd been peering into the rear of her VW van and let out a yelp of pain as she banged her head on the hatch. "Ow." She kicked out at the left tire in frustration, nearly dropping her phone in the process. "Stupid freaking thing," she repeated, yelling now. But there was no one around to hear; this little town in the middle of nowhere was completely deserted.

Flicking off the flashlight app on her phone, she went to stand at the front of her van and take in some deep, calming breaths. Losing her temper would get her nowhere. Pulling her jacket tight around herself, she let the cold breeze wash over her face, cooling her anger. The wind whipped her long blonde hair around her face and she swiped at it angrily. Capturing a handful, she tried to hold on to her wayward locks.

Perhaps she should've paid more attention when Matt was lecturing her about the dos and don'ts of VW maintenance. But she'd been so pleased with her purchase of the remodeled Kombi camper van that she'd been too busy running her adoring gaze over the sleek lines and lovely caramel interior color scheme to listen properly as her older brother talked about air-cooled engines and other uninteresting finer points of what went wrong with these cars.

It'd been a spur-of-the-moment decision. She'd seen the Kombi advertised on a flyer stuck to a lamp pole as she'd been walking down the street near her family home in Melbourne and instantly fallen in love with it. Fallen in love with the idea of the freedom and chance to escape that the van offered. And she'd so desperately needed to get away it'd seemed like the perfect solution at the time. The man who'd sold her the van told her he called her Dotti, and Lacey liked the name so much she kept it. She'd never named a car before, but this cute van with its quirky character and air of joie de vivre seemed to need a name. So it stuck. And it seemed silly not to, as the van even came with a personalized number plate that read DOTTI33.

She sighed and leaned her butt against the front bumper. Poor Dotti; she shouldn't really blame the car. It was her own fault that she was stuck here. If she'd only stopped in Wynyard for the night instead of deciding to push through after dark, she wouldn't be in this predicament. Her destination was supposed to be a small town called Stanley, another forty minutes up the road. She had a powered site booked at the Stanley Tourist Park, but she'd become sidetracked in this cute-as-a-button town called Penguin back down the road and had lost all track of time. There'd been a giant statue of a penguin, and more penguins painted on the side of the garbage bins, as well as wall-art featuring penguins everywhere. Then she'd just had to duck into the Penguin Café to warm up with a coffee and some hot chips slathered with tomato sauce.

Lacey lifted her head and stared out at the night-dark beach. A lone Norfolk Island Pine formed a tall, dark shadow against the inky-blue ocean, its scarecrow branches reaching for the sky, the scene lit by a half-moon rising behind her.

It looked like Boat Harbour Beach might be a gorgeous little bay in summer. Mimicking a wineglass in shape, it'd be protected from the booming waves and howling wind by the headland jutting out into the ocean. But right now, it was cold, deserted, and a tad spooky. Everyone who lived in this small community would most likely be tucked safely in their warm beds. A twinkle of lights stretched out around the bay like a line of fireflies. For a brief second, Lacey wished so hard that she could be one of those people, secure in the knowledge that they were safe in their homes; that they knew where they belonged and had a life mapped out ahead of them. While she was stuck here in this cold, damp parking lot, trying to fix her car. Trying to figure out where she was headed next. Trying to put her life back together.

Her van had started to make coughing noises a few miles up the road. Then it'd started doing funny little stuttering bunny hops, losing power for a few seconds then surging forward again. Lacey had decided to take the turn into Boat Harbour Beach, because it was better than breaking down in the middle of the deserted highway. She'd nursed her van past the small township and into the parking lot at the end of the road, where her Kombi had finally died with a dramatic, loud splutter. A street light cast a weak glow over what looked to be a café at the other end of the lot, but it was all closed up for the night, and there were no other shops or even houses down here.

Lacey stared out at the waters of Bass Strait back toward the mainland. Technically, Tasmania was situated in the Indian Ocean, but as Lacey was learning, the locals were an unconventional bunch and loved to highlight their differences from the mainland. Depending on which local you talked to, she could also be looking at the Southern Ocean, or the Tasman Sea; it was all a bit fluid where these oceans were concerned. One thing she knew for a fact, at the other end of the island there was nothing between them and Antarctica, except a lot of wild, deep ocean and some equally wild weather.

What had she been thinking? Traveling around Tasmania in the middle of winter. She was beginning to regret her decision to keep going, even as the temperature had dropped. The past few months had been spent exploring the area around Hobart and along the wild and isolated east coast. But winter had set in hard down there. Lacey had thought perhaps driving to the northern end of the island might save her from freezing to death, but that didn't seem to be the case. The alternative—heading home to Melbourne where her mother was just waiting to say *I told you so*—held even less allure, however.

Even her sheepskin-lined jacket was no match for the cold sea breeze, which was working its way in through the crevices, down her neck, and up her wrists where the sleeves gaped a little. Shivering, she returned to the back of her van and turned on her flashlight again. One last attempt to figure out what was wrong with her vehicle. Otherwise, she'd be spending the night in this lonely little parking lot, even though the signs screamed, NO CAMPING - FINES IMPOSED, she'd have little choice in the matter. At least she'd have a warm bed to snuggle up in, and she could boil the kettle on her little gas cooker to make a cup of tea. There was a cupboard full of instant noodles which would have to do for dinner.

Peering into the engine bay, she poked at a rubber hose. Was it supposed to hang like that? Maybe it was loose. Maybe she should—

A noise alerted her to a human presence standing right behind her, even before a large hand grabbed her by the shoulder.

"Hey, do you—"

She didn't wait for him to finish speaking—part of her had registered the deep, male voice and knew she was in danger —she reacted with lightning speed, her muscles remembering the defensive maneuver even before her mind could fully comprehend what was happening.

Half turning toward the shadowy figure behind her, she covered the hand that was on her shoulder with one of her own, grabbed a handful of his collar with the other, shoved her shoulder into his chest, bent her knees, swept her foot backward to knock his feet out from under him, and proceeded to execute a perfect single arm shoulder throw.

The man landed on the gravelly ground with a loud grunt of surprise. But she didn't wait for her assailant to get up. As he rolled onto his side, she put a boot into his ribs and another in his face. This time he howled with pain and rage. The only way to stop an attacker bigger and stronger than yourself was to take them down hard. Give them no chance to fight back. She might be petite and look like easy prey to this asshole, but he was about to find out he'd chosen the wrong target.

She moved in closer to aim another kick to his head. Just as she raised her foot, his hand shot out and grabbed her by the ankle and she nearly lost her balance, resorting to hopping on one foot to stay upright.

"Hey," he shouted. "Stop it. I was only trying to help."

"Yeah, sure you were," she yelled but a tiny flicker of doubt crept up her spine. She couldn't see much in the dark; all she knew was he was big, tall and muscled. If he were to get the better of her now, she wouldn't stand a chance. She couldn't let him talk her out of this. Disable the criminal first, ask questions later, that was the way it had to be.

"If you'll just stop attacking me for two seconds, I can explain."

Not likely, she thought, then dropped both knees onto the man's side, hearing the satisfying sound of the air whooshing out of his lungs.

"Right, that's it," the man growled, and suddenly she found herself flat on her back in the dirt.

Oh, shit.

She struggled, trying to lift her knee to smack it into his balls, but he was too heavy. Lifting a hand, she went to scratch at his eyes, but with another grunt, he pinned her wrist to the ground.

"Stop, will you?" he commanded. "I don't want to hurt you."

What did he mean? Of course he wanted to hurt her. He was merely bluffing, to get her under control. Well, two could play at that game. "Get off me, then," she yelled, hoping to buy some time. "I won't hurt you anymore either," she lied.

"Look, lady, I was only trying to help." The man lifted his head and stared down at her, the moonlight shadows playing over the planes of his face. He never loosened his steely grip on her for one second, and she could feel every inch of his muscular body pressing down on top of her. "I'm a cop. I saw that you'd broken down, and I came over to lend a hand, that's all. So, if you'll stop trying to kill me, I'll let you up."

He was what? A cop? She didn't believe him. Not for a second. But... There was something niggling at the back of her mind that might disagree.

"Prove it," she said through gritted teeth. "Show me your badge."

"I'm off duty, I don't have it on me," he replied. "I live in Boat Harbour. I was out walking my dog, that's all."

Something inside her wavered. Was he telling the truth? If so, where was the supposed dog?

"Detective Sergeant Nico Favreau at your service," the man said, easing his grip but not wholly releasing her.

Ah-ha, his name confirmed she had heard a hint of a faint French accent even as he lay on top of her.

"I work for CIB down at Burnie station." As if making a decision, he lurched upward, and she found she was finally free. Scrambling to her feet, she backed away from his looming, dark figure.

Shit, it sounded like he was telling the truth. Double shit; had she just assaulted a cop?

Suddenly a furry, wet thing barreled into the man, jumping up to lick his face. "Get down, Smudge," the detective ordered the frisky dog. This must be the missing mutt. Clearly, the dog had been running in the surf down on the beach. Smudge then turned his attention on Lacey. She liked dogs but Smudge's salty fur was cold against her hands. "Get away, you're wet," the man growled at the dog again, and finally, the damp animal took the hint and stood a few feet away.

By the light of the dim streetlamp, Lacey watched as he lifted his hand to wipe his sleeve across his mouth; then he gingerly touched his nose. Now he was standing, she could make out darker patches on his face. Were they smears of blood? Was that because of her?

She thought back to her lightning-fast attack, rewinding her instinctive actions until she came to the part where she'd kicked him in the face.

Oh, God, had she broken a cop's nose?

"I'm sorry, I didn't know." She took a step toward him. "But you shouldn't accost a woman in the dark like that," she added with a tilt to her head. She had been in the right, she was sure of it. If in doubt, act first, ask questions later. A cop, of all people, should know that.

"Yeah, I'm sorry," he acknowledged. "It was a stupid thing to do." His words had a nasal quality to them and he pinched the bridge of his nose and grimaced.

"Let me take a look." It was the least she could do after she'd attacked him. She might have a handkerchief or something she could offer him in the van. She flicked on her flashlight and aimed it up at his face. He winced and shied away from the bright light. "Sorry," she apologized and dropped it away from his eyes. But it was too late, she'd already seen it. His face was a mess, blood flowing freely from his nose, more blood leaking from a cut above his eye. Fuck. She had caused that. But she couldn't be sorry for her gut reaction. What if he hadn't been a cop? What if he had intended to do her harm?

He swiped at the blood running down his face, most of it ending up on his sleeve. A couple of drops landed in the dirt at his feet, and she directed the flashlight down at the red splotches.

Blood—bright red and glistening.

"It's okay, I don't think it's broken. I just need to stop the bleeding," she heard him say, but she was no longer concentrating on his words, her gaze fixed on the spots of blood on the ground.

Her mind filled with images. Blood. So much blood. All over the linoleum floor. All over the woman's hands. All over the small child lying on the ground. But the woman wouldn't stop. Even when Lacey called to her. She kept plunging the knife into the girl's body, over and over. When Lacey finally reached the pair, it was too late. The girl was dead. Her blue eyes open and staring up at Lacey, pleading with her. Even as Lacey had disarmed the drug-crazed mother, and even as she'd screamed into her police radio for backup, for an ambulance, for someone to come and help her, she knew there was no help for this poor little girl.

Lacey stumbled back a step, a low groan emanating from her mouth as she covered it with her hand. This was the first time she'd seen fresh blood since that horrible incident nearly a year ago. She'd been able to keep those terrible images at bay. Mostly. Except sometimes deep in the night. But now, the sight of that blood had it rushing back. Had her world imploding once more.

She took another step backward but stumbled as her knees gave way, and she landed on her butt on the ground. The edges of her vision blurred, but even when she covered her eyes with her hands, the snapshot of the girl lying on the kitchen floor wouldn't leave her. Pools of red everywhere. The mother laughing maniacally, covered in her daughter's blood. Much later, Lacey had found out the little girl's name. Cindi. That name had become branded into her psyche.

Lacey covered her mouth to stifle a scream that threatened to break free. This was why she could never go back. This was why she could never fulfill her dream of becoming a police officer. She would never be able to overcome this weakness. Never get far enough away. Even running away to some isolated island deep in the Indian Ocean couldn't absolve her of this tragedy. Her mind was lost in a whirl of grisly images and regret. She was no longer in a parking lot somewhere along the deserted Tasmanian coastline; she was in that dingy little fibro house in Melbourne once more, trying to perform CPR on a child who was already dead.

A small part of her became aware that the man was kneeling in the dirt beside her. Keeping a wary distance this time, not touching her, but something about his voice—deep, calming, gentle, but insistent—broke through the miasma of grief and guilt. It brought her back to the present, and she discovered she was rocking back and forth where she sat, her hands clamped over her face. His dog peered around the side of his crouching form, dark eyes liquid and full of compassion. A pink tongue reached out and licked her face, the warm touch easing some of the dread inside her.

"Are you okay? What's the matter? Did I hurt you? Should

I call an ambulance?"

It was that last question that finally made her vocal cords unfreeze.

"No," she croaked. "I just… I need a minute, that's all."

She dragged in a few ragged breaths. Her deep breathing exercises from her yoga practice days coming back. She could do this. She'd done it before. Dragged herself back from the precipice.

She stopped rocking and drew her hands from her face, but she didn't trust herself to stand.

"Are you sure you're okay?" There was compassion and caring in his tone, which surprised Lacey. Most men who'd just had the shit kicked out of them by a woman wouldn't be this considerate of that same woman. It was the final clue that led her to believe his declaration that he was indeed a cop. He'd recovered quickly after a bout of physical violence. But he also had empathy for the perceived victim.

"I'm fine," she said, pouring more conviction than she felt into her words. She had to make him believe she was fine, that way she could get him to leave. All she wanted was to be left alone.

She went to stand, but instead, slipped on the gravelly ground.

He extended a hand to help her up.

She stared up at him.

He didn't move or blink, just waited for her to decide.

She took his hand. Long, strong fingers gripped hers, and she let him haul her to her feet. A jolt of…something shot up her arm. Of what? Awareness? It couldn't be attraction because she didn't even know exactly what this guy looked like. But it was something.

"Look, I'm really sorry I attacked you," she said brushing the gravel from her jeans. Steeling herself, she looked up into his face. She had to tip her head back a long way; he was quite a bit taller than her. Most of the blood was gone now. His nose had stopped dripping, and he'd wiped the rest away with the edge of his sleeve. There was an awkward silence, where he merely looked at her with that assessing gaze of his.

She wanted to admonish him again for sneaking up on her; he'd caused this whole sequence of events really, but she held her tongue. Instead, she said, "But I don't think there is anything you or I can do for my van tonight. I'll call a mechanic first thing in the morning." She straightened her sheepskin jacket around her shoulders and combed her long blonde hair out of her face. "I'll be fine to sleep here for the night, and you can be on your way, Detective." She spun on her heel, heading back to her van, already putting him out of her mind, looking forward to crawling into the rooftop bed and covering her head with the blankets to drown out the residue of the images still accosting the edges of her mind.

"I'm afraid I can't let you do that," the deep voice resonated from behind her.

"I beg your pardon?" She turned around to face him.

"There is a strict no camping rule here." He pointed to the sign.

"Yes, I saw that, but surely—"

"Sorry. If Bert from the council knew I'd let you stay here, he'd have my guts for garters. They're very rigorous with not letting people stay here." The detective dabbed at his nose with his sleeve as he spoke, watching her over the top of his forearm. "If we let one person camp here, then everyone will soon be descending in droves."

"Well, where am I supposed to go, *Detective*?" She couldn't keep the snark out of her voice now. This guy was being ridiculous. And way too self-righteous. And perhaps even a little patronizing. It was one thing to sneak up on a girl when she wasn't expecting it, but to be such a stickler for the rules when it was clear she had no other option just made him a pompous ass.

"I have a property up the road. You can park your van in my backyard if you like."

She stared at him, her mouth hanging slightly open. This guy couldn't be for real. "I'm not staying at your place," she said, sounding each word out succinctly. "I will be fine right here for the night."

"Have it your way." The detective shrugged. "But Bert checks this parking lot every morning, first thing. He'll slap you with a steep fine and order your van be towed when he finds you here."

"Wow, this Bert sounds like a real dick," Lacey muttered.

"No, he's a good man, really. He has the community's best interest at heart. He's just a little overzealous, shall we say."

Lacey stared at the tall man in front of her, then let her gaze drift to her van. She really didn't want to have it towed away; then she'd be completely stuck with no transportation and nowhere to stay. But she didn't know this man from a bar of soap. Just because he said he was a detective, that didn't mean he was a good guy either. She studied him for a few seconds. She was no perfect judge of character, but he didn't strike her as the type to sleaze onto a woman. He'd kept a decent distance from her so that she never felt intimidated or pressured. He came across as solid and dependable. And he was bearing the injuries she'd inflicted on him with a stoicism that told her he didn't hold a grudge against her for landing him in the dirt.

"So, I can park my van in your backyard and sleep in it there. Is that what you're saying?"

"Exactly. All I'm offering is a place to park your vehicle for the night. That's all. You won't get a better offer this late on a Sunday night." Almost as if he could read the thoughts going on behind her eyes, he raised his hands in supplication. "I'll show you my badge when we get back to my house," he offered.

"Fine," she replied irritably. "But I'm not even sure Dotti will start, let alone make it to your house," she grumbled. "My name is Lacey, by the way," she added.

"I'll walk up the road, you can follow me," he said, and she was again surprised at how he seemed to know instinctively she wouldn't appreciate him getting into her van next to her.

To her astonishment, Dotti started after a few attempts and wheezed and coughed her way up the hill behind Detective Sergeant Favreau and his faithful dog as he led the way toward his house. What was she getting herself into now, she wondered as she followed his figure, lit by the beam of her headlights, up the road?

CHAPTER TWO

Nico stared out his kitchen window and considered the Kombi van parked next to his large tin shed. In the pale morning light, he couldn't tell if anyone was moving around in there. If the woman was up, there was no sign, and he decided that trying to stare a hole in the side of the van was doing no good.

He did wonder exactly what kind of problem he'd invited onto his property. The woman hadn't seemed all that…stable. One second she was throwing him like he was a sack of potatoes onto the ground, the next she was practically hysterical, as if she were having a mental breakdown. Then, just as quickly, she'd pulled herself together. This woman had depth. She wasn't just some easy target. Mercurial. Sharp-witted, but also unpredictable. And from what he'd made out of her in the dark shadows last night, she was also quite beautiful. Blonde hair down her back, caramel eyes, a slim figure in her hip-hugging jeans. She was intriguing, to say the least.

And Nico had always been drawn to intriguing. It was the main reason he'd become a detective.

Smudge pushed his wet nose into Nico's hand, as if he thought perhaps Nico had forgotten about him. Nico leaned down and patted the dog's head, smoothing his silky ears. Smudge had taken to Lacey straight away last night, and Nico always liked to think his dog was a good judge of character.

The weather had closed in during the night, and heavy clouds hung in the sky, everything muted by a fine, misting rain. Nico blew on his mug of coffee and shifted his gaze to the rest of his backyard. He had a couple of acres; it was the main reason he'd bought this property in Boat Harbour Beach. Living squashed into a small townhouse or villa in the center of town wasn't his style. It meant a half hour commute back into Burnie every day, but that was a small thing to bear to be able to live in this place.

Thinking of work, he needed to get going soon. But he didn't want to leave without talking to the woman in the van. Lacey, that was her name, he reminded himself. After her van had limped up his driveway and she'd parked it next to his shed, he'd made sure she had everything she needed for the night—handing her a key to the shed, so she could use the little bathroom he'd built into one corner, just in case he ever wanted to convert the shed to another living quarters—and then came inside to clean himself up.

This morning, the mirror had revealed a dark bruise spreading across his left eye, which had taken the brunt of her well-aimed boot. The cut that split midway through his eyebrow wasn't too bad, and he'd applied a bandage to keep it covered. Even though he tried to hide the evidence of his scuffle, he knew he'd still have some explaining to do when he got into work today. How was he going to tell his boss, Charles, that a mere slip of a woman had taken him by surprise and managed to incapacitate him in one fell swoop? It hadn't taken long for him to get the situation under control after that first little underestimation of the woman, despite that, he should never have let it happen in the first place.

After she'd begrudgingly accepted his offer of a place to stay for the night, she'd been determined that she was fine and she didn't need any more of his help.

But still…

He poured another mug of coffee and juggled the two mugs in one hand as he opened the back door. Smudge pushed past Nico's knees and jumped down the rear steps, happy to finally be allowed outside. Frigid air hit Nico as he took the steps and landed on the wet grass below. It was something you had to get used to living in Tasmania. The little island was the closest piece of land to Antarctica and winters were always bitterly cold down here. He was thankful for the woolen turtleneck he was wearing over dark corduroy pants and sturdy boots to keep most of the morning chill at bay.

Smudge was already whining at the door to the van as Nico crossed the grass, leaving dark footprints in the dew. Just before he reached the van, the door slid open, and Lacey emerged, wrapped in a wool blanket. Her hair was tousled from sleep and she gave a large yawn.

"Hey, Smudge," she said, crouching down to pat the dog, letting him lick her face in greeting. She giggled as the dog's tongue lapped over her chin, and then she hugged him close. It was the first hint he'd seen that there might be a more carefree version of Lacey hidden beneath her composed exterior. It was good to know she had a soft spot for animals. A person who didn't like animals wasn't to be trusted. At least not by Nico's reckoning.

"Morning," he said.

"Morning," she replied, a wariness entering her face as she stood and let the dog go.

"I brought you coffee. Not sure how you like it, so it's black, no sugar."

"Thank you. I usually like milk, but that will do," she

replied with a grimace. One hand snaked out from between the blankets to grasp the mug and she took a grateful sip. "Ah, nectar of the gods," she sighed.

He couldn't help but agree. "How did you sleep?"

"Actually, really well," she consented, almost as if she was surprised by her answer.

He wondered why the thought of getting a good night's sleep might be unexpected. Maybe whatever had haunted her last night when she'd become almost hysterical also haunted her in her sleep.

"Nice van," Nico said, deciding to change the subject, casting an appraising glance over her vehicle. It was a two-tone beige and white, pop-top Kombi van. It looked to be in good condition, on the outside, at least.

"Thank you," Lacey replied. "I bought it from a guy who restores Kombis. It's what he does for a living, and he poured his heart and soul into bringing Dotti back to life."

Silently, Nico decided that these restored vans didn't come cheap, but he had no idea of Lacey's financial situation and he wasn't about to start prying. "You call her Dotti?" he asked, peering into the interior, which was also done up in the same beige and white tones.

"Yes, she came with the name, but I like it," Lacey conceded. "It suits her. Would you like to take a look?" Lacey said at last, motioning for him to clamber inside. He had to duck down, there wasn't enough room for him to stand, and he took a seat on the small couch running the width of the van along the back. She followed him in, as did Smudge, who was never one to wait for an invitation. The van was tiny, but he could see how it might suit one person who wanted to live simply. Lacey shut the door to keep out the cold and sat next to him on the couch. The small space suddenly seemed minuscule, almost as if all the air had been sucked out, and he became hyper-aware of her, even wrapped in a thick blanket and sitting as far away from him as she could get. Which wasn't far in this tiny house on wheels. She grasped the mug in both hands to take a sip and he could see her fingers were delicate with short but sculpted nails.

"So, you sleep up there?" He asked the first thing that came to mind just to break the awkward silence, tilting his chin upward.

"Yes, the roof pops up and then I lay out a couple of inserts and roll out a mattress to form a space to sleep. It's quite cosy, really."

"Nice."

"Yeah. And there's a table that folds out from beside the cupboard." She leaned forward and with a quick flick of her wrist, she pulled on a bit of timber, opening out a set of legs that dropped from beneath it, and voilà, a perfect little table to set his mug down on. He watched her surreptitiously as she set up the workspace. The tip of her tongue came out from between luscious lips, working from side to side as she maneuvered the piece of board. He wondered if she was even aware of the action. It may be a subconscious thing for her to do, but it was driving him a little crazy, watching that pink tip move excruciatingly slowly across her bottom lip. Then she was suddenly staring at him, and he realized she was waiting for a response.

"Nice," he said again, for want of a better word. "How long have you been living in...Dotti?" He nearly stumbled over the name. A vehicle was there for one purpose only, to get you from A to B. They were inanimate objects and didn't deserve a name. But each to their own. At least Lacey seemed to have lost some of that initial wariness now she was talking about her Kombi. And that was always good; getting someone to let their guard down was a trick of his.

"Nearly six months now," she replied, settling back into the couch.

"Wow." He was impressed. "That's quite a while to be cooped up in this tiny space. You must enjoy it then?" He turned to face her, and she fixed pale amber eyes on him. Or were they more hazel? Her eyes were just as compelling as the rest of her.

With the table now up, the space felt even smaller and more confined. Smudge curled up on the floor with a sigh, brown-eyed gaze flitting from him to Lacey and back again. The dog didn't seem to be perturbed by the close quarters. So it was just him, then?

Normally, he wasn't affected by a woman's presence. He'd learned to govern his body's reaction. Watch and observe; that was part of his job. But it was also part of his nature. The need to discern a person's character, figure out their goals and motivations, what drove them to make the everyday decisions they did. Because some of those seeming everyday decisions people made, ended up in murder.

But Lacey threw his usual composure into turmoil. He couldn't seem to gauge her as easily as he did most people. Which was unnerving. Perhaps he needed to put some distance between them. Yes, that was it. He wasn't used to being in such close proximity.

"It's called Van Life. Haven't you heard of it? People live simply and freely, on the road," Lacey said.

"What?" He'd lost track of their conversation, and had to mentally pull himself back to the present. "Van life? Yes, I've heard of it." Should he also admit that the idea of living on the road didn't entice him? That he didn't have time to think about frivolous things like taking time off to travel around on a whim.

But she saved him from having to answer by saying, "You don't look like one of those everyday cops on the beat." Those caramel eyes fixed on him again with a shrewdness that hadn't been there before.

She was most likely referring to his hair, which was anything but regulation length. He'd let it grow so that it curled over his ears and touched his shoulders at the back. "I'm a plainclothes homicide detective. We don't need to conform to any particular dress code," he said lightly.

She merely narrowed her eyes at him.

"And what about that scar on your face? Where did you get that?"

He resisted the urge to touch the scar that traveled the length of his cheek. She certainly had no problem diving right in and asking the hard questions. Some of his teammates at work still hadn't worked up the courage to ask him where that scar came from. Or perhaps it was merely a lack of interest. Whatever it was, most people had more manners than to ask that question straight off the bat. Not that he minded her directness. Not one bit. He also didn't mind the scar; he thought it gave him more of a rakish, dangerous edge. Time had healed and faded it until it was now more of a deep crease in his cheek. When he smiled, it could almost be mistaken for a large dimple.

"I was attacked by a dog when I was seven. It didn't bite me, but it pawed at my face, and its sharp claws left a gaping wound." He gave the unvarnished truth, watching her face for a reaction.

She grimaced slightly, and then said, "A nasty thing to happen as a kid, but I'm glad it didn't scare you off dogs for good." She glanced down and patted her knee, and Smudge leaped to his feet and came over to lick her hand, his black body swaying with the rhythmic thumping of his tail.

"Me, too," he agreed. Smudge was one of a few dogs he owned over his lifetime. "He just appeared at the front entrance to the Burnie Police Station five years ago and kept letting himself into reception every time someone opened the front door," Nico told her. "I was the last to leave that night, and the dog was still sitting patiently at the front door. So, I took him to the vet to see if he was microchipped—which he wasn't. The vet thought the dog might've been around three years old, and no amount of searching unearthed his owner. So..." Nico shrugged. He'd been more than happy to adopt the border collie cross, and then when he'd bought this property a few years ago, Smudge had been ecstatic with all the extra space.

But enough of talking about himself. If they were asking questions, he had quite a few of his own.

"Where did you learn to throw a man twice your size over your shoulder like that?" He leaned back and cupped the mug between his palms, stating the question as if it had no real import. But it did. She was very good at defending herself, and he wondered where she'd learned how to do that. And more importantly, why.

"I practice judo. I'm a black belt."

"Right." That was the factual answer to the question, but not the one he was looking for. "You're very good at it," he added, fishing for something more. Because he knew there was more than one level of black belt in judo, and he wanted to know where she fell in that ranking; it'd give him a better idea of exactly who he was dealing with.

"I should be, I've been doing it since I was ten years old," she told him, not falling for his ploy.

"Right," he said again. But at least they were getting somewhere now, because she was talking to him, opening up, even if just a little. He had been thinking that she might've taken the fighting technique up as a form of protection after some kind of event or catalyst. Some women who'd been involved in an assault took up a form of martial arts to help them with empowerment; a way to gain back some of their shattered self-esteem. But if she'd been practicing since she was little, then that wasn't her reason. But something was bothering her. He'd seen enough people who'd either witnessed or been involved in terrible trauma. They had a look to them, as if they'd collapsed under the weight of the terrible pain they were carrying and could never quite build themselves up again to become a normal, functioning human. Lacey had that aura about her. She had some kind of deep, dark secret she was harboring.

Before he could phrase another question, Smudge gave a quiet whine, wanting out of the van, reminding Nico he needed to get to work.

He stood and reached for the door handle, nearly banging his head on the low ceiling. "Sorry, I should get going. I just wanted to make sure you had everything you need." Stepping down out of the van, he drew in a deep breath of misty air. "You're welcome to stay as long as you want," he added.

"Thank you." She'd edged along the couch, pulling the blanket in closer around her as the cold air rushed in. "I'll give that mechanic you recommended last night a call, and hopefully he can diagnose Dotti's problem. I'd really like to get moving today, or tomorrow, at the latest."

"Yeah, Dave's a good bloke. If you mention my name he won't have a problem making a house call." Silently, Nico thought Lacey might be in for a longer stay in Boat Harbour than she planned. If this old van needed a spare part to get her going again the wait to get it shipped over from the mainland could be up to a week, or even more. This wasn't some large capital city, where you could just click your fingers and the parts were already in stock and mechanics were a dime a dozen. Dave would be doing Nico a favor by coming to look at the van. Nico knew he always had his schedule full and was often booked up weeks in advance. Being the only reliable mechanic in this little neck of the woods made him a valuable man to know. Burnie was the closest big town with a few resident mechanics, but Nico doubted any of them would make a mobile visit out here their priority.

"Right, then," he said when Lacey didn't answer straight away. "I normally leave Smudge tied up at his kennel during the day. But if you want to let him off and take him for a walk, that's fine. Just keep an eye on him, he has a tendency to wander off," he warned, already turning back toward the house, whistling up Smudge who'd gone to investigate a nearby tree where he was busily leaving his calling card.

"Oh, ah, Nico?" There was something in her voice that pulled him up short. A hesitancy that hadn't been there before.

He turned back and found her staring at him, as if weighing him up. "I should probably tell you something, in case you decide to look me up when you get to work. Because I know you will. It's what I'd do if I'd invited a strange woman to stay on my property."

Ah-ha. He knew it. There was something in Lacey's past she'd been deliberately keeping from him. He waited as she opened her mouth, then closed it again, as if she had trouble finding the words. Or finding the strength to voice those words.

Finally, she blurted, "I'm also a police officer. I'm a constable in the Victoria Police Force."

He rocked back on his heels. That'd been the last thing he'd been expecting to hear. He wasn't one to be surprised often, but this was indeed a shock.

"I'm on…unpaid leave. Which is why I'm traveling around Tasmania," she continued.

"Okay," he drawled. "Thanks for filling me in." And she was right; he had been going to run a quick background check on her when he got to work. No detective worth their salt would've done any different.

That answered a whole lot of things about her ability to protect herself. She was a trained professional, albeit with a black belt in judo, but trained to take care of herself. The very next question that came to mind was why? Why was she taking protracted leave? Most of the reasons a cop took unpaid leave were usually something to do with their inability to handle the stress of the job—undiagnosed PTSD was a bigger problem in the force than anyone liked to admit —or they'd been forced to take leave because they were being investigated for misconduct. Which one of those did Lacey fall under?

She stared at him, a stubborn tilt to her chin. Clearly, Lacey wasn't going to share that tidbit of information. He could ring around a few of his friends who worked in the force on the mainland and see if he could find out. But for some reason, he didn't want to dig into Lacey's problems. He wanted her to trust him enough to tell him herself. He made an internal promise to himself that he wouldn't do a search on her. Not today, at least.

"Have a good day," he said. "I should be home around six tonight. If you're still here, you're welcome to have dinner with me."

"Thanks." She offered nothing further, so he walked back toward his house, aware of her gaze boring into his back as he went.

Intriguing didn't even begin to describe this woman he decided as he climbed the steps back into his kitchen.

CHAPTER THREE

Lacey bent her knees and threw the flat rock with precision across the water and into the rain. Standing straight, she watched the stone's progress. One, two, three, four. The stone hopped in four graceful arcs before it sank beneath the water. Lacey gave a little twirl and bent to pick up another pebble. She hadn't skipped stones since she was a child, but the discovery of all these perfectly flat little pebbles on the water's edge was too much of a temptation. The ocean was calm this evening, the pattering of raindrops on the surface the only sound. The soft drizzle had kept up most of the day, with no wind to speak of, making the little bay quiet and a tad bleak. Lacey had pulled up the hood on her sheepskin jacket to keep out most of the damp.

Smudge was watching her with some skepticism, gaze alternating from her face, out at the water, then back, as if wondering if she expected him to chase those little stones all the way out there. Because that would be madness; she could see it written in the dog's confused eyes. She patted Smudge's wet head and murmured words of endearment. He was such a sweet animal. So trusting and unfailingly happy. She'd forgotten what it was like to have an animal around. Maybe, when she got back to Melbourne, she'd get herself a puppy. Something to give her unconditional love when she came home from a long day at work. That might help to get her through the dark nights. Maybe.

She lobbed a stick down the beach and Smudge took off after it, happy to finally have something to chase that didn't end up disappearing beneath the waves. She could now see why Bert was a stickler for keeping campers out of the parking lot above this beach. It was a pristine little spot. There was only one other person on the small beach with her this late in the evening. An older lady, wrapped in a waterproof overcoat, had been doing laps up and down in the softer sand at the back of the curving beach, probably her daily exercise. But even she had disappeared a few minutes ago, as the evening drew closer.

The act of skipping a stone, something lighthearted that represented a free time from her childhood, helped to lift the heavy mood that'd settled on her shoulders. The news about her Kombi van hadn't been good.

Dave was a lovely bloke, and he'd seemed to know what he was talking about as he'd looked at Dotti. It didn't take him long to announce that she needed a new fuel pump. It'd become corroded, and he needed to order the spare part from the mainland, which would take days, perhaps up to a week. Even when she offered him more money—because money was no object to her—he'd replied affably that she could pay him triple if she liked, but it wouldn't make the ferry run any quicker, or the courier drive any faster. He placated her by saying that if he got the order in over the phone quickly, because it was only Monday morning, she might be lucky and get the part by Friday.

Lacey was disappointed. Not because she was in any real hurry to go anywhere, more because she didn't want to impose on Nico's hospitality any further. She liked being independent. And hated having to rely on anyone. Hated having to owe someone a debt. Because in her world, if you owed someone something, be it big or small, they always made you pay it back tenfold. Or worse, held the favor over your head until it became a dark cloak of guilt they could use to their advantage. Lacey's mother was the master manipulator when it came to using guilt as a weapon, and Lacey had learned very early on in her childhood that you never got anything for free in this world. There was always a price. At least there was with her mother. Lacey didn't like to tar other people with the same brush, but it was hard not to when she'd had to grow a solid shield around her heart just to protect herself.

She was sure Nico wasn't like that. He was probably just doing his duty as a dependable member of this small community, but she still hated to owe him anything.

So, as payment, she'd decided she would cook him dinner tonight. It wouldn't be anything gourmet, not by a long shot. She was fairly limited to what she could cook on her compact stove. But she'd become proficient in whipping up a tasty meal with hardly any ingredients. There wasn't even a supermarket in this little hamlet. She'd learned that the hard way when she'd gone in search of fresh ingredients and come across the small kiosk that stocked basics like milk and bread, but not much more.

After Dave had given her the unhappy news, Lacey had pulled up Nico's number he'd given her last night and asked if she could stay camping on his land for a few more days. When he'd replied it was no problem, she'd invited him to join her in her van for dinner. She had a little table and two chairs she could set up outside on the grass so they didn't have to eat squashed together like sardines on the couch in the van. They might be cold, but as long as the rain stopped, that was preferable to having to bear Nico's presence so up close and personal again.

She shivered as her body remembered the effect he'd had on her this morning. In hindsight, she should never have invited him inside her van. The only other person she'd allowed into her van and in such close proximity had been Matt, and he was her brother, so he didn't count. But she'd opened her mouth without thinking. Part of her had still felt a little ashamed for the black eye and bandaged brow he was sporting this morning and had wanted to make amends. But then he'd sat his large, imposing body on the couch, and she'd had to press in next to him, and that's when her heart rate had gone into overdrive. She also began noticing all the little things about him she shouldn't. How he smelled like lemongrass—his soap, perhaps. How his hair flopped over his forehead and he had to keep pushing it away, which inevitably drew her gaze to his prominent brows and then down to the scar on his cheek. She'd been mesmerized by that scar. It made him different. Not quite perfect. But she'd never been keen on perfect, so that was fine. And how his long legs seemed to fill the whole of the inside of her van as he stretched them out beneath her tiny table. It'd made her insides go to jelly whenever she'd glanced over to where he was sitting, looking all cool and charming.

Men had been off her radar since…since the incident. She'd been dating a guy right before, but it'd only been a casual thing, and he couldn't understand why she'd suddenly shut down, lost her appetite, and became weepy at just about everything and anything. Klaus couldn't handle her grief and shock and had hightailed if off to find the next bubbly, young girl on his Tinder profile, one who hadn't just suffered an enormous trauma.

Lacey picked up the stick and threw it again for Smudge, who'd come back looking for more things to chase.

It was funny, but Klaus hadn't crossed her mind in a long while. She'd carefully put away all thoughts of the time surrounding Cindi's death, as if that might somehow stop her from being overwhelmed by the images day in and day out.

It hadn't really worked, but then neither had anything else. Which was why she'd decided to take this trip, get herself away from all things familiar, so she could keep jolting her mind with new and different stimuli, trying to replace the bleak images with better ones.

For once, Lacey allowed her mind to drift back to that time just over a year ago. Before the incident. Back then, she'd thought that perhaps she'd finally found a way to have everything she'd always wanted. Had found a way to break free from her mother's controlling ways. Lacey had achieved something huge, not only by applying to join the police force, but surprising herself along with everyone else when she actually survived boot camp and became a fully-fledged new recruit. The fact that she was good at her job also was a bit of a wonder. She soon found she had a deep empathy for the often innocent victims of crime. More so than a lot of her male counterparts. And while she might not be the biggest, strongest, or fastest, able to bring down a fleeing felon with a lunging rugby tackle, she was good at the softer side of policing. Talking down a drug-hazed teenager from a rooftop ledge. Soothing lost or hurt children. Getting an abused wife to open up about her husband's mistreatment and talk them into filing charges to get the dirtbag off the street. Her initial reason for joining up—because it was the absolute last thing her mother would want or expect her to do—had morphed into something much more meaningful and important. She'd decided she could make a career out of policing. And with her judo skills, she could handle the physicality when required.

Until Cindi was murdered by her own mother. That called everything Lacey valued into question, and she couldn't go on as if nothing had changed. As if everything were still normal in her life.

And hadn't her mother crowed about that one. Rubbed it in that she'd always known Lacey wasn't cut out to be a cop. She didn't have the mental stamina and grit needed. She'd practically ordered Lacey to come back to the mansion in Toorak and give up these fleeting notions of being a policewoman, back to where she would be cared for properly and she could get well again.

One morning, a few months following the incident, her mother had delivered the same lecture about how she was too weak to survive on her own for the umpteenth time, and Lacey had stormed out of the house, determined to make a change in her life. Then she'd seen the flyer advertising the Kombi, and it was no wonder she'd jumped on it like a dying woman looking for water in the desert.

Smudge gave a sudden yelp of recognition and dashed up the beach, breaking Lacey from her introspection. "Smudge, come back," she yelled, but the dog was already dashing up the road toward home. Luckily, they were on a back road little hamlet with hardly any cars on the roads. Then she heard the low rumble of a motorcycle engine and knew it must be Nico returning home. Another thing to add to his list of cool traits. He rode a big, black road bike. She'd heard him leave on his way to work this morning, leaning out of her door to glimpse the black beast with the tall man on top as they roared off up the road.

Shit, he was home early. She jogged up the blacktop, following the route Smudge had taken. Thankfully, dinner was mostly prepared. All she had to do was boil the rice to go with her easy, four-ingredient chicken curry. They could nibble on some cheese and biscuits while they waited. It seemed as if the rain had finally drifted away, the clouds parting to reveal a cerulean sky. The ground was damp, but the air was clear.

Slowing as she came to the driveway, she tried to get her breath back under control. And rein in her mind at the same time. None of her erratic thoughts about Nico and his impact on her internal organs was going to show on her face tonight. This was strictly a meal to say thank you to a man who was helping her. End of story.

Nico appeared from around the side of the house, motorcycle helmet under one arm, Smudge gallivanting around his legs. As soon as he saw her, his face broke into a welcoming smile, and she felt her heart knock dangerously against her rib cage. It was just the aftereffects of the run up the hill, that was all. Nothing to do with the way his dark-blue eyes bored right into her, almost as if they could see down to her very soul.

"Evening," he called down to her.

"Sorry, I was just at the beach. But dinner is almost ready."

"Great. I bought us some white wine. I hope that's okay?" He held a bottle aloft to show her.

She gave him the thumbs-up as she climbed the last few feet up the driveway to where the ground leveled out and she could stand next to him.

"I'll get the rice on to boil," she said, noticing how his hair was tied back in a ponytail today. Must be to keep it neat while he was wearing the helmet. But instead of making him look more civilized, it made him seem more roguish. Or perhaps it was the black leather jacket that added to his bad-boy image. Or maybe the gray bruise spreading over the side of his face, reminding her of the battering she'd given him. Whatever it was, she had to glance away before he saw the hot flush spreading up her body at the sight of him. "Come on over when you're ready," she added, not looking at him.

"Will do," he replied as Smudge followed him up the steps to his house.

"Oh, and wear something warm, we'll be sitting outside,"

31

she called over her shoulder and then glanced up at the sky, willing the clouds to keep drifting over the horizon so they weren't forced to go inside her van.

Ten minutes later, Lacey had arranged the chairs and table on the grass to her liking and was just laying out a selection of cheese and crackers up on a small wooden board when Nico strolled over the grass, preceded by Smudge, who's clever nose smelled out the cheese straight away.

"Not for you," Nico said, and Smudge's ears dropped as he backed away from the table. Such a well-behaved dog. Her mother's dog would've snapped up all of that cheese before you could say Jack Rabbit. A spoiled toy poodle called Raymond that Lacey had tried to train but failed because the dog was too smart for its own good and knew her mother would let him get away with anything.

Nico dropped two soft, woolen throw rugs on one chair and placed two wine glasses on the table. "Are you sure you wouldn't rather eat inside?" he asked, raising one quizzical eyebrow. "I've got plenty of room in my kitchen."

Lacey regarded him for a moment. "Why don't we see how we go out here first? We can always move if it rains, or we get too cold. But I was hoping to watch the sunset over the water, and this looks like it might be the perfect vantage point."

Nico swiveled on his heel and glanced out to the vista stretching below them. His block was three-quarters of the way up a low hill and it afforded a lovely view over the ocean. She could see why he'd chosen this property. It had the best of everything. It was large, with a wonderfully restored cottage, plenty of room for a garden and an orchard, and views to die for. The Tasmanian coastline was one of the most wild, yet beautiful shorelines in the world. And while Boat Harbour Beach was a bit more touched by civilization than some places in Tasmania, it was still magical. Even in the dead of winter, this place had a grace and majesty. To her, a winter storm could be just as aesthetically pleasing as a warm summer's day, merely in a different way. If her life had turned out differently, she might even see herself living here.

"You're right, it should be a good sunset tonight." He pointed to the horizon, where the clouds were clearing and the orange orb of the sun could be seen peeking through the growing chinks as it sank lower, racing toward the edge of the world. "And I don't mind the cold. I was more worried about you."

"I'll be fine." She waved a hand in the air. The cold never really bothered Lacey, and while Melbourne might not get as cold as Tasmania, they certainly had their fair share of icy weather. Nico shrugged and twisted the top off the white wine, pouring them both a glass, while she went over and stirred the pot of boiling rice on her small stove. The chicken curry was warming on the burner next to it. The gas stove, along with a small countertop, was designed to slide out of a hidden compartment in the van, and became a handy outdoor kitchen. The van had been so well designed; the guy who did the restoration really knew what he was doing. It had everything a person could need to lead a simple life. There was even a pull out awning she could set up over the side of the van for shelter while she was cooking if it rained. But she was hoping they wouldn't need that tonight.

"Here you go." Nico was suddenly beside her, handing her a glass of wine. "Cheers." He held up his glass, and she clinked hers against his. "Here's to...pretty sunsets," he said, turning to nod at the pinking sky.

"Yes," she agreed. "And to speeding spare parts on their way," she added.

"I already said it's fine for you to stay as long as you need," he said, pursing his lips.

"Thank you." Yes, she understood he didn't mind her staying. But did he understand how uncomfortable it made her feel? She took a seat, trying to put the feeling of indebtedness out of her mind. Draping the soft blanket over her knees, she took a sip of the wine. A buttery chardonnay that was sharp and crisp. It'd go well with the blue cheese she'd put out on the platter. Reaching over, she cut herself a slice, then felt a guilty twinge as Smudge's eyes followed the cheese to her mouth. Nico also took a seat, placing his own blanket over the backrest.

"You must've gone to the cheese shop in Burnie on the way through." Nico made the comment as he leaned forward and cut himself a chunk from the vintage cheddar. He was right; she had stopped at more than one little gourmet shop on the way up the coast. She couldn't go past a good cheese.

"Is there such a thing as a cheesaholic? Because if there is, then I'm one," she told him, popping another bit in her mouth with a grin.

Nico laughed at that. It was a good sound, rich and deep. She liked that sound. "If you're a cheesaholic, then so am I." He raised his glass and they saluted to cheese.

They watched the sunset in companionable silence. The sun had finally dropped lower than the blanket of clouds and was turning the underside of the fluffy mantle a pale orange. Lacey slipped Smudge a piece of cheese when Nico wasn't watching, and the dog's warm tongue licked her fingers with glee. Nico turned to look at her, and she was struck again by the small bandage above his eye. What must his co-workers have made of that? They'd surely have said something. A police detective didn't turn up to work with bruising without expecting some ribbing. They'd want to know who got the better of him. She wondered if he'd told them the truth.

"How was work today?" She asked the question casually enough, not really expecting an answer. But her interest was suddenly piqued. She wanted to know what it was like to work in a small country town. It'd have to be different to the large precinct she'd worked in Melbourne. Was it better, or worse, working a smaller station? Where you knew everyone, and they knew you? There'd been anonymity back in her inner-city station at the Melbourne East Police Station. But there had also been a casual disregard for what she'd been through. A lack of empathy, especially from her male counterparts. As if she needed to toughen up and get over it. And maybe she did. But would her experience have been different if she knew everyone well? Would she have received better care? Treated with respect and perhaps compassion, rather than the toughen-up mentality she'd encountered? It wasn't a concept she'd ever bothered to explore before. Because there'd been no other option. But what if things were different here? Would she have found the strength to continue on and become the cop she wanted to be if she'd been stationed here instead of in the big city?

"Did they ask about your face?" she blurted, suddenly deciding it was important to know the answer.

CHAPTER FOUR

How was work today? Her question reverberated around his head. Work had been…interesting. He studied Lacey for a second before he said, "Yes, they asked about my face."

She had the grace to blush at his words, but she kept her chin held high. "And what did you tell them?"

The hardest part had been reporting first thing to his boss, Chief Inspector Charles Shadbolt. A part of Nico hadn't wanted to stride into his office that morning to tell him what'd transpired before his boss heard it through the grapevine. A voice was screaming at him to hide in the break room and hope no one saw him. Which may have worked for the first ten minutes, but Nico knew he'd be ratted out eventually, and so he'd taken it on himself to report immediately, before the rumors started flying.

Charles had merely raised one eyebrow and studied Nico over the rims of his glasses for many seconds as he told an abridged version of the story before finally saying, "I take it this woman is no threat to anyone else on the team or in the community?"

"No, sir." Nico liked the chief inspector; he always commanded his team with a cool head and a firm hand, as well as getting straight to the point.

"Right. Well, I'm a little unnerved you allowed her to take you by surprise like that, even if she does have a black belt in judo, but let's hope it doesn't happen again." Charles cleared his throat and went back to studying the piles of paperwork on his desk. That was Nico's signal to leave, but just as he turned on his heel to walk out, Charles said, "There's a meeting in the muster room at oh-nine-hundred. Everyone is expected to attend. The district commander will address us. Make sure you're there."

"Yes, sir." Now that was interesting news. It must be something big if the district commander was getting involved. Nico wracked his brains to come up with whatever was on the agenda for today. God forbid, they retrench more officers. He hoped it wasn't more bloody budget cuts. Staff were already stretched to the limit as it was.

On the way back to his desk, other officers had stopped him in the hallway and asked why he looked like he'd come off second best in a boxing tournament. Then right before he made the safety of his office, he'd bumped into Tyrell, the one guy he'd been hoping to avoid. Senior Constable Tyrell Jackson was a lanky African-American, in Burnie on sabbatical for two years. They got on well together and had become routine sparring partners at the local gym after work. So, for the rest of the morning, Nico had to put up with constant referrals from his mate that maybe he should wear a dress next time they sparred and perhaps he'd have more luck getting a punch in. Nico had scowled and tried to take the ribbing on the chin. But it rankled him no end that a slip of a woman had indeed got the better of him.

"Of course I told them the truth," he said to Lacey, a little more gruffly than he intended, and she smiled when he couldn't conceal his embarrassment.

"Sorry I put you in that position," she apologized, but she couldn't hide her grin completely. Then she sobered slightly.

"But I was also wondering if you told them… About me? I mean who I am…was?"

Now they were getting to the bottom of the issue. She wanted to know if he'd revealed her link to the force. He wondered why it mattered so much.

"No, I left that little tidbit of information off the table." Even though it might've vindicated him slightly, at least in the eyes of his boss if he'd known he'd been taken down by a trained police officer.

"Great. Thank you," she replied a little awkwardly, not giving anything else away. When the silence stretched just a little too long between them, she finally blurted, "What's it like working in a regional office?"

"What?" Her question caught him off guard. Damn, she had a habit of catching him off guard both mentally and physically. He needed to put a stop to that.

"Your job. Do you like it? Do you like working down here?" She waved an arm around to encompass his garden and then the ocean farther down the hill.

"Yes, I guess so," he replied. He'd moved down here six years ago to take up the job offer as a senior detective in a special operations branch CIB was setting up, because opportunities were sparse back in Canberra where he'd joined up. Detectives were a dime a dozen up there in the capital. He'd made detective sergeant two years ago, after solving a particularly tricky case. "Tasmania is probably the safest state to work in," he added thoughtfully. "Our crime rates here are much lower than in a major city like Sydney or Melbourne." She was watching him avidly, and so he went on. "The powers that be keep talking about boosting police numbers, especially in rural and remote areas, but you know as well as I do, a lot of that is merely hot air. They're more likely to cut numbers than to give us more manpower. It can be tough working in a smaller station. Longer hours, less resources, that sort of thing. There are also fewer cops who want to work remotely, which also puts the pressure on. Why? Are you thinking of getting out of the city?"

Lacey lifted one shoulder in a half shrug. "No. Yes. Maybe," was her enigmatic answer. "I'm not sure if I'll go back to Melbourne." Then as if she'd suddenly remembered her pot was still on the stove, she jumped up, sloshing wine over the rim of her glass and went to check her cooking. "Shit, I nearly boiled it dry," she said, throwing him a guilty glance over her shoulder.

So, was she thinking of perhaps getting a transfer? Nico watched her back as she moved between the small stove and the van. They could always do with more good police officers around here. But the question needed to be asked, was she actually a good police officer? With no information on her background, he couldn't decide. Being an officer of the law was a demanding career. Not everyone could do it. He loved his job. It was almost as if he'd been made for it in some regards. He'd always had an inquisitive nature. And that, along with his love of practicality and his stubborn refusal to give up until he had an answer to his problems, made him a good detective. Some parts of the job were harder than others, but he loved it when he finally got to solve a case, or discover that one vital missing clue that cracked a case wide open. It was often tedious work, with long, unfruitful hours spent behind a desk, but he did love it.

Lacey clambered into the van and began to pull out plates and cutlery, and Nico's mind wandered back to his time at work this morning; specifically, to the meeting he'd been requested to attend.

When he'd walked into the muster area that morning, an air of gravity cloaked the room as all the officers took their seats without comment. Even Tyrell had stopped ribbing him about boxing in a dress. Nico took a seat near the rear of the room, next to Tyrell and his sometime partner, First Class Constable Sally-Ann Smith, as the room quickly filled. Even though this was considered a regional station, they still had over twenty registered police officers, and that didn't include their civilian staff who helped with the admin, or specialist consultancies like forensics.

Charles stood up on the low stage at the front regarding them all silently over the rims of his glasses. Beside him stood the western district commander Penelope Tander, looking very prim and proper in her full dress uniform, blonde hair pulled into a severe bun, her shoulders back, watching them all from beneath the brim of her dark-blue, ceremonial peaked cap.

"Good morning." The commander addressed the room once there was complete silence. "I'll get straight to the point," she said without preamble, and Nico liked her more already. He much preferred a person who was straight up, no beating around the bush. "Some of you may have already heard the rumors, but there has been talk of a suspected serial killer working down in Hobart."

Nico blinked but showed no other outward sign that he was surprised. Her words had been a revelation, however. Of course he'd heard the gossip. Being a homicide detective, he often knew what was going on in other high-profile cases around the island, and even on the mainland. The police down in Hobart were keeping their cards close to their chests, and no word had been leaked to the media as yet about the possibility of a serial killer, in a bid not to send the public into a panic.

"There have been two murders in Hobart in the past year. Both of them sex workers, with little to no family connections. The second murder was only three months ago, and while there were similarities between the killings, detectives were loath to put them in the serial killer basket." The district commander took a subtle breath, and then continued. "Until three days ago, when there was a third death over in Zeehan. This one has everyone on edge," she warned, her piercing, blue eyes roving around the room, settling on one or two of the officers and spearing them with her gaze.

Nico sucked in a breath, and he heard Tyrell do the same next to him. Zeehan was a small mining town on the west coast of the island over two hours' drive from Burnie. It was normally a sleepy little town full of historic buildings that enticed the tourists, but not much else. It wasn't somewhere you'd think to find a serial killer.

"We have no description of a perp, and no witnesses," the commander continued. "First Class Constable Smith is handing out a copy of the profile the Hobart unit are currently working with." Sally-Ann stood up next to Nico and waved a fistful of papers in the air before she diligently began weaving between the desks, distributing them. "This may seem unprecedented, but we are sharing this information with all stations and operational units on the island. Because we're worried this killer is on the move," the commander finished with a sober grimace. The silence was deafening.

Nico took one of the stapled documents from Sally-Ann and scanned the contents, his heart beating a little faster as he read the details of the three separate crime scenes. Adrenaline coursed through his veins and his mind began to race with different ideas and scenarios as he tried to picture the mind of a killer. He hated he was thinking this way, but it was part and parcel of the job. He was employed to catch murderers. And there was a murderer on the loose. It'd be a huge coup if he could be part of the team who brought this person down; the primary on the case, even.

"Clearly, this won't affect you here in Burnie. We have a team from Hobart heading to Zeehan to investigate the murder there, and to date they already have enough manpower and expertise. The reason we're broadcasting this information is that we want you all to be on high alert. If this turns out to be a serial murderer, and if he is on the move—both big ifs, mind you—I want everyone to be on the lookout for him."

The commander kept referring to the perp as a *he* but Nico knew that was technically incorrect. The killer could be a *she* as well. The likelihood was lower, but it shouldn't be discounted.

Suddenly, Lacey was standing in front of him, holding out a plateful of steaming food. He'd been so caught up in his musings, he'd nearly lost track of where he was and what he was supposed to be doing, and he almost dropped his glass in surprise.

"Here you go," she said. "I caught the rice just in time." She grinned at him.

"Thank you." He readjusted his seat so he could put the wineglass on the ground and take the proffered plate. Enough dwelling on work, it was time to let that go and concentrate on this delicious-looking dinner Lacey had made. It wasn't often a woman cooked for him. Wasn't often anyone cooked for him, actually. Most of the time he ate alone in his kitchen. He wasn't an awful cook, but cooking for one often felt like a waste of time, and so he had his standby favorites of burgers and salad or steak and chips. At least he hadn't sunk to ready-made TV dinners or frozen meals. Not yet.

Some nights he'd eat out with Tyrell after a session at the gym, or they'd meet up with a bunch of cops after a shift and go for drinks at the pub. Occasionally, he'd go out with another of his friends, Gabriel, a young local GP he'd become friendly with through playing in a squash tournament a few years ago. Gabriel liked to think of himself as a bit of a food connoisseur and so he'd choose a different gourmet restaurant to visit each time they went out. Nico was in it for the wine and the company, rather than the food. Then there were the well-meaning older ladies in the community, who'd bring him casseroles or cakes they'd cooked to keep him fed. That'd happened a lot when he'd first moved to Boat Harbour, but once he'd made it clear that he was quite self-sufficient, and not in need of any mothering, most of them had dwindled away to leave him in peace. It was nice to have company though; he could admit that now. Especially the company of a good-looking woman.

"Mmm, this is good," he said through a mouthful of spicy chicken curry. Creamy and with just the right amount of heat. "How did you make this on that little stove?" he asked in wonder as he took another bite.

"It's really simple. I can give you the recipe," she offered with a cheery grin.

"I'd like that." He sat back in the folding chair and regarded the darkening ocean. The sun had set below the horizon and night was falling fast. Lacey had turned on a set of fairy lights strung around the top edge of her van, and they cast a soft glow over their little encampment. They sat in easy silence as they ate, Smudge sitting between them on the grass casting hopeful glances their way. The air was cold and crisp, but with the hot food and half a glass of wine in his belly, he wasn't that worried by the temperature. It gave him a moment of pause, made him stop and realize how lucky he was that he lived in such a beautiful place.

He glanced over to where Lacey sat, the blanket draped over her knees, long legs stretched out in front. She was rugged up in the same sheepskin jacket she'd been wearing last night, her blonde hair falling over her shoulders, the tip of her nose pink from the cold. She gave him a conspiratorial grin and his stomach did a slow somersault. There was something about her. They had a natural connection; she was easy to be around. When she wasn't dropping him to the ground like a sack of potatoes, that was. Admittedly, she was hiding secrets, which always set off alarm bells in his head. But damnit, he liked this woman. He wasn't sure if that was a good thing or a bad thing. One thing was for certain, he needed to learn more about her before he made any more decisions about this budding friendship.

CHAPTER FIVE

Lacey wandered down the edge of the road, not really concentrating on where she was going. This morning had dawned bright enough, but then clouds had come over blocking out the sun as she'd sat in her van eating toast for breakfast. Nico had already left for the day; she'd heard his motorcycle grumble down the driveway before the light was even fully over the horizon. Which left Lacey at a loose end, with nothing to do and nowhere to be. Dave had said the spare part could take a few days to come in, and that he'd call her the second it arrived. So she'd untied Smudge from his kennel and was taking him for a walk, exploring the small hamlet of Boat Harbour Beach, even though it was still too early for most normal people to be out of bed.

The community consisted of a tangle of roads, mostly running parallel to the beach with a mixture of large, modern houses built to take advantage of the views, intermingled with older, heritage homes made of wood, like Nico's. It was no bigger than a few suburban blocks, and the amenities were basic, without even a supermarket. Only a corner store and the café at the edge of the small bay. Locals would have to drive to Wynyard or Burnie to get their groceries, but she guessed maybe they liked it that way. Simple and secluded.

Not too isolated or off the beaten track, but not city living either. She guessed most of the residents knew each other. Small communities always seemed to know each other's business.

She strolled along the edge of the road—there were no walkways out here—watching as Smudge poked his nose into a line of daisies planted along a white picket fence. She looked up and saw a cute cottage, with a well-tended garden, immediately drawn to the idyllic look of the place. She could envisage herself living in such a place. It was so much more homey and welcoming than the enormous mansion her parents insisted on living in. A sign of their wealth and status. Her mother was constantly preening about how much their mansion in Toorak was worth. But Lacey had grown to despise the stately rooms, decorated for style but not for living in, and the empty hallways leading to bedrooms that were never used, or the sprawling pristine gardens that only the paid gardeners enjoyed. Lacey had money put aside in a trust fund, which she could access if she wished. She could buy this little house without even putting a dent in her savings. But what would be the point? She didn't want to settle down. Not here, at least. But she also wasn't sure she wanted to go back to Melbourne. What was there for her now? She could—

"Hello. Is anyone there?" a tremulous voice called from somewhere a little farther down the road. Lacey turned her head and searched for the owner of the voice. "Help. Is anyone there? I need help!" An elderly woman suddenly appeared at a gate to the house next to the cottage Lacey had been admiring.

Lacey broke into a jog, the desperate fear in the old woman's voice driving her on. "What's the matter?" she asked, skidding to a stop in front of the gate.

"Oh, thank the Lord. Come quickly." The woman's face

was drawn back in a rictus of panic and she fumbled to unlatch the gate, then beckoned Lacey into the front garden. "It's Rania. I found her lying right here." She pointed toward the front steps of the second little cottage, this one not nearly as well-restored as the one next door. The garden was also overgrown, with high hedges around the perimeter blocking the view from the road and garden beds full of daisies that were going to seed. But Lacey raced past these to the base of a set of steps from the front veranda. A young woman was lying on the grass, long dark hair spread around her face like a carpet. She was covered in blood. Lacey recoiled at the sight. But then instinct and training took control of her limbs.

She knelt beside the woman, feeling for a pulse. This didn't look good. The victim was unconscious, and Lacey eventually found a weak pulse beneath her fingertips. Smudge, who'd followed her in through the gate, gave the woman a sniff and Lacey pushed him away. "Have you called an ambulance?" she asked without looking up.

"No, I...I just found her. And I don't have a phone. Oh, Lord, is she dead?" This time Lacey glanced up to see the old woman hovering above, wringing her hands together and looking like she might collapse on the spot. She knew how the lady felt; her own heart rate was spiking, and she needed to slow her breathing before she hyperventilated and blacked out. Lacey took a second to try and clear her mind. She should know what to do. She used to be a cop—was still legally a cop. She was trained for this exact thing. But now... Now all she wanted to do was run far away.

"No, she's not dead," Lacey forced herself to say. "Here, take my phone. The pin number is 4557." She handed the lady her cell. "Call an ambulance. And the police," she added. Damn, if only Nico didn't work half an hour's drive away. If only he hadn't left at such an ungodly hour this morning. She really needed him here. Needed a steadying presence who understood exactly what to do in this kind of situation. Because she was about to go to pieces, she could feel it.

"I just came around to prune the gardenias in Rania's garden," the woman said, her gaze fixed on the figure collapsed on the ground as if she couldn't look away. Smudge was hanging back now, as if he sensed something wasn't right, and his ears were down as he stared at Lacey. But she had no time to worry about the dog now.

"What's your name?" Lacey asked, trying to keep her voice steady. Even though she wanted to be far from here, her training as a cop was taking over, like muscle memory for a judo throw she'd learned so well she didn't even have to think about the move anymore. Rule number one was to manage the onlookers and witnesses. Make sure the site was secured, and the bystanders were safe. Then call for help. It was ingrained in her psyche.

"I'm Margie. Herb and I live next door. I like to help Rania with her garden." The words tumbled from the old woman's lips. "But I never thought…" She stopped and covered her mouth as tears leaked from her eyes. Margie was kitted out in Lycra from head to toe, the type that all those mobs of fanatical cyclists wore when they took to the roads on their expensive machines to ride hundreds of miles in one day before they descended on the local café to drink coffee and chat. And now that Lacey looked more carefully, she could see she was fit and slim, even though she must be in her seventies.

"That's good, Margie. My name is Lacey. It's great that you're here, and that you found your neighbor in time. But if you want to help Rania, then you need to call an ambulance."

"Okay." The woman nodded weakly, but began stabbing at the phone, and Lacey transferred her concentration back to the woman lying on the ground and began to catalogue her injuries. The young woman looked to be in her early twenties.

The skin on her face was unlined and Lacey noted detachedly that she was quite beautiful, with honey-colored skin and dark hair and eyelashes. Of middle-eastern descent, maybe.

She was wearing pajamas, as if she'd been roused from her bed when the attacker struck. There were defensive wounds on both her hands and more slashes across her upper arms. Whoever had done this didn't seem to be an expert at stabbing a victim to death. A first-time attacker, perhaps. But it was the two deep wounds in Rania's chest that were of most concern. Blood had leaked from the wounds saturating her clothing and leaving pools of red on the grass below. Rania's skin felt icy to the touch. How long had she been lying here? This didn't look like it'd just happened. Had this poor lady been lying in her garden all night? First things first, she needed to stop the bleeding.

"Margie, I need a rag or a piece of clothing. Something to help staunch the wounds," Lacey called to the woman who was now talking excitedly into the phone. Lacey removed her own sheepskin jacket as she spoke and covered the woman's torso, trying to keep her warm. She was wearing a long-sleeved tee and a sweater beneath her sheepskin, and so she also stripped the sweater over her head and used it to push against one of the wounds on Rania's chest, but it wasn't enough to cover both injuries. The chilly wind now nipped at her through the lightweight fabric.

"Here." Margie handed her the Lycra jacket she'd been wearing, and Lacey used it to staunch the other wound. It wasn't ideal, but it'd have to do. The most worrying thing about the wounds on Rania's chest was that they were no longer bleeding profusely. As if all the blood had already seeped out of her body. There was nothing Lacey could do about that, however, so she pressed down hard on the wounds and prayed the ambulance would get here soon.

It was only then, as she put pressure on the other woman's

chest and whispered to Rania that she was going to be okay, that the other part of her brain finally registered the pools of blood on the ground. As soon as she glimpsed the blood, images of Cindi invaded her mind. The blood was her undoing. Much the same as the other night when it'd dripped from Nico's nose, it was the sight of the ruby-red liquid that tipped Lacey over the edge and she was engulfed in memories so strong they took over her conscious mind.

Her memory was torn back to that fateful day as she arrived at the scene. The blue-and-red lights on top of her cruiser flashing in the background, lighting the scene with their eerie, unnatural pigments. The way everything seemed to play back in slow motion as Lacey ran toward the front of the house where she could hear the animal screams of pain issuing from a girl's mouth. Then Lacey crashed through the door, seeing the mother crouched over Cindi, blood streaked across her maniacal face as she stabbed down over and over again into the fragile body of her daughter, calling on the devil to leave her child's body. Lacey didn't even have time to draw her service weapon; she'd dived on the woman, grappling her away from the child and knocking the knife from her hand, not even caring about the danger to herself in a bid to stop the carnage. Her partner, Mike, had followed her in and helped subdue the mother. Then Lacey had started CPR on Cindi. Even though she'd known it was too late.

It wasn't until the next day that she'd finally, spectacularly, fallen apart, crawling into bed and refusing to come out. Refusing to go back to work. Refusing to talk to anyone. Finally, the police counsellor had got through to her and talked her down from the precipice of mad depression. But it wasn't until after weeks of counseling that she'd felt a little more human.

Life as Lacey knew it was never the same, however. She wasn't the same person anymore. What hurt the most, what'd shattered her confidence, was the feeling of complete and utter helplessness. That she was too late to stop the tragedy. Too late to save the little girl. Her badge and her gun and the fact she had the power of the law on her side were all useless when it came to saving Cindi. This was the reason she couldn't go back to policing. She'd never be able to trust herself again. To trust that she wouldn't fall to pieces when she was needed the most.

The mother had been in an ice-induced rage and was completely and utterly devastated when she finally came down off her high and realized what she'd done. But that didn't stop her from being sent to jail for the next thirty years. And it also didn't stop Lacey from blaming herself every single day since then for not getting there a minute earlier, so she could've perhaps saved the little girl.

"The ambulance is on its way," Margie reported, but Lacey barely heard the older woman's words. All she wanted to do was to curl into a fetal position on the grass until everything disappeared. She couldn't do this. This woman was going to die, and it'd be all her fault. A second death on her hands. A low moan escaped her lips.

"Lacey, did you hear me?" Margie touched her shoulder and Lacey flinched away. "Are you okay, luv? Oh, Lord, is Rania going to die?" Margie's voice rose an octave as she observed Lacey's distress.

She had to get herself under control, if only for this elderly woman's sake. She couldn't leave Margie to tend this situation all on her own. Lacey drew in a shuddering breath. And then another.

"I'm okay," Lacey rasped. "What was that about the ambulance?"

"They're on their way. But they have to come from Burnie and it might take them half an hour to get here, so I called the local doctor. He lives in Wynyard, its only ten minutes away."

"Good. Well done," Lacey praised Margie, while clenching her teeth and marshaling her mind back into a semblance of order. She leaned over Rania and felt for a pulse again, listened for signs of breathing. They were there, but her breath sounded like it was rasping in her lungs now. Not a good sign. She hoped that doctor got here soon.

"Margie? Where are you?" a loud voice bellowed over the side fence.

"Oh, Herb, thank the Lord. Quick, come over to Rania's, she's been hurt," Margie replied.

Ten seconds later, a fit-looking older man appeared in the garden. He was wearing Lycra like his wife.

"What do you need me to do?" he asked, seeming to assess the situation almost immediately. "I'm ex-military," he added by way of explanation, his eyes flicking over Rania but not coming to rest on her, as if afraid to look too closely.

"You could get me some blankets," Lacey replied. "Then you could wait out the front and direct the first responders in here. I believe your wife has called a local doctor."

"Yes," Margie piped up. "I called Dr. DuPont. He was just about to leave for work, but he said he'd be here in less than ten minutes."

"Good, good," Herb told her efficiently. "I'll get you some blankets." He bounded up the stairs into Rania's house with the energy of a man half his age, Margie hot on his tail, seemingly revitalized now her husband was taking charge. Leaving Lacey alone with the terribly injured woman.

Rania's breath became more raspy in the still morning air, like a rattlesnake had taken up residence inside her chest.

Things seemed to happen a lot more quickly then. Herb came back with a handful of blankets, which she carefully spread over the woman, trying to keep her warm and treat her for shock. Then he said he was taking Smudge over to his garden, to get the dog out of the way. It seemed he must know the man, as Smudge followed him happily enough. Nico had warned her that Smudge didn't take to strangers.

A few moments later, there was a commotion from the road outside the gate and a young man strode in carrying a black duffle bag, which he dropped near Rania's head. "I'm Dr. Gabriel DuPont," he introduced himself, while at the same time assessing Rania, lifting her makeshift bandages to look at the wounds and taking the woman's pulse. Lacey could hear Herb and Margie talking to someone else outside the front gate. Perhaps the neighbors had finally cottoned on to the fact something was going on in their sleepy little community.

"She doesn't sound good," Lacey whispered. "Her breathing has become labored and much louder in the past ten minutes."

"I've got it," the doctor replied calmly. He was young, probably only a little older than her. Clean-shaven and good-looking in a nerdy sort of way. With a flop of sandy hair that he needed to brush away from his eyes whenever he bent over Rania. He undid his black bag and removed his emergency items. He took out a blood pressure cuff, along with a syringe, bandages, and various vials and packets of medicine. It looked like he was going to insert a line in her arm, hopefully to administer some life-saving drugs. Lacey sat back on her heels, stupidly grateful that this young doctor was here to take over. She could now leave everything in his capable hands.

Margie came up and tapped her on the shoulder. "Here, luv, your phone is ringing." Lacey had forgotten the older woman had it. She stood and took it with a small smile of gratitude and looked at the caller ID. "Nico," she answered a little breathlessly, stepping away from the doctor and his patient.

"I've just heard about the injured woman," he said. "I'm on

my way right now." By the sound of it, Nico was calling from a hands-free and speaking inside his motorcycle helmet; she could hear the muffled thrum of the motor. The tightness in her chest eased ever so slightly at the sound of his voice. "Are you okay? You're not hurt at all?" How did he know she was involved? For all he knew she should still be tucked up in bed in her Kombi van. "The radio dispatcher mentioned your name," he added.

Ah-ha, that was how. She guessed there probably weren't too many Laceys in the vicinity.

"No. I'm fine. The next-door neighbor flagged me down while I was out for a walk with Smudge."

"Yes, good old Margie, she's always poking her nose into other people's business. But this time it seems like a good thing that she did." He gave a short, humorless bark of laughter.

There was a flurry of movement near Rania, and Lacey's focus was diverted. What was going on?

"Excuse me. Lacey, is it?" The doctor lifted his head, and she caught his gaze and nodded. "Do you know CPR?"

Oh, shit. That didn't sound good.

"She's stopped breathing," the doctor said calmly. "I'll give the chest compressions. Can you do the rescue breaths?"

"Yes." Her mouth answered the word, but her body was screaming, *No, no, no! Not this again. Please. No!*

"What's going on?" Nico demanded down the phone, but she didn't have time to answer, merely hit the end button and dropped to her knees beside the girl's head, ready to follow the doctor's instructions.

CHAPTER SIX

The ambulance pulled away from the front gate, no lights or sirens on. The small crowd stood and watched it go in somber silence.

The girl, Rania, was dead. Not even the skill of a trained doctor could keep her alive. Nico glanced over at his friend, Gabriel, who stood with shoulders slumped, hands still covered in dried blood. Margie sobbed into Herb's chest, and a few other neighbors who'd gathered when the ambulance had first arrived now stood around, slightly shell-shocked and looking grave. This sort of thing just didn't happen in their sleepy little hamlet. Certainly not blatant murder, which was what this looked like.

Nico had arrived well before the ambulance, but there was nothing to be done for the girl. Gabriel and Lacey had still been performing CPR, but the look on the doctor's face said it all. It was too late. Once the paramedics had arrived and taken over the fruitless effort, Gabriel told him she'd lost too much blood. It probably wouldn't have mattered if they'd got her to hospital, she still would've died.

Another team had arrived in their police cruiser soon after Nico, and were now cordoning off the area with police tape and shooing people away from the scene, ready for forensics to take over. A specialized team was already on their way from Devonport. Nico had arranged it all over the phone, as he watched the paramedics fight to get Rania back. He acknowledged even before they did what'd happened here. The girl was dead, and this was now a murder scene.

Nico lifted his head to search for Lacey. She'd been standing by Gabriel as they loaded the body into the ambulance, but now she was over by the hedge on her own, arms wrapped around her middle, eyes as huge as saucers. She was only wearing a thin long-sleeved shirt, and was also covered in Rania's blood, but she seemed not to notice, her awareness turned inward, her eyes not focussed on anything. The haunted look on her face said it all, and without thinking, Nico made his way over to where she stood. The paramedics had handed her back her jacket, but it hung bloody and forgotten in her hands.

"You okay?" he asked softly.

She just shook her head and seemed to withdraw even further into herself. He was reminded of her reaction the other night after she'd pounded the shit out of him, when she appeared to have some kind of panic attack. She clearly didn't deal with trauma well. Did that have something to do with why she was on sabbatical from the force?

Without asking for permission, Nico put his arm around Lacey's shoulders. Warily at first, because he thought she might flinch away from him. But she leaned into him instead, and he could feel the slight trembling running through her body. Whether it was from the cold or from shock, he wasn't sure. She was quite a conundrum. On the one hand, Gabriel and Margie had both sung Lacey's praises, saying that she'd acted quickly and proficiently, doing everything that needed to be done with ultimate professionalism. But now he could see the cracks beginning to appear as the need to act wore off.

"You did a great job," he said, pulling her in tighter and

resting his chin on top of her head. "I know this was a terrible thing to go through. But you did it all by the book. You have to believe you did everything in your power to help that poor woman."

She moaned and shook her head slightly, as if his words caused her pain. "No, I didn't. She died, Nico. She died and there was nothing I could do about it." Lacey buried her face into his leather jacket as great sobs shivered through her.

He held her and let her cry. It was the best thing for her right now, to get all that emotion out. But again, it made him wonder. It was unusual for a police officer to show such raw grief, especially in public. Even one who'd only been on the beat for a short time, which seemed likely for Lacey. You learned to guard your emotions better when you were a cop. And while you might not become inured to death and violence, most people learned to put on a brave face. It wouldn't do to show the public how affected you might be by a brutal murder or other violent crime. They'd never trust you to protect them if you did. Maybe that explained why she wasn't cut out to be a police officer. He'd love to know her story, find out what had caused her to be this way. But he'd have to let her tell him in her own time.

Suddenly, almost as if she'd flicked an internal switch—or as if she could hear his thoughts—her sobbing subsided and she withdrew her face from his chest.

"Sorry," she apologized. "That was out of line." She backed away, swiping a hand under her nose. "I'm keeping you from your duties."

He was about to argue that it was part of a police officer's duties to offer comfort when it was needed, when the sound of a revving car engine caught both of their attention.

A car screeched to a halt outside the cottage and a young man leaped out, wild-eyed and breathless. "Where's Rania?"

Nico took two strides and held up his hands to stop the

man rushing straight in through the gate.

"Slow down," he commanded, but the man tried to push past him.

"Herb called me. He said Rania was hurt." The guy searched the gathered crowd and the elderly next-door neighbor stepped forward, his sniffling wife still tucked under one arm.

"That's right, I did." Herb's eyes crinkled up in sorrow. "I thought he needed to be told. Karim is Rania's boyfriend," he added by way of explanation to Nico. "But, oh Lord, my boy, I'm so sorry."

The young man's face drained of all color as he stared at Herb. Nico still rested one restraining hand on Karim's arm.

"What are you saying, Herb? What's happened?"

Nico drew in a breath. It was up to him to deliver this news. It was part of the job. "I'm sorry to have to tell you that Rania is dead." It was always better to do it quick and clean. Drawing it out did no one any good.

"No." The man's dark eyes went crazy with panic and pain. "No, that's not possible. She was still asleep in bed when I left. No. No. Noooo." Karim pulled free from Nico's grasp and looked around him, as if Rania might suddenly appear miraculously from behind the hedges. "Rania. Where are you?"

"Come with me," Nico said, using his most conciliatory voice, taking the young man by the arm. "Come and sit down." Karim didn't resist, even though he continued to call out his girlfriend's name.

As Nico led Karim to the curb and helped him sit down, he exchanged a knowing glance with Lacey. She seemed to realize exactly what he was thinking. If this was the boyfriend, he needed careful examination. Thirty percent of homicide victims were killed by someone they knew. This distraught man could be merely putting on a show. Making it look like he was innocent, when in fact he knew exactly what'd happened. It may well turn out this was a crime of passion. Perhaps he hadn't meant to kill her, but in a fit of rage…And then he'd calmly gone off to work and left her to die.

Nico crouched down next to the boyfriend, patting him gently on the shoulder. Charles had already told Nico he was the primary on this case and it was now Nico's top priority. Anything to do with the serial killer was to be put on the back burner. This was his crime scene now, and he needed to think strategically. Needed to put Lacey out of his mind and open his intellect to take in all the clues and all the possible scenarios surrounding this murder instead.

But against his will, his gaze kept drifting to the forlorn figure huddled next to the hedge.

* * *

It was late, but that didn't stop Nico from knocking on the door of the Kombi van. He needed to see how Lacey was coping. And a light still gleamed from inside, so she must be awake. It was almost midnight, and it'd been a long, long day for him, as it had for everyone else involved in the investigation.

"It's open," she called, and he yanked on the sliding door to reveal a bright interior.

She was tucked beneath a blanket on the couch, a small heater warming the van, making the space cozy and inviting. Smudge was curled up on the floor and wagged his tail a little sheepishly in welcome, but didn't budge from his warm spot. "Come in." She beckoned him inside. "And close the door, will you?"

He did as he was asked and then took a position on the couch as Lacey drew in her feet leaving him just enough room.

"Rough day, huh?" she asked as her gaze settled on his

face. Was it that obvious?

"For everyone," he agreed. He noticed her face was pale and drawn, her mouth pinched in a tight pucker, and knew she was just as affected as he was.

"Can I get you a drink?" She held up a glass that contained a good measure of golden liquid.

"That might be the best offer I've had all day," he said. "Stay there," he added as she began to rise. "Just point me in the right direction and I'll get it." There couldn't be too many places to hide booze in this tiny abode.

She directed him to a small, partially hidden cupboard beneath the countertop where he found a bottle of whiskey and held it up to the light, having to duck his head as he moved around the van. "Sheep Dog," he said, reading the name aloud. "Peanut Butter Whiskey. What is that?" he asked, screwing up his nose.

"It's delicious. Try it," she replied with a hint of a smile.

He found a glass in a rack above the countertop and poured himself a generous amount, then took a dubious sip. The alcohol slipped down his throat and he immediately welcomed the burn deep in his stomach. It was slightly sweeter than a normal whiskey, with a definite hint of peanut butter. But he had to admit, it wasn't bad. He maneuvered himself back onto the couch and raised his glass in a salute. "To Rania," he said simply.

"To Rania," she agreed, a slight wobble to her voice, and they clinked their glasses in the memory of a woman whose life had been taken too early. They sat in silence for a minute, both contemplating the events from this morning.

"I'm not even going to ask how your day went," Lacey spoke as he took another sip. The stuff was growing on him.

With her experience in the force, she'd probably have a good idea how things had gone. Gathering a squad of professionals he trusted to be part of his team. Setting up a murder board in one of the two situation rooms at the Burnie Police Station. Briefing his team on the details they had to hand so far. Organizing Tyrell and another officer to do a round of door knocking through Boat Harbour Beach to gather any pertinent information or take witness statements from people who might've seen something but hadn't yet come forward. Investigating friends and acquaintances of the young couple, Rania and Karim, trying to piece together a picture of their life with each other. Coordinating with a liaison from forensics and another from homicide in Hobart. The endless interviews he'd conducted. Having to deal with Rania's family, who'd flown from Hobart, still shocked and disbelieving, wanting answers that Nico couldn't give them. Not yet. He'd also had to deal with the boyfriend's family, who lived in Devonport, less than an hour's drive away. Karim's devastation had morphed, and he'd become increasingly troublesome as the day drew on, as he slowly became aware that he could be suspect number one in this case. The family had called in a lawyer and Karim had clammed up. They'd closed ranks around him and taken him back to a hotel in Burnie to be secluded with them, much to the shock of Rania's family, who thought they would have an ally in their time of need. But instead, Karim's family had withdrawn, probably to protect themselves and their son against the growing media attention and questions that'd inevitably arise.

Had Karim killed Rania? The timing fit. Karim stated he'd left for work at three am that morning. He worked at a bakery in Wynyard and that was his usual start time. He could've stabbed Rania and then left her to die, giving himself an alibi by turning up to work on time. Nico was still waiting for the coroner's report detailing the time he thought the stab wounds had been inflicted, and how long Rania had been alive after the attack. But Gabriel had said she could've been alive for some hours before her neighbor found her and raised the alarm.

One question that'd niggled at the back of Nico's mind all day—ever since the paramedic had pronounced Rania dead and stopped performing CPR—was a question he didn't really want to ask. Was this girl another victim of the suspected serial killer from Hobart? The MO didn't seem to fit the profile. The only similarity being the victim was a young woman; everything else, including the way the victim was killed was completely different. The other three women had all been in the sex worker industry and had been strangled to death. But he couldn't rule out a link. Not completely. So, he'd requested more information from the team in Hobart who were dealing with the serial killer case. And he'd put Sally-Ann in charge of collating the information received.

"It was a hard day," he admitted, taking another sip. "And you're right, I don't really want to talk about it." What he wanted to talk about was how Lacey was coping. He really hadn't wanted to leave her this morning, looking so forlorn and alone. But he had a job to do. He'd taken a brief statement from both her and Gabriel, then rushed back to the station to coordinate everything. He'd require a more detailed account, and was hoping to get her to come into the station tomorrow for an interview. But tonight, it felt important that he ask after her mental state of mind. She'd broken down in his arms this morning. Add that to her freaking out the other day at the sight of his blood, and he decided he needed to know what was going on with her. He was no longer prepared to let her keep her secrets.

He settled his glass on his knee and looked her in the eye. "I know this morning was traumatizing for you. It would've made most people upset and distressed. But I feel like there's something else going on. Something you're not telling me.

Your reaction was…more than I expected." He wanted to say, *Over-the-top,* but refrained. "I'm guessing it has something to do with why you're taking leave from the force?" He decided not to beat around the bush and go directly to the heart of the problem. Now she was involved in a murder investigation, like it or not, he was going to have to reveal her connection to the Victoria Police. But before he did that, he'd like to get up to speed on her history.

She wouldn't meet his gaze. Eventually, she said, "I guessed you'd probably ask me that." Twirling the glass between her long fingers, she tilted her head back to stare at the roof, and he waited for her to speak. "Yes, I requested stress leave from the force because I witnessed a crime that I couldn't come to terms with," she said quietly. "The short version is that I was called out to a domestic dispute by a worried neighbor, and it turned out a junkie mother was having a psychotic episode and thought the devil had inhabited her daughter's body. So, she decided to stab her to death to rid her of the demon. I arrived too late to save the little girl. She was only five years old." As if sensing Lacey's pain, Smudge stood and rested his chin on her leg, staring up into her face. Dogs were so damned intuitive to human emotions, and Smudge especially didn't like it when someone was upset. And this time, Nico sympathized with the dog, because he wanted to do exactly the same. Rest a reassuring hand on Lacey's knee, to comfort her, until that bleak despair left her eyes.

"My partner and I tried CPR. We tried everything," she continued, and he could imagine the desperate scene as the two police officers tried to resuscitate the little girl. It sent shivers up his spine merely thinking about it, and he couldn't imagine what it must've been like to actually experience it. "But she was dead, and nothing we did could bring her back. And now Cindi seems to have inhabited my soul. She goes everywhere with me, condemning me from the shadows."

Whoa. This went way deeper than he suspected. Lacey was indeed traumatized. Everyone dealt with trauma differently. Some people could put it behind them, and some found it almost impossible. This time, he gave into his impulse and laid his hand gently on her knee. She glanced up quickly, but didn't move away.

"I'm so sorry you had to go through that." Some police officers went their entire career without having to deal with such a terrible incident. Most weren't so lucky, however. Unfortunately, Lacey had experienced this early on in her career, before she'd had time to build that wall around her heart and mind that was required if you were to keep doing the job with any sense of normality. And it may well have destroyed her. "Did you receive any counseling?" he asked gently.

"Mmm hmm." She nodded. "And it helped. But not enough to let me go back to the force. When I said I was going to resign, my commanding officer gave me the whole year off. Leave without pay. He said he hated to lose a good officer, and he hoped that with enough time and space I might be able to return. Back then, I agreed with him. But it's been almost a year now, and I don't think I'm any better." She hung her head and stared into Smudge's big, brown eyes, running her fingers over his soft ears. Nico wished he could provide as much comfort, but if the dog was helping, then that was all that mattered. There was only one thing he could think of that'd truly help.

"We have a good psych here in Burnie we use for any officers in need of help. His name is Imran. I'm sure I can arrange a session with him for you. Would you be interested if I could wrangle it?"

She looked up, but her eyes were narrowed, and he thought she might decline.

He continued before she could open her mouth to argue. "I think you need to see a professional after what you've just been through. It's clearly opened up old wounds." He wanted to berate himself for letting her get dragged into this murder. But there was absolutely nothing he could've done about it. Never in a million years would he have predicted a murder of a young woman would take place less than a block away from his home.

"I was going to ask you to come in and give a formal statement tomorrow morning, anyway. Imran is a friend of mine. I'm sure he could fit you in."

"Are you sure he'd see me? I'm technically a civilian."

"Yes, I'm sure. Most of his patients are civilian," Nico replied. He would make it happen, even if he had to go to Imran and beg him for a favor. Lacey clearly needed help, and while she might think she was dealing with it by herself at the moment, he knew from experience that she probably wasn't. Mental health wasn't to be taken lightly. Nico of all people understood that. His own father had suffered from PTSD. His father had been a corporal in the French Foreign Legion, and had spent time fighting in the Gulf War, bringing his internal scars back home with him. But he'd tried to tough his way through it instead of accepting help. And nearly destroyed his whole family in the process.

"Okay then. If you're sure. It might be a good idea."

"Good." Nico let out a sigh of relief. And Smudge, who seemed to sense a turning point in Lacey's grief, stood and shook himself, walking over to the door as if to say he needed out. It was definitely time for Nico to get some shut-eye. It was going to be another long day tomorrow. Thinking about his warm bed, reminded him that Lacey would be sleeping out here in her little van.

He was glad Lacey had consented to see Imran. But now he'd like to see her safe inside his house, and he wondered if he might push her that little further. Or would she baulk at his offer? Lacey had a stubborn streak, so he needed to phrase this next request in terms she couldn't disagree with.

He stood and put his glass on the small countertop. Then he turned and raised an eyebrow, as if the idea had only just occurred to him. "Do you want to come and sleep inside? I've got plenty of room."

"Thank you. But I'm happy out here in my own little space."

Just as he thought. He put his hand on the door, but wasn't prepared to give in yet.

"I really think it'd be a good idea. Especially with a potential murderer in the area."

Lacey gave a snort. "I think I've already proven that I can take care of myself." A ghost of a smile played over her lips.

"I guess you have," he acknowledged, resisting the urge to rub his eyebrow where she'd landed her boot the night before last. "But I'd still rest easier if I knew you were safe inside the house, where it's warm and secure. I've got a spare room already made up, so it's no trouble. It's at the other end of the house, you'd have your own bathroom." He didn't add that he'd also be close by if she needed him. Because, for him, that was important. If she suddenly had nightmares, or worse, had some kind of breakdown during the night, he didn't want her to have to face it alone.

He could see the idea of an indoor bathroom appealed and that she was wavering, so he played his ace, touching his dog lightly on the head and saying, "I'm sure Smudge would love your company too." Smudge had always been an outside dog. He seemed to prefer not being cooped up inside. Nico would tie him up at his kennel every night. But this year, as the weather had turned colder, Smudge had been less keen to be ushered outside at night. Even going so far as refusing to budge off the mat in front of the fireplace when Nico called him one night to go outside. There'd been a wild storm raging that night, and while it hadn't bothered the dog in previous years, this particular night, he'd raised beseeching brown eyes up at Nico and he'd had to relent. Smudge had spent most nights inside since then, and Nico was okay with that. The dog would be coming up to nine years old now, and while that wasn't terribly old, he was perhaps starting to feel the bite of a cold winter in his bones more than he had in his younger years.

"Could Smudge sleep in my room?" Lacey asked, her eyes brightening. If he had to bribe the woman using his dog to get her inside, then he was all for it.

"Of course. I can move his bed right in next to yours, if you like."

"Would you like that, boy?" Lacey looked at Smudge, who trotted over and licked her hand as if to say, *Yes, he'd like that very much*. It looked like Smudge had won the lady over. Nico suddenly found himself wishing that she'd look at him with the same adoration in her eyes. Which was stupid. There was no way he could be jealous of a dog. And no way he intended to get more involved with Lacey. He'd learned through his many years of dealing with victims of crime that people who'd been traumatized by violence were just too vulnerable to date. He wouldn't do that to her. It wouldn't be fair.

CHAPTER SEVEN

Lacey moved around the big kitchen, helping herself to another mug of steaming coffee, while at the same time actively avoiding Nico, who was cooking eggs in a skillet on the stove. It was early, but the sounds of Nico up and about had urged her out of her warm bed. She was still wearing the sweatpants and T-shirt she'd slept in, over which she'd pulled on a ratty old, but very comfy, cardigan. Not her best look, but she'd never been one to worry too much about what other people thought of her. Nico was looking just as rumpled in his own sweatpants and a long-sleeved top.

"I hope you like geese eggs," he called over his shoulder. "I inherited a small flock of geese when I bought the farm. And they're good layers," he added.

"I've never tried them," she admitted. The sound of a gaggle of geese had woken her yesterday morning, but she'd yet to lay eyes on the birds. They must spend most of their time grazing in the small orchard at the back of the property. Geese weren't her favorite animal; a rather angry male had chased her as a child and she'd never warmed to them, even as an adult.

"They're the same as a big chook egg, really." Like an expert, he flicked the pan with his wrist and turned the eggs over easy.

Such an interesting man.

On one hand, he was a dedicated cop, serious and forthright. But he definitely had a gentler side. It was obvious in his love for his dog, and his love for this little cottage with all its rambling gardens and incumbent wildlife. She took a seat at the small table in the corner of the kitchen and watched Nico's back as she sipped her coffee. His long-sleeved top was almost like a second skin and made Lacey acutely aware of each ridge and bump of his muscular back, shoulders and arms. He filled the room with his presence, working the kitchen with ease and familiarity. She wasn't sure what to make of him. And wasn't sure what to make of her feelings for him. She'd finally admitted that she was attracted to Nico, but that didn't mean the sentiment sat lightly on her shoulders. She didn't want to be attracted to him. For so many reasons. But utmost was the fact that she was on a self-imposed hiatus from her job as a cop, running around Tasmania trying to get away from herself, and not sure if she could ever go back to face reality. Meanwhile, he was the exact opposite. He was firmly rooted in reality. He'd taken up residence in this community and it seemed he was good at his job, enjoyed being a detective. He had everything a person should have at his stage of life.

Well, perhaps he had one thing missing from his life. She had yet to discover if he had a significant other. A partner. A girlfriend. He'd never mentioned anyone, but that didn't mean there wasn't a woman on the scene. Shaking her head, she took a sip of scalding coffee and directed her gaze out the kitchen window, away from that tantalizing back and broad shoulders still hunched over the stove.

Surprisingly, Lacey had slept well last night. Better than she might've imagined after her distressing day. Perhaps it was Smudge's presence, gently snoring from his fluffy bed on the floor beside her. Or perhaps it was knowing there was a six-foot-two man sleeping a few doors down who'd come running to her rescue if she needed him. Not that she needed him. But still…

There was a knock at the front door, and Smudge took off down the hallway, barking at whoever had the gall to interrupt them this early in the morning. Nico exchanged a glance with Lacey, then with a shrug, went to answer the door.

"Margie, hello," Lacey heard Nico exclaim when he opened the door, and Smudge gave a welcoming bark of greeting. Lacey peered down the hallway to see the diminutive woman standing on the front porch, an eager smile on her face. She wondered if Margie was a regular visitor, or if this had something to do with yesterday. A cold breeze was blowing in through the open door, and Lacey shivered, suddenly glad she hadn't had to spend another night in her van.

"Do you mind if I come in?" Margie didn't wait for Nico to answer, barging right past him. "I wanted to check on your young friend. And I've brought you some food in case you haven't had time to cook. It's just a courgette and mushroom slice." Nico threw up his hands in mock despair behind Margie's back and closed the door.

"Hello, luv." Margie bustled into the kitchen, placing a casserole dish on the countertop. "I came to see how you're feeling today. You know…after the…" Margie waved her hand in the air and her face dissolved into a mournful expression.

"Thank you," Lacey replied, and was shocked when Margie embraced her in an unrestrained hug.

"It was such a terrible thing to happen. Just terrible." Margie let Lacey go and turned to Nico. "And what about you?" she demanded. "I know you're a big, gruff detective on the outside but this must've affected you too." Lacey had to stifle a laugh as Margie stared up at Nico, and without warning, took him into an embrace as well. She was so tiny the top of her head barely even reached the middle of Nico's chest. He looked bewildered for a second before he wrapped his arms around the older woman and then raised his eyebrows at Lacey in mock bafflement. Lacey had to applaud the woman's caring nature; she was worried about them and had come to do her civic duty to make sure they were coping.

"And what on earth has happened to your poor face?" Margie asked as she withdrew from Nico's arms and stared directly at his bruised eye. Lacey winced as Nico sent her a look.

"Someone took me by surprise," he admitted. "But don't worry, I soon gained the upper hand."

Lacey put her hands on her hips and glared at Nico. He had *not* gained the upper hand. But he'd been gentlemanly enough not to dob her in, so all she could do was pout at him from behind Margie.

"Well now, if you had a woman in your life to look after you, then maybe that kind of thing wouldn't happen." Margie cast a not-so-subtle glance in Lacey's direction, and Lacey felt the blood rising up her neck. At least it answered her question as to whether Nico had a girlfriend or not.

She was about to open her mouth and protest that she and Nico were not an item, and would never be an item, when Margie jumped to the next subject, saying, "I still can't believe my poor Rania is dead." The old woman took a seat at the table, wiping away a stray tear.

Nico turned back to the stove to tend to his goose eggs before they burned, and Lacey retook her seat next to Margie.

"I'm just cooking us up some eggs for breakfast," Nico said to Margie. "Would you like some?"

"Oh, no thank you, luv." Margie gave him a weak smile.

"Herb and I have already eaten. He's gone off on his bike with the Crank Masters. But I couldn't face a thirty-mile ride this morning. Not when my head is full of murder. It's all been a little overwhelming. I don't know how Herb can do it."

Lacey sympathized with Margie. Not that she'd even ridden five miles on a bicycle before, let alone thirty. But she guessed that's how the older couple stayed fit. She'd seen how it could become a passion for some people, it just wasn't her idea of fun.

Nico placed a plate of eggs and toast in front of Lacey, and she drew in the delicious smell as her stomach rumbled. She'd hardly eaten yesterday, her stomach had been in knots and her appetite had been nonexistent. But these golden yellow eggs made her mouth water. Nico drew out a third chair and sat down with his own plate of food.

"Thanks for checking on us, Margie. But as you can see, we're fine. I'm taking Lacey into town with me today, so she won't have to stay out here all alone." He smiled genially and shoved a huge forkful of eggs into his mouth. Nico had omitted the part about him wanting to interview her a second time, as well as her seeing a psych, but she was fine with that. She suspected he was keeping his comments intentionally free of details because he didn't want Margie spreading any kind of rumors around the community. She might be well-meaning in her anxiety about Lacey's and Nico's welfare, but Lacey didn't doubt there was also an element of voyeurism to her visit.

Taking Nico's lead she switched the subject back onto the old woman. "And how about you, Margie? How are you coping?" Her question set Margie off, the words tumbling from her lips about how she'd hardly slept a wink last night, and how she'd had to spend most of the afternoon consoling Pam, who lived on the other side of their cottage, who was terrified that a murderer was now on the prowl, and how she thought they all deserved police protection. Lacey listened and nodded along, while eating her tasty eggs and toast. Nico did the same on the other side of Margie.

Suddenly there was a loud honking from outside the kitchen window. Smudge got to his feet and barked at the back door. Lacey had never heard the big birds this close to the house before, and while geese were notorious for making great guard dogs, this sounded serious.

"Excuse me. Better check on the girls." Nico got up, leaving the remains of his uneaten eggs on his plate, grabbing his jacket from a peg on the wall, and striding out the back door, Smudge hot on his heels. Lacey hoped the birds weren't being chased by a wild dog or some such catastrophe. Watching Nico don his jacket made Lacey remember her own sheepskin jacket, still covered in Rania's blood. Even if she got it dry-cleaned, would she ever be able to wear it again?

Margie waved a hand, but didn't stop speaking, as if geese in trouble were of no real consequence. Lacey tuned back into Margie's chatter just as she said, "And that poor boy, Karim. He must be devastated. His family came around to the house yesterday to get some of his belongings, but the police wouldn't let them in. Said it was still a crime scene. Sad state of affairs if you ask me. Karim wasn't with them. He must not want to come back to the place where he lost his soulmate. They were such a lovely couple together. So young and in love. You should've seen them." Margie sighed and took a breath. But just as Lacey opened her mouth to speak, Margie was off again. "My Herb says that the police probably have Karim pegged as their number one suspect." Margie looked up as if to make sure Nico was still outside, before she continued in a conspiratorial whisper. "But I just can't believe that. Not for a second. Herb would've seen or heard something that night if it'd been Karim who killed her. If they'd had an argument or something, you know? Herb's been suffering from insomnia a lot lately. I keep telling him he needs to see the doctor and sort himself out. So many times I wake up in the wee hours of the morning and my Herb is missing from our bed. I used to get up and go looking for him. Sometimes he'd be out in the shed tinkering with his bike, but other times he was nowhere to be found, so I gave up in the end. It's too cold lately to be chasing my husband around in the dark." Margie gave a soft giggle. "So, you see, my Herb would've heard if anything untoward was going on next door the other night."

"Mmm hmm." Lacey made a noncommittal noise, and Margie went on to tell Lacey all about Karim's family, how he looked so much like his father, tall and handsome. Karim's family were refugees from Syria, part of a resettlement of people who'd been forced out of their homeland. They'd landed in Hobart seven years ago, where Karim had finished school and then moved up here to become a baker. As Margie talked, something tickled at the back of Lacey's mind, and she let herself examine the thought. Margie had said Herb was often missing from the bed. And sometimes she didn't know where he went. That he probably would've heard if something had been amiss that night. Was he actually out of bed on the night Rania was killed?

Nico reappeared through the back door, bringing a blast of cold air with him, and Margie finally stopped talking and looked at him expectantly.

"I think it was some domestic dispute over the best spot to lay an egg," Nico said with a laugh, removing his jacket and then taking the plates from the table and putting them in the sink.

He turned and looked directly at Margie. "I hope you don't mind but I need to shower and shave and get ready for work," he said quickly to head Margie off as she opened her mouth to talk again. "We'll take some of that delicious-looking slice for lunch, as well." He cast Lacey a meaningful glance as he spoke. She was supposed to be going into town with him today, which meant she needed to get ready too. How on earth was she supposed to get away from this old woman who could talk the hind leg off a donkey? Margie was well-meaning, but boy, she barely drew breath.

"Yes, we do." Lacey stood and pulled her cardigan closer around her shoulders, hoping Margie would take the hint.

"Oh, of course you do." Margie slid her chair back and stood. "You young people are always so busy. Especially you, Nicolas. I'll get out of your way so you can catch that murderer, then people can sleep soundly in their beds at night again."

Nico ushered Margie down the hallway, nodding in the appropriate places, while the old woman continued to ramble, even as she walked through the front door.

"Bye, Margie." Lacey waved from down the hallway as Nico finally got the door shut and then leaned against it with a sigh.

"I swear, that woman is actually a secret weapon in disguise. Her superpower is to talk someone to death."

Lacey pursed her lips, trying to hide her smile. She knew Nico didn't mean it, but she understood his frustration. He'd had to deal with her a lot longer than Lacey.

"I'll go jump in the shower," she said, instead. "I can be ready in fifteen minutes. Is that okay?" It was lucky Nico had two bathrooms. It meant she didn't have to think about him stripping naked and stepping into the same shower as her, mere minutes after she'd left.

"Great," he replied, and they both went their separate ways.

* * *

True to her word, Lacey emerged fifteen minutes later from

the spare bedroom, dressed and ready to go. She had on her thickest woolen sweater under her spare rain jacket, finished off with jeans and boots. The rain jacket was big and bulky, but it'd have to do until she could get her sheepskin dry-cleaned or replace it. She found Nico in the kitchen, finishing up washing the dishes.

"I'm ready to go," she said to his back. Then a sudden thought occurred to her. "Oh, are we taking your motorcycle?" She was definitely going to need another layer of clothing if she had to spend half an hour on the back of that black beast. The idea made her cringe.

"I was going to take the Jeep. It's parked in the shed," he said, turning and letting his appraising glance rest on her face. "But we can take the motorcycle if you want," he added with a sly grin.

That grin made her suddenly imagine herself sitting on the tiny booster seat with her arms wrapped around his middle, leaning into his strong body as they flew around yet another sharp corner, her thighs gripping his lean hips. She licked her lips and shook her head. "Nope. Not at all," she replied.

"The Jeep it is, then." Now she thought about it, there had been some kind of four-wheel drive parked on one side of the shed. She'd seen it when she'd used the bathroom, but hadn't paid much attention. Letting out a quiet sigh of relief, she followed Nico out the back door.

She waited while he tied Smudge to his kennel, the dog's ears drooping as they walked away. While Nico raised the roller door and backed the vehicle out, she quickly checked her van to make sure all was still as it should be.

Hopping into the passenger seat, she rubbed her hands together and willed the heater to do its thing a little faster. It was cold enough for snow today. Nico joined her after he closed the roller door and they were soon on the road to Burnie. Rolling, grassy hills flew past on either side, a hint of the blue ocean to their left appearing every time they dipped into a valley.

The idea of visiting the Burnie Police Station had sudden butterflies swirling in her stomach. To keep them at bay, Lacey asked the first question that came to mind. "Does Margie often arrive at your door unannounced?" Lacey was curious. Margie had seemed quite at home in Nico's kitchen.

Nico ran a hand through his hair, ruffling his long locks. "It's not uncommon," he conceded. "She came a lot when I first moved here. As did some of the other... Let's just call them the blue-rinse-brigade. The older women in the district like to help out where they can. It's a community spirit. This is what happens when you live rurally. Everyone knows everyone else's business."

"Yes, well, Margie certainly seemed to be on the hunt for some gossip this morning," Lacey replied, arching an eyebrow.

"Yeah, I got that. She was hoping I'd drop a juicy detail or three about the murder that she could spread around to the other girls."

"It wasn't the only reason she was here," Lacey said with a frown. She needed to tell Nico what Margie had said while he was out tending the geese, but it felt a little like betrayal. Margie was sweet and well-meaning, had really only been looking for some reassurance. Nico's eyes never left the road, but he stiffened in his seat, and she could feel the tension ramp-up around him. "She happened to mention that she was worried about Herb. He's suffering from insomnia, and she's constantly waking up in the middle of the night to find him missing."

Nico nodded thoughtfully at her words, and she could see his mind spinning. Exactly the same way hers had when Margie let the information slip.

"Did she say if he was missing from bed two nights ago?"

he asked without preamble.

"Not in so many words. But she hinted at it," Lacey replied, worrying at her bottom lip with her teeth. It meant that Herb didn't have an alibi for the night Rania was killed. "But surely...?" Lacey couldn't even begin to phrase the question. "He would've said if he'd seen or heard anything unusual that night. He's a lovely old man. They're a caring couple, looking out for their younger neighbors. Community-minded and active. They love their cycling and keep their garden neat. What possible motive could he have to hurt Rania?" There, she'd said it. She'd voiced her concerns over the friendly old man.

"I don't know," Nico mused. "But he's healthy and extremely fit for his age. He's certainly physically capable of hurting someone. And if he was awake during the wee hours of the morning, why didn't he just tell us? Even if he didn't see anything?"

Lacey felt a sudden heavy weight settle on her chest. How could he even think that helpful old man could be capable of such a thing?

"I'm going to have to ask him in to the station to answer some more questions," Nico said, but she could see by the downturn of his lip that he wasn't happy with the idea. He was only doing his job. If she still worked in the force, she'd be encouraging him to do this exact thing. But somehow it felt wrong.

CHAPTER EIGHT

Nico led Lacey out the front door and down the steps of the police station, then onto the pathway below. He turned left, and they walked side by side toward the harbor and the main shopping center. They passed the SES regional headquarters, a beautifully restored old colonial building and then strolled past the city council chambers before finally coming abreast of the first line of shops. Burnie boasted quite a few heritage buildings, scattered amongst the modern concrete structures. As did a lot of the country towns in Tasmania. It was one thing Nico liked about living on the island. They'd maintained a lot of their colonial history, unlike the bigger cities on the mainland where the old buildings were torn down to make way for the shiny new ones. The main street was busy, almost bumper to bumper with traffic, but it was nearly lunchtime, which accounted for the rush.

Lacey said nothing as she paced along beside him, and he wondered what was going through her head. It'd been an arduous morning, and it was probably going to be an even longer afternoon.

"You okay?" he asked.

"Mmm hmm." She nodded her reply.

"Sorry you had to relive all that over again."

"Don't be silly. You were just doing your job."

Her face was pale and drawn, and he was glad Imran had granted him this favor and slotted Lacey in for a consult. He'd tried to go easy on her in the interview, but it was being recorded—which she knew and understood the reasons for— and the answers she gave would be vital to the investigation. So he had to delve deep to make sure he got every little fact correct, insignificant, or not.

He hadn't learned a lot that he didn't already know. Lacey had been very comprehensive, even in her preliminary interview at the crime scene yesterday. She'd detailed how Margie had called her into the garden, how she'd found Rania, still alive, but unconscious with copious amounts of blood around her. Then Gabriel had arrived and taken over, inserting a cannula and administering life-saving drugs, while also bandaging the wounds. He'd established that Lacey never entered Rania's house—a good thing because one less person to contaminate the scene always helped—but revealed both Herb and Margie had gone in to retrieve blankets to keep Rania warm.

Then Rania had gone into cardiac arrest, and Lacey had helped Gabriel as best she could. They performed CPR for twenty minutes until the paramedics arrived. Nico could vouch for that last part of her story, because he'd arrived soon after Rania had coded. He'd stood there watching, helpless and frustrated, because he could do nothing more apart from holding back the bystanders.

He glanced across at her again. Her features seemed to have brightened slightly now they were outside, and she had the sights and sounds of the main street to fill her mind. After what Nico had learned about Lacey, how badly affected she'd been by that terrible act she'd witnessed, he was even more proud of how she'd conducted herself over that first half an hour as she fought to keep Rania alive. A lesser person may have let the trauma overwhelm them and refused to help. Or run away completely. But Lacey had stayed. She said it was her police training that'd taken over. But Nico knew there was also a strength of will there too. She would've made a good cop. Nico was beginning to see hints of what Lacey's commander had seen in her. If only she could get back to that person she'd once been. But that may be impossible.

"Up here." Nico guided Lacey toward a set of stairs next to the local newsagent that took them up to a first-floor suite of offices in another faithfully restored, red brick building. It was sort of a mini healthcare center, with his friend Gabriel taking one office, Imran with his psychology practice in another. There was also a sports physiotherapist and a nutritionist filling out the other two offices, with one main reception desk for all four practices. It was very modern and clean, if a tad sterile.

Imran was standing at reception as they walked up the hallway. He had on his serious, professional face, mustache perfectly groomed as always, and dark eyes watchful. Lacey had fallen a few steps behind Nico, as if suddenly nervous. He turned and looked her directly in the eye, not giving her a chance to change her mind. She needed this. And he needed to know she was being taken care of mentally. Without a doubt, he could take care of her physical safety, but protecting a person's emotional health was a tricky subject, best left to the professionals. Sure, he could offer her a shoulder to cry on if she needed it, but he wasn't about to offer solutions to her PTSD. He'd watched his mother try and battle with his father's demons, try to help him again and again, without success. Until his father eventually shut her out. Shut all of them out.

"I'll see you in an hour," he said, making sure his own serious and professional mask was also up. It wouldn't do for Imran to see that Lacey was special to him. That man had a million and one ways of getting into your head, and Nico didn't want him digging around in there asking about his love life if he could help it.

"Yes." Lacey drew her shoulders up and lifted her chin to look him directly in the eye. Good. She could do this.

Imran nodded to him in greeting and gave Nico a searching look, noting the bruises on his face with a shrewd frown but not commenting, before turning to lead Lacey into his office. Nico watched the door close and then turned and walked back toward the stairs.

"Nico." He was halfway down the hallway when a hand landed on his shoulder, and he spun around to find Gabriel standing behind him.

"Hey." Nico gave his friend a smile in greeting.

"How are you?" Gabriel asked, slapping Nico on the back with gusto. "I mean things must be crazy up at the station right now." His features pooled into a look of commiseration. "Are you here to see Imran?"

If Gabriel wasn't such a good friend, Nico might've taken exception to such a personal question. Instead, he shrugged and said, "No. I was showing Lacey the way up here."

He didn't include the details about which of the practitioners she was seeing, but Gabriel clearly filled in the blanks, because he said, "Poor thing. I don't blame her. I might book in for a few sessions myself. That was pretty intense yesterday. I mean, I've lost patients before, of course. But seeing Rania like that. Trying so hard to get her back. It just…" Gabriel's eyes went cloudy as his memory seemed to fill with the hectic moments trying to revive Rania. Then, as if he remembered where he was, he shook himself and said, "It was hard," he finished.

Nico could see it in the other man's eyes. Rania's death had affected him deeply. That was interesting; he hadn't been aware Rania was one of Gabriel's patients. But he shouldn't be surprised. He was the only GP in Burnie. Some people preferred to travel to Devonport, or even Launceston to see a health professional, however.

"I'm sorry," he said. Because he was. He was sorry they'd all had to experience this. This kind of thing would leave a permanent scar on a community. It also put everyone on edge and caused hysteria, making him that much more determined to catch the killer.

"I know." Gabriel shrugged. "I'm sure a lot of people will be affected. I've already had other patients asking after her. And I hear they're planning a vigil for her in a few days' time. A candle-lit service to highlight violence against women, down on the waterfront."

"Hmm." Nico had heard the same rumors. If it helped to start the healing process, then he was all for it. He'd make sure to be there too, in a professional capacity. In the unlikely event that the killer came along to gloat. He could study people, gauge their reactions. Even the smallest details could often be significant.

"Are you free for a late lunch?" Gabriel suddenly asked. "I mean, after Lacey has finished. I'd really like to catch up with you both. Talk it over with someone who understands. I can get Sarma to shuffle my patients."

No, Nico didn't really have time for lunch. He had a murder investigation to run. But Gabriel was his good friend, and if he could help him, even a little, then of course he'd be there. He thought about Margie's courgette slice awaiting him back at the station and shrugged. That could wait till tomorrow.

"Sure. Lacey is due to finish at two. I'll meet you in reception then," he said. He hoped Lacey wouldn't mind that he'd answered for her as well.

"Great, I'll book us into The Foreshore, I could go for some of their Cajun salmon right now," Gabriel replied, then turned on his heel to go back to his office. Nico was fine with that; the food at the restaurant was good.

"Oh, Gabe," Nico called. "I need you to schedule in a time to come down to the station. We still need your detailed statement."

Gabriel grimaced, but nodded his assent.

* * *

Exactly an hour later, Nico was back in reception, slouched against the wall, eyes trained on Imran's door. But even while he waited for Lacey to emerge, his mind wouldn't stop analyzing facts and figures. It'd been a very interesting morning. So much information was now being amassed on Rania's life it was going to take a while to sort through it all. Calls to the murder hotline that'd been set up straight after her death were running hot.

One call in particular had sparked Nico's interest. It was from a co-worker of Rania's at the motor mechanic shop where she worked as the receptionist. The man had said his name was Danny, and he was the head mechanic. He thought they should know that one of the third-year apprentices had been showing an unusual amount of interest in Rania. Had become fixated on her, if Danny was to be believed. Danny said he thought Rania might have even registered a complaint with the police after she'd caught him peering in her kitchen window one evening and had finally had enough of his antics. Nico had one of his team checking the system to see if he could find a record of that complaint. Danny had seemed almost keen to rat out this apprentice, and it made Nico wonder why. Was there some sort of personal vendetta going on there?

It'd take some time and digging to figure out the dynamics of the mechanic shop, but in the meantime, Nico had requested this apprentice, Floyd Hamilton was his name, come in for an interview first thing tomorrow morning.

Just then, Lacey emerged, and his eyes locked onto her face, forcing his rumination on the investigation into the background as he tried to gauge her mood instead. She saw him immediately and offered a bright smile, and his heart lifted. Which was odd and a little alarming. That her smile could have such an effect.

Today, her long, straight hair was left loose, tucked behind her ears to stop it falling in her face. She was wearing pretty much the same outfit as she had for the past few days, minus the sheepskin jacket—which they'd dropped in to be dry-cleaned this morning—jeans, and a blue woolen sweater, with boots. No-nonsense, warm, and casual attire. She moved to drape her rain jacket over one arm as she turned and shook Imran's hand. While the clothes were her everyday wear, somehow she managed to look sexy in them. Her long legs looked great in her well-worn jeans, and the sweater barely skimmed her hips, accentuating her flat stomach and nicely proportioned breasts. Not too big, and not too small.

He dragged his gaze away from her. What was he doing? Documenting this woman's desirable features while she was talking to a psych helping her come to terms with watching a woman die yesterday. Was he some kind of sick pervert?

"You're here." Gabriel's voice sounded from behind and Nico turned, grateful for the distraction. "Ah, and here comes Lacey," Gabriel added, looking over Nico's shoulder. "Just in time."

Lacey joined them, and Nico wanted to ask her how it'd gone. But he didn't want to put her on the spot in front of Gabriel, so he merely smiled down at her and said, "Gabe has asked us to join him for lunch. I hope you don't mind."

"Not at all," Lacey replied. "I'm actually starving. Even though I wonder how I can be hungry at a time like this," she added quietly.

"Don't be silly," Gabriel said, taking Lacey by the arm and

leading her down the hallway, leaving Nico to trail behind, feeling a little out of sorts as Lacey laughed at something Gabriel said. He shouldn't begrudge his friend; he and Lacey had gone through something horrendous yesterday. They now had an enduring connection.

They walked the short distance to The Foreshore Restaurant, located farther down the main road on the West Beach Waterfront, with a first-class view out over the ocean—which was still stormy, with whitecaps dotting the waves as far as the eye could see. Gabriel hung onto Lacey's arm the whole way.

The waitress ushered them to a premium table next to the large windows looking directly out at the view. The restaurant was only half-full, reminding Nico it was getting late for lunch.

Lacey ordered the spicy prawns with Asian salad and he ordered the buttermilk chicken burger, while Gabe ordered the Cajun salmon, just as he'd mentioned earlier.

They admired the view for a few moments before Lacey excused herself to go to the powder room. Both men watched her go, but when Nico looked back, he saw Gabriel's eyes fixed on his face, watching him watching her. Damn, had he been caught staring at Lacey? Gabe raised an inquiring eyebrow and gave a knowing smile, but said nothing for which Nico was forever grateful.

A quick change in subject was required, and he asked Gabe if he was up for a game of squash in the next few days. A few fast rounds in the courts would help get rid of some of this pent-up energy. Help him to loosen that itch between his shoulder blades that meant he was storing too much stress.

They were still talking about squash—Gabriel was thinking of buying a new racquet—when Lacey reappeared at the table. Almost at the same time, their meals arrived and conversation ceased as they all tucked into their food, making the odd appreciative noise.

Gabe laid his fork down and dabbed at the corner of his mouth. "I was wondering if the coroner has come back with cause of death yet?" He asked, then held up a hand as Nico frowned at him. "I know you wouldn't normally give those kinds of details away, but this time I have a vested interest, and I was hoping you might loosen your protocol just a little. I'd like to know for sure there was nothing else I could've done to save her," he added with a tight grimace.

Lacey looked up, a question mark in her raised eyebrow as she, too, waited for Nico's answer. Even though, with her experience on the force, she probably already knew what he was going to say. His friend certainly was right, Nico always kept the particulars of any investigation close to his chest. It was the first time Gabriel had ever asked him directly about the specifics of a case.

"No, it's too early for that," Nico replied, placing his fork carefully on the table. Of course Gabe would want to know if he could've done more to help Rania. He'd probably always feel a little responsible, no matter the coroner's findings.

"I'm assuming she went into hypovolemic shock," Gabriel mused, then seeing both Nico's and Lacey's confused glances, he added, "It's when the organs start to shut down due to loss of blood or other fluids. I pumped her full of epinephrine to try and increase her blood pressure, and then put her on a saline drip, hoping to force more liquids into her, but it wasn't enough. Usually the heart is the last organ to shut down, but if there isn't enough blood to pump around the body, the blood pressure drops and... Well, you saw what happened."

"Yes, we did," Lacey replied, also putting down her fork, as if she'd suddenly lost her appetite.

"People are already pointing the finger at the boyfriend, you know," Gabriel said conversationally. "It's all some of my patients are talking about. This is the biggest mystery to happen in this neck of the woods for a long time."

For some reason, Nico bristled at this throwaway comment. Of course people wanted to accuse the boyfriend. It was the easy answer. But he knew there was a lot more to this case; a lot more digging to do. Nico's team needed to wade through the backstory of Rania's young life first, to find anyone who might hold a grudge against her, or want to hurt her for whatever reason. Her family were refugees from Syria, as were Karim's. Could they have brought some sinister secrets with them when they fled the country? Maybe it wasn't Rania the killer had been after. Perhaps they were trying to send a message to her family, or to Karim. There were so many components to sort through when starting a murder investigation. And there were a lot more suspects high on Nico's list than just Karim. This Floyd fellow was definitely on his list now, but Nico was also keeping the idea of a serial killer in the area on his radar. He was sure the list would get much longer before he could start eliminating people.

And you couldn't just go around pointing the finger. It was dangerous. Especially if the media got hold of the rumor, which they no doubt already had. Shit, he hated this side of the investigation, the innuendos and the amateur sleuths who thought they had the case already tied up in a pretty bow. The media, who Nico often referred to as a pack of vultures—in private, of course—were already baying at the door, demanding answers. He'd had to station a cop out the front of Rania's place to keep away the rubberneckers, as well as the overeager reporters hanging around outside hoping to get a juicy tidbit from one of the neighbors. One zealous reporter had been found snooping in the back garden, about to break into the house, so he could video the inside of the victim's place and get the scoop on the other stations. It wasn't going to get any easier anytime soon.

Gabriel took another bite and then turned to face Lacey. "Was she still conscious when you got there? Or did she ever regain consciousness while you were with her?" he asked, his gaze fixed intently on Lacey's face.

Lacey cocked her head to one side. "No. Why?" There was a sudden gleam in her eye. Like the cogs of her cop brain were beginning to whir inside her head.

"I was just wondering if she said anything that could identify her killer, that's all." He shrugged and then gave a self-deprecating laugh. "But I guess Nico has already asked you that. And I guess if it was Karim who stabbed her, then the truth will come out sooner or later."

Lacey narrowed her eyes, but before she could respond, Nico said, "Karim is no more a suspect than anyone else in this investigation." He didn't bother to keep the warning note out of his voice. Gabriel was going too far. Listening to gossip was one thing, it was inevitable in a case like this, but actively engaging in that gossip was another thing altogether. It really sounded like Gabriel had decided Karim was guilty. And while the evidence might be running in that direction, nothing was set in stone. Nico needed cold, hard facts before he'd consider someone a definite suspect. "Perhaps you need to remind your gossiping patients that everyone is innocent until proven guilty. Or at least that's what the Covenant of Civil Rights says."

Gabriel looked up at Nico's sharp tone. "Oh, yes, I completely agree. Sorry, I was being insensitive. It's just that this thing has occupied my entire mind for the past twenty-four hours and it's hard not to keep from getting sucked in. I apologize if I overstepped the mark." Gabriel smiled and Nico felt a trickle of shame run down his spine. He shouldn't be getting angry at his friend. He was only human, just like everyone else. And of course, he wanted answers too.

"Perhaps we should steer clear of any more shoptalk for now," Nico said, by way of placation.

"Sure, of course," Gabriel replied, seeming not to take offense at Nico's reprimand. He went on to change the subject, talking about how snowed under with patients he was at the moment, and outlining his idea for perhaps expanding the little health center, by bringing on another GP or maybe a chiropractor.

Lacey didn't say anything, merely picked up her fork and continued to eat.

Half an hour later, all three of them walked back up the main street, all patting their full bellies and wrapping their jackets tighter around themselves. The wind had picked up today and felt like it was whipping in straight from the Antarctic.

"Oh, do you mind if I just pop in to see if my jacket is ready?" Lacey said as they passed by the dry-cleaner.

"We'll wait out here," Nico said, moving to stand in the leeway of the shopfront, out of the wind. Gabe took his lead and did the same thing. They stood in companionable silence for a few moments, Nico's mind already going over what was next on his list when he got back to the office. He'd asked Margie and Herb to come in and give formal statements, they were due in an hour, but he needed more background on how long Rania and Karim had lived in that house and—

"You like her, don't you?" Gabriel said softly, breaking his train of thought. He gave Nico a sideways smile. Before Nico could even open his mouth to deny it, Gabe went on. "Don't worry, you're secret is safe with me. I think it's a good thing. You need a woman in your life."

"There's nothing going on between us," Nico growled, annoyed at his friend's gentle ribbing.

"Yet." Gabe winked and patted Nico on the back. "She's hot, mate. You shouldn't let her slip through your fingers."

Nico shook his head in denial but his friend's words echoed in his head. He had to admit, Lacey was a good-looking woman. Yes, he was physically attracted to her. But it was complicated. Complicated because he was providing Lacey with shelter while her vehicle was fixed. She'd also revealed part of her damaged soul to him, and he wanted to help her with that. Then there was her involvement in this murder investigation. Apart from all that, she'd be moving on as soon as her van was repaired, and as soon as he told her she was no longer required as part of his investigation. Which technically, he didn't. She'd given her witness statement; she was free to move on. He didn't want to take advantage of that. This wasn't the right time to be having a relationship. Not for him, and not for her. He had no claim on Lacey. And she had no claim on him.

CHAPTER NINE

Lacey looked over from the passenger seat and smiled at Gabriel. "Thanks for giving me a lift home." She winced inwardly as she caught herself using the word *home*. It was Nico's home; she was simply staying there until she could move on again. Hopefully soon. Gabriel was concentrating on the road, which was full of twists and turns, and merely flicked her a smile in return. His car was some cute little stylish MG. Not her cup of tea; give her a practical four-wheel drive or her van any day.

The lift had been Lacey's idea. It struck her when she saw Gabriel walking down the hallway with Nico late that afternoon on his way to give his witness statement. She'd been stuck at the police station all day, and she knew Nico wouldn't be leaving anytime soon. She wouldn't want to pull him away from his vital work anyway. Gabriel lived in Wynyard, and Boat Harbour was another fifteen minutes farther down the road. It'd be a little out of his way, but she thought he'd probably be okay with the suggestion. So, she'd cornered Gabe when he came out from the interview room, and he'd happily agreed, telling her to come to his office in half an hour and they'd leave.

Nico hadn't looked all that pleased when she'd told him

her plan. But it was her only option if she didn't want to spend the next three or four hours waiting for him to finish up for the night. She knew how it went. When there was a big investigation, sleep was often in short supply for the first few intensive weeks of fact finding interrogations.

She was also feeling emotionally exhausted from her session with Imran. But he'd definitely helped her to put everything into better perspective. She'd told him about Cindi, and how she'd thought she might be getting better. Until the sight of Nico's blood had given her flashbacks. And then again how she'd frozen when she'd first seen Rania. But he was optimistic when she revealed her police training had taken over and she'd gone on autopilot until Rania was put in the ambulance. Imran had reiterated that she should continue with the breathing exercises and added a few of his own to the mix. He'd also given her a prescription for some antidepressants, which she had in her bag but wasn't sure if she was going to use yet. She had another appointment booked with him for two days' time. But would she still be in town by then?

The road straightened, and Gabriel took one hand off the wheel. "So, Nico tells me you're traveling around Tasmania. You have a sweet remodeled Kombi van. That sounds like a cool thing to do."

"Yes, I've seen some really interesting places," she replied.

"What's been your favorite so far?" he queried.

"Probably Wineglass Bay, down on the Freycinet Peninsula. That was spectacular."

"I've never been," Gabe admitted. "It's hard for me to take holidays right now. But it's on my bucket list. I'll get there one day."

Lacey nodded her agreement. "It's probably better to go in summer, then you can swim. The water was too cold for me. But the walk into the bay was amazing. And there were even kangaroos on the beach. I've never seen that before." Images of the gorgeous bay invaded her mind. The glassy, flat water with the beach curving around it like a lover. The red rocks, white sand, and aquamarine ocean. It was no wonder it was considered one of the jewels in Tasmania's crown.

"You're right, summer would be a better time to go. It's bloody freezing at the moment. Don't you get cold sleeping in that little van of yours every night? Get a little lonely?"

"Not really. I have an electric heater which warms up the space nicely. And once I'm in bed, then I'm always toasty. It's very snug." For some reason, she decided not to tell Gabe that she'd been sleeping in the main house.

"Hmm. Well, I'm sure Nico would be happy to warm you up, if you need it."

She gave him a sideways glance. What was he implying?

"He likes you, you know. I can tell. We've been friends long enough I can see the signs when Nico is interested in someone," he said, as if it were the most natural thing in the world to suggest that Nico was keen on her.

"Oh…um…" She was at a loss for words. She hadn't expected Gabe to just blurt that out, and she was completely caught off guard. "We're not… I'm not…"

"It's fine," Gabe laughed. "Sorry, I didn't mean to embarrass you."

"No, you didn't," she lied. What did she say to throw him off? She didn't want anyone getting the wrong idea about her and Nico, not even his best friend. "But I'm moving on soon, once my van is fixed, and I…" What? "I'm happy with my own company right now. Especially with everything that's just happened. It's all been a bit stressful," she finished lamely.

"Yes, it has," he replied lightly. "And I completely understand. But sometimes we all need a little…stress relief." The cheeky wink he gave her before he went back to watching the road made her groan quietly inside.

Was it really that obvious? How attracted she was to Nico?

She stared out the window as she considered Gabe's words. Should she partake in a little *stress relief* with Nico, as Gabe put it. A fling, a hookup, a quickie. Maybe that would put to rest the constant awareness she had of Nico whenever he was in the room. Maybe if she scratched that itch, she might be able to concentrate properly again.

Lacey drew in a quiet sigh of relief. It wasn't like she'd never had a one night stand before. She'd already given in to temptation once while in Tasmania. She'd been down in Hobart and met a sexy sailor at a bar near Constitution Dock, got a little tipsy and when he'd asked if she wanted to check out his boat—a big maxi yacht, which it turned out he was only crewing, he didn't own it—she'd taken him up on his offer.

Lacey turned to study Gabriel out of the corner of her eye as he drove. He was a nice guy. Extremely good-looking, smartly dressed, intelligent, had a job her mother would absolutely covet, and his slight French accent was to die for. But he didn't interest Lacey in the slightest. Nico barely had any of his French accent left. He said he'd moved to Australia when he was only ten, and he'd been so desperate to fit in with the rest of the Aussie kids at school he'd purposefully lost his accent. Pity. Lacey was a sucker for that smooth, honey-like cadence. Hmmm, Nico with the imperfect scar on his face speaking French to her…

She pushed the thoughts of Nico aside and asked Gabriel, "What about Cradle Mountain? Have you been there? Now that is definitely on my bucket list." The famous mountain wasn't too far from here. Around two hours' drive inland if Google Maps was to be believed.

"Yes, that's one place I have managed to get to. Nico and I hiked part of the Overland Track two summers ago. It's so beautiful up there. I hear it snowed on the peak yesterday. Now that'd be an amazing sight to see."

"Oh, really? Perhaps I should head up that way once my van is fixed." Now they were back on safer ground, Lacey let out a quiet breath. She'd been planning on continuing her trek to Stanley farther up the coast, and save the hiking for later on, but perhaps the sight of Cradle Mountain covered in snow shouldn't be missed.

For the next twenty minutes they debated the pros and cons of taking her Kombi into a mountainous area where the roads might be blocked with snow against the chance of seeing a white-capped peak. Their conversation was easy and natural, but Lacey made sure to lead the topic onto other good places to see when she cruised around the island, while trying to ignore the elephant in the room. Rania's death. She didn't want to answer any more questions about the scene when she'd first arrived, or rehash it all over and over with Gabriel. And she could feel he wanted to talk about it, like most normal human beings, it was a natural response. But she was all talked out on that particular subject. Besides, she knew all the members on Nico's team would be under strict orders to keep vital information under wraps. Not to leak it to the public or the media. Not that she was on Nico's team, and not that she was even officially still on the force. But old habits die hard.

Gabe dropped her in Nico's driveway and watched to see that she got safely up to her van before reversing back onto the road and giving her a wave goodbye. Smudge's barking got her moving toward the back door. Poor dog had been tied up all day. She was welcomed by a tail-wagging fur-ball, who jumped up and licked her face as she tried to unclip his lead. He probably needed a walk, but she was too tired. Instead, she let him run around the back paddock—it was too big to be called a yard—for a few minutes. He was lifting his leg on everything in sight, as she went to check on her van. Everything was still in order and she looked longingly at her couch and the pop-top roof bed. Perhaps she should just return to her van and not stay in the house, as Nico had suggested. Surprisingly, she missed her tiny home. But she'd promised to cook something for dinner, then Nico could reheat it, no matter what time he finally arrived home. And she had to admit it was much warmer inside. With a lot more room to move around. Decision made, she whistled Smudge to come inside.

After flicking on all the lights as she went through the house, Lacey prioritized turning on the gas heater in the main living room and the little electric heater in the kitchen to warm the place. Nico had an open fireplace and plenty of chopped wood around the side, but she couldn't be bothered to take the time to light it.

Then she moved around the kitchen, opening the refrigerator and checking in cupboards, until she found an assortment of ingredients with which she could make a meal. Nico kept his cupboards well stocked, which was a little surprising. Most men she knew lived on frozen meals and takeaway, but it seemed that Nico cooked when he had the time. Vaguely, she wondered what he would've done if she hadn't been here to prepare the meal. There were plenty of tins of soup in the larder; maybe it would've been minestrone and toast for dinner. For a second, she imagined him sitting at the kitchen table alone, eating with only Smudge for company. The life of a detective could often be solitary and isolating. Well, she could do better than that.

Lacey had gathered together the makings of vegetarian pasta. Pumpkin, walnuts, and spinach—that looked like it might've come from Nico's back garden—a tin of tomato puree and some nutmeg. Yum.

Smudge watched her moving about the kitchen with

hungry eyes. It was funny just how at home she felt in here. Almost like she'd lived here all her life. Nico had told her the cottage had been renovated when he bought it, but he'd done a good job of decorating the place, and the kitchen had all the essential appliances but with an eclectic collection of pots and pans and crockery that suited the rustic style.

It was past seven when she sat down to eat. Smudge had a bowl of dog food and a little dollop of pasta to top it off. She ate in silence, only the sound of Smudge licking his lips and the branches of a shrub tapping against the windowpane to break the quietude. But that was okay, she was used to silence after all her time alone in her van.

Taking a mouthful, she thought about Nico, wondered what he was doing now. The random thought that it'd be nice to have him here, sitting at the table with her made her fork stall halfway to her mouth. Two nights. That's all it'd taken. For her to become used to having him around. To enjoy his company. To miss him. Uh-oh, she might be in trouble here.

* * *

Lacey was just drying the final dish and putting it away in the cupboard when her phone buzzed on the countertop. She answered it without checking caller ID, thinking it might be Nico. Shit. Bad idea. Her mother's voice echoed down the phone. "Lacey, is that you?"

"Of course it's me, Mum." Lacey held back a sigh. Who else would it be?

Her mother always chose the worst times to call. Admittedly, Lacey had been even more slack than normal; she hadn't called home in over two weeks. But she had her reasons. And now she had the ultimate excuse; she was caught up in a murder investigation.

"Yes, well." Her mother sniffed loudly. "I'm calling to find out how you are. Because, God forbid my daughter would ever phone *me* and let *me* know." Lacey held back a second sigh, this one a lot closer to escaping. And so it began. The guilt-tripping.

"Yep. Sorry, Mum. I've been busy…traveling. Not a lot of reception in these places, you know," she replied, keeping her tone light. No point in putting her mother on the defensive straight away. Because once you annoyed Elora Carmichael, it took a lot of hard work and groveling to get her back onside again.

"Well, where are you? How have you been?" Elora asked, her words snippy.

"I'm in a little town called Boat Harbour Beach. It's right on the coast, set amongst all these rolling, green hills. There isn't even a grocery shop, that's how small the community is. It's a real pretty little place, I think you'd love it."

"How on earth could you think I'd like a place without the convenience of a grocery shop?" her mother huffed, pouncing on the one thing she could complain about. "That sounds like the worst kind of backwater. Whatever do you see in these little two-bit towns, Lacey?"

This time, Lacey did let out the sigh, long and low, holding the phone away from her ear, so hopefully her mother didn't hear it. How could she forget so quickly that nothing she did or said ever made her mother happy? Now she remembered why she hadn't called in two weeks. It was to avoid this constant barrage of negativity.

"No, you're right, you wouldn't like this place," Lacey agreed. Which was probably exactly why Lacey liked it so much. Time to change the subject. "But how have you been, Mum? What have you and Dad been up to?"

"If you called more often, then you might know. Your father and I have suffered through a bout of Covid. And it was terrible. I've never been so sick in all my life."

"Oh, I'm sorry to hear that." She winced as she spoke. Her mother always overplayed her illnesses, it was just one more way to garner attention. But she would expect that attention. Lacey tried to force the words past her lips, and not sound too trite while doing so. "I hope it didn't last too long. Are you feeling better now?"

"No," her mother snapped. "I'm still not myself. This disease takes away your very will to live. I'm exhausted all the time." There was a slight pause and Lacey braced herself. "It would've been nice if you were here, so you could've helped take care of us. As it was, poor Sammy had to do everything. Run my errands for me. Everything. But I didn't want her to catch it, too, so I made her stay down the other end of the house, and I got Greta to bring us our food and medication."

"Yes, poor Sammy," Lacey agreed, screwing up her nose with the effort of making it sound like she agreed with her mother and she wasn't in fact being as cynical as hell. But really she should be saying poor Greta. Her mother's full-time house cleaner was an absolute saint in Lacey's eyes to put up with her mother's demands. And Sammy. Lacey could just imagine what her little sister had done for their parents while they were sick. A big fat nothing. Sammy was the golden child as far as her mother was concerned. And she was becoming a spoiled little brat as far as Lacey was concerned. Still living at home and sponging off her parents, lolling about the mansion, pretending to be training to become a beauty therapist, but only going to classes when she felt like it.

But she could tell by the icy silence on the other end of the phone that her mother hadn't bought it. Lacey cursed inwardly. She hadn't been sincere enough.

"At least Sammy is here, where she belongs, helping out. Not traipsing around an island in the middle of nowhere avoiding her issues. Unlike some people I could name." Her mother drew breath, but Lacey knew there was more to come.

Then her mum let her have it, questioning how Lacey could stay away from her family for so long, asking when she was coming home to rejoin civilization, telling her how she was letting her family down, making them look bad in the eyes of their friends and the rest of society by her lack of ability to cope. It was the familiar lecture on how she was the worst daughter in the world. Lacey held the phone away from her ear, so she didn't have to hear it. She'd been informed often enough about her lapses in daughterly duty to know how this conversation would go. A one-sided tirade.

Lacey's time traveling around Tasmania had given her a certain sense of freedom. Time and space away from her mother had been a liberating experience. It finally made her wonder why her mother was such an ordeal to live with. So, she'd done some research. And she'd thought she may have hit on the answer when she'd read a book about narcissistic personality disorder. It'd been quite an eye-opener, and it explained many of the horrible things her mother did and said. But none of those reasons could ever excuse her mother's behavior. And she would never change. So it was up to Lacey to decide how she would handle their relationship going forward, which was becoming more and more toxic over time. One solution was to take herself away from her mother's sphere of influence, hence why her trip to Tasmania was such a good idea. It lessened the amount of guilt trips Lacey had to endure, but it didn't really solve anything. Certainly not long term.

"Mmm hmm," Lacey murmured into the phone when it sounded like her mother might've finally wound down. It was no use arguing with Elora when she was like this; it only gave her more ammunition. Lacey usually capitulated until she could change the subject. Which she was about to do.

"Is Dad around? I'd like to talk to him and see how he's feeling as well," Lacey ventured. There was no way she was going to tell her mother anything about what she'd just been through in the past few days. But someone in her family needed to know. She'd fill her father in on the details and let him decide the best time to tell Elora later on down the track, when she wasn't in one of her moods.

"Oh, I see. My conversation isn't good enough for you. Of course, you want to talk to your father. You always were daddy's girl." Lacey bit her lip in an effort not to scream. How did you argue against that kind of mentality? Her mother was a nightmare. She wasn't a daddy's girl, far from it, but at least with her father she could have a logical conversation, not filled with emotional blackmail bombs going off every ten seconds. "Barry," her mother yelled down the phone, nearly deafening her. "Lacey is on the phone. She wants to talk to you."

Perhaps the more tactful thing to do would've been to hang up and ring her father on his own cell phone. But Elora would most likely have cottoned onto that eventually, and Lacey would still be in the shit for going behind her back.

"Hi, luv, how are you going?" her father's familiar baritone came down the line. She and Barry had a pretty good father-daughter relationship. It was only when it came to her mother that she felt Barry let her down. He never argued with Elora to her face. He would merely let her go on with whatever mean thing she was saying at the time. Behind Elora's back he was caring and supportive, but he'd never once stood up to his wife, and it made Lacey so mad. It also created a lack of respect for her dad. She knew why he did it. His capitulation was for his own protection. So that he didn't become the target for Elora's next vicious attack. But in his own way, he was enabling Elora's behavior.

Lacey had often wondered why he stayed with her. Speculating that it was because of the money seemed small and mean of her, but it might just be true. Barry Carmichael had made his millions establishing a chain of very successful discount pharmacies. He'd started off as the pharmacist in his own chemist shop forty years ago and had built it up into over ten separate shops, with more coming soon. But if he divorced his wife, she'd get half of all his wealth. Possibly more, if her lawyers were good enough. Barry was at work more than he was at home, limiting the time he had to deal with Elora. Probably on purpose.

"I'm doing okay, Dad," Lacey replied. "But a few things have happened lately, and I need to tell you what's going on." Lacey launched into the story of how her van had broken down and she'd ended up being stranded in Boat Harbour Beach. Then she went on to tell him about her walk that fateful morning and how she'd become embroiled in a murder investigation. He listened quietly, only interrupting her twice to get more pertinent details. She mentioned Nico, but only in passing, telling Barry that he was the detective sergeant in charge of the investigation. He needn't know Nico had also offered her sanctuary after her van had broken down.

Finally, when she wound down and stopped speaking, he said, "That sounds horrific, and my heart goes out to that poor family of the murdered girl. But you need to take care of yourself first, Lacey. You know how…fragile you are at the moment. What are you planning to do? Perhaps it's time you came home."

"I don't know, Dad. But please don't tell Mum what's going on. Not yet."

"She'll need to know soon. Because if she finds out some other way…" Her father didn't need to finish his sentence; Lacey knew her mother would never forgive her if that happened. "The poor murdered girl has already been on the news over here, but you know your mother rarely watches TV."

"I know," Lacey replied glumly. But even a few days of peace from her mother's constant *I told you sos* when she found out would be a welcome interlude. "I'll call her in a few days. I promise."

"Okay." Her father's voice was full of uncertainty. He didn't like keeping secrets from his wife. Could she trust him to hold on to this one for the next few days? "And, Lacey. Let us know what your plans are soon too. You know I don't often ask things of you, but I really think it's time you abandoned this trip. This girl's death...well, it feels like a sign."

"Mmm hmm," Lacey murmured, not wanting to disagree with her father. Because the sad truth was, she didn't know what she planned to do next. The more she thought about it, the more foolish it seemed to keep going with her travels. How could she continue while her involvement in this whole murder hung over her head? Seeing Imran today had helped bring her back from the edge, stopped her slipping into her previous habit of retreating from the world. But perhaps she should go home and arrange to see her old psych on a more regular basis. Try and get back into a routine. Rejoin the real world.

CHAPTER TEN

Nico unlocked the back door and was met by an ecstatic Smudge, who forgot his manners and jumped up to lick his face. Nico let it slide, because his mind was taken up by other things. Such as coming home to a house with the lights on and a delicious smell emanating from the kitchen. Coming home to someone else. A warm house, that felt like someone lived here.

It'd been an especially trying evening. He undid the band from his hair, shaking it free, and scrubbed a hand over his tired eyes. Working in these rural stations was often fulfilling and never dull. But it also had its drawbacks. Like having to deal with locals who he liked, and interacted with every day, only to treat them with seeming indifference while he was executing his job. He'd just come from down the hill, where he'd been paying a visit to Margie and Herb. And it hadn't been pleasant. But that was the job, he had to keep reminding himself of that.

He entered the kitchen and was greeted by the sight of Lacey leaning her hip against the countertop and talking into her phone. Sending him a tight smile, she went back to listening to whoever was on the other end of the phone, her knee jiggling impatiently. He drank in the sight of her, taking the chance to flick his glance from top to bottom. She'd kicked off her boots and was wearing socks beneath her tight jeans which outlined her shapely legs and hips as she shifted from one foot to another. Her blonde hair hung long and straight around her shoulders, softening her features and hiding the side of her face. Her dark-blue sweater hugged her curves. The scene of Lacey standing in his kitchen set off something warm and nebulous inside his gut. Like he wanted to go up and touch her just to make sure she was real. He'd seen her wearing this same outfit around the police station for most of the day, but for some reason she looked different. Like she belonged here.

Smudge still gamboled around his knees, so he bent to give the dog a proper pat. Shrugging out of his jacket, he hung it on a hook next to Lacey's by the back door and removed his service weapon from its holster and stowed it in the small gun safe in a top cupboard in the kitchen. He was just about to head into the living room to give her some privacy, when he heard her say, "Yes, Dad, I understand. I'm sorry, but I really have to go. I promise to call you again soon." With that, she hung up and pushed her phone into her back pocket with a dramatic sigh.

"Sorry. That was my dad." She rubbed her forehead and grimaced and he wondered what they'd been talking about. Her parents must be worried sick about her being a prime witness in a murder investigation. His mother still worried about him, even after all this time of him being a detective.

"Don't apologize," he replied.

"You're home a little earlier than I expected," she said, lifting a corner of her mouth. "I made pumpkin and spinach pasta. Would you like some?"

"Sounds divine." His mouth had already been watering from the smell drifting through the kitchen. "I'll just light the fire, if that's okay?"

"Sure. That'll be nice. I'll heat up your dinner."

He lit the fire most nights. It was a gentler heat than gas, which he normally kept for the odd occasion when he couldn't be bothered to fetch the wood and strike a match. But it might be nice to sit in the living room with a crackling fire, a glass of red, and Lacey's company.

Smudge accompanied him outside. He knew the dog was dying to go for a walk, but perhaps he'd take him later, after dinner. It only took him a few minutes to set the fire and light the kindling, and he soon had a bright blaze going in the hearth. Just as he stepped back, warming his palms against the flames, Lacey entered the room, a plate of food in one hand and a bottle in the other.

"I've already eaten," she said apologetically. "But I found your stash of wine in the cupboard, and I'd love to join you in a glass. I hope that's okay?"

"You read my mind," he replied with a grin, taking two crystal glasses from a wooden side table behind the couch. They were an heirloom, belonging to his grandmother on his father's side. French cut crystal and probably quite expensive, but he rarely used them. Tonight was as good as any time to bring them out of hibernation.

Lacey took a seat in one of the winged chairs, placing his plate on a small coffee table, while he opened the wine.

"We should probably let it breathe," he said with a shrug. It was a good Tasmanian pinot noir—the island was renowned for its cold-climate boutique wines. "But to hell with it." He poured them both a glassful, then raised his glass and clinked it against the edge of hers, the crystal giving out a pure, clear tinkle.

"This is a little more civilized than eating outside on fold-up chairs," Lacey admitted, taking a sip and leaning back in her chair.

He didn't disagree, but he was too busy digging into the

delicious pasta to answer.

"How did your afternoon go?" He could hear the compassion in her voice. She understood a little of the stress he was under right now. He hadn't seen a lot of her after they'd had lunch together. He'd been busy with other witnesses and amassing facts from all the various statements so far. His intention had been to go and find her midafternoon, just to check in and perhaps take her to coffee, but then things had got hectic. Floyd Hamilton had been brought in for an interview earlier than expected, all belligerent and demanding to know what he'd done wrong, and Nico's good intentions had fallen by the wayside. It bothered him, knowing she was hanging around the station, waiting for him to finish up, and so he should've been glad when she organized her own way home tonight, putting him out of his misery. Briefly, he wondered how the drive home had gone with Gabriel.

"I saw Herb and Margie come in this afternoon. Could they offer anything new?" she asked, snapping his mind away from Gabe. Her question was harmless, built on curiosity and nothing more, but he tensed at her words, swallowing hard. Had she guessed something had happened in that interview? Was it written all over his face?

Should he tell her? She was a cop—or had used to be, at any rate—and she'd know to keep anything he said to herself.

"Actually... Yes, they did." Or specifically, Herb had said some things that had set his whole team abuzz. Nico tried to decide what to tell Lacey. He was already on edge after Gabe's uncalled for probing. And he wasn't used to sharing his thoughts with anyone outside the members of his team. But Lacey had once been a cop. And he'd already talked over other details of the investigation with her. In the end, he determined he could trust her. Especially because he'd like her evaluation on what Herb had said. She might be able to offer a different point of view, an altered insight into Herb's bombshell claims.

He took another mouthful of the delicious pasta—he could get used to Lacey's cooking; he could've sworn he didn't have the ingredients to whip up something this tasty in his cupboards—to give himself time to phrase his next comment.

"Herb revealed some interesting insights into Rania and Karim's relationship today."

"Wow," Lacey breathed and leaned forward in her chair, causing her hair to tumble forward over her shoulders, reflecting the glow of the flames and shimmering like gold in the firelight, momentarily distracting him from his line of thought. "Like what?" she asked.

He should probably start at the beginning, so he put his fork down. "We talked to the couple separately, of course. Myself and Senior Constable Jackson were doing the interviews. You met him this morning. Tyrell is a good officer."

Lacey merely nodded, rolling her wineglass between her palms and watching him intently.

"Margie came in first, and she retold the events of that morning with good accuracy. Everything fit with her first statement." Lacey would understand the significance of that. If a witness started to change their story, they were either unreliable, or lying. Neither of which would stand up in court. But Margie's account was solid, and Nico believed everything she said.

He snatched another mouthful before he continued. "But by the time Herb came in, he seemed a little...on edge. You know?" Nico wasn't sure why, but he picked up some sort of vibe coming off Herb that hadn't been there the other morning. Or perhaps it was all such a mess of local bystanders and cops and paramedics, he just hadn't been watching for the signs at the time. But now, Herb had had time to stew, sitting in the waiting room while they interviewed his wife. Maybe he was worried about what she might've said to the cops.

"Anyway, when I asked him what he knew about Rania's relationship with Karim, he clammed up. I was just asking if he thought they were happy together, normal procedural question, you know what I mean? But he went all weird and wouldn't look at me, saying he didn't know. Then, I pushed harder. After your conversation with Margie, I was hoping he might admit to being awake that night. Admit to his insomnia. Perhaps let on that he had seen something, so I didn't have to initiate the conversation. Instead, he said Karim wasn't the saint everyone said he was."

"What does that mean?" Lacey asked.

"He finally revealed that Rania had broken down one evening and told him everything. He'd found her walking up and down their street late at night, crying. Margie was still in bed, so he'd taken Rania back to her house and they'd sat on the front steps. And that's when she'd told him she didn't know what to do anymore. That Karim was using drugs—she thinks it was cocaine—to get him through the early starts and long hours at the bakery. They'd had a huge argument about it, and Karim had taken off. But it didn't sound like this was their first argument. Herb had heard raised voices a few times before, when he'd been up because he couldn't sleep." He took a breath and shoveled some more food into his mouth, giving Lacey time to digest his news.

The fact Karim might be a cocaine addict was a big one, and of course he'd be investigating that right away. If he'd been on a bender, or in a drug-fueled rage, and they'd had an argument, it could easily have driven him to stab Rania in a fit of violence. But Nico wasn't about to start jumping to conclusions. They'd bring Karim in first thing tomorrow to question him. But until then, he could only speculate.

And the mystery only got deeper. "Rania begged Herb not to tell Margie because the old woman adores Karim, and she didn't want her to think less of them as a couple," he added, watching for Lacey's reaction.

"And Herb agreed to that?"

"Sadly, yes."

"So, there's no one to back up his claims?"

"Not at the moment, no."

Lacey didn't say it, but he knew by her wrinkled forehead that she was thinking much the same as him. He liked the way she picked things up so quickly. Liked her sharp mind and her logical thinking. It was no wonder she'd decided to become a cop. He looked up to see her intelligent amber gaze regarding him with interest. Their eyes locked for a few seconds longer than was strictly necessary, and Nico felt a surge of heat through his groin. Although she was sitting in the armchair and he was on the couch, she'd shuffled forward as her interest took hold, and now their knees were almost touching, her hair hanging like a silken sheet within reach if he let his fingers do what they wanted. He could almost smell the shampoo she'd used to wash her hair this morning. *Look away, Nico, before you embarrass yourself.* He cleared his throat and took a sip of wine, breaking their contact as he did so.

There was more to his story, so he concentrated on that instead. "The most important part is that he also revealed he had some of Rania's stuff stored in his shed. Said she'd asked him to look after it for her, because she didn't trust Karim."

"Oh, no." Lacey clapped a hand over her mouth, her eyes wide. She understood the second that he said the words how much it changed everything. For Karim. For the investigation. And for Herb. There could be vital evidence in whatever was in Herb's shed. Herb might not realize it yet, but this wasn't good for him. So far, Nico didn't think Herb had a motive to kill Rania, but he certainly had the opportunity. Perhaps there was something else going on between the old man and the young woman no one knew about yet. And perhaps that stuff might hold the evidence. "So you think Herb is trying to implicate Karim?" she said, almost in a whisper.

"I'm not sure," Nico replied with an unhappy grimace. If anything, this news complicated things even further. "It really seemed as if he didn't want to tell us any of this at first. As if he really was trying to protect the boyfriend. And Rania's privacy. As if he didn't believe the guy was capable of murdering his lover. It wasn't until I suggested I'd be prepared to issue a search warrant for his house and shed, that his face kind of crumpled and he blurted out the whole truth." Herb might be old, but he wasn't stupid. He would've known it was better to tell the police what he knew now, rather than let them uncover it later, which would make him look guilty as hell.

"He said he's got three boxes of Rania's stuff in total, but he says he doesn't know what's in them. That he would never pry into her private business."

Lacey raised a skeptical eyebrow at that, but Nico thought Herb might've been telling the truth on that count. He was an old-fashioned man with old-fashioned values.

"Anyway, I ordered a search warrant for the property, which I helped to execute this evening. I've just left Herb's place. Senior Constable Jackson is in charge now, and the boxes should be at the station waiting for the team to go through first thing tomorrow."

"Poor Margie. Poor Herb. They probably don't deserve to be mixed up in this." Lacey sighed and put down her now-empty wineglass. He knew what she meant. It would've been a scary thing for the old couple to go through, watching their house being searched by a team of police. Wondering what it all meant for them. Nico had been professional and brisk when he'd first knocked on the door to the cottage. When

Margie's surprised face had crumpled into dismay and then despair as he read out the rights on the search warrant, he had to stop his immediate reaction to put his arm around her shoulder and comfort her. He'd had to remind himself to do his job. That by doing his job, he was protecting the innocent, even if it didn't feel much like it at that moment.

"Perhaps not. But with this information, along with Margie's admission that Herb might not have been in bed where he was supposed to be on the night of the murder— Herb never confirmed whether he suffered from insomnia, or whether he was awake that night—you know what it means, don't you?"

Lacey nodded her head sadly. "Yes. Do you think he realizes he's a suspect yet?"

"Not sure." Nico refilled Lacey's glass and his own, then leaned back into the couch and stared at the fire, the flames having died down to bright glowing coals. This was the hardest part of being a small town detective. Sometimes the people he knew and perhaps even loved were involved in the crimes he was called on to investigate.

"So, that's where you've been tonight?" she asked, compassion in the lines around her eyes.

"Yes." There was no need for more of an answer. She would probably comprehend how hard that'd been for him.

"How was Gabriel this afternoon?" Nico decided it was time to stop talking shop and change the subject.

"What?" Lacey looked up sharply. "Oh, yes. It was lovely of him to drive me home. We talked about all the good places I have yet to see around Tasmania." But it wasn't her words he was concentrating on. Rather her body language. Had her face just turned pink? Or was it the reflection from the flames?

What had Gabe said to her? It wouldn't surprise him if Gabe had been trying to matchmake. Nico gave a soft sigh.

Damn Gabe and his meddling ways.

"You talked about Tasmania?" he asked a little dully, trying —and failing—to get his mind operating again. But it wouldn't cooperate. All he could think about was what Lacey might've said to Gabe in response. Was she just as attracted to him? The idea was riveting.

"Yes," she replied, but he hardly knew what she was agreeing too. She took a sip of wine, leaving a ruby-red drop of liquid trembling on her top lip. He became mesmerized by that droplet, couldn't look away. She noticed his gaze and her tongue came out to lick the wine away. But goddamnit, her attempt to remove the liquid just made the whole thing that much more seductive. Now he was noticing how lush her lips were. How her bottom lip was slightly fuller than the top. And how her front teeth were straight and white as she opened her mouth a little, as if about to speak. She stared at him, those big tawny eyes fixed on him. She had long, sandy eyelashes that framed her eyes. Was it the second glass of wine making him a little crazy?

He leaned forward, not really aware of what he was doing, only knowing he was drawn toward this woman. He looked down to see their knees were almost touching. When he glanced up again, she was suddenly closer, also leaning in to him. Their eyes locked and he couldn't look away. The silken sheet of her blonde hair drifted past her face, and before he knew it, he was running the strands through his fingers, feeling the softness against his palm. Her skin looked velvety in the firelight as he traced the contours of her face with his gaze. He wanted to kiss her. Desperately. The urge thrummed through him like a smoldering fire. He forgot all about the fact she was leaving soon. Forgot all about the murder investigation they were both tied up in. Forgot all the important things and focussed on her, and her alone. His hand wandered to her thigh. It was firm and warm beneath his fingers.

His concentration narrowed until there was just her and him in the room. He moved closer. Or was it her who moved? A tickle of her warm breath flowed over his lips, they were so near now. So near he could see the golden flecks in her eyes glowing in the firelight.

He let himself go.

Leaning in, his lips almost touched hers.

There was a loud banging on the front door.

No!

He willed whoever was there to go away.

Lacey licked her lips and he watched, fascinated by her pink tongue.

"I know you're in there," a deep voice bellowed. Followed by more banging.

Shit. Both he and Lacey sat back at the same time.

"Who the hell...?" he growled. But the moment had been shattered into a thousand shards.

"Let me in," the voice bellowed again, and this time, Nico caught a hint of menace. As well as a slight slurring. Whoever was knocking on his door at this late hour of the evening was drunk. And Nico wasn't happy. Not happy at all.

Pushing out of his chair, he stomped down the hallway, ready to tell this person to rack off.

Lacey was right behind him as he strode toward the door, and as the banging got louder, he suddenly wished he'd taken the time to collect his firearm. The front door was original to the cottage, but had been restored along with the rest of the building. It was solid wood, but sported two glass leadlight panes in the upper half. Whoever was on the other side of the door, they were rattling it so hard he was worried the glass might break. Fleetingly, he wondered if he should perhaps replace the door with something more security conscious. And get a peephole installed. Because right now he was opening the door blind, and had no idea what or who was going to greet him on the other side. He flicked on the porch light and saw a large man silhouetted in the glow.

Putting his hand on the door handle, he pushed Lacey behind him, ignoring her protests, and opened the door just enough to see who was standing on his front porch, keeping his foot firmly jammed up against the inside.

It was Karim Khaled, Rania's boyfriend.

"What are you doing here?" Nico demanded, keeping a firm hold on the door. He cursed inwardly. Of course Karim would know where he lived. Most of the residents of Boat Harbour knew where the local detective lived. If this guy tried to force his way in, he'd have a harder time than he imagined. Lacey stood on tiptoe and peered over Nico's shoulder. Karim leaned against the doorjamb, looking as if he could hardly support himself. This guy was more than drunk, he was completely blotto. Not a good sign.

As soon as Karim's gaze landed on Lacey's face, he stood upright and became more animated. "You," he said, pointing at Lacey. "You were there. When she…" He didn't seem to be able to bring himself to say the word. Nico tried to push Lacey farther behind him, but she resisted. He knew she was probably fuming at his overprotective gesture, and would most likely tell him in no uncertain terms that she could protect herself. Which she could, he could personally attest to her self-defense skills. But this was his house, and he was in charge here.

"They said she was alive when you found her. She must've said something to you." Karim took a staggering step forward and Nico put a hand on his chest to prevent him from coming inside.

"Stay away," Nico commanded. "Or I'll have to arrest you." Arrest him for what exactly, Nico wasn't sure yet, but he couldn't allow the guy to come into his house. He was so drunk he could hardly stand, and his words were coming out slurred and unintelligible.

"Rania. She must've said something to you," Karim repeated loudly, staring at Lacey over Nico's shoulder. "They're going to frame me for murder." At that, the man giggled wildly, as if it were the funniest thing in the world. Then he sobered again. "But she must've told you who did it. You must know." Karim made a stumbling lunge, trying to reach Lacey over Nico's shoulder. Nico swung into action, grabbing the man's wrist as he reached for Lacey and twisting it savagely up and back, forcing the man to turn around so he could march him out of the door. Karim tried to struggle and break free, but Nico landed him on the floorboards with a thump, putting his knee directly into the man's back. He'd used reasonable force to restrain the man, but the guy was so drunk, he suddenly stopped fighting.

"Call for backup," Nico commanded without taking his eyes off the man underneath him.

He could feel Lacey hesitate behind him, as if loath to leave him, but then she did as she was told and ran inside for her phone.

Now he was incapacitated on the ground, Karim's menacing behavior evaporated.

"I didn't kill her," Karim sobbed. "I loved her. I wouldn't kill her. You've gotta believe me."

Tell that to the judge, Nico thought. Lacey soon returned with her phone to her ear and a pair of zip ties, which she handed to him so he could restrain the guy. Karim had gone completely limp now, but was still muttering that he was innocent. Nico ignored him.

"There's a car in the area," Lacey reported, putting her phone in her back pocket. "They should be here in ten minutes."

"Good," Nico growled, wanting to get this guy off his front

porch.

"I didn't do it," Karim continued, tipping his head sideways, to try and catch Lacey's eye. Suddenly a light of perception entered Karim's gaze, his face clearing a little. "You need to look at that little fucker, Floyd. He had a thing for Rania. I had to punch his lights out to get him to leave her alone. I bet he did it. You should look at him." Karim rolled over onto his side, directing his last comment to Nico.

But Nico's attention was diverted as a car pulled into the driveway, bright headlights spotlighting the scene on the veranda. It was too soon for the police cruiser to have arrived, and Nico tensed.

"Who's there?" he shouted as he heard car doors slamming. He could only make out silhouettes of people approaching through the bright lights. "Stay where you are," he commanded, wishing for the second time that he'd stopped to grab his service weapon before answering the door. He put his foot on Karim's back to make sure he didn't escape. This night could go from bad to really ugly in just a few seconds. Lacey stepped forward and stood at his elbow, almost as if she were ready to defend him if need be.

"Oh, no, Karim. Why you do this?" a female voice cried and Nico relaxed slightly. It was Karim's mother. She stopped at the bottom of the steps.

"My boy! My boy!" Karim's father joined his wife, and they both looked up with pleading faces. Squinting into the lights, Nico was pretty sure it was just the two of them.

"We are sorry, Detective Sergeant. He disappear. We tried to find him. But we don't know where he go."

Nico remembered the father's name was Hamid. He'd met them at the station when they'd brought Karim in for questioning. Karim was now staying with his family in a hotel room as they grieved for a young life lost and worried about Karim's future.

"Stay where you are, Hamid," Nico warned again, although he was now less worried about being rushed by a hoard of angry family members. "I'm sorry," he said in his most professional voice. "But I'm going to have to take him into custody. He threatened a police officer."

"No. No. Please no." The mother got down on her knees and wailed. "He's a good boy. He won't do this again."

Nico stiffened his spine. He couldn't allow the woman's pleading to get to him. The parents might think the sun shone out of their son's ass, but Nico knew better. This guy was at the very least a cocaine addict, and at the worst a cold-blooded murderer. Lacey took a step forward as if to go to the woman, and he laid a hand on her arm to stop her. She flinched at his touch but stayed where she was. Her closeness reminded him of what they'd been doing mere moments before. They'd been about to kiss. And it would've been good too; he just knew it. She would've tasted sweet, like honey, and of the red wine they'd been drinking, and her lips would've been soft and welcoming.

Now he was going to have to send this young man off in a police car to be charged with being drunk and disorderly, and perhaps even assaulting an officer. Then there'd be all the damned extra paperwork he'd have to fill out tomorrow. Karim moved sluggishly at Nico's feet as if the booze had taken hold of his mind again, then groaned loudly before vomiting onto the wooden decking.

This was not the ending to his evening Nico had been hoping for.

CHAPTER ELEVEN

Lacey stared out the kitchen window into the early morning light. She'd let Smudge out to relieve himself, and she'd been standing here for a full ten minutes. Fuming. Angry. At Nico. She tried to damp down the churlish emotions, but they kept rising to the surface. She'd hardly slept a wink, as the whole scene on the front porch replayed in her mind in luminous technicolor all night. Karim, drunk and slurring, demanding to see her. Then as she went to talk to him, Nico had pushed her behind him, as if she were nothing. As if she were some weak woman and he was the man in charge. She didn't like being told what to do. And she didn't like it when men let their egos and their testosterone get the better of them. She was a trained judo expert. She could look after herself.

And she'd wanted to talk to Karim. To find out what he meant when he said he was being framed. Who he meant by this guy Floyd he'd mentioned. Because for some reason, she believed him. Had believed his demands that he was innocent. A cop was supposed to take an unbiased view. Not to believe or disbelieve what a witness said, but to go on what the evidence told you instead. But there was also the unwritten rule, that a cop was trained to go on gut instinct. Even if it wasn't an official term, a lot of police talked about how they got a feeling when someone was telling the truth. Or when they were lying. And she knew Karim was telling the truth. But Nico had kept pushing her aside. He wouldn't let her follow her instincts. It'd been eating at her all night, the way he'd effectively dismissed her, disparaging her abilities. And the anger had grown in her belly.

"Good morning." Nico's deep baritone preceded him into the room. She closed her eyes for a second, trying to force down the emotions, continuing to face the window. "How are you this morning? I'm sorry you had to see all that," he continued.

"Hmm," she replied noncommittally. Turning to face him, she tried to put on a smile, but it wouldn't come.

He must've misjudged her reply for one of worry, because he said, "You know you're safe now. Karim is locked up. At least for the next day or so until he gets bail."

It was possibly the worst thing he could've said. She wasn't afraid of Karim. It was the exact opposite; she'd wanted to help him. And Nico had stepped in and taken the man down. To protect her.

To be fair, Nico had seen her at her worst, after she broke down at the sight of his blood, and then again after Rania's death. Yes, she suffered from PTSD; she could say that now without cringing. And yes, she needed psychiatric help to deal with the fallout. Maybe that made her weak in Nico's eyes. And she hated that.

"I'm not some damsel in distress who needs to be rescued. I know how to look after myself," she blurted.

It took him a few seconds to process her words. "Ah," he replied as a knowing light entered his eyes. That one syllable made her even madder. How dare he *ah* her, as if she were the one being unreasonable.

She took three steps and got right up in his face. "Look, Detective Sergeant. I know you think you were doing the right thing by 'protecting' me last night." She emphasized the word with air quotes. "But I don't need you putting your body on the line to keep me safe. Do your job and let me do mine."

Oops, that'd just slipped out. She was no longer a constable on the police force. She had no job to do. But this whole murder thing was forcing her back into that mode. Almost against her will, she was starting to analyze the details; the crime was practically all she could think about night and day.

"Let you do yours?" he repeated softly, and Lacey was suddenly aware that she was rammed up against his chest, standing on tiptoe, her nose barely inches from his. She was so close she could make out every detail of the scar on his cheek, every discoloration of the bruise on the side of his face, see every flash of indigo in his blue eyes as he stared back at her. Her heart was pounding erratically, and she wasn't sure if it was adrenaline from confronting him, or because she could now feel every single minute detail of his muscular pecs that were thrust up against her breasts.

She was frozen in place. Ensnared in his gaze, her irritation evaporating in an instant at the hunger she saw in his eyes. What exactly was she angry at him for again?

His arm snaked around her waist and held her captive to his chest as they continued to stare at each other.

As if it had a will of its own, her hand reached up, and she traced his scar with her fingertip. Drifting down, she felt her way around the edge of his jawbone, which was covered in stubble, to his chin, then outlined the shape of his bottom lip. They'd been so close to kissing last night. A residual heat, left over from her unrequited craving, surged up her legs, to settle in between them. She desperately wanted to finish what they'd started.

Her gaze fixed on his mouth. There. That was where she

wanted to be. Like a tractor beam was pulling her in, she stood higher and reached for his lips.

Her mouth collided with his, and as if he'd been released from a bond that'd been holding him immobile, he responded with deepening need, grabbing her around the waist with both arms and lifting her higher so he had better access to her lips and her feet were dangling off the ground. Lacey became lost in Nico's mouth, using her tongue to explore, tilting her head to get a better angle. He sucked and nibbled, taking her bottom lip between his teeth and pulling. Then his tongue dove back in to devastate her mouth again.

She could feel the length of him pressed up against her, unable to ignore the shape of his hard erection pulsing into her belly. How could she get closer? She needed to get closer. Wrapping her arms around his neck, she levered herself up, so she was level with his face, appreciating his muscular shoulders beneath her biceps.

Then he broke their kiss, drew back to watch her for unmeasured seconds with his cobalt eyes. A slight smile curved his luscious lips, and she wanted to know what he was thinking. She opened her mouth to ask, but he buried her words beneath another scorching kiss, this one so hot she might well end up in a puddle of lust on the floor.

So this was what it felt like to be kissed by a Frenchman. They certainly had a reputation for being the world's best lovers, and Niko was proving every last one of those rumors to be true. There was a fire, such passion, in his touch, in the way he looked at her. As if she were the only woman in the whole wide world. As if she were the most beautiful woman in the whole wide world.

How could she have gone from fiery anger to a lust so strong it nearly consumed her in less than two seconds? They were both blazing emotions; perhaps it wasn't as large a jump from one to the other as she thought. Lacey had heard of make-up sex, but never experienced it. Now she was beginning to understand what it meant. This kiss had been hot, their connection so immediate. It was if she already knew him on some deep cellular level.

There was a noise outside the back door. A little woof of displeasure. Smudge was not happy at being left outside. It was enough to break her absolute focus and bring her back to the present. Slowly, he let her feet touch the floor again, and she remembered she was rumpled and sleep mussed as well as barefoot, being cradled in Nico's arms in the early morning light.

She withdrew slightly, and he let her stand up straight but didn't relinquish his hold, letting his arms drape around her waist.

"I should apologize," Nico said, not looking at all apologetic. "For taking advantage of you." For the first time she noticed how disheveled his hair was, and that he was also barefoot. "But I've wanted to do that since the day you dropped me on my ass in the gravel."

Really? She found that hard to believe. She almost snorted, but the intensity in his dark eyes stopped her.

"And I think maybe, so have you."

This time she did snort. Arrogant man. Who did he think he was, presuming to know what she wanted?

His lips touched hers again, soft, but still demanding, sending a scorching fire through her veins and straight to that place between her legs. Goddamnit. Perhaps he was right. There was something that'd drawn her to him right from the first night. But she was never going to admit that.

"So, I'm not going to say I regret what we just did."

But. She could feel the *but* coming.

Smudge whined again, and Nico gave a soft smile. "But, I need to let the dog in. And then I should get to work," he said, this time allowing her enough space to step away from him. Funny, but he made the *but* sound almost reasonable.

"Yep, sure." She busied herself getting a mug out of the cupboard by the coffee machine.

He moved back into her space and gently tipped her chin up so that she was looking at him. "I meant it, Lacey," he said in his gravelly voice that turned her insides to mush. "I know this might be…complicated. But I don't regret that kiss."

"Neither do I," she found herself saying.

"Good."

He turned and went to let Smudge in, who bounded around their legs, searching for attention, almost as if he knew they'd been up to no good.

Lacey went to put some socks on and when she returned, Nico had made them both a coffee and toast. They discussed Karim again over their slices of Vegemite toast, and surprisingly, all of Lacey's anger had leached away. It was like they'd been sitting here all their lives at this little table, considering the facts in an open murder case. Like they were a couple who did this every morning. Nico was itching to get to the station. Karim should be sober by now, and he wanted to interview him again. Then decide whether to lay charges. Lacey wasn't sure any charges were warranted, because in all honesty, the guy had been too drunk to do much damage. To either of them. But that wasn't the point. He couldn't be allowed to go around town threatening officers of the law in their own home. And begrudgingly, she agreed.

"Do you know who this Floyd is? The guy Karim was talking about last night," she asked, suddenly remembering Karim's words.

Nico studied her for a few seconds before giving a slight shrug, as if to say she already knew everything else, was already in too deep, so why not give it all to her.

"Yes. Floyd Hamilton is an apprentice at the mechanic shop where Rania worked. She made a complaint about him following her around. Sort of stalking her, I gather. We interviewed him yesterday afternoon, but he said he knew nothing about her complaint. Denied he was ever obsessed over her. He also never mentioned anything about an altercation with Karim. But that's definitely a question I'm going to put to Mr. Khaled this morning."

"Wow. She had a stalker? And Karim beat him up?" She pursed her lips. "Well, that changes a few things." Lacey felt a sudden rush of ideas flood her brain. If this apprentice was fixated on Rania, perhaps believed himself in love with her, and then Karim disgraced the guy by hurting him and then threatening him with more violence, it gave the man motive.

"I know," Nico said, catching her eye and raising an eyebrow, as if reading her mind. She loved how they seemed to think in parallel. Like their minds were in perfect sync.

Nico slugged down the dregs of his coffee and went to have a shower. Lacey shivered and pulled her cardigan tighter around her shoulders. The past two mornings, Nico had turned on the gas heating. But they'd been too... preoccupied today, and the house was left with a morning chill hanging over it. Lacey decided to light the fire. If she was going to be stuck here all day while Nico was at work, she may as well make the place cozy.

A little later, after Nico had gone to work, rumbling down the driveway on his motorcycle, Lacey had showered and lit the fire. She was standing at the kitchen window again, staring out at the garden, mulling over everything she knew about the investigation. About Herb with his covert boxes belonging to Rania, about Karim being a cocaine addict. And now about this new suspect, a possible stalker named Floyd.

She shook her head, reminding herself this was not her investigation. She had the whole day ahead of her to fill. It was a nice vista out the window, the green lawn, stretching away to a small, rambling orchard at the bottom of the hill, with two raised vegetable beds off to the left full of the last of the end-of-season veggies. The geese wandered through the orchard, white bodies lumbering through the long grass, and she could just make out their honking calls through the windowpane. A bank of trees lined the far left-hand fence, marking the edge of a patch of native bushland that'd been set aside as a state park. And to the right, she could make out the corner of her Kombi parked alongside Nico's large shed. The whole place was rustic and a bit rambling. It was quite idyllic. In fact, she could absolutely live here.

Whoa. What was she thinking? She was absolutely not going to live here. Tasmania was a place where she could find solace while traveling around the immensely beautiful natural wonders. She'd never in a million years intended to live here. It was an escape. Nothing more, nothing less.

And just because she'd kissed Nico, that didn't mean anything either. Certainly not anything permanent. He was a nice guy, and she was attracted to him, but she needed to get moving. And as soon as her van was fixed, that's what she intended to do. Which reminded her, maybe she should call Dave and check on how the spare part was going.

Right then, her phone rang, the shrill tone shocking her out of her musing. Careful to check the caller ID to make sure it wasn't her mother, she answered with a wary "Hello" when the number came up as unlisted.

"Hi, Lacey, it's Dave." Speak of the devil. She was relieved when his friendly voice sounded down the phone. Perhaps his ears had been burning, or perhaps she'd conjured him up by simply thinking about him.

"That's a little weird," she said into the phone. "I was just thinking of you. Have you got good news for me?" She almost held her breath as she waited for the answer.

"Yes. Your fuel pump is arriving on the ferry tomorrow. But the courier won't get it to me till late in the arvo. The best

I can do is come around and replace it for you Saturday morning. I hope that's okay?"

Her heart sank a little. Today was Thursday. It'd be nice to get Dotti fixed sooner rather than later. But if Dave was prepared to come around on a Saturday to fix her, then she should be grateful. She would finally have her wheels back.

"Thanks, Dave. That'd be great," she said, forcing a smile into her voice, ending the call.

This would also give her two more nights with Nico. But that thought was too complicated to contemplate right now. That scorching kiss was too much to contemplate. She could still feel the ghost of his teeth nipping at her bottom lip. Still feel the imprint of his fingertips on her ribcage like they were bruises. She'd wanted him so badly the desire had boiled behind her belly button like lava, causing her stomach to cramp. That had never happened before. It was unsettling just how fiercely he affected her.

* * *

The fire was crackling, the house cozy and warm, and Lacey was waiting up for Nico to come home. The remains of a vegetable pie in the oven, ready to reheat, and a bottle of red stood on the table, ready to be opened. But it was already past ten. Should she keep waiting? That question was easy to answer. Because of course she was waiting up for him. Her stomach did a little flip at the mere thought of seeing Nico walk through that door. She'd been thinking about him all day, random images of them kissing in the kitchen that morning interrupting her at the oddest of times. And as much as she told herself this was never going to work, not long term, her stupid heart leapt every time she thought of him. She needed to see his face. Needed to see that he truly didn't regret that kiss. Needed to know if his heart skipped a beat every time he saw her too.

She'd spent the day walking Smudge down at the beach.

And had run into Margie and Pam, another neighbor, talking for much longer than she thought possible. Did it become a necessity that you be able to talk about something ad infinitum without drawing breath once you turned seventy? Lacey thought it might be, because with those two old women around, she couldn't get a word in edgeways. Margie still wanted to talk about how terrible it was to have been the one to find Rania, and how she'd been unable to sleep at night because her mind kept rehashing the event over and over. Lacey sympathized with her, but she also urged her to move on. Perhaps even seek some counseling if she couldn't do it on her own. But Margie waved a dismissive hand at Lacey's suggestion, saying that she didn't need to see a quack, and she was fine with her and Herb bumbling their way through it.

Lacey doubted that, but kept her mouth shut.

Herb was nowhere to be seen, which was a shame. She'd love to see if she could wheedle out more about those boxes stored in his shed. But Margie was unusually cagy about the police raid on her house, not mentioning it once, then frowning and quickly changing the subject when Pam broached the subject of more police cars outside the cottage the other night, wondering what they were up to. It made Lacey decide that Margie wasn't such a foolish old woman after all, and she was at least keeping some of her cards close to her chest. Perhaps she regretted telling Lacey about Herb's nightly wandering and had learned her lesson. Although Nico would never have revealed his source, Margie may have put two and two together and figured out who'd given away her secret.

Eventually Lacey made her excuses and edged away.

The rest of her day had been spent wandering the garden, picking some vegetables for tonight's pie, staying away from the fierce, honking geese. Nico had warned her they were very territorial. Almost as good as having a guard dog. But they shouldn't chase her, as they'd recognize her by now. Lacey wasn't prepared to take the chance, giving them a wide berth.

Then she Googled Stanley, the next place to visit on her agenda. It wasn't very far, less than an hour's drive, and she wondered if she should pick somewhere farther down the road to stay on Saturday night, once Dotti was fixed. Or should she change her plans and head inland to see Cradle Mountain capped with snow?

All in all, it'd been a restful day, pulling some weeds and pottering around the kitchen, cooking. Something she hadn't done in a long time. It felt domestic and homely, with Smudge following her around like a shadow.

Lacey glanced up and spied the wine bottle on the kitchen table through the doorway. Drat it, she needed a drink, and she was tired of waiting.

But just as she cracked the seal on the bottle, the now-familiar grumble of Nico's motorcycle sounded outside. Then she saw the flash of a bright headlight as Nico pulled his motorcycle into the shed. Her heart leapt into her throat, and she found herself smoothing her hair and hoping her outfit—jeans and a sweater—looked okay. Which was stupid.

She grimaced at her teenage-like behavior, determined not to let any of it show when Nico walked through that door. She would be friendly and happy to see him, nothing more. She turned the oven on to heat the pie, while she fetched two of the crystal glasses they'd used the other night.

Then in walked Nico, motorcycle helmet under one arm, his hair pulled back in a ponytail, but still mussed from the wind. His nose was pink from the cold, the bruises less pronounced now, becoming a faded yellow, and she watched as he shrugged out of the leather jacket he wore when riding his bike. It certainly gave him a little of that bad-boy edge.

Along with the scar and the long, dark hair, it wasn't too much of a stretch of the imagination to think of Nico as one of those dangerous alpha-male-types, who might belong to a biker club or tough street gang. She was quite glad he was the exact opposite, but there was a certain kind of attraction…

And her traitorous heart somersaulted in her chest, something going dark and liquid in her belly at the sight of him. A small part, one that she hardly acknowledged, hoped that he'd scoop her up and kiss her again.

Lacey mentally kicked herself for her disobedient thoughts and held out the wineglass. "Welcome home. Dinner is in the oven," she said, then she cringed, immediately realizing that she sounded more like a wife welcoming a husband home than practically a stranger in his house. Damn. She wished the words back into her mouth, but hid her dismay behind a bright smile.

Something flashed in Nico's eyes, and he looked as if he was about to say something, but instead, he gave her a tired smile and gulped down half of the glass of wine.

"Thanks," he said, leaning down to pat Smudge before removing his gun from his side holster and locking it away in the safe.

"Long day at work, huh?" she asked, then mentally slapped her forehead because she still sounded more like the wife than the stranger.

"Yep. We charged Karim for being drunk and disorderly and assault of a police officer, but he'll probably get bail tomorrow. The parents weren't happy."

"I can imagine." She beckoned him toward the living room and the fire. "Dinner will only be ten minutes. Come and sit down." Her deceitful body could sense him only a few feet behind her, feel the heat of his big body, and she had to crush the sudden desperate wish that he reach out and touch her, trace a gentle finger down the curve of her neck, then curl his fingers around her throat and turn her so he could delve his tongue into her mouth…

Nico fell heavily into the couch with a sigh, as she mentally berated herself. He wasn't going to kiss her again. She didn't want him to kiss her again, she kept reminding herself.

"You cooked dinner again? And lit the fire." He looked impressed. "I could get used to this." Then as if he realized what he'd just said, his eyes went wide.

"Ah, that came out wrong. I'm not saying… I didn't mean to imply… I know you're not…" He gave her a stricken frown and leaned forward, nearly spilling his wine.

She laughed at his troubled face and efforts to backtrack. He'd fallen down the same domestic rabbit hole she'd jumped into. It was some consolation that he'd done the same thing. "Relax." She raised her glass and clinked it against his. "I don't think you're a misogynistic pig. Not yet, anyway." As long as he didn't think she was trying to weasel her way into being his wife after a few days spent in his house. She watched as he settled back into the couch, Smudge resting his nose on Nico's feet and looking up at him adoringly.

"I had nothing else to do, and I kind of enjoyed doing nothing today. It was nice for a change not to be planning my next route, or worrying if I was going to run out of petrol, or finding out the cockroaches have made a nest in my pasta and I have nothing to cook for dinner," she admitted with a laugh.

He laughed along with her, and the mood lightened. "I mean it, though. I didn't expect you to do this," he said again.

"I know."

The timer on the oven dinged, and Lacey got up to see to the pie. As she was laying a large piece onto a plate, alongside a serving of salad, she heard Nico's phone ring.

"Hi, Mum," she heard him say. Should she take his plate through to the living room, or wait for him to finish his conversation? She didn't want to interrupt, but then, she also didn't want the pie to go cold.

There was more murmured, one-sided conversation that she couldn't quite hear. Making a decision, Lacey picked up the plate and carried it to the living room, placing it on the side coffee table nearest to where Nico had been seated. He was now pacing to and fro in front of the fireplace, head down so she couldn't see his expression. She made wild gestures trying to show him his dinner and that she'd leave him to it, when he looked up and locked eyes with her. Then he shook his head, pleading wordlessly with her to stay.

"Hold on a sec, Mum, slow down. What are you saying?"

Nico's face was ghost white as he held the phone to his ear, his gaze never leaving Lacey's. It was too late for her to give him privacy now; she could tell his mother had given him some terrible news. So, she stayed, glued to his every word. Even though she felt uncomfortable, as if she were a voyeur, listening in on his family's secrets.

"I don't understand what you're saying. It can't be true. This must be a hoax. Dad is dead. We buried him in a wooden box in the ground. I was there at the funeral, and so were you."

Lacey had to stop a gasp from breaking from her throat. Nico's dad was dead? They hadn't covered any of his family dynamics yet in any of their talks. He'd mentioned his mother a few times with an affectionate smile. But she'd never had time to ask about the rest of his family. But if his father was dead, what was his mother saying about a hoax?

She listened to him try to calm his mother down over the phone for the next ten minutes, him pacing back and forth on the rug, her perched on the edge of her seat, watching him with concerned eyes, the pie forgotten on the table.

Finally he promised to call his mum back first thing tomorrow morning and then he hung up. Falling into his seat on the couch, he laid his head back and pursed his lips.

Lacey wasn't sure what to say.

"Sorry, I didn't mean to put you in an awkward position," Nico said at last. "But I'm not sure exactly what to think. If what my mother says is true… But it can't be." His eyes took on a faraway look before he said, "I was hoping to get your insight, if you don't mind?"

"Sure, not at all," she replied quickly, laying a hand on his arm. This was so unlike the composed, earnest man she was used to. Professional Detective Sergeant Favreau was nowhere to be seen. Instead, a very agitated and bemused Nico sat before her, scrubbing hard at his chest, as if his very heart was pounding too hard, trying to escape from his body. Lacey was worried about him. Naturally, she would help in any way she could.

CHAPTER TWELVE

Nico's first impulse when his mother had started speaking was to leave the room, or let Lacey leave the room, as she clearly wanted to give him some privacy. But as his mother's words sank in, he needed Lacey's genuine presence to anchor him. For once, his cool reason deserted him completely. What his mother was saying was crazy, but also very personal, and his normally logical mind couldn't seem to grasp the entirety of what she was telling him. Lacey had already heard his half of the conversation, so there was no hiding it from her. Lacey's rational mind would help him to unravel the knots of untruth his mother had just told him, when his own brain was spiraling like a Texas tornado.

Lacey was looking at him expectantly, but he wasn't sure where to begin. So he took another swig of his wine, surprised to find he'd emptied the glass in one gulp.

"Would you like a refill?" she asked.

He shook his head, needing to get this off his chest; his mind was still whirling, going to dark places he normally kept tightly secured. A voice in his head kept chanting, *Your father is dead, your father is dead*. There had to be some other explanation. His mother had got it wrong. She must've got it wrong, that was the only explanation.

"Why don't you start by telling me about your mum," Lacey said helpfully, and he realized he'd been sitting in a silent daze, staring at the wall, still trying to comprehend his mother's words. He sat up straighter and brushed the hair from his eyes. He could do that. He and his mother were close; they spoke on the phone at least once a week. She was a solid base with which to start this story.

"My mother is usually a very reasonable person," he said as an image of Catarina Favreau formed in his mind. Smartly dressed in a pantsuit that showed off her petite figure, her blonde hair, always neatly done up in a loose chignon, with a smattering of grays showing through; he thought they suited her, gave her a certain gravitas. "Catarina was a seamstress back in Paris, and she started her own business when we moved to Canberra. Cultivating her way into the wealthy and powerful circle of clientele, most of whom worked in politics. It was a thriving business, and she even employed two other women to help out in her heyday. But now, she's practically retired. She still does the odd job, more as a favor than for the money, stating that her eyesight is failing, and her stitches aren't what they used to be."

"She sounds like a strong woman," Lacey said. "It takes guts to start up a new business in a foreign country, especially with a young family to look after."

Yes, it had. Their father had dragged them away from France on a whim, but his mother had never complained, merely got on with the process of surviving and building a new life. He'd never put it into quite those words before, but Catarina was definitely a survivor. She'd put up with Serge for all those years, after all.

"She still lives in Canberra," he added. "She made a good life for herself there, after Dad died. Has been seeing a man called Andy for the past five years. Says she's never going to marry again, but she enjoys his company." Nico had only met

Andy twice, on trips back home to see his mother. He was a solid guy who owned a small accounting firm. Andy had grown-up kids of his own, and he and Catarina maintained separate houses and saw each other a couple of times a week. Nico liked that his mother valued her independence. It might be a reflex to having spent so many years living with Serge's domineering ways, but that was better than letting herself be sucked into another man's life too easily.

"Once she got over the shock of my father's death, she's been happy and self-sufficient. My younger sister, Gaëlle, stayed in Canberra, and she lives nearby." It was good that Gaëlle had chosen to stay in the same town. It didn't absolve himself and his older brother from moving away to follow their careers, but it helped to soften the blow. His little sister had a steady job working in a government department, and she'd just started seeing a man called Oscar, who Gaëlle had told him in a hushed whisper one night over the phone that *he might be the one*. His mother was secretly hoping for grandchildren from Gaëlle soon—she'd given up on Nico ever settling down; she knew his job practically precluded him from that. And Brice...well, who knew what was going on with Brice. He liked money more than he liked female company, so he may never marry either. "My older brother, Brice moved to Sydney to follow his career, and then I joined the force, and eventually moved here. So, it's good Mum has Gaëlle to keep her company. The four of us were a pretty tight-knit family. Still are, in lots of ways."

Lacey inclined her head in understanding but didn't interrupt him.

Nico drew in a breath. He knew he'd been avoiding the true topic of this conversation. Because his father hadn't been part of that tight-knit group. He'd always been a loner, floating around the edges of the family core.

"My father, Serge, spent fifteen years in the French Foreign

Legion. He was involved in the Gulf War in 1991." Perhaps that helped to explain some of Serge's behavior. That was where his mother said Serge had changed. Something had happened over there to permanently alter his character. Serge had always been strict and a tad remote before that according to Brice, but he'd only been five when Serge returned from his stint in the war, and didn't recall much. Catarina agreed that it was when Serge returned from The Gulf War that she first became truly scared of him. His temper seemed to be on a knife's edge in those years afterward, and he was also drinking heavily.

"I was only two years old when he came back from the war, so I don't remember much. He left the Foreign Legion a few years later and then we moved to Canberra when I was ten." Serge had believed a better life awaited them all in Australia. Maybe he hoped to evade his demons by moving half a world away. At the time, Nico had been too young to understand his father's motivations, and so had become resentful and sullen at having been forced to leave his culture and his friends behind.

"We'd only been in Canberra for five years. Had just started to feel like we belonged there and then Serge died when I was fifteen," Nico said bluntly.

"Oh, I'm sorry. That's a hard age for a boy to lose a parent." Her voice was soft and compassionate. He looked up, surprised that she'd grasped his pain so quickly, and nearly got lost in her amber eyes. A quick flash of that kiss this morning buzzed through his brain, but now wasn't the time to be reliving stolen kisses that perhaps shouldn't have happened. Zeroing in on Lacey's words, he decided it *had* been a hard time, but not for the reasons she was probably thinking.

"Hmm." He shrugged. Maybe he needed that refill after all. Talking about his father was bound to drag up all those unhealthy memories he'd been trying to keep at bay for so many years. The red wine was on the table between them, and so he poured himself a generous glass and topped up Lacey's as well.

"Gaëlle took it hard," he agreed. "She was only ten at the time, and I think she was worried she'd lose her whole family. That once Dad was gone, our family would fall apart. But Brice—he'd just turned eighteen—he stepped up and became the man of the family. He made sure we were all okay." Brice had been about to complete high school and had big plans to move to Sydney and make his fortune. He'd put all that on hold to make sure he took care of them. Nico remembered clearly the day they'd received the news of Serge's death, how Brice had faced the two policemen at the front door with solemn dignity. Taking his mother by the shoulders and supporting her to the couch, while the police told them the barely believable news.

"Do you mind me asking, how he died?" Lacey asked gently.

"His car hit a tree. It burst into flames. The coroner said he died on impact."

Lacey covered her mouth with her hand. "Oh, that's terrible."

He frowned. It *was* a pretty violent way to die. But then it also seemed like a fitting way for Serge to go—in a fiery flash of glory. Nico was sure Serge would've liked that. There'd been rumors Serge may have even planned it that way. Committed suicide in the grandest way possible. But that'd never been proven, and no one in the family ever discussed it openly. At least the Foreign Legion widows' fund had helped them in the months after Serge's death. It'd been a financial lifeline. If Serge had actually committed suicide, at least his time in the Legion had made sure they were well cared for after his death.

"That was seventeen years ago, but I can still remember the funeral like it was yesterday." The images were seared into his brain. The French flag draped over the coffin, honoring a fallen hero. Which made Nico feel physically sick. His dad was far from a hero. Everyone else had been somber, some openly sobbing, patting him on the back, pity in their eyes for the three kids who'd lost their father at such an impressionable age. But all Nico could think was that they were finally free. And then afterward he was filled with shame that he'd felt no sadness at his father's passing. The man who was supposed to love him and Brice and Gaëlle, but who had treated them more like his own personal little army instead. Barking military commands at them and using his belt as a form of punishment, making sure they understood the rules. Rules were very important to Serge. The times he wasn't teaching them how strict discipline was good for the soul, Serge was aloof and uncaring, flitting through their lives as if they were of no importance to him. It was a relief to have that finally come to an end.

"I'm sorry," Lacey said simply. He forced himself to meet her gaze again, expecting to see pity in their depths. The well-meaning friends and neighbors who'd been at the funeral had all looked at him with pity and sadness, making him feel all the more angry and resentful. They didn't understand. No one would ever understand. But Lacey wasn't looking at him with pity. It went deeper than that. It was as if she could see through all his bitterness, shame, and hurt down to the boy who'd just wanted his father to notice him but knowing that, in his father's eyes, he'd never come up to the standard Serge demanded. He could never please his father, no matter what he did.

"I can see his death left a mark on you. How could it not," she added. "But I think you came through it a little stronger. More determined, maybe?"

He pursed his lips, unsure where she was going with this, and she tilted her head to the side to consider him. "A loved one's death always changes us, leaves us a different person to who we were before they died. But you endured, Nico. You became a detective in the police force. A protector of the innocent. That's a good thing. Isn't it?"

He took another gulp of wine as he turned her words over in his head. Lacey was trying to find the positives in his father's death. And there were positives, of that he had no doubt. Not least of which he was free to pursue the career he wanted. Serge had always pushed and pushed, telling him that he would join the army when he was old enough. Then specialize into the ranks of the SAS or some other elite squad. Nico had silently resisted his father's command, until at last, he was able to choose for himself after Serge's death.

He'd never really dissected his motives for joining the force. All he knew was that it was an ethical, solid job, and it allowed him to use his sharp, logical mind for the power of good. Back when Serge had been alive, both Nico and Brice had done their best to protect their mother against their father's harsh demands and cold manner. Serge was never physically violent toward her, but his words often cut like knives. Nico had sometimes ended up in shouting matches with his father after he said something particularly mean to Catarina. Perhaps a small part of him had been worried that he might turn out to be like his father. And joining the police was a way to stop that. To force himself to turn his intellect to ways to help people, rather than allow his mind to become corrupted.

Nico knew he had a sharp tongue and there were a few times when he'd been fighting with Brice that he'd said unforgivable things just to prove a point. He desperately didn't want to become his father. The military and the police might not have been worlds apart in some people's eyes, but to Nico, they were like night and day. A policeman would never be forced to go to war. Would never be forced to see the carnage a war could commit on a land and on a people. Would never have to see a dead mother or a child as collateral damage because they were trying to kill an enemy who hid amongst the community like a coward.

"Yes," he finally agreed. "It is a good thing." She was right. Something good had come out of his father's death.

"So, what is this terrible cryptic message you got from your mum about him?" she prompted. "I mean, obviously I listened to your conversation. But that was because you wanted me to stay," she added in a hurry. "And I got the gist that something your father said or did has come back to haunt you? Is that right?"

"Yes. And no." He knew he was being as cryptic as she'd accused his mother of being, but it was hard to force the words between his lips. He just needed to say it. "My mother ran into some old friends today. A couple she and my dad got to know when we first moved to Canberra. Marco worked with Dad at the military college, and we sometimes had him and Priscilla around for a barbecue on a Sunday, or drinks on a Friday." Nico remembered them well, mainly because they were possibly the only friends his parents had. The only people Serge could tolerate. Serge had been able to secure a job as a consultant to the Royal Military College, Duntroon. His skills and experience were highly valued by the academy to help the young cadets get ready to take up professional roles in the army. And perhaps he respected Marco as a fellow officer and comrade—Marco had served in the French Army, not the Foreign Legion, but at least on a similar par, in Serge's eyes. They'd been good friends for at least three or four years. Then Marco had been offered another job, and the friendship had evaporated.

"These friends moved to somewhere in Victoria well before

Dad died." Nico stopped and thought about Marco and Priscilla. They were good people. But Marco had something about him, the same dangerous edge that Serge possessed. The same edge that only someone who'd lived through a war and seen atrocities other people hadn't gave them.

"They were just passing though Canberra on their way to drive to Sydney. It was completely random that Mum ran into them in a café."

"Mmm hmm," Lacey encouraged, touching his knee as if to give him support. He suddenly recognized he wanted that support, and so grabbed her hand and held it on his thigh, appreciating the warmth spreading from her palm and slowly up to his stomach and chest, soothing some of the ache that'd settled there.

"This couple didn't know that Serge had died. Mum never contacted them after the funeral, and I'm not even sure she knew where they'd moved to. Anyway, when Mum told them of his death, they were completely shocked, and asked when it'd happened. As she told the story, they became more and more agitated, until Marco finally blurted that they'd seen Serge a few years ago, in the little town on the Victorian coast they're now living in, called Lorne, and he couldn't possibly have died seventeen years ago."

Lacey covered her mouth with her hand, but her eyes never left his face. Even now, as he was speaking the words, he almost couldn't believe them.

"Mum didn't believe them at first, tried to laugh it off, saying they must've mistaken someone else for Dad. But Marco was absolutely positive it was Serge. Of course, he was a lot older and grayer, but Marco said they chatted for at least ten minutes, mainly about what Marco and Priscilla had been up to."

"And they're one hundred percent sure it was your father?" Lacey asked, her hand leaving her mouth, index finger tapping on her chin instead.

"That's what Mum says. They said they even have a photo of him somewhere. Said they could send it to her if she liked, when they got back home. Priscilla took it of him and Marco standing together. The other man didn't know she'd taken the photo, she sort of snapped it as they were saying their goodbyes. As a memento for Marco." Nico was loath to call *that man* Serge. It couldn't be his father. Alive and walking around Lorne less than three years ago. It just couldn't be. There must be some other explanation. But a small part of him believed Marco. The man was ex-military, observant and quick-witted, with a blunt manner. If he said he saw something, then he probably did.

"There has to be a valid explanation," Lacey said as if parroting his thoughts. "I mean… I'm guessing there was a body found in that car wreck?"

Nico nodded glumly. There'd definitely been a body in the coffin; his mother had asked to view it before the funeral, needing closure, even though the sight must've been horrific. But a charred body wouldn't have had any defining features left. Catarina wouldn't truly have known if it were Serge or not.

"And I'm guessing the body was identified somehow. With DNA evidence, or a dental record?"

This time he shrugged. "I'm not sure. I was too young at the time to even know to ask those questions. And I don't think my mum did either."

"So… They might've buried the body without formally identifying it?"

Nico merely shrugged again. The process was slightly different in every state, and had also been different when Serge died over seventeen years ago. If the coroner was happy that there was no question it'd been Serge in that car, then he may not have called for an autopsy. He may just have released the body to the grieving family and let that be the end of the story.

"But, why...?" Lacey was just as lost for answers as he was.

Why? If it had been his father in Lorne that day, then why? Why would he fake his own death? Why would he desert his young family? Let them think they'd lost a father and a husband?

Other questions also clamored for answers. Such as *who* and *how*. If it wasn't Serge in the car, then who was it? And if it was someone else, how had Serge engineered the fake?

"My mum broke down when Marco told her, and they had to call Gaëlle to come and collect her," he told Lacey instead. The idea of his mother so hysterical caused him to shrink a little inside, wishing he could've been there for her.

"Oh, no." Lacey's hand tightened on his knee, and his throat constricted. Because she felt his pain. Felt his need to go to his mother and make this all okay again. He'd promised to ring her again in the morning. He was in the middle of a murder investigation, which meant he couldn't up and leave to go and visit his mother. This was his crime, his killer to apprehend. But if his mother needed him...he would make it happen, even if he only flew in for one day.

They sat in silence for many long minutes, until Lacey finally said, "You need to get a copy of that photo."

"Agreed."

"Can you track this couple down and talk to them yourself?" she asked, going into full cop mode.

"Probably. If I wanted to." And that was the crux of the question. Did he want to pursue this? Did he want to find out if his dad was actually still alive?

"You could also talk to the coroner in charge of your father's death. Or at the very least pull the files on the case."

"Yes." They were all valid comments. And he could follow

up on all of them. Or none. Depending on how much he wanted to know.

"What about your mum? Will she want you to pursue this?" Lacey asked.

"I don't know." He grimaced as he thought about Catarina. After all this time thinking they were free of Serge, would she want to know he was still alive? And if she did, he'd probably have to honor her wishes. And then there was the rest of the family. What would Gaëlle and Brice want to do?

Gaëlle had still been with Catarina when she'd called him. Nico had heard her soft voice in the background, encouraging their mother not to get too worked up over her supposedly dead husband.

What would it mean to them as a family if Serge was suddenly found healthy and breathing? He clearly hadn't wanted to be found, if he had indeed faked his own death. Which hopefully meant he had no intention of coming back to haunt his family.

Up until tonight, his total focus had been on solving Rania's murder. And Lacey, of course. She took up the part of his mind that wasn't fully devoted to the investigation. Even when he tried to push her out of his brain, she was there, the way her body affected his, the way her soft curves called to something deep inside, the way her voice lingered in his head long after she'd left the room. It was all-consuming, and he wasn't sure what to do about her yet. But this new information about his father would put a damper on everything he was already dealing with. Steal his attention away from what mattered most. He had to find this killer. His whole career might hinge on this investigation. Not to mention the fact he wanted to make this a safe community once again. One where people didn't have to lock their doors and windows at night and watch their neighbors with suspicion.

Nico blew out a breath and closed his eyes. What to do now?

CHAPTER THIRTEEN

Lacey had another appointment with Imran today. But rather than have to spend the whole day trapped in town, waiting for Nico to finish work, or someone to give her a lift back to the house, Nico had suggested she borrow his Jeep and he would ride his motorcycle into work. Dotti wouldn't be fixed until tomorrow, and so Lacey had reluctantly agreed to his offer. She was already imposing so much on him; she really didn't want to take any more.

But then perhaps she'd been able to give back just a little last night. Nico had been distraught after his mother's call. Unable to think clearly. It seemed as if Nico had needed her clinical evaluation of the events. Needed her to help him dissect the information and come up with some answers that made sense. Although nothing really made sense in his story. His father was dead. Nico had seen his flag-draped coffin being lowered into the ground. It was almost inconceivable to Nico that his father might've faked his own death. She could hardly grasp the concept herself. But Nico had really struggled with the hypothesis, and she'd been the one to ask all the hard questions, helping him to find a way through the hazy fog enveloping his mind.

She'd seen it happen once before, when a friend of hers in

the force had been too close to the victim. A relative had been raped, and he couldn't disassociate himself enough to be able to evaluate the facts properly. He'd gone to pieces during the investigation and his bias had led him to assault the man he believed was responsible for the rape, only to find out later he wasn't the culprit. It was the main reason an officer was usually excused from a case where they had a personal interest.

But she found it interesting that Nico also fell into that box. Up till now she'd thought of him as without any flaws. A good detective with great deductive skills. He hadn't said so himself—she knew he wasn't the type to brag—but she'd asked around the precinct the day she'd been in for the interview, and Senior Constable Tyrell Jackson had been only too keen to spill the beans on his friend. Over the past two years, Nico had cracked the last two homicide cases he'd headed up, leading to the arrest and incarceration of both criminals. And he'd also been heavily involved in the team that tracked down and charged the man who'd abducted and then murdered two teenage girls down in Devonport. It was a big case, and his name had been put out there as the one who'd found the vital clue that'd lead to the killer's arrest. The accused man was still waiting to go to trial, but everyone was convinced they'd nabbed the killer. Nico knew what he was doing. It sounded like he was a well-respected detective and had moved up the ranks quicker than most, gaining the rank of Detective Sergeant just after his thirtieth birthday.

Tyrell had been only too eager to congratulate Lacey on the way she'd thrown him to the ground the night her van had broken down. At least the bruises on Nico's face were fading now, but she was still embarrassed whenever she saw the healing scar through his eyebrow, knowing she'd been responsible.

Lacey looked down at the set of car keys in her hand. She

should probably get going, or she'd miss her appointment with Imran. But something kept her feet glued to the spot in the kitchen. She didn't want to leave.

When Lacey had mentioned to Nico in passing that Dotti should be fixed by tomorrow, he'd raised an eyebrow, but hadn't commented. She wished she knew what was going on in that head of his. She hadn't told him it meant she'd also be moving on. But it was implied. Yet, he hadn't asked her to stay.

Confusion reigned in her heart and in her body. One kiss, that was all they'd shared. One kiss wasn't a relationship. But she couldn't deny the sizzling attraction between them.

There was also a far less-defined need urging her to stay. The fact that Nico had confided in her about his father perhaps being alive after all these years. He'd trusted her enough to let her in on his family's dark secret. She knew things about him now that no one else knew. It gave her a deeper insight into the man who was Nico Favreau. And it made her want to stay to help him sort out this problem. She didn't want to abandon him in his hour of need.

This morning Nico had been back to his normal composed self. They'd talked it over and over last night, but Nico had committed to no real plan by the time they'd both gone to their separate bedrooms well after midnight. She knew what he should do if he wanted to follow up on this information and find out once and for all if any of Marco's allegations were true. But when she'd brought up the subject this morning, he'd shrugged it off and said he needed to think about it some more. He wanted to deal with this in his own way, and she needed to respect that.

Time to head to Burnie. She gathered her jacket from the hook near the door and whistled up Smudge. The dog gave her a sour look when they went toward his kennel; he'd got used to not being tied up during the day with her around.

Lacey patted Dotti affectionately on the way to the shed and Nico's Jeep, promising the Kombi that she'd take her for a drive tomorrow, once she was good as new. The wind was blowing a gale today, and the sliver of ocean she could see from the backyard was dotted with whitecaps. The sky was clear of clouds, but had turned a brutal blue. She pulled her sheepskin jacket closer around herself, thankful when she stepped into the shed and out of the wind. Her hair was a snarl of tangles already, and she regretted not taking the time to put it into a braid. She'd had to force herself to put the jacket on this morning, telling herself that the bloodstains were gone now, remaining only in her imagination. It smelled clean, clinically so, and not at all like a well-loved piece of clothing. The jacket still reminded her of Rania, but it was her favorite and the warmest, and logically, she knew the only way to get past the anguish was to wear it until it no longer reminded her of the dead woman. Her thoughts turned to the candlelit vigil being held tonight in memory of Rania, celebrating the young woman's life. Lacey had said she'd go, but still hadn't completely committed to it in her own mind.

The drive took a little over half an hour. But Nico hadn't warned her how hard it'd be to find parking in the main street. Lacey drove around for ages looking for a spot, and because she wasn't used to driving Nico's big Jeep, it was all the more difficult. Finally she gave up and drove around into the back streets behind the main shopping precinct where she wound down an alleyway and by some fluke found a spot in a small parking lot at the rear of the healthcare center buildings. She spotted Gabe's little sporty MG and decided she was in the right place. This must be where the shop owners parked. Hoping she wasn't about to get a fine for illegal parking, she locked the car and looked for a rear entrance into the building. There was a door, but it was marked as an emergency exit, so she decided to go back down the alley—jogging now because she was running late—emerging into the bustling main street again.

Imran was also running a little overtime with his current patient, so Lacey took a seat in the waiting room, running her fingers through her hair to try and tame it. There was no sign of Gabriel. He must be with a patient. Or perhaps he was off on a lunch break.

Waiting for Imran gave her time to gather her thoughts. It was interesting, but now she thought about it, she'd had so much else on her mind recently, she surprised herself by how little time she'd had to dwell on her innermost feelings.

Her PTSD hadn't really bothered her over the past few days. Even yesterday, when she'd spent most of the day by herself, pottering around Nico's house, she hadn't been drawn back down into those spiraling depths of depression. Her time alone spent in the warmth and comfort of the cottage had acted as a healing balm, and it was an interesting development. Part of the reason she'd found traveling around Tasmania was good for her mental health was that she didn't allow herself time to stop and stagnate too long in one place. She was constantly on the move, which kept her mind occupied with the small details of life on the road. This was the first time she'd had time and space without anything to do. Even after being confronted with Rania's terrible wounds and then her death, Lacey thought she was coping quite well. She was interested to hear what Imran thought about her insights. Whether he agreed she might be finally getting stronger. Or could it be the opposite? Was this the calm before the storm? Was she actually headed on a collision course with her darkest depression yet?

Suddenly, Imran was standing in front of her, and she realized he must've been calling her, but she'd been so lost in thought, she hadn't heard him.

"Sorry." She jumped up with a guilty smile.

"Good to see you again, Lacey." Imran shook her hand she was comforted by his warm palm on hers. Imran was good at his job. He projected a caring aura, and his dark-brown eyes were kind, but his handshake was firm, conveying a strength of character. She felt as if he would be there to catch her if she fell.

* * *

An hour later, Lacey emerged from Imran's office, a lightness in her step. He'd given her words of cautious encouragement, telling her she was on the right path, but to be careful not to get too overconfident. His consult had done her more good than she could've imagined, mainly because he helped her to talk about Rania, about how her death had affected her. She was starting to see now that Cindi's death had completely overwhelmed her because of the sheer innocence of the child, the utter unfairness of a mother taking her own daughter's life. But she'd also been engulfed by misery because there'd been nothing she could do to save the girl.

While Rania's death had many similarities—she'd been attacked with a knife, and was lying bleeding to death on the ground—the other circumstances were completely different. Rania was a grown woman, and while her death was terrible and senseless, Lacey didn't get that same wholly defeating feeling of helplessness as she did when she thought about Cindi's passing. The little girl had been so innocent. So trusting. She trusted her mother not to hurt her. And when that trust failed, she trusted that a policeman would come and save her. No one had stepped up for Cindi that day. In the end, no one had been there to save that little girl. It wasn't fair that Cindi didn't get to live a life filled with endless possibility. It was the unfairness of it all that'd cut Lacey's heart in two.

But Rania was a grown woman who'd had a chance to live her life—albeit not a long one. Lacey had tried her best to save Rania, had done everything by the book; everything humanly possible. But in the end, Rania's death hadn't solely rested on her shoulders. Gabe had been there. And if a licensed doctor couldn't do anything to save her, then…

This new insight gave her hope. Hope that one day she might return to the police force. That she might be able to ease herself back into working the beat. That not every violent crime she came across was going to cause her to lose her shit. Cindi would always be with her, Imran had warned her of that, but given time, she might come to a sort of truce within herself about not being able to save the young girl. Deep down, she would always blame herself, but that didn't mean she couldn't be of use to other people who also needed her.

Hope was a fleeting thing, Lacey knew that. But it made her feel as if there was light at the end of the tunnel.

"Excuse me," a woman said from behind, and Lacey looked up to find she was standing at the top of the stairwell, staring into space.

"Sorry," she apologized, stepping out of the way.

The woman gave a tight smile and descended the stairs, Lacey following in her wake. She was at a bit of a loose end now and wondered if she should pop in and see Nico. Or would he be too busy to see her? There were still hours before the candlelit vigil, and Lacey had yet to make up her mind whether to stay in town for it or head home now.

Lacey pursed her lips and tilted her head, considering her options.

She would most likely be leaving tomorrow, as long as Dotti was fixed.

One more night.

One more night with Nico.

Suddenly, her decision was made for her. She wasn't going to the vigil. She already knew that she'd probably garner a lot of attention if she went, being one of the last people to see Rania alive. Attention she didn't want or need. She had her own way to honor Rania, and it didn't include crowds or other people's expectations. And these things sometimes got heated. What was supposed to be a peaceful memorial to a woman taken too soon could be hijacked by people with other agendas. She'd already heard talk about making this vigil about women's rights and women's safety. Which wasn't a bad thing. But the last thing she needed tonight was people deciding that Lacey was a good candidate for their cause and pushing her to the forefront of their political action. Nope, she needed peace and quiet tonight.

She would make something delicious and that would be it. Her last hurrah. For her last night in Nico's house. She had a hankering for a slow cooked chicken tagine. Nico would like it, she was sure. Lacey pulled up short, halfway down the stairs. Was it bad of her to have taken up the domestic role so easily in Nico's house? Always being the one to cook because he was never home in time? Taking on the role of the little woman, always in the kitchen. It was a simple routine to fall into. And not one she'd ever found herself in before. She shrugged and decided with only one night left she could leave those thoughts for later.

There was a fresh market on the edge of town where she could gather the ingredients for her tagine. Yes. Now she had a plan, she felt invigorated.

At the bottom of the stairs, she was about to turn left to head out into the main street when she spotted a door that said *Emergency Exit Only* off to the right.

Was that the door that led into the rear parking lot? It was worth a try, as it'd save her a five-minute walk if it was.

Tentatively, she pushed the door, half expecting an alarm to sound. But there was nothing except sunlight streaming in through the gap. Quickly, she ducked around the door and let it bang shut behind her, only to find she was in the rear alley all right, but not in the parking lot she was seeking. She must've come out farther along than she thought. Bugger. The alley smelled bad and there were a stack of dumpsters lined up along the opposite wall. The parking lot should be to the left, so she turned and walked in that direction. She stuck to the dank pathway that hugged the opposite side of the alley, where it backed onto the rear fences of suburban houses behind the shopping precinct. Now that she was walking the alley, rather than driving down it, she noticed things she hadn't seen from the Jeep. Each shop had its own rear entryway, and some were kept clean and tidy, like the one to the clinic, but in others, there were garbage bags piled up in a heap or a stack of empty beer bottles left to litter the dirty concrete. Some even had little covered alcoves, where Lacey imagined an employee might stand to have a smoko break and keep out of the rain.

The roar of an engine heralded a dump truck, which appeared at the other end of the alley and began the process of picking up a large dumpster. Lacey was nearly to her car now; she could see where the alley opened up ahead into the parking lot. She stopped on the path to watch the truck tip the large dumpster over its head. The sound of breaking glass and the roar of the garbage landing in the truck was almost deafening.

Out of the corner of her eye, she caught a slight movement, and turned to see two figures partly hidden in the alcove of one of the shops. The weathered sign above the door said *Bakery*. Lacey squinted into the gloom, wondering what the couple were up to. It looked like they were…

Oh. Lacey let out an embarrassed giggle. They were full-on kissing. Snogging, her little sister, Sammy, would've called it. So engrossed in their tryst they didn't seem to notice anything else going on around them, including the garbage truck.

She hurried on by, not wanting to embarrass them with her presence; they probably hadn't heard her approach over the sound of the dumpster being emptied.

Then she caught the side profile of the person closest to her.

It was Gabe. Wasn't it?

She stopped to study him. The truck was nearly finished emptying the dumpster; she'd have to hurry if she didn't want them to hear her retreating footsteps. Yes, it was definitely Gabe; she recognized his clean-shaven face, high cheekbones and well-coiffed hair.

And the woman he was kissing…was a man!

A young man with dark, curly hair and smooth cheeks, as if he wasn't even old enough to shave.

Lacey nearly stumbled backward. Gabe was gay? Not that it was a problem. But Nico had made out that Gabe was very much a ladies' man. And the way Gabe had come onto her in the car the other night, she'd never have suspected he was gay. Or perhaps he was bisexual. Maybe he liked both equally. And that was fine with her as well. Nevertheless, it was an interesting discovery. No wonder there hadn't been any sign of Gabriel in the clinic. He'd been otherwise occupied.

Lacey charged ahead, eager to get to her car now, glancing back over her shoulder.

Had Gabe seen her? She didn't think so. Not that she was specifically trying to hide from him. But something about the circumstances of the tryst, that they'd chosen a dingy back alley as their rendezvous and were trying to stay hidden in the alcove, pointed to the fact that perhaps they didn't want to be seen.

Changing her mind about not bothering Nico, she decided she'd go and see if he was free for a late lunch. Let him know she wasn't going to the vigil, and that she was cooking something delicious for dinner. He could make her apologies if anyone asked about her at the vigil, because she knew Nico would definitely go, being the detective in charge of Rania's murder. Reversing the Jeep out of its parking spot, she glanced in the rearview mirror. The alley was empty.

Maneuvering her way down the narrow passageway, her mind was only partly on driving the big, unwieldy car. The rest was occupied by this new revelation about the country doctor. Did Nico know of Gabe's predilection? More to the point, should she be the one to reveal it, if he didn't?

CHAPTER FOURTEEN

Nico tapped the large whiteboard affixed to the wall with the tip of his pen, considering the photo of Karim Khaled's face. Things were not looking good for the young man. Evidence was piling up against him. He chewed the end of his pen as he lifted his eyes to the ceiling, brooding on the new information they'd just received.

Even though Floyd Hamilton denied it, Karim was adamant he'd gone to the young man's house and knocked him around, trying to scare him so he'd leave Rania alone. This had been backed up by Danny, the head mechanic, who swore that Floyd had come into work the next day with a black eye and bruises all over. Floyd had been sullen and wouldn't talk about who'd used him as a punching bag—Nico was still to get to the bottom of why he refused to admit to the beating, perhaps it was a pride thing, or perhaps he'd merely wanted to save face in front of Rania—but it was further confirmed by Floyd's flat mate that it'd been the young Syrian boyfriend of the hot receptionist who'd come to the house that evening, full of aggression and brutality. Karim probably thought that by revealing this to the cops, he was implicating Floyd in her murder. But it might do Karim more harm than good, as it was more evidence of his violent streak.

Evidence that spoke of how he was controlling in his relationship with Rania.

They'd also had the results from the coroner this morning from Rania's autopsy. Tyrell had given Nico the rundown, as he hadn't had time to read the full report himself. Cause of death was a heart attack, which was exactly what Gabe had described earlier. The loss of blood had been so great, and her blood pressure had dropped so low, her heart went into cardiac arrest. The timing as to when she'd actually been stabbed and when she finally succumbed to her wounds, was a little more circumspect. The coroner commented that judging by the size of the stab wounds and where they were situated—they'd missed all vital organs—he could surmise how much blood she'd lost over time, and he estimated she could've been alive for two or three hours before Margie found her. He stressed this was an estimation, however. His report also listed all drugs found in her system. There was a blood thinner, an analgesic, and adrenaline. Which all sounded reasonable to Nico. All the drugs must've been administered by Gabriel as he was trying to save her life. Gabe had also hooked her up to a saline drip, in an attempt to increase her blood pressure but that'd come too late to save her life.

There was a quiet knock at the door. Nico was the only one left in the command room at present; the rest of the team were either out following up leads, or had gone for a much-needed lunch break. He turned to see who it was.

Lacey's slim form was silhouetted in the doorway and Nico did a double take. Not only because he hadn't been expecting to see her, but because of the way his stomach jumped like a frog in a sock at the sight of her. Messy, blonde hair fell around her shoulders, whipped up from the wind outside. The hair framing her face turned her eyes a light, sandy color, and for a moment, he was lost in their pale depths.

"Hi," he said with a smile.

"Hi," she replied, glancing quickly around the room.

"How did you get in?" he queried.

"I have friends in high places," she said with a smirk. When he raised an eyebrow, she explained, "Sally-Ann is on front desk duty. She knew I was here to see you."

Ah. That explained it. He really, really hoped Sally-Ann hadn't said anything inappropriate to Lacey. She'd only met Lacey the once, but she'd already latched onto the idea that Nico should get back in the dating saddle, and she was more than vocal in telling him he should ask the lovely young woman out. Nico had told her in no uncertain terms they were merely friends, and he was letting Lacey stay at his place because she had nowhere else to stay; he would've done the same for anybody. Sally-Ann had merely slapped her thigh and let out a knowing laugh that made Nico grit his teeth.

"Have you got time for a quick lunch?" she asked.

For her, the answer was a resounding yes. But not wanting to appear too eager, he raised an eyebrow and seemed to consider her words for a few seconds. Waiting until his heart subsided to a slightly more normal beat, he finally said, "Of course," in his most proficient voice, as if he hadn't just been shaken by her appearance. "How about a sandwich and a walk along the shorefront? I could do with a little fresh air."

"It's more than fresh out there," she answered, finally giving him a smile. "But I get that you need to blow the cobwebs away," she added.

He liked how she understood his need without having to be told. Along with everything else, he was having trouble getting the disturbing details of his mother's call last night out of his head. He'd phoned Catarina again this morning to see how she was coping. At first she was agitated, but she calmed after he promised he'd look into it, told her to leave it with him for a few days. All he wanted was to focus on this murder investigation, but thoughts of his dead father kept interrupting at the most inopportune times. Thoughts of how he could get hold of that photo and confirm for certain the man in it was Serge kept circling his head. But he simply didn't have time to go to Victoria and check out Marco's claims. Perhaps if he got outside and let the wind whip through his hair, it'd give him some much needed perspective.

"Lead the way," he said with a flourish, and his heart started that stupid double-tap again when she smiled at him, eyes dancing and white teeth flashing. What was he going to do about his attraction to this woman? It was getting stronger every day.

He checked in at the reception desk on his way out to make sure there were no messages or any new calls come into the hotline and let Sally-Ann know he'd be out for half an hour. He grimaced as she winked at him from behind Lacey's back.

They decided to grab a ready-made baguette from the bakery a few shops down from the health clinic—his was beef and mustard; hers was salmon and brie. Nico had been frequenting this little bakery ever since he'd started work in Burnie, and the baguettes were always fresh and delicious. But Lacey gave the guy behind the counter an odd look as Nico put in his order. Jayden, the apprentice, seemed not to notice Lacey staring at him. The young man was in his second year with the bakery and Nico often chatted to him about his passion, hiking the wilderness trails throughout Tasmania. Jayden was fit and athletic and loved to hike whenever he could, and Nico was a tad jealous. He'd love to spend more time exploring the Tasmanian back country, but he never seemed to have enough time. Clark Constantine, who owned this bakery as well as the one in Wynyard, where

Karim worked, was nowhere to be seen today.

Clark had been as helpful as he could answering Nico's questions about Karim as an employee. He'd been just as shocked as everyone else to hear about Rania's death. Clark had said he didn't think Karim was capable of murdering his girlfriend; they'd seemed so in love. But there had been an edge to Clark's remarks, and when Nico dug deeper, the other man conceded he had wondered about his employee's behavior lately. He'd been pretty wired a few times when he'd arrived at work for the four am start. Clark said it felt like the guy was almost manic. No one started that early in the morning by bouncing into the building like they'd just won the local meat raffle. Even with his two cups of extra-strong coffee, Clark had said he never felt that bright and perky in the morning.

Jayden handed him the two baguettes and Nico steered Lacey out of the tiny shop. "Are you okay?" he asked.

"Hmm?" She made a preoccupied noise and glanced over her shoulder toward the bakery. What was going on with her?

"You were staring at Jayden," he said, handing her the salmon and brie baguette.

"Was I?"

"Mmm hmm," he replied. "Something you want to tell me?" Like did she have the hots for nineteen-year-old apprentices with a mop of dark hair and equally dark eyes? The stab of jealousy was so sharp it took Nico by surprise. But he schooled his features and waited for her to answer.

She glanced up at him, her amber eyes going dark as she seemed to consider something for a second. Then she shook her head. "No. Sorry, I don't know what got into me." She laughed, as if she'd been thinking something silly.

There was a new walkway that'd been built along the waterfront of West Beach that he guided her toward. The wind was blowing hard from the northwest, making the already chilly day feel icy. But he didn't mind the cold; it was a nice change from his overheated office. Lacey zipped her jacket up to her neck and lassoed her hair into a tight ponytail, but didn't complain. They strolled past The Foreshore Restaurant, where they'd eaten lunch with Gabriel the other day. Lacey attacked her sandwich with relish, making appreciative sounds that reminded him of how she'd moaned in the back of her throat the other morning when he'd kissed her. *Quick*. He had to get that thought out of his head, or he wouldn't be able to walk along in public for much longer.

"God, this is the best baguette I've ever tasted," she said through a mouthful of bread.

"I know," he agreed. He debated for a second whether to tell her what was on his mind. He'd already confided in Lacey more in the past few days than he had in anyone else over the past few years, so it was only natural to tell her this latest tidbit. "The man who owns that bakery also owns the one Karim works for in Wynyard."

Lacey stopped mid-chew to stare at him. "Really?"

"Really," he replied, taking a satisfied bite of his baguette. The picture of Karim's life was coming into focus. And it was making him more and more likely to be their prime suspect. When asked by the media, their official line was that Karim was assisting police with their enquiries. He hadn't been charged with anything. Yet. His little outburst the other night hadn't made things any easier on him. Karim would most probably make bail this afternoon, which irked Nico no end. But Nico felt it might not be long before they had enough evidence to take Karim back into custody.

"Clark admitted he'd had suspicions about Karim's drug taking when we interviewed him yesterday," he said through a mouthful.

Lacey looked thoughtful for a second. "Which corroborates Herb's story about what Rania told him."

"Exactly," he replied. "We have an undercover contact who works with the drug element in the area and we tracked down Karim's dealer yesterday. He wasn't happy about us collaring him, but he talked eventually."

Nico took another bite of his lunch as he thought about the facts building against the young man. He should feel a sense of satisfaction, but instead he felt vaguely indignant that it could be this easy. There was uncertainty hovering at the back of his mind, but he wasn't sure what was causing it.

"We still haven't found his cocaine stash," Nico revealed. "But when we confronted Karim today with the evidence we have so far, he finally admitted to his habit. His parents are heartbroken."

"I can imagine," she replied. "Their golden boy isn't so golden anymore. It must be a hard thing to learn about your only son."

"Yes. Especially because they were relying on his income to help the family."

"Hmm." Lacey stopped walking and stared out at the stormy ocean. "I still can't get out of my head how piteous he sounded the other night when he came to your place. How desperate he was for us to believe he wasn't guilty."

Nico wasn't sure if he agreed with Lacey, because that pathway led to doubt and self-reproach. She might be able to show the man compassion, but he couldn't let mercy get in his way of finding a killer.

"We're cops," he reminded her gently. "We can't let bias get in the way—"

"Yeah, yeah, I know. Don't let pity cloud your reason," she interrupted him, a scowl marring her perfect face. "God forbid we ever show an ounce of kindness."

"That isn't what I meant," he replied.

"I know." The frown cleared from her face. "And I know you're not like that." She touched him on the arm. "These are my issues, not yours. Perhaps it's one of the reasons I would never have made a good cop."

"Or maybe it's the exact reason you *would* make a good cop," he countered. "We need someone who's going to keep us honest." Policing was a male-dominated profession. It was a harsh fact of life. There were more female cops joining the ranks every day, but it was by no means an equal share yet. And a lot of those male officers were prone to responding to a highly charged situation with aggression and violence. It was an instinctive reaction. But some cops—women especially—were better at de-escalating a situation, calming everyone down so that a resolution could be found. Nico would bet Lacey was one of those officers. Even if she was also good at using her lightning-fast judo skills when called for.

Lacey gave him a sideways glance, but didn't comment, and he wondered what she was thinking.

"But there are still other suspects. I'm assuming you haven't already decided he's guilty, and that's the end of it? I mean, what about this Floyd guy?"

"Of course there are," he replied, trying to keep the slightly offended tone out of his voice. Plenty of theories were abounding in the command room, his team proposing all kinds of scenarios, both plausible and completely wild. While Herb was definitely another person of interest, the boxes belonging to Rania they'd seized from his house were yet to turn up anything definitive so far. They chiefly contained spare clothes, some personal documents which were mainly from her earlier life. Things like school transcripts, her birth certificate, even her passport. All things she might need if she was going to run away from Karim, as she'd indicated to Herb, so the boxes seemed to corroborate his story…so far.

Some bright spark had then suggested that perhaps Herb

had been carrying on an illicit affair with the victim, and Rania was preparing to run away with him. Many people laughed at that theory. But the same bright spark had suggested that perhaps Margie had found out about the affair and murdered Rania in a jealous rage. Nico had placed that one firmly on the extremely unlikely pile of hypotheses, but he knew from experience not to discount anything completely. So now Margie was on the list as well.

The young mechanic apprentice was also there, as Lacey had pointed out.

Then there were all the people they were yet to start investigating. Supposed friends of Karim's family, who still had ties back to a rebel Syrian army. Karim's father, Hamid, had once belonged to that army, although he'd supposedly broken all connections with them when his family had escaped the war-torn country. There was a large community of Syrian refugees in Hobart now, where most of them had settled when they'd been moved to Tasmania. There were rumors of a sort of Syrian mafia-style gang emerging, led by a man who by all accounts had been an acquaintance of Hamid's back in Syria. Had Hamid somehow gotten on the wrong side of this gang? Were they targeting his family for something he'd done wrong either in Australia, or even back in their home country? Or had Karim somehow offended this gang? They were linked to drug smuggling and Karim was a known cocaine addict. Did he owe them money? The questions were vast and many.

Nico was about to open his mouth and tell her about some of these other theories, when he was overcome by a stab of guilt slicing through his gut. There was one person on the suspect list that she wouldn't like to hear about.

Her.

Nico thought back to this morning when Charles had asked him into his office for an update. Nico had informed him of the growing list of suspects, and Charles had stopped him and asked point-blank if Lacey Carmichael had an alibi for the time the crime was committed.

Nico had been rocked back into his seat by the blunt question. Never in a million years would Nico suspect Lacey. Apart from the fact she'd only arrived in the area a day before, she had absolutely no motive to kill Rania. The two women were complete strangers; Lacey had no connection to the victim.

Nico had also made sure early on to check out Lacey's story of traveling around Tasmania, and it was all true. But Charles was just asking the hard questions, as any good chief would. Then he'd reminded Nico about the potential serial killer they had on their hands and politely mentioned that Nico himself had been the one to state that not all serial killers were men. Nico had to hold back the laugh that'd built in his throat. His boss implying that Lacey might be a serial killer was the most ridiculous thing he'd ever heard. But he'd plastered on his serious face and promised he'd dig deeper into Lacey's alibi until he was one hundred percent sure she was who she said she was. It was at that point he revealed Lacey's connection with the Victoria Police Force. Lacey had asked him to keep it quiet if he could, but proving to Charles that she shouldn't be on the suspect list was too important. The time for keeping her secrets had passed.

"I know you do," Lacey said, breaking into his thoughts, and he was absurdly pleased when she decided not to ask who they all were. Because he didn't think he'd be able to tell her *she* was on that list too. Albeit, as more of a token, than a real person of interest.

He debated whether to tell her about the possible serial killer. Would that just spook her? Or would she be able to offer some more of her succinct insight?

As he turned to Lacey, he caught a moving shape out of the

corner of his eye and grabbed Lacey's arm to drag her out of the way just in time as a young man flew past them on a skateboard.

"Hey, Jayden, watch where you're going," Nico yelled after him indignantly.

"Sorry," Jayden yelled back over his shoulder with a contrite grin. Although, Nico knew the teenager wasn't really repentant. He rode that skateboard everywhere, usually like the devil was on his tail. One day, he was sure to cause an accident, run into some little old lady taking a stroll and knock her over. Nico made a resolution to talk to him next time he went past the bakery.

"Was that the same guy from the bakery earlier?" Lacey asked a little breathlessly.

"Yeah. Jayden is the apprentice. He must've just finished his shift." Oh, to be young again, he thought. To have that much energy and passion. He was probably off to do some ten-mile hike before dinner. And oh how jaded he sounded. Nico had to remind himself he wasn't that old. Not really.

"Jayden, huh?" Lacey stared after the young man, her eyes narrowing the same way they had when they'd been in the bakery earlier.

"Does Jayden have anything to do with Gabriel?" she asked cryptically. "I mean, are they friends? Or acquaintances perhaps?"

"Apart from Gabe buying a cinnamon bun from the bakery most mornings—he calls it his one little vice—I don't think they hang out in any of the same circles. Why?"

"I think he might have more than one vice," Lacey murmured softly.

"What do you mean?"

"I'm not sure if I should tell you this. I mean, you may already know. And if you don't, you may not want to know."

"You're talking in riddles," he chided.

"Shall we head back? I'm cold," she said, changing the subject.

"Only if you tell me this secret I don't need to know about my friend." Nico was becoming worried by the unsettling astuteness in Lacey's gaze.

She swiveled on her heel, and he followed suit. It was nice not to be heading directly into the cold wind. He swallowed the last two bites of his baguette and tucked his hands into his pockets, waiting.

Finally, Lacey blew out a breath and said, "This is probably none of my business, but I saw Gabriel kissing that young apprentice in the back alley this morning after my appointment with Imran."

"What?" Nico almost shouted the word. That was the last thing he'd been expecting her to say. "Are you sure it was him? And Jayden?" The idea was preposterous. Gabriel was into women. Always had been. He was forever gawking at the pretty ones, making sure they knew he was checking them out. And he'd had plenty of girlfriends over the years. Admittedly, none of them had stuck around, but that just meant Gabe wasn't ready for commitment. Didn't it?

"Yes, it was them." Lacey fixed him with her steady, amber gaze, and he believed her. She was observant and had a sharp eye. One thing a good cop needed to be. So that was why she'd been staring at Jayden earlier. She'd recognized him.

Did that mean Gabriel was gay? And if it did, why was he trying so hard to stay in the closet? Did he think he might scare away patients or tarnish his reputation in town?

"So, you didn't know, then?" She was walking close to him now, her elbow bumping his in solidarity, and he enjoyed the human contact.

"No. That's a revelation to me," he replied thoughtfully.

"There's nothing wrong with Gabe wanting to keep his sexual preferences quiet," she said. "I can think of a lot of reasons why he'd do that. Small towns are full of prejudice. Even in this day and age, not everyone is comfortable finding out their local doctor is gay. But... Jayden strikes me as particularly young. Not that I'm judging," she added quickly.

She'd hit at the heart of the very thing that was making him uncomfortable too. Gabriel was nearly thirty-five. Jayden was technically still a teenager. He was practically cradle snatching. Maybe the pickings in Burnie for a gay man were slim and he had to take what he could get, but still, it didn't feel right.

"Thanks for telling me," he said, reaching down and squeezing her hand for a few seconds. "I'm sure that was a hard decision to make."

"Not really," she admitted. "I wouldn't have kept anything like that from you. Not for long. You're a friend and these things fester if they're not let out into the open. But don't worry, my lips are sealed. I won't let on to anyone else."

"That might be best," he replied. "That throws a different light on something I saw a few weeks ago, though," he added softly.

"What was that?" She turned her face up to his, and he was momentarily caught by the soft pink color of her lips.

"I saw Gabe and Jayden in the parking lot at the supermarket. It looked like they were arguing about something. I thought nothing of it at the time, I was heading out the exit in my car, and so didn't stop. But now...?"

"A lover's tiff, perhaps?"

Lacey was spot on with her thinking, and he nodded his agreement. He wondered what they'd been arguing about.

Nico pondered this news as they walked back past The Foreshore Restaurant. What would he do with the information? A part of him wanted to confront Gabe, tell him it changed nothing, that he would always remain a good friend. And part of him didn't want to say anything. Because it'd make things awkward between them. Nico relied on Gabe's friendship, perhaps more than he liked to admit. This news would change their dynamic, even if it were only in subtle ways. Mostly because Nico now knew Gabe had been keeping a secret from him. Even though he understood why, it still burned that he thought he knew his friend so well, only to find out he didn't. Then there was the smallest part of him that was miffed, wondering how he could've missed the signs. Some detective he was if he couldn't even tell his friend was gay.

"He might not be gay. He could be bisexual," Lacey mused beside him. "Or even pansexual. Is that what they call it nowadays?"

"Yep," Nico agreed through pursed lips.

Lacey's mouth twisted into a half smile, but she didn't comment.

They walked back up the busy main street toward the station, maneuvering through the crowds without further comment. Nico was still trying to digest this news as they passed the clinic, and he unconsciously glanced up at the entrance, as if the doorway might hold some answers. Now that he thought about it, he wasn't surprised to learn Jayden was gay. While the young man loved his outdoor pursuits, he had a gentle manner about him. He never seemed to partake in those bawdy, slightly misogynistic jokes Clark sometimes found extremely funny either. And he'd never had a girlfriend to Nico's knowledge, at least.

"Will you come in for a second?" Nico asked as they reached the front door to the police station. "I was hoping to give you a few boxes to take home for me. I can't fit them on the motorcycle." It was a shame Lacey had decided not to attend the vigil tonight, but he could understand why she didn't want to be there.

"Sure," she agreed.

It was nice to step out of the wind and into the shelter and warmth of reception. Nico buzzed her in past the front desk and she followed him down to the command room. Sally-Ann was no longer on duty, for which he was eternally grateful. The last thing he needed was for her to see them together again; it'd only add fuel to her matchmaking fire.

Nico had his hand on the door to his office when the chief inspector appeared in the hallway.

"Ah, Nico," he greeted him jovially. "And this must be the lady who tried to help Rania." Charles held out his hand and waited for Nico to introduce Lacey.

"Yes. Yes," Nico hurriedly agreed. "Lacey Carmichael, meet Chief Inspector Charles Shadbolt."

"Hello, sir." Lacey straightened her shoulders and looked Charles right in the eye.

"Nice to meet you." Charles continued to shake her hand contemplatively. "I've heard a lot about you."

"You have?" Lacey's face blanched.

"Yes. And I was wondering if you might have a few spare moments to pop into my office for a chat?"

"Oh, ah, of course, sir."

"Good. Good." Charles glanced at Nico over the rims of his glasses, but his face was unreadable. "Follow me," he directed.

Lacey cast him a look of concern before she followed the chief into his office. Nico stared at the closed door. What the hell was Charles playing at?

CHAPTER FIFTEEN

Lacey stirred and got to her feet. She'd almost fallen asleep in the comfortable wing chair by the fire. Smudge was lying on the rug in front of the hearth, fast asleep, his little feet twitching in some doggy dream. She needed to look at the chicken tagine, which was simmering on the stove, the enticing smell making Lacey's stomach rumble.

After checking on dinner, she went to stand and stare out the kitchen window. It was becoming one of her favorite places, where she could look out into the backyard and contemplate the vista, watching the ever-changing weather. It was just coming on dusk. The wind had almost blown itself out now, but dark clouds had settled over the horizon, blocking out any sign of a sunset. The candlelit vigil for Rania was due to start soon. She ruminated on how it might go and how many people might attend.

Without her summoning the thought, her mind returned to the police station this afternoon. Chief Inspector Shadbolt was an interesting man. A little intimidating, but that was to be expected. You didn't become chief of a large police station like Burnie without stepping on some toes. Bald as a badger, wearing wire-rimmed glasses, the chief was slightly overweight, but with his height, he carried the extra pounds well. He had an almost kindly face and reminded her a little of Patrick Stewart, the actor who played Jean Luc Picard from that *Star Trek* movie. But there was an extra sharp edge to Charles. A don't-fuck-with-me edge. Lacey remembered her commander, Anthony Blaxland, back in Melbourne had that same hard edge.

The look on Nico's face as Charles had led her into his office had been priceless. Filled with apology as well as uncertainty, as if he wasn't sure he should allow his boss to lead her like a lamb to the slaughter but also knowing there was nothing he could do to stop it. It'd been accompanied by a sharp flash of curiosity. What did the chief inspector want with her? A question close to her own heart. What could the Burnie police chief possibly want?

She'd sat in the chair he indicated and tried not to quake in her boots, waiting for him to speak first, while he sat slowly behind his desk. After adjusting his glasses and then looking down his nose at her over the rims, he said, "Detective Sergeant Favreau told me some interesting facts about you today."

Lacey flinched inwardly but kept her face blank. The chief wouldn't be doing his job properly if he didn't take an interest in everyone involved in a murder scene. So he knew she'd been a cop and was now on leave without pay. Probably never to return to the force. And that thought filled her with a wave of shame. Shame that this intimidating man knew she'd failed at being a cop. At some deep level, that hurt. She hated to fail at anything. That was probably her mother's influence. It was very hard to keep her mother's voice out of her head, especially in those weeks and months after Cindi. Telling her to get over it, to get back on the horse and ride like the wind because that's what the Carmichaels did. They never gave up. Where would her father have ended up if he'd given up at the first hurdle? He surely wouldn't be a multi-millionaire. And she wouldn't be living in the lap of luxury if her father had given up either.

"I hear you did everything in your power to try and save that poor girl, Rania. And I want to personally thank you for that," Shadbolt continued, and Lacey banished her mother's voice from her head.

"I was just doing what anyone else in my position would've done, sir."

He shook his head. "That's not strictly true. Margie was there, and she was running around wringing her hands and doing nothing useful, by all accounts."

"Yes, but—"

Charles held up his hand and she bit off her retort.

"Learn to take praise where it's given." He tilted his head to one side and considered her. "You did a good thing. You need to accept that."

"Yes, sir," she said, trying not to sound unconvincing.

"I've also looked into your previous employment records." This time Lacey couldn't keep her grimace hidden. She sat a little straighter in her chair, bracing for the worst. "It seems you were a good young constable, with lots of potential." He studied her closely, and she wondered where he was going with his comments. This wasn't what she'd been expecting at all. "I've talked to your previous commander, and he agreed that if you left the police force completely it'd be a loss for us all."

"Oh?" She was clueless as to what to say next. Her ex-boss had said something similar to her, but she'd let the words wash over her, not being in the correct headspace to hear them. She'd never thought of herself as a good cop. That first year in the force had been a baptism of fire, and she'd thought she was doing well just to keep her head above water. She also didn't think she'd been on the beat long enough to prove what sort of cop she was going to be, but perhaps she'd underestimated herself. Perhaps her commander had seen something that she hadn't.

"I understand you went through something horrific, and everyone deals with those traumatic events differently. But if you ever feel like you'd like to rejoin the force…" He was still staring at her with that unwavering gaze. "Well, this station is growing, believe it or not. Crime is increasing in the area, which may not be a good thing, but at least the powers above have deemed we need more staff to handle the load. We're about to recruit two more constables. I was wondering if you might be interested in one of the positions?" He held up his hand as she opened her mouth to reply. "Don't say anything yet. Just take some time to think about it, okay?"

This was the last thing she'd expected when she'd traveled to this little town. A job offer. Could she really work here? With Shadbolt as her boss? Would she ever be strong enough to go back to the police force? Become the person she'd always dreamed she could be?

"Ah… Thank you, sir." She stood and shuffled her feet nervously. "I will… Think about it, I mean."

"Good." Shadbolt gave her a warm smile, the first she'd seen from him, and then reached for a pile of papers on his desk, effectively dismissing her.

Closing the door behind her, she walked down the hallway in a daze. This was the most unexpected thing. Nico appeared in his doorway, an inquiring lift to his mouth, and she'd mumbled that she'd tell him all about it when he got home that night. He'd handed her two boxes, and she'd driven home in his Jeep, her mind only half on the road.

And even now, three hours later, she was no closer to an answer. Should she tell Nico about the offer? He might convince her to stay. Or, he might try and talk her out of it. And she wasn't sure which option she dreaded more.

Her gaze fell on the shed at the edge of the driveway. Shit.

She'd forgotten to bring in those boxes Nico had given her from the Jeep. Better get them now, while there was still a hint of light in the sky. Most of the garden was already in shadow, the anemic light from the setting sun barely reaching the roof of the house now. Soon, the place would be plunged into desolate darkness. At least she had the fire well alight. Smudge was still dreaming on his mat by the fire, so Lacey decided to leave him there; they'd already had a long walk down by the beach this afternoon.

The geese were making a hell of a racket. Honking away up in the orchard. Vaguely, she wondered what'd got into them as she slipped on her jacket and closed the back door behind her. Walking across the grass to the driveway, Lacey stopped to contemplate her beloved Kombi parked next to the shed. Dave was coming tomorrow to fix Dotti. She still hadn't decided what to do once her van was drivable. The logical thing would be to move on. To continue her travels around Tasmania. If you'd asked her last Sunday—nearly a week ago, boy how time was flying—she would've been adamant she'd move on just as soon as was humanly possible.

But that was before she'd got to know Nico. Should she factor him into the equation? Nico absolutely hadn't asked her to stay. And why would he? His job as community-minded champion, offering her sanctuary in her hour of need, was at an end. As soon as she became mobile once more, there was nothing to keep her here in Boat Harbour.

Of course, Nico already had her contact details, so if he needed her for anything connected to the murder, he'd know where to find her.

But now there was also the job offer to contemplate. Her head was spinning with the possibilities. A voice in her head screamed that the best thing to do was to jump in her van and disappear. Run away. Then she wouldn't have to decide. She wasn't saying no, and she wasn't saying yes, she was just letting fate take her where it would.

She let out a sigh, her warm breath turning to mist in the cold evening air.

The geese were getting closer, their honking getting louder. Lacey looked up to see the little flock waddling down the path from the orchard. It looked like they were heading straight for her. Did they think she was going to feed them? She watched them with growing trepidation. Or were they coming to attack her?

Suddenly, Smudge barked from inside, a deep, urgent bark, as if he were desperate to get outside. As if he were warning her of—

A figure flashed in her peripheral vision. She spun around in time to see a man wearing a balaclava running at her. He must've been hiding behind the shed.

He was on her, knocking her to the ground, before she could do anything. Then he landed on top of her, pinning her down. What the fuck was going on? Why was someone assaulting her? What did this man want? Her money? Her car? Her judo skills were of little use to her now, but she did the best she could. Levering her left heel against the ground, she arched her back, attempting to dislodge the man, while at the same time, desperately trying to get her leg free enough that she could bring it up to knee him in the balls. A highly effective way of disabling an attacker, if only—

"Stop!" the man commanded, his voice deep and menacing.

Was there something about that voice she recognized? But she wasn't about to stop. Not in a million years. Smudge was still barking, she could hear the nebulous noise as if it were far, far away. Fighting to get one of her arms free, she tried to get a look at the guy on top of her, but the balaclava covered his face, and his eyes were turned away, looking at the house, so she couldn't even see what color they were. The man was of a medium build, but he was wearing bulky clothes, so it was hard to get a reading on his exact size and musculature. Her heart was hammering like a bird fluttering in a cage, but she wasn't afraid. Just desperate to get free.

"Stop," the man commanded again. He moved on top of her and she felt something cold and sharp press against the skin of her throat.

A knife. The man had a knife. Now her panic finally turned to fear. She froze in place, not daring to move.

Rania had been killed with a knife.

Fear turned to terror.

Was this the same man who'd killed Rania?

Was this Karim?

If only she could get a look at his eyes, perhaps she might be able to tell if it were. Karim had dark-brown eyes.

But the man wouldn't look at her. Instead, he lifted his head to stare in the direction of the honking sound.

It was getting closer. So close, it sounded like the geese were nearly on top of them.

"What the fuck...?" the man swore, then lifted the knife from her throat as if to ward off something. Then the air was filled with beating wings and hard, pecking beaks as the flock of geese descended on them. Protecting their territory. Protecting what was theirs. Lacey tried to cover her head to stop the birds battering her, but they seemed to concentrate more on the man. They had one goal, and that was to drive this man away. The figure in black got to his knees, covering his eyes with his forearm, much the same as she was. But the geese kept coming at him, using their wings to batter him, and pecking mercilessly at his face and arms.

Lacey shuffled backward away over the gravel, but the geese paid her no heed. As if she were part of their flock, and the man was the intruder who needed to be got rid of. Were geese really that smart? Nico had told her they would act like guard dogs. But this...? She would never underestimate the big birds ever again. The man stumbled to his feet, waving the knife in the air, but the birds continued to hound him. He lifted his head and gave her one long, penetrating stare and then he turned and ran.

The geese continued to chase him, leaving her sitting on the driveway. Safe. Had the geese just saved her life?

Smudge was going absolutely crazy inside the house, barking at the top of his lungs. Lacey pushed herself off the ground and ran toward the door. She wasn't waiting around out here to see if the man came back.

She rushed through the door, banging it shut and locking it. Then she leaned against the wood, breathing heavily. Smudge growled menacingly at the door, then tried to jump up and lick her face, but she pushed him away, too shocked to pat him right now. That'd teach her to take the dog outside with her next time. No man would've been able to sneak up on her like that with Smudge around.

Still leaning against the door, she slid down until she was on her haunches, finally bringing Smudge in for a cuddle. At the same time, her mind was frantically processing what'd just happened.

Was that a random attack? A mugger trying to steal her car? Or taking advantage of her being alone out here and rape her?

Or was this somehow connected to the case?

Could that have been Karim, back to finish what he started? Nico had mentioned he might get bail this afternoon, but she hadn't confirmed it before she left. Was he high on drugs again and perhaps decided that she was the person responsible for framing him for Rania's murder? Or had he indeed murdered her, and now he was coming after Lacey as well? As some sort of perverted repaying of a debt.

She'd been so sure he was innocent.

But now, nothing made sense anymore.

Smudge was licking her face, and she wrapped her arms around his neck and buried her face in his fur.

Fuck.

That'd been close. But she'd survived.

She got to her feet but her legs were like jelly and she wobbled into the kitchen, holding onto the wall so she didn't fall. Peering out the window, she surveyed the garden and driveway, checking to make sure the guy was really gone, but it was too dark to make out much. All of a sudden, ghostly white shapes waddled past the window and Lacey recoiled in fear, until she realized it was the victorious geese returning, the leader flapping her wings in a show of strength, clearly happy at seeing the intruder off the property.

The way the geese were acting made her believe she was safe. For now. That guy wouldn't be back in a hurry. If at all.

Now, she needed to call Nico.

CHAPTER SIXTEEN

Nico paced around his house, double-checking all the windows and doors were secure. Smudge was following in his wake, an apologetic tilt to his ears as if he were embarrassed he hadn't been there to ward off the intruder. Nico peered out the window in the front room. Good, the squad car was there, just like he'd commanded. Nico knew their rural station didn't have enough manpower to keep Lacey under guard forever. But Charles had given permission for a car to stay at least tonight and perhaps over the weekend. Nico was frustrated he couldn't keep Lacey under lock and key forever, just to keep her safe, but there were limits to his powers. He walked back down the hallway.

Nico was practically vibrating with anger. Most of that anger stemmed from a feeling of impotency. Lacey had been attacked, and he hadn't been around to help her. What's more, she'd been attacked right outside his very house. His house! How dare they? He hadn't seen this coming, and that just made him more furious. What kind of detective was he if he couldn't keep his key witness safe? He should've put her under protective custody. He should've—

"Stop beating yourself up over this," Lacey said tartly as he returned to the kitchen. She was sitting at the small table cradling a cup of tea. Her amber eyes were fixed on him, a fierce frown marring her gorgeous face. "There is no way in hell this is your fault. Neither of us could've predicted someone might attack me. This could also be completely unrelated to the murder."

Damn her intuitive nature. How could she read his mind so succinctly? But Nico disagreed with her on all points, so he merely grunted in reply.

"I mean it," she said. "No one could've foreseen this, so sit down, will you?"

"I've already ordered a squad car out to Karim Khaled's house," he growled in reply, pulling out a chair and taking a seat. But then he was up again, pacing around the kitchen, unable to keep still. "If he doesn't have a fucking watertight alibi, he'll be back in jail before he can say not guilty."

"So he made bail then?" Lacey nodded thoughtfully to herself.

"Yes. At around four this afternoon." Which would've given him plenty of time to get high and then come around and hurt Lacey. "If that bastard tried to hurt you…"

Nico couldn't remember the drive home; it was all a blur. He'd been at the vigil, which'd been about to start down by the waterfront. The Khaled family were noticeably absent, but perhaps they'd chosen to lie low and not attract any more attention, which was a good idea in Nico's book. One less security problem to worry about. But as soon as Lacey called, he'd jumped into his car and raced home, making calls to his team as he went, directing a car to Khaled's house and another two cars out to Boat Harbour to search for the fugitive and process the scene. Nico was determined to find this guy, whoever he was. One of the teams was out the back right now collecting evidence. They'd already spoken to Lacey and processed her hands and body for any telltale evidence the attacker may have left behind.

At least Lacey had been clear on one point. Her assailant had definitely been a man.

Lacey suddenly stood, put her cup on the table, and placed herself directly in his path so he was forced to stop pacing.

"Can you please hold me for a moment?" Gone was the fierce frown and the hard voice. She looked up at him with pleading eyes. "I'm still feeling a little shaky."

"What? Of course." He wrapped his arms around her and pulled her in close. Why the hell hadn't he thought of this? Of course she'd be in need of comfort. She'd just survived an attack on her life. He hated to think what might've happened.

"I still can't believe I was saved by a flock of geese," she murmured into his chest, and he could hear her attempt at humor in her voice. But when she finally looked up at him, her eyes were glazed with tears. "Sorry. I seem to be making a habit of crying on your shoulder."

"With good reason," he scoffed. "This is the second traumatic event you've been through in a week."

"Hmm." She buried her face in his shoulder again and they stood like that for untold minutes as she took his proffered comfort. He allowed himself to feel her body pressed up against his. Allowed his heart rate to subside. Allowed himself to know that she was safe and real in his arms. He rested his chin on top of her head.

This woman was confusing his feelings, making him doubt himself and lose his focus on the job. All things he didn't need or want. And yet... He hungered to have her in his arms more than anything. Wanted to get closer to her. So close they were melded together. Wanted to kiss her until the fear and anger diminished. Whether that was his fear and anger, or hers, he couldn't really say.

Smudge lay with his head on both their feet as they stood locked together. The three of them must be a sight to behold.

At last, Lacey withdrew slightly so she could look up into

his face. "Thank you," she said. "I feel better now. Stronger."

"Good." He tucked a strand of hair behind her ear. Her eyes widened slightly at his touch. And then she did the one thing that he couldn't resist. Her tongue came out to moisten her lips, drawing his gaze unerringly downward to her pink, lush mouth. The urge to kiss her before had been strong, born from a desire to comfort. But now his desire turned to pure lust as it ramped up to scorching levels.

He couldn't stop it, his mouth landed on hers without conscious thought. He let his tongue run over the corner of her upturned lips, then lightly over her teeth before he delved the depths of her mouth. She softened against him, her mouth pliant, consenting to his need to plunder her. The feel of her fingers in his hair at the back of his neck sent shivers of anticipation down his spine as she pulled his head down to get better access to his lips. Their first kiss had been explosive. And needy. This was just as needy, but more… sensuous. More adult. Like they'd progressed from a quick and dirty exploration to a more measured and considered discovery. Which was even more sexy somehow.

He ran his fingers across the small of her back, then up under her sweater to find all that glorious skin. Warm and soft and inviting. He spread his fingers across the breadth of her back, feeling the bumps of her spine beneath his palm. She was small and fragile beneath his big hand. But he knew she was quite the opposite. Knew that she could land him on his backside in one practiced move if she so wished it. A woman with hidden strengths.

The idea excited him even more. A woman who could be his equal. It was something he'd never encountered before. Something he might never encounter again. She could be life-altering, if he let her in.

He tilted his head on the side to give him better access to her alluring lips and she stood on tiptoe, meeting him halfway. A small sound escaped her throat. A groan of pleasure. That sound turned his blood to fire in his veins. She wanted him. Possibly as much as he wanted her. Pushing his hips into hers, he ground his erection into her belly, letting her know just how much he desired her. Together, they stepped backward, until her shoulders hit the wall behind. He cradled her head in one hand, his other hand still roaming the naked skin of her back. He found the fastener to her bra and prised it open with a flick. Pushing her against the wall, he bent and lifted her thighs, so they rested on his hips. Now her core was pressed to the front of his jeans. But there were so many clothes between them. They needed to—

There was a loud knock at the front door, startling them both. He drew in a sharp breath and lowered Lacey to the floor. Keeping one arm tucked around her waist, he called out, "Who is it?" Were they destined to always be interrupted by someone at the door? Just one time, he'd like to finish what they started.

"First Class Constable Gorman, sir," the voice called through the wood. "We've processed the crime scene. Would you like to hear what we've found?"

"Yes, yes," Nico answered gruffly. "I'm coming." He needed a few moments to be decent again. It wouldn't do for one of his junior officers to see him with a raging hard-on. Although he didn't mind the fact Lacey did that to him, he needed his professional face back on.

Lacey stepped away from him, combing her fingers through her hair and straightening her sweater after refastening her bra. He gave her one, long look, loving the pink flush in her cheeks and the way her lips were still swollen and lush. Nico took his time walking down the hallway, readjusting himself a few times, until he was happy that he was respectable. Studying the silhouettes of the figures outside, he made sure it was actually the two police officers standing on his front veranda before he unlocked the door.

"What have you got?" Nico asked.

"We found a knife in the ditch at the end of the driveway. We think the assailant might've dropped it when he was being chased by the...ah, birds." The first class constable could hardly hold back his smirk. The two officers hadn't believed Lacey's story at first, about being rescued by a flock of birds. But when Nico invited them to take a trip up to the orchard to see how those *birds* might react, the cops had demurred. Nico then told them about the other instances where the large geese had defended his property; twice from marauding foxes who thought they'd make an easy meal, only to be sorely mistaken. And the first time he himself had stepped onto the property when he came to inspect it before buying it, they'd chased him back down the driveway. That story had even made Lacey giggle. It seemed First Class Constable Gorman was still dubious, however.

Lacey had followed Nico down the hallway and was now peering over his shoulder.

"That's great news." Nico's heart rate-accelerated as he lifted his chin. "Let me see it," he demanded. This was an important find, and Lacey knew it as well, if the way she leaned into him, almost shoving him forward to take a look, was anything to go by.

The first class constable beckoned his partner forward, and he held up a plastic evidence bag containing a large kitchen knife with a black plastic handle. Lacey covered her mouth and stepped back, clearly having seen enough. Nico's mind immediately went into overdrive. It was a common knife, available in any number of shops around the state. Which would make it harder to track. But not impossible.

He didn't allow his anticipation to rise too far. But he was hoping he already knew where that knife came from. When forensics had gone over Rania's house after the murder, they'd reported the large carving knife seemed to be missing from a set of knives all lined up in a special wooden block on the kitchen bench. He needed to know if this was the missing knife.

"Do you think this was the weapon the attacker used on you?" He half turned to look at Lacey. Her face had gone pale, and he was suddenly sorry he'd been so brusque, but the question needed to be asked.

"I don't know," she admitted. "It was nearly dark. I felt it against my skin, but I never really saw it close up. He was waving it around his head to ward off the geese, so... Perhaps it might be. The knife he had was certainly big. Bigger than a pocket knife, or a paring knife."

"It's okay." He hugged her tightly to his chest for a fleeting second. "That's all good information. And I'm just happy he didn't get to use it on you."

Other scenarios were also circling inside his head. If this was the murder weapon used to kill Rania, it could blow this case wide open. If it wasn't, then it might prove the attack on Lacey was random after all.

"We need to get this into evidence as soon as possible," Nico instructed. "I want it measured against the stab wounds inflicted on the murder victim. And against that wooden knife block in Karim and Rania's house."

"Yes, sir." Gorman gave him an appraising look, and Nico knew the first class constable had had the same thoughts running through his head. Good. It meant Gorman would make a good cop if he was able to put that together so quickly. It also meant Nico wasn't completely crazy. He allowed a small kernel of hope to blossom in his chest. That he might yet get his man.

* * *

"Nico, are you awake?" Lacey's voice was soft in the dark

room.

"Yes. Is everything okay?" He sat up in bed, suddenly afraid that perhaps Lacey had heard something outside that he'd missed. Had the attacker come back to finish the job? He'd been tossing and turning, uneasy about going to sleep, but knowing he needed some shut-eye to function properly. The squad car was still parked out the front of his house, however, so he wasn't sure what he was worried about.

He glanced at the digital screen of his bedside clock. It was one-thirty-three am. He heard the shuffle of feet and the creak of his bedroom door as it opened wider. Lacey was silhouetted in the doorway from the glow of the lamp he'd left on in the living room. She was all soft curves and tousled hair. Smudge stood at her feet, slowly wagging his tail, also asking for entry. Nico had commanded his dog to sleep in Lacey's room as her companion and guard, and Smudge was more than happy to do so. But he wasn't about to be left out in the hallway now.

"I can't sleep. And I just wondered...?" He heard the hesitation and unease in her voice. And he understood she was probably being haunted by replays of tonight's attack.

He also knew what she was asking. But did he dare let her in his bed? He only wore a pair of briefs to sleep in. He was practically naked. Would he be able to keep his libido under control? And could he be held responsible if anything did happen? But he couldn't leave her standing there, anxious and alone.

"Come here," he replied softly, making room for her. He held the covers up so she could slip in beside him, then pulled her down so her head was on his shoulder. Her hair fell in a soft fan across his chest and he luxuriated in the feel of it. Smudge lay down beside the bed with a soft grunt.

"Thank you," she said, her breath warm on his neck. "Sorry, I just..."

"It's okay if you need help to get through this, Lacey. I already said I'd be there for you," he chided softly.

"I know." She moved slightly, snuggling deeper into the bed, resting her legs against his. He almost jumped at the feel of her bare skin; she must only be wearing sleep shorts and not her sweatpants like she normally did in the morning. Great. Add her lack of clothes, to his state of undress and he could barely think straight. The thought of all those acres of skin right there for him to explore was momentarily distracting. Her shapely calves, her firm, slightly muscular thighs… *Hold that thought.* He tamped down on his runaway mind. She'd been in his bed for less than a minute and already, her body was affecting him so that he couldn't think straight.

But then, she also smelled so good. A hint of her shampoo and something else understated and musky, like the pages of a favorite book, or the smell of the air after it rained on a dusty road.

"I couldn't get the feel of that knife against my skin out of my head," she whispered into the dark.

Her words brought him back to reality, drawing him away from the precipice of the desire building in his gut. Replacing it with that simmering sense of rage he'd felt earlier.

"Well, at least Karim is back in custody," Nico replied, voice gruff.

Karim hadn't been able to come up with a solid alibi for his whereabouts during the time of the attack. He'd told the officers sent to check on him he'd been out walking, trying to clear his head after finally getting bail. He'd needed to get away from his family's constant worried diatribe; he couldn't think straight with them jabbering in his ears all the time. And he'd wanted to go to the vigil for his girlfriend, but had been warned by various people that he might become the target for the less tolerant people in the community. The ones who already blamed him for Rania's murder. But Karim denied he'd been anywhere near Nico's house. He argued he had no mode of transport, and he surely hadn't walked to Boat Harbour and back to Burnie in that time. Which, sadly, made a lot of sense. But stranger things had happened. Karim could've had an accomplice. Or perhaps stolen a car—although no reports of a stolen vehicle had come through tonight—or he could've borrowed one.

Nico wondered if what Karim was saying was true, and he hadn't actually been responsible for the attack on Lacey. If so, had he really been wandering the streets alone, like he said? Nico found it hard to believe. Easier to believe that perhaps he'd been out trying to score a hit of cocaine. An equally bad idea in Nico's books.

"We'll review CCTV footage around town and see if we can pick him up during his nightly wanderings," Nico added. If they could, they might be able to rule Karim out as the assailant.

"Mmm hmm," Lacey replied. "I've been thinking about it. And I don't believe the guy who attacked me was muscular enough to have been Karim," she said thoughtfully. "Much as it gives me the shivers, I keep replaying those seconds when he was holding me down, with his body on top of mine, trying to see if I remembered anything. Even the smallest detail." Lacey shivered then, and he pulled her closer.

"You're a very brave woman, and you continue to astound me," he said, without a hint of irony. Instead of pushing the traumatic attack out of her mind, she'd been actively reliving it, so she could get her facts straight. To help the case. And to give him something more to work with.

She lifted one shoulder in a shrug, dismissing his comment. Which made him a little sad. Why couldn't she see what an amazing woman she was? He wished there was some way he could help her to restore her faith in herself.

She continued with her evaluation of the man who'd attacked her. "But while the man was much heavier than me —and let's face it, most men are—he wasn't solid. I've seen Karim. He must work out in the gym lifting weights, because he's a big guy. I mean I'd guess that one of his biceps would be bigger in circumference than my thigh. Would you agree?"

He nodded. Her assessment was pretty spot on.

Her left hand was resting lightly on his chest. She made circles with her index finger, running lightly over the curling hairs. Her touch set off a vibration somewhere deep inside him. He had to force himself to tune back into her words.

"He had on bulky clothing, but that didn't stop me from being able to get an idea of what was going on underneath when he was lying on top of me. And I'd have to say the guy was of medium build and medium height. Personally, I'd rule Karim out as a suspect," she finished.

Okay, that was interesting. "I'll take your judgement into consideration," he replied. And he would. But he certainly wasn't ruling Karim out just yet. If the guy was capable of murdering his own girlfriend—and that was still a big *if*— then he was definitely capable of trying to hurt Lacey.

Nico hadn't forgotten there might be a serial killer in the vicinity. Could that same person have killed Rania? But if they had, why go against his previous MO? Maybe he'd got sloppy. The lust for the kill overcoming his need to be careful. Had that same serial killer come after Lacey as well? Could Karim be that serial killer? There were so many facets of this investigation. He just wished he knew how they all fitted together.

"What about this Floyd guy, what does he look like?" Lacey was still trying to deduce who attacked her.

"Hmm?" He was only half concentrating on her words; her touch was still distracting him. "He's small, around your height," Nico answered. "You might call him weedy. With shifty eyes and a bit of bum-fluff on his chin that might pass as a beard." Nico had taken an immediate dislike to the apprentice; there was something about him that reminded him of a weasel, but he couldn't tell Lacey that.

"I don't think it was him," she replied after a few moments of consideration. "This guy was definitely taller than me. Anyway, that's enough picking over the facts. I came in here because I didn't want to think about it any longer." Lacey's finger stopped tracing circles. "And do you know the one thing that helped me to forget? About the assault tonight? And about Rania dying?" She levered up onto her elbow so she could look down on him.

"No. What?" But his stomach quivered at the hungry light reflected in her eyes.

"Kissing you." She never moved, just locked her amber gaze onto his. Inviting him in. If he wanted to take the bait.

Lunging upward, he caught her around the waist and flipped her over onto her back, so that he lay on top of her. Yes, he did. He gave in to temptation. How could he not? She was sexy as hell. Like an intoxicating drug, igniting his desire with a searing flash of heat. He'd been prepared to deny himself, to keep himself under control. But now she offered herself to him, he couldn't deny her.

"I can certainly do more kissing, if that will take your mind off things. I'm here to help. To serve and protect." He tried to make his tone light, to give her one last out, if she wanted it. But she shifted, wrapping her long legs around his waist and grabbing a handful of his hair in her fist.

"I like that you're here to serve and protect me," she replied huskily. God, she was making him so hard with just her words.

"Me too." he agreed. "But there might be more than just kissing if you keep looking at me like that."

"I'm okay with that," she said.

Any more comments were lost when she drew him down by his hair so she could claim his mouth. He gloried in the feel of her lithe body beneath his. Let himself sink into her. Sink into her soft curves and soak up the feeling of lying with a woman.

It'd been a while since he'd got naked with a woman. Back when he'd first started this job in Burnie six years ago, Sally-Ann had flirted outrageously with him. But when it became clear by his polite but firm rejections that she wasn't the one for him, she'd started a one-woman quest to find a suitable partner for him instead. Sally-Ann had introduced him to Claudia two years ago, and he'd had a long-term—by his standards anyway—affair with the lady for around six months. Claudia owned a pilates studio in town, and had been sensuous and uninhibited, with warm, brown skin, and a supple body that could do so many interesting things. Claudia had ended it because she said he'd stood her up one too many times, and she needed a man she could count on to be there when he said he would. He hadn't tried to stop her, because it was true, he put the job over her, every time. Sally-Ann still liked to throw him to the wolves now and then by inviting him out and then subtly turning up with *a friend* in tow. But none of them stuck. He was too engrossed with his job to give time to a woman. Especially a woman who didn't understand why the job was so all-encompassing. It was why Sally-Ann was so happy to see him let Lacey stay at his house. She lived in eternal hope that one day Nico would find his match.

And maybe he finally had.

Lacey wriggled beneath him. "I have too many clothes on," she said, struggling to grab the hem of her T-shirt and pull it over her head. He was more than happy to help, and the shirt was off in seconds. Lacey lay back on the bed, letting him take in the glorious sight of her naked breasts, the light sneaking in through his partially open door just enough to make out the details.

"Mmm, beautiful," he whispered, tracing his index finger down in a line from the hollow at the base of her throat, over her sternum, and between her breasts. They were small, but pert and flawless. He'd never been a man interested in big breasts. And Lacey's were perfect. He cupped one breast in his hand and then lowered his tongue onto the nipple, tasting and sucking.

She arched into him, murmuring, "Oh, God."

He spent untold moments exploring her breasts, running his hands over her body, caressing her flat stomach, down to the hemline of her sleep shorts, enjoying the sounds of satisfaction Lacey made. She was practically purring like a cat when he slowly tucked a finger in each side of her pants and drew them down over her hips and past her knees, past her ankles—

"Do you have a condom?" Lacey suddenly sat up.

He grinned. Was that actual fear in her eyes? "Yes," he replied, putting her out of her misery. A good detective was always prepared. And he was a stickler for protection. He reached over and yanked open the top drawer of his bedside table. "How many would you like?" he asked, grabbing a handful and dropping them on the bed.

"One is good for now," she said, snatching one up, her breath coming in short and sharp gasps. "Your turn," she said pulling greedily at his boxer briefs, fumbling ineffectively at them.

He stepped off the bed and helpfully dropped his boxers around his ankles.

"Not bad," Lacey said, raising her eyebrows. Her gaze roamed over his chest, down his legs and then came back up to rest on his erection. "Not bad at all."

Smudge suddenly stood, tail wagging hopefully. Nico had

forgotten his dog was in the room. "Out," he demanded, pointing his finger at the door. Poor Smudge slunk through the gap and headed for his customary place by the fireplace. Nico didn't think Lacey would appreciate his dog watching on eagerly as they made love.

Lacey giggled when he climbed back onto the bed. But her mirth quickly subsided as he took the condom from her hand and ripped it open with his teeth.

As he sheathed himself, she lay back on the bed, blonde hair falling all around her like a halo. An angel. That's what she looked like. Until she reached up grabbing at his hair with one hand and grabbing at his erection with the other, greedy for him, before urging him inside her. Then he was glad she also had a little of the devil in her.

CHAPTER SEVENTEEN

Lacey couldn't look at herself in the bathroom mirror. She could hardly believe how she'd acted last night. And looking in the mirror merely reminded her. When she did finally lift her head and stare into the steamy glass, she saw her mouth still swollen from kissing, the mark on her neck where Nico had branded her in the heat of passion, and a blush on her cheeks that hadn't been there yesterday. Damp strands of hair from her shower hung around her face, the blonde locks still tangled and messy from their night spent rolling in the sheets.

She looked exactly like a woman who'd been ravished.

And she didn't know how she felt about that.

It was true; she was the one who'd gone to Nico's bed last night in search of comfort. She certainly hadn't been actively seeking to have sex with him, that hadn't been her goal. It was as she told him, to drive away the nightmarish images that kept playing on repeat behind her eyelids. She'd fought with her feelings of fear for many hours, knowing a good police officer should be able to handle such things. But in the end, her craving for comfort, the sort of comfort only Nico could offer, became too strong to ignore. All she'd really hoped for was a few hours of blissful sleep, safe in his arms.

But perhaps there was also a wish, buried in her subconscious that things might get…heated.

And heated they had definitely become. Nico was good in bed. No, better than good. He was amazing. He was gentle when he needed to be gentle, but also demanding and bold when his passion took hold. Not asking anything of her that she wasn't prepared to give, but not holding anything of himself back either. And that body. Oh, my. She couldn't get enough of his body. Not big and muscly like Karim. Nico was toned and lean, with a set of abs that she couldn't stop running her fingers over, just to feel the ridges. And hands that were big and strong; his long, clever fingers leaving an everlasting impression on her skin.

It was after nine in the morning when they finally emerged from their warm, safe cocoon in Nico's bedroom. Smudge had been whining by the door for a while before Nico grunted that he needed to "let the bloody dog out", and had gone to do exactly that, stopping to kiss her thoroughly on the lips on the way out. Poor Smudge; not only had Nico kicked him out of the bedroom, but he'd been so patient waiting to get outside to relieve himself. Without Nico in the bed, Lacey had suddenly felt awkward being alone in his bedroom and decided to take the opportunity and shower and change. Grabbing her clothes, she'd fled to the bathroom.

Lacey turned her head to study her profile in the mirror, letting her gaze drift down to analyze the rest of her body. She was wearing her underwear but hadn't yet donned jeans or a sweater. Studying herself critically, she tried to see what Nico might find attractive. Her stomach was fairly flat—probably a result of not eating properly over the past few months, more than any regular exercise regime—and her breasts were on the small side. Elora had always tried to get her to wear those padded, push-up bras, proclaiming that a woman needed to enhance her assets if nature didn't provide.

And for a while, Lacey had worn the uncomfortable underwear just to please her. Until she began traveling around Tasmania and left the sphere of her mother's influence. Now she wore soft, cotton sports tops, which were more comfortable than sexy. But Nico had been adamant he liked her breasts just the way they were. And she thought she believed him. Moving her gaze down, she noted her skin had a sort of creamy hue, from not seeing the sunshine for so long, and her—

There was a knock on the bathroom door, and she jumped guiltily. "How are you doing in there? Is everything okay?" She'd been in here much longer than was strictly necessary, and he must be worried about her.

"Yes. I'm just getting dressed," she called out, hopping on one foot as she tugged on her jeans.

"I didn't mean to rush you," he said through the door. "Just checking you're all right?" She could hear the edge of uncertainty in his tone. He'd probably returned to the bedroom, expecting to find her still in his bed, and wondered where she'd got to. She felt like a coward, because she'd been unable to face him. Tugging her sweater over her head, she threw open the bathroom door and smiled winningly.

"All good," she said. "The shower is free, if you want it."

"No, that wasn't what I meant." Nico stood in the hallway, his hair pushed back from his face, the scar on his cheek more pronounced in the harsh lighting. While he was definitely a man in his prime, this morning she could see through his confident exterior to the man beneath. And he looked older somehow, fatigue gnawing around the edges of his bravado. It was as if their night together had allowed her access to a deeper level of Nico, to the man he kept hidden from most people. Now she was beginning to learn some of the secrets he concealed behind his eyes. Knew that he was scrupulous with details, almost a perfectionist. And he hated it when he got things wrong. Like letting her come home alone, only to be attacked. She knew he took that hard. And it was part of the stress she was seeing on his face this morning.

Suddenly, she didn't know what to say.

An awkward silence descended, just as she'd feared it would. Sleeping together had changed things between them. Shit. She stared at him, grasping for words, but none came. Nico's dark-blue eyes narrowed; then he pursed his lips, and it was as if a shutter had gone down inside him.

He turned and walked to the kitchen. She followed hesitantly in his wake.

She needed an explanation as to why she'd vanished from his bed. Why she was suddenly tongue-tied and shy. Needed to say something to get the real Nico back. But what? She didn't know if last night was a one-off thing. Arising from her weakness and her inability to cope, and so she'd sought comfort in his arms. And had he given her what she needed because that was the kind of man he was? Always wanting to help. Always wanting to fix things. She was so confused.

Instead of addressing her concerns, she turned the conversation to safer ground. "Dave is coming this morning. Soon, I think," she said as Nico stopped by the coffee machine and flicked on the switch.

He looked up, eyes hooded, hiding his true feelings. "Oh. I'd almost forgotten," he said blandly. "With everything else that's happened… I thought perhaps you might…" He trailed off. What? Perhaps she might stay longer? Not get her van fixed? She had to get her van fixed. That was a no-brainer. But whether she moved on or not once it was roadworthy, that was the elephant in the room. Why had things just got more complicated, not less?

Things had changed between them last night. They'd proved their physical chemistry was off the charts. And that'd been after only one night. What might they achieve if they did it again? And again? What if they started a relationship? They might be great together. Was that what she was scared of?

But she was getting too far ahead of herself. She didn't even know if Nico wanted her to stay for one more day, let alone for the foreseeable future. And even if he did ask her to stay, did she want to?

There were commitments at home. She couldn't keep traveling forever. She'd have to face reality sooner or later. Have to face her mother. And her father. Oh, God, that reminded her. She still hadn't told her mother about being a star witness in a murder case. Lacey had promised her father that she'd tell her soon. Tonight. She would ring her tonight. Whether she called Elora from Nico's house or from her van in the caravan park in Stanley was immaterial. Her mother was going to freak out, but Lacey would just have to handle it. She was a big girl. The same way she would have to handle whatever it was that Nico wanted to say to her.

"Might what?" she prompted.

He put the coffee cup he'd been about to fill down carefully on the countertop and cleared his throat. "I thought you might stay for a while. At least until we've investigated who attacked you last night."

"But that could take months," she admonished softly. "Surely, you don't want me to stay for months."

"No," he said a little too quickly. Then he added, "Well, as long as you don't want to stay for months, because you're quite welcome."

"Really? You'd let me stay here? In your house? For months? So you can make sure I'm safe?" No matter how hard she tried to keep her voice even, it rose by the end of her last sentence. The high pitch made Nico glance sharply at her.

Then he shrugged and looked a little bewildered, and a slow anger began to burn in her guts. She didn't know if they had anything together. And if they did, what the hell it might mean. But one thing she did know was that she wanted Nico to want her to stay for him. Not out of any sort of duty or guilt. Not just so he could protect her. That wasn't nearly enough. She wanted him to ask her to stay because he had feelings for her. Or at least so they could explore whatever it was growing between them.

But she couldn't put her anger and confusion into words. Nico didn't owe her anything. Much like she didn't owe him. Perhaps he was just as confused as her, but she wished he'd say something. Anything. She stared at him, not trusting herself to speak.

There was a knock at the front door, breaking their impasse, and a grave voice called out, "Hello, Detective Sergeant Favreau? It's Constable Hickey. I have a man here who says his name is Dave, and he's come to fix your Kombi van."

Saved by the bell. Again.

Smudge ran to the door, barking. Nico raised an eyebrow, asking if she wanted him to get it, but she waved him away. Dave was her problem.

"Coming," Lacey called as she trotted down the hallway and opened the door, keeping Smudge at bay with her knee.

"Is that correct, ma'am?" It was one of the same constables who'd found the knife last night. Stocky and thick-necked, he made her think of a bulldog. A bulldog that was protecting her, she reminded herself. Had this poor cop even been home to sleep? Or was he pulling a double shift? He narrowed his eyes at her and used his chin to indicate Dave, who was standing nervously behind him.

"Oh, yes. Sorry, I should've told you. You can definitely let him in, Constable Hickey." At least it was good to know the local constabulary were doing their job. But if she moved on, she assumed she'd forfeit all this kind of protection. Another thing to think about. Did she even need protection? She was beginning to think last night's attack was merely random, and had nothing to do with the murder investigation.

"Right, then." Hickey gave Dave one more long, appraising look before he stepped down off the veranda to return to his cruiser.

"Something going on that I don't know about?" Dave asked conversationally as she ushered him through the door and down the hallway, Smudge gamboling at his feet.

Lacey grimaced. She wouldn't be able to keep the attack a secret for much longer, so she may as well tell him. "Yes. We had an…intruder here last night. He tried to assault me. But he got away. I'm fine, by the way," she added hurriedly.

"Really?" Dave's kind, brown eyes went wide as he turned to face her in the kitchen.

"Yes, really," Nico replied with a growl. "Morning, Dave," he added, almost as an afterthought.

"Has this got something to do with the murd—"

Nico cut him off. "We're not speculating about anything until we have all the facts."

But he and Lacey both knew if Dave had jumped to that conclusion, then so would everyone else. By lunchtime, the whole community would be abuzz with gossip and innuendo. Lacey groaned silently. Maybe she was better off leaving after all. At least she wouldn't have to face all those half-truths and speculation, or people staring at her as if she was some kind of freak. As if she'd invited this sort of unwelcome attention on herself. She'd had enough of that to last her a lifetime after Cindi died.

Nico's frown deepened as he stared at Dave, almost as if the poor man was the root of all their troubles. None of this was Dave's fault. He was just here to fix her vehicle. All the other problems that existed between her and Nico were of their own making.

"Got the spare part, I see," Lacey said brightly, pointing at the white box in Dave's hands. "Shall we go out and see if it fits?"

"Of course it'll fit," Dave huffed. But he followed her and Smudge out the back door and down the steps. Lacey pulled on her jacket as they walked toward her Kombi. It'd be good to get Dotti going again. Good to hop back in and go for a drive. Gain her independence once more. She hadn't realized how much the lack of her own set of wheels could make her feel trapped. Even though Nico would've driven her wherever she wanted to go, it wasn't the same as getting in her own car and just going.

"Sorry it took so long," Dave said, bending to lift the rear door to the engine.

"It's not your problem," she replied. "Actually, I need to thank you again for coming out on a Saturday."

"Don't worry about it. I often work on Saturdays, it's the nature of the job. The joy of being self-employed."

"I guess so." Lacey watched as he tinkered around inside the engine for a few moments.

"I've just got to pop down to my truck and grab some more tools." Dave stood and pointed at his truck parked at the end of the drive. "Your mate, the cop, wouldn't let me come farther than the front gate."

"Sorry," she apologized. "He's just doing his job."

"That he is." Dave cast her a long look before turning to walk down the driveway. He must have a million questions, but she was thankful he had enough manners not to ask them.

"Drive your truck up here," she called out after him, and he waved his understanding.

She rubbed her hands together and blew on them to warm them up. The threat of snow had dissipated for now. Reports confirmed that Cradle Mountain still had a dusting of white lying on its peak, but it'd melt away soon enough. Gray clouds hung over the bay as Lacey turned to look out over the ocean. But even with the threat of rain, the bay was still pretty in the morning light. The muted colors of the bruised grays of the clouds were reflected in the darker graphite of the water, tipped with silver flashes as a wave broke the surface. A watercolor painter's delight.

It was the sort of day that she'd love to take a long walk along the beach and then come back and curl up next to the fire with a hot chocolate. Or even better an Irish coffee with a good slug of whiskey. Lacey glanced toward the house. Would Nico be up for that sort of day? If she went back in and asked him, what would he say? It might be nice to spend one last day together. Then she could make her decision. To stay. Or go.

Dave would be fine out here; he didn't need her hanging around watching him fix her van. Making up her mind, she shoved her hands in her pockets, waving at him as he reversed his truck in next to her Kombi. Whistling up Smudge, she waited for him to come charging back down from the orchard, where he'd been exploring some fascinating smell, and laughed as he skidded on the linoleum as he ran through the door.

"Hey." Nico looked up from where he was reading something on his laptop at the kitchen table. Lacey's heart fell. She'd forgotten how busy he was. He was the lead detective right in the middle of a murder investigation.

"Hey," she replied.

"I made you a coffee." He pointed to a mug on the countertop.

"Thank you." She picked it up and sipped it carefully, trying to gauge his mood. The shutters seemed to still be firmly in place, but she took a chance anyway. "Are you going in to work today?" She hoped she sounded conversational.

"I'm not sure. Why?"

"I thought it might be nice to take Dotti for a drive, and stretch her legs. Maybe stretch my legs as well. I feel like a nice, long walk along the beach. You can join me if you like."

He tipped his head to the side, his long hair falling over one eye as he considered her. "I can probably take a few hours off. I'll need to make some calls this morning, and check my emails, that kind of thing. But I could be free around eleven."

"Perfect. I could make us some lemon slice to take with us." Lacey had noticed a few lemons on a tree up in the orchard. "As long as the geese let me near them," she added with a laugh.

"They see you as part of their flock now. They wouldn't have protected you if they didn't." His comment brought an air of seriousness back to the room. Damn, she wished she hadn't reminded him of the attack.

"True," she replied, not rising to the bait. "I'll pick some lemons and leave you to it." She set off out the back door again, Smudge at her heels. It was good to have a plan, even if it only put off the inevitable. A drive and then a walk on the beach would be good for her. Good for both of them. Afterward, she could make a decision.

CHAPTER EIGHTEEN

"This lemon slice thing is amazing," Nico said, his voice muffled by the sweet treat he was stuffing into his mouth. He licked his fingers and took another piece. It'd been a while since he'd had home-baked goods. Especially this delicious. Sometimes Margie or one of the blue-rinse brigade would take pity on him and bring him a batch of freshly baked Anzac biscuits or a chocolate cake. But this slice was still warm and oozing from the oven. And made from his own lemons, what's more.

"More coffee?" Lacey held up the thermos full of fresh coffee she'd made on his machine.

"Yes, please." He held out his cup for her to refill. They were sitting in the little fold-up chairs outside the Kombi in a parking lot in the little township of Stanley, having morning tea before they set off for their walk. Smudge was sitting next to him, hopeful eyes flicking from him to Lacey and back again. No way was Smudge getting any of his delicious slice. It was too good to share. Clouds hung low and somber over the headland at the end of the bay, hinting of rain to come. But Lacey said she had a good rain jacket, and a little rain never hurt anyone. He was wearing his thick woolen turtleneck and a waterproof jacket, as well, and he agreed with her. In fact, it'd be nice to get out into nature for a while.

It was the first time he'd stopped to take a breather in he couldn't remember how long. Well, not counting last night's escapades in his bedroom. But that was different. Parts of his body were still tingling from being with Lacey. She'd reignited all kinds of nerve endings he'd forgotten existed. Unearthed all kinds of emotions he'd also thought long buried. Then she'd gone and made it awkward, and he couldn't figure out why.

He glanced over at Lacey, sketching her profile as she stared out to sea. Her little ski-jump nose and her full mouth, with long, caramel eyelashes fluttering on her cheekbones. The smile on her face hadn't faded from the drive over here. She was so happy to have her wheels back. And he had to admit the drive in the vintage van, with its restored interior and big wide windshield giving a panoramic view of the road, had been kind of fun. Dotti added an air of gaiety to the whole trip. He could see why Lacey loved her.

It was Nico who'd suggested they come to Stanley. "There's a loop walk, which takes us through the back of the dunes, and then down onto the beach right near The Nut, and we can walk back to the car. It's about three miles," he'd told her as she was packing a small picnic basket in the kitchen before they left.

"That sounds perfect," she'd said with a smile. That same bright smile he'd first been attracted to a week ago. White teeth and amber eyes alight with joy, cheeks flushed pink. "I really want to see The Nut, so this will be a great opportunity."

Nico had almost forgotten about the tourist icon. A large rock protuberance, the remains of a volcanic plug, at the end of a headland jutting out to sea. Most people liked to climb to the top, or there was a chairlift for the less adventurous, but this walk went down the beach, showcasing The Nut from afar.

He still had plenty of emails waiting to be answered and he really should pop into the station to collect a few more files, so he could review them tonight. He was also sweating on the analysis results of tests to the knife Constable Hickey had found. But it was Saturday. And even though the knife had been sent to forensics in Devonport, Nico knew he wouldn't realistically have an answer until at least Monday, even though he'd put a rush on it.

It was Saturday, he reminded himself again. He could afford to take a few hours off on the weekend. He wasn't a robot. He couldn't run on fumes forever. Or that's what Sally-Ann kept telling him. She was constantly scolding him for all the long hours he spent at the precinct, telling him it was no life if you were all work and no play.

So today, he was playing.

"Ready to take that walk?" Lacey stood and emptied the dregs of her coffee onto the grass at the edge of the parking lot.

"Sure," he replied, even though he'd been quite happy sitting there contemplating nature. He helped her pack up and lock the van, snapped Smudge onto his lead, then they went to find the trailhead. Nico led the way, zipping his jacket up against the sneaky wind, with its cold, probing fingers. Winding their way through the long, coastal grasses, he followed the trail into the rolling dunes.

Technically, dogs probably weren't allowed on this trail. But Nico wasn't prepared to leave his dog behind. Smudge was well-behaved, and he'd keep him on his lead until they got to the open beach. Besides, it was another layer of added protection. Just in case. That was the other reason he'd agreed to come on this walk; to keep an eye on Lacey. Not that he'd admit it. She seemed a tad touchy about his overriding urge to keep her safe. As if he were insulting her capabilities or something. Far from it, Nico respected her ability to defend herself. But she'd been taken by surprise last night. Who was to say it couldn't happen again?

They walked in silence for a while, the wind whipping through his hair and biting at his cheeks with its cold teeth. Lacey had tied her hair back in a plait to keep it from turning into one giant snarl.

"How's the thing with your mum going?" Lacey suddenly asked from behind.

"What?" Her question caught him by surprise and he nearly missed a step.

"The phone call the other night," she prompted. "I was just wondering if you've heard anything more about your father?"

She had every right to ask, but just the mention of his father made him tense up.

"I talked to my mother quickly yesterday morning," he said, forcing his shoulders back down. He'd called Catarina in the space between a meeting with Charles and a media interview. He knew he'd probably sounded distracted, but he also knew he couldn't put it off for too long, or his mother would lose her patience and start calling him instead.

"And," she prompted quietly.

"And she's still freaking out about the idea that Serge might be alive." Catarina had still been close to hysterical when he'd spoken to her. It was hard for him to hear his mother like that. Nico loved his mother, he didn't like that she was hurting. "So, yesterday afternoon, I hired a private investigator to look into it." There was no way he could spare the time at the moment to rush across to mainland Victoria, to the little town of Lorne to start the search himself. So he'd done the next best thing. He hoped it'd be enough to placate his mother and sister. At least for the next little while, until he had time to use his own contacts and delve into this mystery himself. "The guy was recommended to me by another police detective mate in Melbourne. Supposedly, he does good work. Charges like a wounded bull, but my mate said that if there was anything to find, then this guy would find it."

"That's good," Lacey chimed in from behind his left shoulder.

"At least it's something. I couldn't keep ignoring it. Catarina would've gone batshit crazy if I had. This way, I can tell her when the guy comes back with the info that there's absolutely no basis to any of Marco and Priscilla's claims, I can put my mother's mind at ease."

"Yes, and your own," Lacey replied softly.

He didn't reply, but she was correct. He was doing this as much for himself as he was for his mother and the rest of his family.

They walked some more in silence, Smudge enthusiastically investigating every little bend and shrub on the trail, until Nico had to remind him they were walking to get somewhere, not just out for a dog's pleasure. The wind was weaving its magic, blowing the cobwebs away and leaving him feeling refreshed and revitalized.

The trail opened up, and Lacey moved up so they could walk side by side.

"This was a good idea," he told her.

"Yes. It's so pretty out here. The crashing waves, and the wind whipping though the grass. There's something therapeutic about a fresh, ocean breeze. Something about that salty tang that brings you to life," Lacey agreed.

It was true. And it was something he often failed to appreciate; the fact he lived on the coast and saw the ocean every single day.

The trail curved around and passed between two grass-covered dunes, then they emerged out onto the open beach. Nico leaned down and released Smudge from his lead. The dog raced down to where the waves were breaking on the shore, barking like an idiot.

"I need to feel the sand between my toes," Lacey sang, dancing down onto the sand. "Come on, take your shoes off," she goaded.

But he shook his head. The sand was damp from the rain, and it looked sticky and cold. But nothing could stop Lacey. Even though the wind was freezing, Lacey removed her shoes and rolled up her jeans, then pranced through the damp sand to the edge of the waves with Smudge. Dipping her big toe in the water, she squealed and ran backward. "Oh, it's freezing."

"I could've told you that," he replied, but he laughed along with her, feeling suddenly lighter than he had in weeks. Months, even. For once, he had something else to think about besides work. The simple pleasure of spending a winter's day at the beach. Spending time with a woman who could teach him a thing or two about being more spontaneous. Teach him how to live a little.

He kept pace with her up on the drier sand, while she and Smudge skipped through the wavelets. The Nut slowly grew larger as they progressed down the beach. As they walked back, the clouds got lower, almost touching the top of The Nut. A light mist began to drizzle down on them. But he didn't even mind, just pushed his damp hair off his face, and tucked his hands into his pockets. Lacey came up the beach to join him, the misting raindrops shining like tiny jewels in her hair.

"Stay. For a few more days," he suddenly blurted. Bugger. He hadn't wanted to sound as if he were pleading. But he needed her to know how he felt. He didn't want her to leave. Not yet. And it had nothing whatsoever to do with the murder investigation. And everything to do with her. His feelings for her were complicated and maybe he needed a little more time to process them.

She glanced up at him, her features unreadable.

"Maybe I will," she replied, tossing her braid over her shoulder and glancing behind at her footprints in the wet sand.

"I'd like it if you did. I..." Damn, how did he say this without sounding like a dork? He wasn't used to entreating a woman to do anything, and he wasn't about to let Lacey turn him into some spineless man whose emotions got the better of him. "I'm not just asking you to stay because of the case. Because I want to see you under police protection," he said, trying not to grind his teeth. This was harder than he thought it'd be. "I want you to stay because..." Why couldn't he say the words?

"Shadbolt offered me a job," Lacey blurted into the silence.

"What?" He stopped and turned to stare at her. Why was this the first he was hearing about it?

"Yesterday, in his office."

They'd never got around to discussing why Charles had asked her into his office. Nico had been much too preoccupied with Lacey's attacker to remember to ask. He'd assumed Charles was merely confirming her backstory. Making sure she really checked out, just as Nico had told him. But wait, hadn't Charles been the one to remind Nico to make sure Lacey's credentials were verifiable? How could he be putting her on the suspect list in one breath and then offering her a job with the next? Charles must not truly presume Lacey to be a realistic suspect to be offering her a job. So what had his little lecture been all about then? Just a way to get Nico to dig a little deeper into her life? But why? Charles had feigned innocence when Nico had told him about her career in the Victoria Police Force, but Nico had a growing feeling that Charles had this information tucked up his sleeve all along.

"He said your station is short-staffed and they're hiring two more constables. He said I should consider applying for one of the positions."

"Wow." Nico was a little lost for words. "Are you going to? Apply, I mean."

"I don't know." She lifted her shoulders in a shrug. The rain was getting heavier now, and she pulled up her hood, effectively hiding her face. "The offer came out of nowhere. Shadbolt said he'd talked to my old commander, Anthony Blaxland, and from what he heard, he'd be happy to have me on his team."

"Wow," Nico said again. "Would you want to stay down here, though? I thought you were keen to get back to Victoria."

"Hmm," she hummed an indistinct answer, then shot him a look. "I don't have any solid plans. But yes, I was eventually supposed to go home."

He just stopped himself from saying *wow* for the third time. This was an interesting development. And Nico was unsure how he felt about it.

Yes, he had just asked Lacey to stay on. For a few more days. But if she took up this job offer... What would that mean? To him? To her? To their relationship? If in fact they even had a relationship. One night of fun between the sheets —albeit the best fun he might ever have had with a woman— did not a relationship make.

And the biggest question of all, did he want Lacey working in the same precinct as him? Would he be able to cope with that?

In the end, it was Lacey's decision. He might be able to sway her one way or the other, but only if he could make up his own mind about what he wanted first. And was it even fair to influence her?

He tried not to let this news rattle him. The walk in the rain had been refreshing, easing his stress. And he and Lacey had been getting on well. After the weird tension between them this morning, it'd been nice to feel that easy camaraderie return.

They loaded Smudge into the van, and Lacey offered him the keys. "I thought you'd never ask," he said with a grin, jumping at the chance to drive this old heritage vehicle.

It wasn't as easy as it looked, and Nico had to concentrate to get the gear changes right; even though his Jeep was a stick shift, this old gearbox required a gentle hand and some extra coaxing. But they were soon jaunting down the road, and he had to admit there was a feeling of freedom driving this old girl along the coastline, almost as if the car was enjoying the drive as much as he was.

As they drove up his street, they were laughing at the comical look on Smudge's face as he tried to draw in as much air as he could through the small gap in the window they'd left open for him, when Nico slowed the van suddenly. There was a car parked in his driveway. It was Gabriel's little MG. Gabriel was pacing back and forth at the front of his car, being watched by the constable on duty, who followed his pacing with a wary gaze.

Nico pulled up alongside the MG and wound down the window. "Gabe," he greeted his friend with a big smile.

"Where the hell have you been?" Gabe jogged around to the driver's side. "I just heard someone attacked Lacey. I was so worried." His friend peered in through the window, so he could stare at Lacey. "This cop wouldn't let me near your place, so I've been waiting here for the past half hour for you to come home."

"Sorry, we've been for a walk along the beach," Lacey called, leaning past Nico.

"Good. Right. Okay then." Gabriel took a step back. "I'm just glad that you're both okay." He ran a hand through his hair and appeared to regain some of his equilibrium.

"Yes, we're fine." Gabriel's reaction seemed a little over the top, and Nico studied his friend. It was the first time he'd seen the doctor since Lacey had revealed his little secret. Gabe looked exactly as he always did. Dressed in black trousers and a woolen black overcoat, clean-shaven, he was the epitome of the fashionable modern man. But now Nico saw the way his friend dressed in a new light. Gabe always took a lot of care with the way he looked, but Nico had never questioned his friend's tendencies before. Nico drew in a breath. *Act normal.* That's all he needed to do.

"Why don't you come in for a coffee," Nico suggested. "I'll park the Kombi and tell the constable to let you in." He felt a stab of guilt that he hadn't told Gabriel about the attack yet. But even though he considered Gabe his best friend in this town, he didn't need to tell him every little detail.

"Thanks. But no thanks." Gabriel glanced up at the house and then back at Nico. "I've got another engagement. I just wanted to make sure you were both good. When I heard the news, I was shocked. How could someone attack Lacey at the house of our local detective? Whoever it was must have some balls."

Nico couldn't disagree. The guy was either terribly stupid or terribly desperate to attack Lacey in the open and in the backyard of a well-known officer of the law.

"But I would like to talk more with you both. What about lunch tomorrow at my place? I'll cook up a roast lamb, you can bring the red wine. What do you think?"

Nico glanced over at Lacey and she nodded her consent. Why not? It might be good to catch up with his old friend. See what was going on in his head. Nico wasn't all that keen to bring up the question of Gabe's sexuality, but he guessed it needed to be addressed at some stage. He'd need to do some more work tomorrow, perhaps even pop into the station, but he could fit that in around the lunch. See, he was getting better at this work-life balance thing.

"Sure. We'll see you around midday, then," Nico agreed.

"Great." Gabriel seemed pleased they'd accepted his invitation. "See you tomorrow." He shot the constable a hard glare before he got back in his car and drove away.

Nico eased the Kombi up the driveway.

"I love a good Sunday lamb roast," Lacey commented as he reversed the van in next to the shed. Then the smile fled from her face. "It sounds like word has definitely got around about the assault, though." She bit her lip and turned to face him.

"Yep. This is a tight-knit community. You can't keep anything secret for long." Nico paused for a second. "Gabe seemed really worried about you," Nico commented.

"He knows I'm important to you. That's probably why," she countered.

"Or maybe he's not gay after all," Nico replied obtusely.

CHAPTER NINETEEN

Lacey sipped her coffee as she stood and stared thoughtfully out the front window of Nico's house. There was a good view down over the small township right through to the bay and the ocean. This room had been set up as the formal dining room and it seemed a bit of a waste to have the room with the best view relegated so that it was barely used. If she lived here, she'd rearrange things, move in a few cozy armchairs and create a nook from which to appreciate the vista below. It was cold in here—Nico usually kept the door shut—unlike in the lounge room where the open fire crackled, and Lacey wrapped her cardigan across her middle. She'd come in here while Nico was having a shower, looking for a different perspective from the usual one found through the kitchen window.

Sunday morning in Boat Harbour Beach was a quiet affair. Not a soul was around, not even the old woman who was usually prowling up and down the beach. The same gray clouds from yesterday draped across the sky, blocking out the sunshine and making everything drab and colorless. But Lacey liked the soft winter tones, they were as much a character of this coastline as the wild, bright colors of summer.

The squad car was finally gone from the front of the house. She'd watched the two police officers drive away ten minutes earlier, their shift at an end, and no one had replaced them. Nico had warned her he didn't know how long their protection would last. The chief inspector's patience for using a precious resource to guard her had probably run out. She felt like it'd been a waste of time; she didn't need to be babysat around the clock. She'd already proved she could look after herself. Between her and the flock of geese and a highly trained detective, she felt pretty safe, even if the attacker tried again.

"Here you are. I was wondering where you'd got to." Nico wrapped his arms around her waist, kissing the side of her face. It was such a couple thing to do, and Nico did it with such ease but it caused a sharp pain in Lacey's chest. Because they weren't that easy, familiar couple. Not yet, anyway. He smelled fresh and clean and still damp from the shower.

"I like this room," Lacey said. "It has a wonderful view. I understand why you bought this place. You can see for miles from here."

"Yes, you can," Nico mumbled, his face buried in her neck. Slowly, he came around in front, took the mug from her hand and placed it on the windowsill, and wrapped both arms around her waist. "I liked the view in my bedroom last night much better, though."

She couldn't help it, she blushed at his comment. Last night had been another exploration into an erotic wonderland. They were definitely sexually compatible; she could say that much about them as a couple.

When they'd returned from their walk along the beach, Lacey hadn't been sure where she stood with Nico. He'd seemed taken aback by her news of a job offer at Burnie Police Station, but then who could blame him. She'd half been expecting the same awkwardness from earlier that morning to descend once they returned to the house, but it was as if a truce had been called. He said he'd cook dinner that night and not to worry about it. So, she spent the next few hours reading a book that she'd started weeks ago but never managed to find the time to finish. Nico occupied his afternoon on his computer, and then he shuffled through a pile of documents for another hour, a look of perplexed frustration on his face. When it came time to prepare dinner, Nico shooed her out of the kitchen, saying she'd done more than enough cooking over the past few days and it was his turn.

With half an hour to kill, Lacey had decided to bite the bullet and call her mother. She'd been putting it off for too long. At first, Elora had sounded pleased to hear from Lacey. *Her impossible daughter*, as she'd called her. But if that was the worst insult Elora could come up with, then Lacey was happy to let it slide. Her mother's tone soon changed, however, when Lacey dove straight into the reason she was calling. To inform Elora about the incident *her impossible daughter* had unwittingly been caught up in, and how she was now a prime witness in a murder investigation. At first, Elora had been shocked, but her concern for Lacey didn't last long. It quickly morphed into concern for how Lacey's involvement would make the family look. How Elora herself may be implicated in the whole thing, and then finally rage that Lacey hadn't told her about this on the very first day.

When she found out Barry had known for days, Elora had become speechless with rage. Her mother's outbursts were hard to bear, but it was when she became silent that you really had to watch out. Lacey wasn't in the mood to spend hours placating her mother. She didn't allow Elora to derail the conversation and kept to the point, which sometimes worked with Elora and sometimes it riled her up more. But by this stage, Lacey didn't care. She had a dinner date with

Nico and she wasn't going to ruin it by letting her mother get under her skin.

Lacey had been polite but direct with her mother, asking her to pass the news onto both her siblings and then telling her she'd call again in a few days. Perhaps Elora might've calmed down by then and they could have a half-decent conversation. Time often dulled her mother's barbarous comments but it couldn't be guaranteed. Lacey had given her mother one compensation. Elora had demanded she come home straight away. But Lacey wasn't ready to do that. Yet. She agreed she needed to face her family soon, however. So she'd given her mother a solid date for when she'd return home. She only hoped she could keep that promise. Afterward, she texted her father to warn him there would be fallout from her conversation. She had no doubt Elora could be coming for her husband next, to vent her frustration on him.

Then Nico had called her through to the kitchen and she'd sat at the small table and been served delicious pork and fennel sausages from a local producer and mashed potatoes with mountains of butter. Exactly the kind of meal a lazy Saturday called for. Over dinner, her gaze had kept tangling with his, but she was unsure what it meant. She desired him. Would jump at the chance to sleep with him again, but she wasn't sure where they stood after their conversation today— to call it an argument was too harsh a word, but they'd certainly been at odds with each other's ideas.

And then afterward, as she was washing up the dishes because Nico had cooked, he'd come up from behind and nuzzled her neck, much the same as he was doing this morning.

"Leave those," he'd commanded, voice husky.

And she'd suddenly known where she stood, at least for that night. He wanted her, couldn't keep his hands off her.

And she wanted him too. They'd left a trail of clothes on their way to the bedroom, and Smudge had followed along in their wake, sniffing their dropped clothing and looking confused. Nico was fast running out of condoms. He was going to have to replenish his stock soon if they were to keep this up.

Now, standing in front of the window, Nico kissed her, his mouth hungry on hers. Telling her he wanted her again. And she was happy to comply. He set her body alight with just the simplest of touches. The thought someone might see them in their lover's tangle highlighted in the window was quickly buried by the surge of heat that coursed through her body.

Lacey pulled back to look at him. She ran a finger lightly over the scar on his face, drinking in his features. Etching them into her memory. She may as well tell him what she was thinking. It might put his mind at ease for the next little while.

"I've decided to stay another week," she said, tilting her head slightly so she could look deep into his eyes. "Then I'm going to continue my travels. I'm going to head inland to see Cradle Mountain." It was true when she'd told Gabe the other day that it was on her bucket list. It was the one place she wanted to see before she left Tasmania. "And then I told my mother I'd be home by the end of the month." Which gave her one week to spend with Nico and another two weeks traveling before she had to be back on that ferry to Melbourne. "My family are desperate to see me. They're worried about all this stuff going on. And I guess my mother is right. I can't keep traveling forever. I owe it to them to go home and spend some time with them."

A small frown line appeared between his brows at her news, but she didn't know him well enough to understand what it meant yet. Was he irritated? Or concerned for her welfare? Or sad that she was leaving? Or all three?

"If that's what you want to do, then I think it's a good idea.

My mother would be the same if I were in your shoes." The frown line disappeared, and he sounded so understanding. But she wondered what was really going on behind those indigo eyes of his.

"What about the job?" Nico asked quietly.

Fair enough question, but one she had no clear answer for yet.

"I don't know yet. That's one of the things I need to sort out. I'd like to clarify a few things with Shadbolt first. And I was hoping a week here might give me the space I need for things to become clearer. I don't think the job will be advertised for a few weeks yet, anyway."

"That makes sense. Take as much time as you need, Lacey. Like I said before…you can stay as long as you want."

"Hmm." And there it was again. That slight hesitancy, like he couldn't quite bring himself to ask her to stay forever. To stay for him. So they might pursue this thing between them.

Lacey stared out the window as she considered her next words, but something caught her eye. "Is that Herb and Margie?" Lacey peered at the road leading down the hill. "Are they coming up here?"

"Shit." Nico turned his head to check out the older couple climbing the hill. "Yes," he added with a sigh. "Just when I was hoping we could take this back to bed."

"I'd better get dressed then." Lacey disentangled herself from Nico's arms and fled to the bedroom. Hopefully, their lazy Sunday morning wasn't about to get ruined.

Nico had already let the older couple in and they were milling around in the kitchen when Lacey appeared fully dressed and feeling more up to facing them.

"Good morning, luv," Margie said, giving her a sly smile. "We saw you two in the window. You were kissing," she added guilelessly, and Lacey had to stifle the urge to groan loudly. Of course they'd seen them in the window. Now it'd be all around town that Nico and Lacey were an item before they were ready to let their secret out. "I think it's wonderful," Margie gushed. "It's about time, Detective. You need a good woman in your life."

"Hmm." Nico stood with his arms crossed, hip leaning against the countertop. This time, the small line between his eyes had been replaced with a raft of frown lines as he made it clear he wasn't going to be drawn into Margie's matchmaking.

Herb stood behind his wife, but he looked a lot less agreeable. He too, was frowning, and now he stepped up beside his Margie. Dressed as usual in their matching Lycra outfits, Herb was wearing a backpack over his shoulders; the older couple looked like they were about to go out for a cycle. When Lacey looked at them, all she saw were two kindly people, who liked to stay fit and who were happily living out their senior years to the best of their ability. She certainly didn't see anyone who might be capable of murder. But she could tell that was what Nico saw. Or at least he was taking it into consideration. Should she be doing the same? If she were to go back into the force, she needed to start thinking like a cop again. Was she prepared to be suspicious of everyone she met from now on?

"That's not why we're here, Marg," Herb said.

"No, you're right," Margie piped up. "We just wanted to talk to you, to see how the investigation is going. See if you've found out anything new."

"Margie," Nico sighed in exasperation. "You can't come up to my door and ask me to tell you what's going on. It's a conflict of interest, can't you see that? I need to be completely unbiased in this investigation. I can't give out confidential information. Not to you, and not to anyone."

"Yes, but... Surely you can tell us something. We're your friends. You live amongst us, in this community," Margie stuttered, while Herb gave Nico a look like thunder.

Lacey suddenly understood what a fragile line Nico walked sometimes. The boundary between being part of a community and policing that same community was often blurred.

"You'll have to wait, like everyone else. Chief Inspector Shadbolt will be holding another media conference on Monday afternoon. If we have anything new by then, you can hear all—"

"Pardon my French, but cut the crap, Detective," Herb interrupted. Margie's friendly smile fell from her face, and she laid a hand on her husband's arm. "You can't keep us in the dark like this. I know you think I'm a suspect, and I demand to know what's going on. My son told me I should get a lawyer. Is that true?"

"Now, Herb, calm down," Margie urged.

Nico's frown wavered. Lacey's heart went out to the couple. This thing must be turning their whole lives upside down. Her grandmother on her father's side was still alive and lived in Melbourne, and Lacey shuddered to think how something like this might affect her nan. They must be consumed by worry.

"Why don't you sit down, and I'll make you a cup of tea," Lacey suggested, trying to diffuse the situation.

"No," Herb practically shouted. "I will not sit in somebody's house if they think I'm capable of doing anything to hurt that sweet woman." He was practically shaking with rage. "All I was trying to do was help her. Protect her. Like I hope someone might do if it were my daughter in trouble." Herb stood up to his full height, nearly matching Nico, his features hard and inscrutable.

"Oh, Herb," Margie said on a sob.

This was getting out of hand, and Lacey glanced at Nico, whose face seemed to soften slightly.

"Look," Nico said, holding his hands up in the air. "I know this must be frightening for you, and I regret you have to go through this. But a woman has been murdered, and it's my job to uncover every stone and investigate every lead to find out who did it. I'm sorry, but I can't give you what you're hoping to hear. I have to follow due process. But I'm sure you'll be cleared of any suspicions soon, and I'm doing everything I can to make it happen."

No one said anything for many long moments, and Herb stared at Nico for so long Lacey thought he'd been struck dumb. But finally, his face crumpled, losing the hard planes and deep-edged lines, becoming an old man again.

"I guessed you'd say something like that. But this is just so…"

Herb didn't need to finish his sentence; they could all hear the anguish in his voice.

"Come on, luv, let's go." Margie took his hand to lead him out of the kitchen.

Herb seemed to hesitate, sending a searching gaze between Lacey and Nico. "I wasn't sure whether to give you this or not." Herb removed his backpack and unzipped it.

"Are you sure?" Margie asked as she watched him draw something out of the bag. "I don't—"

"Yes," he said, cutting her off. "I think it's time to give this up," Herb acknowledged, holding out what looked to be a journal with a pretty embroidered cover.

"You've had this in your house the whole time? And you never told us?" Nico closed his eyes and gritted his teeth, and Lacey knew he was trying to rein in his temper. There could be a vital clue in this journal, and Herb had kept it from the police. It was a little mind-boggling. The older couple might not realize it, but Nico could charge them with withholding evidence and obstructing an investigation. She hoped he wouldn't do any of those things, and instead, be happy that

Herb had at last brought the journal and other documents to him. Vaguely, she wondered where Herb had stashed this last piece of evidence, because Nico had his house and shed thoroughly searched.

"Yes," Herb admitted. He handed it ceremoniously to Nico, who pulled his sweater sleeves down to cover his hands before taking the book.

"Can you get me an evidence bag from my duffle please," Nico requested of Lacey. She went to the black bag he carried everywhere with him, currently in the vestibule by the back door, keeping one ear open to the continuing conversation.

"I've been holding onto this, because Rania asked me to keep it secret. Keep it safe and not show it to anyone. She said there was stuff in there that might get her in trouble. And maybe other people as well," Herb said as Lacey returned with a plastic ziplock bag. There was silence as Nico placed the journal into the bag and closed it up. What the hell had Rania written in that journal? Could the answer to who was the killer be in there?

"Who do you think she meant by other people? Do you think she meant Karim?" Nico questioned.

Herb hitched his shoulders up. "I don't know. Could be. But I never read it. I kept her secret safe, just like she asked me to."

Lacey couldn't help but stare at Herb. He really hadn't even taken a peek? For some reason, she believed him. And perhaps that was why Rania had chosen Herb to be the guardian of her private words. Because she knew he was a man of honor. An old-fashioned guy who kept his word.

"Well, if Herb's noble enough to give you the journal, then I may as well tell you something I remembered, too." Margie squared her shoulders and looked Nico directly in the eye. "I wasn't going to tell you, because you haven't been very forthcoming yourself." She continued to glare at him. Nico tactfully held his tongue but Lacey could see his patience was wearing thin as a muscle jumped in his jaw with the effort not to command the information from her right this second.

"What did you remember?" Lacey asked quickly, keeping her voice calm and shooting Nico a look over the top of Margie's head.

"A young man paid Rania a visit one evening about two weeks ago. I was out watering the garden, and I saw him go in her front gate. He came out again less than ten minutes later, and so I didn't think much of it. I'd actually completely forgotten about it until I saw that same young man at the bakery in town yesterday. It was that apprentice, I think his name is Jayden."

Lacey considered Margie's surprising words. What would Jayden want with Rania?

"It would've been better if you'd told us this yesterday, as soon as you remembered," Nico said equably enough, but the way he was clenching and unclenching his hands gave away his tightly controlled temper. "Can you remember the exact day and time this happened?" he added quickly when Margie narrowed her eyes at him.

"I think it was Thursday two weeks ago. Probably around five-thirty pm. Rania would've just got home from work, but Karim's car wasn't in the driveway. He often goes to the pub for a few beers with his mates on Thursday."

"Right. Thank you, Herb. And Margie," Nico said, touching Margie quickly on the elbow. "I know you've been trying to do the right thing all along. And this is definitely the right thing."

"Humph," Herb said in reply.

Nico showed the other couple out, and he and Lacey watched them trudge back down the hill again.

"Are you going to look at the journal now?" Lacey couldn't help but ask.

"I want to. But it's almost time to go to Gabriel's."

"And I still need to shower," Lacey replied.

"I'll get a squad car to come and collect this straight away," Nico said, eying the bag with the journal as if it might bite. "I want to submit this into evidence today. Do everything strictly by the book. I don't want to be accused of tampering with the evidence, or not following protocol. I'll get Tyrell to look at it first thing tomorrow morning. And I'll also bring Jayden in for an interview tomorrow, too."

"Margie might be right, Jayden's visit might be completely innocent. He works with Karim, after all. It could've been as simple as him bringing a message from Karim." Lacey pursed her lips as she considered Nico.

"Probably. But you know we need to follow up all leads," Nico agreed. "And this feels like it might be important but I'm just not sure how Jayden fits into this investigation yet. Especially because we know he's probably gay. So what was his interest in Rania?"

Lacey went off to shower and change and was ready in fifteen minutes, her mind still churning with the new information Margie and Herb had just supplied. But they still had to wait another ten minutes for the cruiser to come by and collect the bag.

They jumped into Nico's Jeep with two bottles of Nico's best red wine and headed toward Wynyard.

The morning had gotten off to a rocky start, and she hoped that lunch with Gabriel would put things back on track.

"Are you going to tell Gabe that I saw him and Jayden the other day?" she asked as he zoomed around the curves in the road much faster than she would've been game to if she was driving. She admired his strong hands as he drove, long fingers wrapping easily around the steering wheel. She was beginning to love those hands. Love what they could do to her.

"I don't know yet. I'm not sure it's the right time. And now we have this other sighting of Jayden, it might be better to keep our cards close to our chests until we've figured out what he was doing at Rania's."

"I'll follow your lead," she assured him. "Personally, I think the longer things are left to fester the worse they turn out in the end." But she wasn't one to talk. How many times had she chosen the easy path of not telling the whole truth to her mother, only to have it come back and bite her in the ass later? She understood Nico's reluctance, however. Gabe was his friend, and if Nico wanted to let him keep his secrets, she wasn't one to argue.

Gabriel welcomed them into his home with a bright smile and hugged them both. Which surprised Lacey a little and even seemed to surprise Nico at his outward show of affection.

"I'm so glad you guys could make it," he gushed. "And I'm so glad you're okay," he added to Lacey, taking her aside and staring into her eyes.

"Yes, yes, I'm all good," she replied, a little embarrassed.

"And who would've thought your geese could be so aggressive," Gabe added as he led them down a long hallway to the back of the house and into the open-plan kitchen and dining room.

Lacey cast a sideways glance at Nico. The grapevine had been busy, if everyone knew it'd been the geese that saved her.

Instead of taking the bait, she switched the topic. "Nice house," Lacey exclaimed. It was very modern and sleek inside. Lacey much preferred the character and charm of Nico's house.

"I like to think that it's befitting of an up-and-coming young doctor on the go like myself," Gabe said with a flourish, taking the bait hook, line, and sinker.

Before Lacey had seen Gabe kissing the young man in the alley, she wouldn't have thought anything of his theatrical wave. But now, she saw it in a slightly different light.

He spent the next few minutes showing her around his newly renovated house, and she could see how proud he was of his place.

"Anyway, lunch is ready," he told them as they rounded back into the kitchen from a tour of the main bedroom. "You guys were a little late," Gabe admonished.

"Sorry. We got caught up," Nico apologized but didn't elaborate.

"Well, sit down, and I'll serve up." Gabe waved them to the table, which had been set with gleaming white plates, silver cutlery, and real napkins. There was even a row of candles burning as decoration.

"This is lovely," Lacey said, raising an eyebrow at Nico over the table when Gabe wasn't looking. He gave her a quelling look in return.

The lamb roast was to die for. The meat melted in her mouth, the gravy was smooth and delicious, and the roast potatoes crispy on the outside and soft on the inside. They chatted about normal things, like how the Burnie City Council's bid to allow a construction conglomerate to build a high-rise apartment block on the beachfront had all the locals up in arms and petitioning against it. And how one of Gabriel's patients, Cecile Turner, was trying to set him up with her niece. By all accounts, a lovely young woman who was into running triathlons and had just got out of a bad relationship, so a steady, reliable doctor would be good for her. Gabe had grimaced at that.

After a delicious lunch, washed down with a few glasses of red wine, they all leaned back in their chairs and patted their full stomachs. It was good to see Nico so relaxed for a change. He was clearly at ease in his friend's company.

Gabe stood and cleared the plates. "Let me help you with the dishes," Lacey offered.

"That'd be great, thank you. And, Nico, do you remember when you promised you'd have a look at my old television, and maybe see if you can set it up with that Apple TV box thing. I'm such a technophobe," he stage-whispered to Lacey, by way of explanation. "And Nico is so good at these things."

"Sure," Nico agreed and took his glass of wine off to the living room.

Lacey was soon elbow deep in sudsy water, with Gabe stacking the dishes for her and then picking up a dishcloth. They washed and talked, and she asked him for the recipe for his delicious gravy. The pile of dishes shrunk quickly as they chatted.

"What are your plans now?" Gabe asked suddenly, taking a plate from the rack and drying it.

"What do you mean?"

"I was just wondering if you're going to continue your Tasmanian odyssey? I know you were really keen to keep going once your van was fixed." He met her gaze, light-blue eyes curious. "Or have you and Nico... You know, got something going?" He gave her a quick wink.

"I'm going to continue my trip," she replied, ignoring his innuendo about her and Nico getting together.

"Oh. When will you leave?"

"At the end of this week," she said, placing a saucepan into the drying rack.

"Oh, right." The doctor's face clouded over for a few seconds as he seemed to become lost in thought. Then, as if he could feel her gaze on him, he said hurriedly, "I mean, I feel sad for Nico. I'm sure he's going to miss you," he said with an inquisitive grin. "And I'm sure you'll miss him, too?"

The doctor was digging for information, but Lacey merely shrugged. She wasn't prepared to share her thoughts and feelings about Nico with this man, and she definitely wasn't going to let on how much she cared for the enigmatic detective. That was for her and Nico to sort out. No matter how good a friend Gabe was to Nico, Lacey wasn't comfortable saying anything more to him.

"You don't want to hang around longer to see if Karim really is the killer, then? Don't want to watch Nico take all the glory when he finally gets his man?" Gabe said it in a teasing tone, as if he were making a joke, but Lacey took sudden umbrage at his words, and her mood changed. Why did Gabe continue to push Karim forward as if it were a done deal that he be found guilty and sent to jail? Lacey was no longer as sure as she had been that Karim was innocent, but it still made her mad. And his snide, underhanded comment about Nico getting his man smacked of sarcasm. It touched a nerve in Lacey, made her indignant. Gabe was supposed to be Nico's friend.

"Karim isn't the only suspect," she said, turning to glare at him. "Nico already told you that. There are plenty of other people his team are investigating." She felt a sudden need to defend Nico.

"Oh, yeah?" Gabe made it sound like he didn't believe her, throwing the dishcloth over his shoulder and raising one eyebrow in mock disbelief.

"Yeah," she huffed, suddenly indignant, needing to knock Gabe off his high horse. "Did you know Rania had a stalker? One of the apprentice mechanics she used to work with. He's got a damn good motive, if you ask me. He could definitely be the killer. Then there's—" Lacey snapped her mouth shut. She was about to name Herb and Margie, tell him the old couple who lived next door were keeping all kinds of queer secrets, ringing all kinds of alarm bells. But she'd gone too far. Nico had told her things in confidence. And while she knew Gabe could be trusted, she shouldn't be giving out confidential information to anyone, not even him.

"Well, it's good to know the police are following up every lead. I know Nico is always very thorough," Gabe said smoothly, folding the dishcloth in half and hanging it on a rail above the stove. "But it's always the boyfriend or the husband in the end. Or at least it is in all the murder mystery movies I've ever watched," he said, still maintaining the joking air, as if he wasn't really all that interested. But Lacey didn't miss the sardonic curl of his lip.

Removing her rubber gloves, she glanced down the hall; she could still hear Nico banging around in the living room. She hoped he'd just about finished, because she'd like to head home now. She'd had enough of people who already thought they had an open murder investigation solved. Even if Gabe was supposed to be Nico's best friend, Lacey suddenly wanted to get away from him.

It was time to get out of here.

There were plenty of other things she wanted to do this afternoon, and all of them took place in Nico's bedroom. She hoped Nico felt the same.

CHAPTER TWENTY

Nico paced back and forth across the command room, gnawing at his bottom lip. He hated Mondays, and today in particular was the worst kind of Monday. All kinds of shit was going down today.

He'd arrived at the station bright and early this morning feeling buoyant and ready to get back into this case. After he and Lacey had returned from lunch at Gabe's, he hadn't got nearly as much work done as he was hoping. Lacey had distracted him the moment they walked in the door, taking him by the hand and leading him straight to the bedroom. He hadn't been surprised, as the sexual tension in the car while they'd driven home had been almost palpable. Lacey had laid her hand gently on his knee as he drove, her light touch telling him everything he needed to know. She wanted him. And he wanted her. She was all he'd thought about the whole time he was eating lunch at Gabe's. He could hardly believe he'd allowed this woman to worm her way so deeply into his psyche. And she was leaving at the end of the week. Which was the one driving factor that'd led him to decide *stuff work*; for once, he was going to spend a Sunday afternoon with a fascinating, sexy woman. Admittedly, he had left her curled up all warm and snug in his bed and done a few hours work later in the evening, but he'd been feeling relaxed and less stressed.

Until this morning, when he came back to reality with a loud thump.

Things were progressing at lightning speed. He'd requested Jayden Melman, the baker's apprentice to come in for an interview. That was scheduled for later this afternoon. But Jayden's statement may not even be relevant, as his team thought they now had enough evidence to arrest the killer.

The results had come back on the knife found dropped near Nico's place after the attack on Lacey. It was a positive match for the stab wounds found on the murder victim's body. And it was also a positive match to the set in Rania's kitchen. In other's words, it seemed they'd found the murder weapon.

But that wasn't the end of it. Karim Khaled's partial fingerprint was also found on the knife handle. The *only* fingerprint found on the knife. The man who'd attacked Lacey on Friday night had been wearing gloves. If that man had been Karim, why would he be stupid enough to leave a fingerprint when he stabbed Rania, but not when he attacked Lacey? It was a riddle he was yet to untangle.

He had a junior officer still trolling through hours and hours of CCTV footage, to see if Karim's claim that he'd been out walking the night of Lacey's attack could be verified. But so far they'd had no joy. The one camera that could possibly give him an alibi on the corner of the street where his hotel was situated had been offline for maintenance at the time.

Together with the mounting details about Karim's drug habit, the constant fights between himself and Rania, and the young man's anger management problems, including his altercation with Floyd, Charles had deemed it was enough hard evidence to arrest Karim and formally charge him with murder.

Nico had begrudgingly agreed and dispatched Sally-Ann and First Class Constable Gorman to do just that. He never asked any of his people to do anything he wasn't prepared to do himself, and truth be told, he'd much rather be the one snapping the cuffs on Karim right now. But Shadbolt mentioned that he'd like a reason to promote Sally-Ann, and so Nico had taken the opportunity to give her more responsibility. He agreed with Charles; Sally-Ann would make a great senior constable, it was time for her to move up. And he trusted her implicitly to get the job done. Making the arrest in a high-profile case such as this would surely put Sally-Ann on the radar.

But instead of sitting back in his chair with a satisfied grin while he waited, there was an uneasy sensation hanging heavy in his gut.

Because that knife had come from Karim and Rania's house. So, of course it'd have Karim's fingerprints on it. It was almost too convenient. If Karim had killed Rania, had the couple perhaps been arguing late that night, Karim potentially high on drugs, and the argument had escalated? He'd grabbed the knife and stabbed her out of an uncontrollable rage. It'd been a spur-of-the-moment thing, which was why he'd been sloppy enough to leave a print the first time. Then what? He'd just left to go to work, leaving Rania to bleed to death? Taking the knife with him? Why hadn't he checked if she was alive or dead? Had someone interrupted his killing spree? It didn't add up. But then, murder often didn't. It was often messy and spontaneous. Nico paced back and forth across the command room, flipping from self-doubt—did the evidence really point to the truth?—to being convinced they had the right man.

Then there was Rania's journal. What would that reveal?

He had Tyrell feverishly scanning the journal right now and had told him to come to him immediately if he found anything incriminating.

Perhaps there was solid proof in there that Karim was the murderer. Maybe Rania had written that she was afraid for her life, especially when he was on drugs. Perhaps she had been planning to leave him, as Herb had suggested. Perhaps he'd even tried to kill her before, and that was why she was secretly trying to leave him.

An image of Herb and Margie in his house yesterday appeared in his mind. Nico still wasn't one hundred percent convinced that Herb was telling him the truth.

Just because the man was in his seventies didn't rule him out as a murderer. It was rare to find a senior citizen who was a killer, but it did happen. There was the famous serial killer Sam Little, who'd been arrested when he was seventy-two. Then there was the Granny Ripper, an elderly Russian woman who was declared mentally ill after she murdered several people in her building. And the old couple in their eighties from Missouri, who delighted in killing drifters who came onto their farm. And Herb was extremely fit for his age. Maybe he and Margie were in it together, like the Missouri couple. So no, Nico definitely wasn't ruling him out.

There was a knock on the open command room door and First Class Constable Gorman stepped in, a grim look on his face.

"What?" Nico asked, but he was already dreading Gorman's answer.

"Floyd seems to have gone AWOL."

"What does that mean?" Nico snapped.

"His boss reported that he didn't turn up for work this morning. So I took it on myself to take a drive past his house. His flat mate confirmed that Floyd got in his car and drove away yesterday afternoon, and he hasn't seen him since."

"Shit." Nico began to pace again. Now Floyd was missing. By this stage, he could already be on the mainland. "Get an

Australia-wide APB out on him, with instructions to arrest him if they see him," he commanded. There were lots of reasons for people caught up in a murder investigation to run, but most of them weren't good. Floyd could just be scared and had taken off. Or he could know something vital to the case. He could even be the killer, and Nico had let him slip through his fingers.

"On it, boss." Just as Gorman stepped out of the room, he was nearly bowled over by First Class Constable Hickey as he burst in.

"They've just arrived, sir." Nico didn't need to ask who he was talking about. It was Karim. "They're bringing him up to interview room three."

"Right. Thanks." Nico straightened his back. If Karim was here, Nico needed to concentrate on him for now, and leave Tyrell to hunt down Floyd. "Has he requested a lawyer?"

"Yes, sir." Hickey gave a grimace of distaste, but the young constable would learn in time that even a criminal had rights, and lawyers were a necessary evil. A lawyer might try and stymie the interrogation, but Nico was good at keeping his cool, asking the right questions, and making sure he didn't put the lawyer offside. Things needed to be done by the book. He absolutely hated it when a known criminal got off on some vague technicality when a cop became sloppy and let procedure slip in an attempt to get a confession, and he was determined not to let that happen.

Striding down the corridor, he cursed Floyd Hamilton one last time, then put him out of his mind. Perhaps, if Karim confessed, they wouldn't need to track down Floyd after all.

* * *

Nico sat down at his desk, taking a sip of his coffee with a sigh of relief. Interrogations took it out of him. It was mentally draining, and he was glad it was over. For now. Although they didn't have a confession from Karim, yet, Nico was hoping it'd come.

Karim had been distraught when they first brought him in. Spouting the same mantra he had the other night when he'd appeared at Nico's house. "I'm innocent. I didn't do it. I'm being framed."

But they all knew Karim wasn't innocent. Far from it. And soon, he'd admitted that Rania and he would sometimes fight. But didn't every couple fight? When Nico pressed him, he revealed his drug habit was the reason he and Rania fought, because she wanted him to stop—just like Herb had suggested. Karim had already admitted he had a cocaine habit, but today, Nico delved more deeply into the reasons he used the drug.

"Did it make you angry when she asked you to stop?"

"No," Karim had said. "It made me sad. I was sad because I wanted to stop taking it too. But I couldn't. I need it. I can't get through a shift at the bakery without it."

"So you use coke as a pick me up?" Nico asked. He knew a lot of users experienced reduced fatigue, increased confidence, and diminished inhibitions when they took the drug.

"Yes, exactly." Karim had seemed relieved that Nico understood.

But it also had less favorable effects, such as erratic and reckless behavior, anxiety, and aggressive or violent actions.

"And you never experienced cocaine paranoia? You never got angry or lost control when you were using?"

Karim hesitated, then shook his head vehemently. But they both knew he was lying.

"What about when you attacked Floyd Hamilton? Did you lose your temper then?"

"It is yet to be proven he did actually attack Mr. Hamilton," the lawyer interjected. "You don't need to answer that question, Karim."

Karim scowled for a second and dropped his gaze to his lap, and Nico thought he would stay silent. But suddenly, he said, "That fucker deserved it. He was peeping on my woman. She was afraid of him. I did what any real man would do. I showed him who was boss. Not to mess with me. Or Rania." Karim lifted his gaze and glared at Nico. "You would've done the same thing if someone was stalking your woman."

Nico didn't answer Karim's accusation. And if he had, he would've denied it to the boy's face, telling him that taking the law into his own hands to solve a problem was illegal. But inside, he quailed at the thought of someone hurting Lacey. Would he do the same thing? He'd been ready to smash the face of whoever it was who'd attacked Lacey to a bloody pulp the other night. So perhaps he was being a hypocrite.

Nico spent the rest of the interview concentrating on Karim's anger-management issues, trying to goad him into letting it slip that he had grabbed the knife and taken to Rania to stop her incessant yelling. At first, Karim denied he and Rania had fought on the morning she died. But Nico kept pressuring him, asking him to recount that morning in exact detail, until it became apparent Karim's memory of the event was a little hazy. That he had long moments of blackout right after he'd injected himself. Nico knew that regular cocaine users could suffer from short-term memory loss and blackouts.

Could Karim have really stabbed his girlfriend and then left her to die without remembering doing it? It was an interesting concept. But it'd be incredibly hard to prove.

Nico took another sip of his coffee, then checked his phone and saw he had a missed text from Lacey. It'd been sent at midday, asking was he free for lunch today, and if so, would he like to meet her, as she was popping into town for another appointment with Imran. Maybe her last before she left town.

It was now midafternoon. Wow. Had he really been in that interview room for over three hours?

He texted her back, apologizing for not replying earlier and telling her he was sorry he missed lunch, and he might also be late home tonight.

He waited for a reply but got none.

He wondered how the interview with Jayden was progressing. Or had it perhaps finished already? He'd asked Sally-Ann to take that over while he interviewed Karim. While Sally-Ann's directive had been to find out exactly what Jayden had been doing at Rania's that night, Nico had also instructed her to question him about the fight Nico had witnessed between Gabe and Jayden a few weeks ago. He wasn't sure if there was any connection between the two events, but his gut instinct was telling him to ask anyway. Had Jayden revealed the link between himself and Gabe? And if he had, Nico wondered what Gabe would do once the news got around. Standing up, he ran an agitated hand through his hair. He should check on Sally-Ann's progress. But just as he went to step out of his office, one of the junior constables poked her head around the doorframe. "Hey, Detective Sergeant Favreau?"

"Hmm?" He lifted his head, but was only half concentrating. It was Lucy Drimble, one of the juniors on his team. "We just got a call on the hotline from an elderly neighbor who lives near your house, Dorothy Melman."

"Yes?" He narrowed his focus on the pretty young woman. Blonde and athletic, she'd only come off probation three months ago, but she was already a favorite with many of the male officers.

"She said your dog was running wild up and down the street."

"Damn," Nico replied with a sigh. "Did you tell her the hotline was only for crime-related incidents? Specifically, for information on Rania's murder?" Annoyingly, there were constant calls on the police hotline that had nothing to do with the murder, people using the line to make petty complaints or air their neighborly grievances.

"Yes, sir. But she wasn't listening. She was most annoyed that your dog was barking and causing a ruckus."

"Shit. Sorry," he apologized quickly for swearing. But his attention had swapped from Dorothy's misuse of the hotline to worry about Smudge. Why was his dog running wild in the street? Lacey should be home by now. And if she wasn't, she would've made sure he was tied up securely to his kennel. Damn. Now what was he going to do? He couldn't very well leave work to sort out his unruly dog.

"No probs, boss," Lucy said. "Just thought you'd want to know."

"Thank you," he replied as the young constable went back to answer the phones. A thankless job, but someone had to do it. Nico remembered a time when he'd been the most junior officer in the station and all the boring jobs had landed in his lap. It was a rite of passage.

He returned to the problem of his runaway dog. He tried calling Lacey, but her phone merely rang out, eventually going to voicemail. He left a short message to call him back as soon as she got it.

Where was she? Her appointment was supposed to have been at twelve. It was now after three. She should be home by now. But then, maybe she was enjoying a leisurely drive along the coast in Dotti. There was no real reason for her to rush home.

Who else could he call to go and corral his dog? He couldn't leave Smudge running around the small township. He could get hurt, or hit by a car, or if he got spooked, he might even run away. The thought of his loyal dog missing and perhaps hurt had his heart racing.

The fleeting thought that perhaps he could see who was patrolling the area and ask them to go get Smudge entered his head. But he quickly disregarded that idea. It was a blatant misappropriation of resources. Besides, Smudge would only go to someone he recognized. He was wary of strangers.

A brilliant idea flashed across his mind, and he dialed a number quickly. Smudge would recognize Herb and Margie. But they didn't answer their home phone, and he left a message. Then he tried Herb's cell phone, but again, no answer. Where was everyone? Had everyone in Boat Harbour gone on strike? They could be out on one of their eternal bicycle rides, but it was getting a little late in the afternoon for that. Were they purposefully avoiding him? Perhaps they thought he was ringing about the case. Damn it.

He began to pace. He knew it was a bad habit, but it helped him think.

He dialed Lacey's cell phone again, frustrated but not surprised when she didn't answer.

Then he began to wonder. He rang the clinic and asked to speak to Imran. The receptionist, Sarma, recognized him, and apologized but said he was with a patient. Sarma had worked at the clinic for over a year now, and Gabe said she was the best, reliable and dependable.

"Maybe you could help me, then," Nico requested of the young woman. "I'm trying to track down a young lady by the name of Lacey Carmichael. She was supposed to have an appointment with Imran this morning."

"Yes, she had an appointment booked, but she never showed up," the receptionist answered, sounding more than a little distracted. Probably sick of patients who reneged on their scheduled consultations.

"Okay. Thank you for that," he said and hung up. Why would Lacey text him right before her appointment and then not turn up?

Inspiration struck, and he redialed the clinic number. "Hello," he said brightly when Sarma answered. "It's Detective Sergeant Favreau again. Sorry to bother you, but is Gabriel available right now? Or could I leave a message if he's with a patient?" Perhaps Gabriel had seen Lacey today, or heard from her. It was a long shot, but he was stumped by her absence.

"Dr. DuPont isn't in today. I'm sorry, he called in sick, and he's cancelled all his patient list." Sarma sounded a tad frazzled, and Nico didn't have to wonder if she'd been the one to cancel all of Gabe's patients; it would've been a thankless task.

"Oh, right. Thank you." Nico hung up. That was weird. Gabe had seemed perfectly fine yesterday when they'd left him. Not coming down with anything. Was it something he'd eaten? Both he and Lacey were in good health. Or maybe that's why Lacey wasn't answering her phone. Maybe she'd come down with the same thing that was afflicting Gabriel.

Nico let out a frustrated growl.

There was nothing for it. He was going to have to drive to Boat Harbour to collect his dog. Perhaps then he might find out where Lacey had got to as well. If she was lying in bed puking her guts out, he'd do everything he could to make her comfortable, but then he'd have to get back to work. This was not a good day for him to just up and leave in the middle of everything. At least they wouldn't be interviewing Karim again today. The lawyer had called a halt to proceedings on account of the young man's agitation. Then the lawyer had asked for Karim to have a psyche evaluation, which annoyed the hell out of Nico but he had to play by the rules. No way was he letting Karim get off on grounds of insanity. That boy was as sane as the rest of them. He might have a cocaine habit, but he knew exactly what he was doing. But he still wanted to debrief Sally-Ann on Jayden's interview. And there were a million-and-one pieces of paperwork to be completed before tomorrow.

Tyrell had no word on Floyd, so there was nothing they could do on that point unless he was sighted.

He poked his head into Charles's office. "I have to pop out for an hour. I'll be back as soon as I can."

Charles lowered his eyebrows over the top of his wire glasses but said nothing. He trusted his staff to know what they were doing.

Nico jumped into his Jeep—he'd driven that to work now that Lacey's Kombi was on the road again. He pushed the limits of his vehicle and the speed signs to get to his house in nearly record time without the use of actual lights and sirens.

First, he drove past Dorothy's house at the end of his lane, but there was no sign of Smudge. He'd go home, and if his dog wasn't there, he'd patrol up and down the streets until he found him.

But as he pulled into his driveway, Smudge bounded down from the backyard, excitement and relief written all over his doggy features.

"Hey, boy." Nico stepped out of his car to greet his canine friend. After a few seconds making sure Smudge was unharmed and giving him reassuring pats, he lifted his head and stared up the driveway. "What the hell is going on here?" he asked. But the dog didn't answer.

The Kombi van wasn't parked in its usual spot by the shed, and his heart sank a little. It looked like Lacey was definitely out. Had she just forgotten to tie Smudge up when she left? Or had he broken free somehow?

The door was locked and the house dim and quiet when he entered. There was a note left on the kitchen table. It was in Lacey's handwriting.

I've decided to move on early. There's just so much of Tasmania still left to see. Thanks for your wonderful hospitality. I'll be in touch in a few days.

What the…? He read the note again.

Thanks for your hospitality?

Thanks for his fucking hospitality? Was that what she called what they'd done together? Hospitality?

What the fuck? Lacey had been adamant that she was going to continue her trip, it was something she needed to do, and he'd accepted her decision. But they'd also had an unwritten agreement that they'd enjoy the time they had left to the utmost. Whether Lacey would come back after she finished her tour and then visited her family was a question neither of them had touched on yet. But for her to leave like this, without any real explanation, it was coldhearted and bizarre.

He shoved the note into his jeans pocket and went to look around the house.

All of Lacey's stuff was gone. The house felt empty and cold.

She was really gone.

And there was nothing left for him to do but go back to work. He decided to take Smudge with him. His dog could stay in his car for a few hours where it was safe while Nico ploughed through the pile of paperwork that came with arresting a suspect. Smudge was more than pleased to be invited into the car and sat in the back seat like he was the king of everything he surveyed. Nico couldn't help a smile at his dog's appreciation of the small things in life. He could learn a thing or two from his dog.

Almost as an afterthought, Nico went past Herb and Margie's place. But their big Nissan four-wheel drive was missing from the carport and no one answered his hasty knock on the front door. He guessed that was why they hadn't answered their landline. But surely Herb would answer his mobile, no matter where he was. Nico left their house, a puzzled frown on his face, and continued toward Burnie.

Five minutes later, his phone rang, and he answered it using the hands free.

"Hi, boss," Tyrell said, but Nico caught an edge of something in his tone.

"What is it?" Nico asked without preamble. His temper was on a knife-edge, this whole day had gone to shit and it wouldn't take much more to tip him over into a fury.

"You asked me to let you know if I found anything interesting in Rania Samann's journal."

"Yes," Nico practically snapped. What was the guy getting at?

He was just about to tell Tyrell that it could wait, as he was on his way back to the office, when the constable blurted, "I think Rania found something out about our local doctor. Something incriminating. Something he didn't want made public."

"When you say doctor, do you mean Gabriel DuPont?"

"Yes, sir. In an entry from around three weeks ago, Rania says that she went to visit Karim at the bakery in Wynyard, but the bakery had just closed for the day, so she went to look for him around back and saw Dr. DuPont and the male apprentice baker in a... She called it a lover's embrace. The doctor was shocked that she'd seen them and shouted at her, but Rania ran away."

A silence hung between them as Nico digested the news.

Tyrell continued. "There are more entries a few days later, when Rania talks about her conflicted thoughts about whether she should tell Karim, or anyone else what she saw. But then the doctor cornered her in the parking lot in town the next day and asked her if she'd informed anyone. When she said no, the doctor was very relieved and then begged her to keep it to herself. Saying she'd ruin his career if people found out. Rania agreed to keep his secret."

"Is there anything else?" Nico growled.

"Not really, sir. After her encounter with Gabriel, she seems to switch to talking about the fact Karim is becoming more violent, and the escalating fights they're having. The last entry in the journal is around a week and a half ago, when she says she's going to give the diary to her neighbor for safekeeping, because she's afraid of what Karim might do if he found it."

"Right. Thanks." Nico's mind was whirling with theories and hunches.

"What do you think it means?" Tyrell asked.

"I'm not sure. But I'm in the vicinity, so I'm going to call into the doctor's house on the way back and ask him some questions."

"Is Dr. DuPont a suspect now?"

Lacey had seen exactly the same thing as Rania. Gabriel kissing Jayden. And Gabe had called in sick today. And now Lacey was missing.

"It's a possibility," Nico replied with a grunt. "If he was desperate enough to keep his gay lifestyle secret at all costs…" Was Gabe that desperate? Surely not. Not in this day and age, when people barely blinked an eyelid if they found out someone was gay. The LGBTQ community didn't have a big presence in a country town like Burnie, but they also weren't Neanderthals. People watched TV and knew what was going on in the world. It was 2023 for God's sake. Why would Gabe think it'd ruin his career if people found out he was gay?

He ended the call and drove like a bat out of hell to Gabriel's house. No one was home when he got there, and Gabe's car was missing. Nico banged on the door repeatedly and then stomped around the house peering in windows. If the doctor really was sick, surely he should be at home in bed. So, where was he?

Nico went over what he knew in his head. Floyd Hamilton was missing. Herb and Margie Garret were missing. Now Gabe was missing. Gabe hadn't even been on his radar of possible murder suspects. But now…he definitely was. He knew he should've pushed Charles harder to keep a squad car stationed outside his house. His gut had told him that Lacey was still in danger.

And where was Lacey? He pulled the crumpled note out of his pocket and studied it again. It was her handwriting, but it didn't feel like her words.

A cold, hard lump settled in Nico's gut. Something was wrong. He could feel it.

He called Tyrell back. "I need to track Lacey's van," he said, not bothering with a greeting. "I want an alert sent out on her registration number." Nico gave Tyrell the personalized number: DOTTI33. "And I want all CCTV cameras in the area surrounding Boat Harbour searched as well."

"That's going to take a lot of manpower," Tyrell said carefully.

"I don't care," Nico snapped. "I think Lacey might be in trouble, and I think the person involved may be linked to Rania's murder. I want everyone on this, pronto. This now takes precedence over everything else. Do you understand?"

"Yes, sir," Tyrell replied briskly.

"I want the Garrets located as well, if possible. They're missing too," he added, almost as an afterthought.

Dotti shouldn't be too hard to spot. She was a one-of-a-kind vehicle. Nico was going completely on gut instinct, something he swore he'd never do. He was a logical man, who liked to analyze everything first and come up with the right answer, not jump to conclusions. That was why he was so good at his job.

But he'd run out of time, and all rational thought was flying out the window. Lacey was in trouble, he could feel it right down in his solar plexus. He could barely breathe, the band of fear was so tight.

CHAPTER TWENTY-ONE

Lacey came back to consciousness slowly. Opening her eyes was an immense effort; it felt like she had ten tonne blocks on each of her eyelids. At first, things were blurry, and it took her a few moments to process her surroundings. It was the unmistakable sound of a VW Kombi engine that finally confirmed where she was. She was lying on the floor of her van, being jostled around as the car traveled down the road.

She tried to sit up and couldn't, and that's when panic set in. For a second she thought she'd lost control of her limbs. But then she realized that her hands and feet were tied up. What was going on? Her memory was hazy, but she shut her eyes and forced her mind to go back in time.

A vague recollection of answering the back door at Nico's place to find Gabe standing there flashed across her memory banks. She'd let him in but told him she couldn't talk long as she needed to get to an appointment with Imran. Smudge had been acting a little strange, sort of growling at Gabe, which was unusual, because the dog knew Gabriel well.

Gabe had flashed his winning smile at her and said, "That's fine, this won't take long at all." And that's when things had become murky.

Why had things become so confused? She concentrated

even harder and suddenly she remembered.

"Oh." She let out a little gasp of surprise. Gabe had stabbed her with something sharp. She remembered a quick pain, like a needle stick in the side of her neck.

That fucker had injected her with something to make her sleep. Some kind of fast-acting sedative. Even now she felt woozy, as if the world were made of soft plastic. She needed to get herself together. Needed to get out of this situation. Whatever situation this was.

"Gabriel," she tried to shout, but it came out all raspy and weak. Clearing her throat a couple of times, she shouted again, this time, with more effect. "Gabriel." It had to be him driving her car, right? At the moment, all she could see was an indistinct shape sitting in the driver's seat when she lifted her head.

"Ah, good, you're awake." It was Gabriel's smooth voice all right. She'd recognize that accent anywhere.

"Let me go. What the fuck are you doing?" She rolled onto her back, bracing her feet against the side of the van and lifting her head so she could stare between the two front seats. "What do you want with me?"

"What do I want?" For a second, Gabe's face appeared in the gap between the seats before he quickly returned his gaze to the road. "In a perfect world, I want to turn back time and make sure I'm not in that alleyway kissing Jayden. If you never saw us, then none of this would be happening."

So he *had* known she was in that alleyway. That she'd seen him and the young apprentice. She hadn't been as discreet as she'd liked to think. He must've caught sight of her as she retreated down the alley. But why was he making it sound like all this was her fault somehow?

"I'm not sure why that matters so much to you," she said, struggling to wrench her wrists free of the bindings, but to no avail. "I don't care that you were kissing another man. In fact,

I care so little about it, that I haven't even told anyone I saw you. And even if I had, no one else cares about your sexual preferences, either." She crossed her fingers as she told the lie. Did telling Nico count? Her instincts about keeping his secret safe had been right, however. Gabriel didn't seem to want the rest of the world to know about his partiality for young men. A lot of homosexual men had their own reasons for staying in the closet, and she wouldn't judge him for his demons.

"But you see, that's where you're wrong," Gabe replied. She could just make out the side of Gabriel's face as he looked forward through the windshield. His mouth was a grim line of determination.

"I'm not wrong. No one cares about your taste in men or women, or anything in between," she yelled, then was flung sideways as they took a sharp curve in the road, the tires screeching against the tarmac. Gabriel was driving a little crazy, throwing her poor old van around the corners as if it were his modern, sleek sports car. The roads around Tasmania were notoriously narrow and winding, and she hoped he didn't crash.

"Sadly, you *are* wrong," he said once he had the van under control again. "If I'm to survive, then you can't be allowed to tell anybody what you saw. I have to keep you quiet. Which means…"

She waited for him to elaborate, but he wasn't forthcoming. "Which means what?" she demanded after the silence had stretched on, but a strange prickle of premonition caused goose bumps to rise all over her skin. If he wanted to keep her quiet… Did Gabriel intend to kill her? Surely not. Not this mild-mannered, Frenchman. Not the guy who looked like butter wouldn't melt in his mouth.

Instead of answering her question, he said, "Don't worry, we're nearly there."

"Nearly where?" Where was he taking her?

"We're going to Cradle Mountain," he said brightly. "You told me it was on your bucket list. But sadly you might not get to see it from the place I have in mind." His bright smile faded, and right then, Lacey decided Gabriel was perhaps a little unhinged.

"What won't I be able to see?" The man was talking in riddles, and Lacey was sick of it.

"The mountain," he clarified. "I'm not sure we'll be close enough when we stop to see it from the road. I hear there's still snow on top." He gave a satisfied grunt. "It took me longer than I anticipated packing up all your stuff. You are a messy little miss, aren't you? But I made sure I got it all. We don't want Nico thinking you plan on coming back because you left something behind. Even so, we should still get there in time for the sunset. For the grand finale."

At this point she couldn't care less if she saw Cradle Mountain. With snow, or without snow. It was time to put an end to this pretense of a kidnapping attempt. "Look, Dr. DuPont." She put great emphasis on his name, hoping to guilt him into listening. "Why don't you just pull over and stop this charade. You're never going to get away with this—whatever it is you have planned for me. People will be looking for me by now. The jig is up."

"Oh, no they won't," he said with a lopsided grin. "You probably don't remember, but you wrote a note before we left, telling Nico you'd decided to restart your travels around Tasmania a few days early."

"What? I would never do such a thing," she scoffed. She certainly didn't remember writing any note.

"But you did. There were two drugs in that syringe. One was a sedative, but the other was a psychedelic which makes a person lose their autonomy and opens them to suggestions, removes a person's free will. It's called the zombie flower drug, and the cocaine lords in Columbia use it to control their kidnap victims. Cool huh?" He turned to look at her again. No, it wasn't cool at all. That bastard was gloating at her. She wanted to spit in his face.

"So, no one will be looking for you," he added softly. "I've covered all my bases, this time at least. It's a distasteful business, but if I'm going to do something, then I'll make sure to do it right."

She vaguely wondered what he meant by *this time*. But before she could put her thoughts into words, he said, "I know a place. A high cliff. It'll be quick. Pity about your cute van, though."

She froze as his words sunk in. He was planning on pushing her off a cliff? Or running her and her van over a cliff face? Could it be that simple? It seemed perhaps he had thought through this plan after all. "Nico will know," she hissed at him. "Nico will hunt you down. He's very good at his job."

Gabe flinched at the name, but didn't turn. Instead, he said, "Nico won't work this one out. I've fixed it. I've made it so someone else looks guilty. Floyd was so gullible. It was so easy to convince him to drive out to the lookout and meet me. He'll join you in your last flight over the edge. I'll get rid of two birds with one stone."

Lacey was completely stumped. Why was Gabe talking about Floyd? What did he have to do with anything? He was just the apprentice mechanic who'd been obsessed with Rania. Was Gabe going to kill him too? A sudden flush of guilt ran through her. She'd mentioned the apprentice to Gabe just yesterday as a suspect Nico was looking into. She hadn't said his name, but was Gabe adroit enough to work out who it was from her description? Had she inadvertently given Gabe a scapegoat? Or was she giving herself too much credit? Had Gabe known about Floyd all along?

There were too many options to consider when it came to

Floyd. Too many unknowns. Focus on herself. That was what she needed to do. She had to believe that Nico would work this out. That he would come and save her. Would stop Gabriel. And then she was suddenly wracked with doubt. Was she talking Nico up too much? Was Gabe actually going to get away with killing her? Blame it on this Floyd guy somehow? And then return to society as the highly regarded local doctor as if nothing had happened? Her blood turned cold, and she shivered, suddenly feeling very vulnerable and alone.

But Nico wasn't here.

It was just her against the deranged doctor. Her throat constricted, and she held back a sob. She really, really wanted Nico to come and save her right now. But he was probably still at work, with no idea she was even missing. She'd have to work this one out herself. She'd once been a cop. She had skills she could call on. And one of those skills was her sharp mind. Even Nico had commented that she had a scientific mind, was capable of digging to the heart of the problem when others couldn't see through the haze. Perhaps her perceptiveness came from her compassionate side. Because that's what she'd been good at during her short time in the force. Finding out what people were thinking, their deepest desires, to help her work out their motives. What was Gabriel's motivation? He was clearly terrified about being outed as a gay man. But why?

"Why does it matter so much that you're a homosexual?" she asked.

"Don't say that word," Gabriel snarled. "That's a dirty word, and I'm not a dirty person." He seemed to take a few seconds to gather himself before he continued, "I like women. I'm going to marry a nice girl someday soon, and settle down and have a gang of kids. That's what my mother wants. She'll be so happy when I do."

So, his mother didn't know he was gay. Was that why he was so fucked up about his sexuality? Because he wasn't able to please his mother? Even if he wasn't gay, he was at least bisexual, and this clearly caused him terrible emotional pain. She needed to tread softly here. It seemed all his insecurities may stem from the way his mother brought him up.

"I get it," she replied, and in some ways she did. "Our mothers are often hard to please." And she should know better than most. "But sometimes we just have to come to terms with the fact that'll we'll never be perfect in their eyes."

"No, I am perfect," Gabriel argued. "My mother thinks I'm perfect. I love my mother. She and I... We're very close. When my dad left us, I was only nine. But my mother needed a man desperately, and so I became her man. She showed me what love was really all about."

Something in the way he said *became her man* had the hairs on the back of her neck standing up. When most guys said they had to step up and fill their father's shoes they meant by being the person who carried out the garbage, who fixed things when they were broken, who got things done, kept the wolves at bay. But it felt like he meant something else. His mother had showed him what love was? The way he said it was spine-chilling in a way she didn't want to think about.

"Okay, okay, I get it, you're perfect," she soothed. Gabe was majorly fucked up, and it had something to do with his childhood. But Lacey didn't have time to delve into how he'd got this way. All she needed was to find some way out of her predicament. And digging into his younger years wasn't helping. She needed to appeal to his human side. To the compassionate doctor inside him. The one who'd taken the Hippocratic oath to do no harm. To help people. What if she... Her thoughts trailed off as the memory of his words from earlier came back to her. When he'd said he'd got it right *this time*, had he meant he'd tried this before?

"Oh, my God. You were the one who attacked me the other night," she gasped.

"Hmm," he hummed in acknowledgement, almost as if he were pleased she'd worked it out. "But this time I made sure to sort out those fucking birds. I learned from my mistakes. All it took was a few scattered bits of fruit to keep them busy, and they never even cared about me being on the property after that. Humph, guard birds they certainly are not." Lacey watched his profile as he pursed his lips in delight. It seemed he had learned from his mistakes. He was a cold, calculating killer, after all, with all the aces up his sleeve. And she was at his mercy. "Shame that bloody dog sneaked out the door before I could catch him. But he won't be able to tell anyone what he saw." Gabe gave another unhinged grin.

Poor Smudge. Was he wandering around Boat Harbour looking for her? Waiting for Nico to come home? She hoped Smudge was safe. Safer than she was at least. Her mind returned to her own predicament. Her mind was her best weapon against him. She tried to make sense of the puzzle of the last week and a half. It'd all started with Rania's death.

Oh, God. Did he have something to do with Rania's murder? Had she perhaps stumbled across Gabe and Jayden just like Lacey herself had? What had she done with the information if she had? Perhaps tried to blackmail him? No, surely not. Lacey mentally shook her head. Gabriel couldn't have killed Rania. She'd been there with Gabe when he'd tried to revive the poor woman. They'd done CPR together. It made no sense that he would attempt to stab her to death, then return a few hours later and help try and save her. Lacey just couldn't get her head around it all.

Lacey lay back and looked up at the sky racing past the windows above. A tear leaked from her eye and ran down the side of her face and into her hair. She was going to die soon if she didn't do something. Her judo skills were of no use to her all trussed up like a Christmas turkey. What else could she do to help herself? An image of Nico's face appeared before her. The scar on his cheek that made him that little bit imperfect. His gorgeous, deep-blue eyes. The way he looked at her and it felt like he could see down to her soul. She didn't want to lose him. Didn't want to lose this thing they had. Her heart ached when she thought about him.

What would Nico do in this situation? She tried to imagine, but all she could hear was his voice in her head. *You're a strong woman. Stronger than you know. You didn't become a cop for no reason. You have skills. You have knowledge. Put them to use.*

Could she find the strength to become the cop she wanted to be?

He was right. She shuffled her shoulders up until she was propped partially into a sitting position against the base of the couch. She knew the inside of Dotti like the back of her hand. There must be something in here that could help her escape.

Of course. There was a drawer full of kitchen utensils right above her head. All she had to do was get to it without Gabe noticing what she was doing. Lacey tilted her head up to look at the drawer. But with her hands tied behind her back and feet bound so tight together she was losing feeling in her legs, she might as well be thinking about scaling Mount Everest. How was she supposed to get up there, get the drawer open, and fish out a knife without the use of her hands? And while the van was still being driven so erratically around the bends that it was all she could do to brace herself to stop from being rolled around like a billiard ball? A small sob escaped her lips. Shit. Shit. Shit.

CHAPTER TWENTY-TWO

Nico threw his motorcycle around another bend. His motorcycle was so much faster than his car on these winding roads, and right now, Nico was pushing the bike to extremes, not caring about the speed limit, not caring about his own safety. Hoping to catch up to the Kombi van. He had to find Lacey. Before it was too late.

As soon as he'd hung up from the call to Tyrell, he'd driven home and swapped the Jeep for his motorcycle and riding leathers, keeping his gun strapped to his shoulder holster underneath. And waited. Waited for news. Lacey's van would be easy to spot, and if she was on the road in the vicinity, his team would find her. He had complete faith in them. Couldn't allow an ounce of doubt. They would find her. And he'd drive all the way to Antarctica to get to her if need be.

Smudge hadn't been happy to be locked inside, but he couldn't take the dog with him, and he needed to know at least one thing he cared for was safe tonight. One thing he cared for. That word stuck in his head. He *cared* for Lacey. More than cared for her. Whenever she was around, he felt euphoric, as if he could conquer the universe. But it was a feeling he didn't know what to do with. Because he wasn't sure what the future held for them. And that was the heartrending part. For the past few days he'd been ignoring the future and concentrating on the present. Enjoying just being with her, enjoying the amazing sex and the easy way they fit together, but also the way she challenged him mentally, made him see more in the everyday little things. But now, with the possibility that Lacey was in trouble and he might never see her again, he suddenly found that he couldn't imagine a time without her warm smile in it. Which confused him. Because up until now, he'd been playing it cool. Letting her make all the big decisions. Staying a little aloof. Not pushing her away, as such, but definitely not making any commitments.

Lacey going missing had suddenly made it crystal clear in his head that she was more important to him than he let himself believe. He needed her. He wanted her. He wasn't going to go as far as saying he was in love with her. Not even inside his own head. That word had so many complicated connotations tied up inside it. He'd watched his father tell his mother and both his sons that he loved them. Fiercely and forever. But Serge's love had always come with strings attached. Often physically violent strings for him and Brice.

He'd never allowed himself to fall in love before. He wasn't really sure what his version of loving someone looked like. And he was a little scared to find out.

There'd been one time when he thought he might've been in love. But that was back when he'd been young and naïve, only twenty-one, and in his first year as a probationary constable. Marietta had been ten years older than him and so beguiling. So bewitching. He still couldn't believe how she'd sweet-talked him into marrying her. Just so she could gain citizenship. How could he not have seen how duplicitous she was? At least he'd come to his senses and divorced her less than five months after they'd spoken their marriage vows. No one outside his family knew of his quick, failed marriage. And that was the way it was going to stay.

He'd failed sorely at marriage once, and it only provided more proof that he wasn't good at love. With Lacey, he might come close to love, perhaps. He certainly felt a devotion toward her. A tenderness he never knew he was capable of. But what would happen down the track, when he revealed he didn't have the ability to truly love someone? She'd find out he was a fake, eventually.

As he waited to hear from his team, he leaned against his motorcycle parked in front of the shed, ready to go at a moment's notice, and watched the sun get lower in the sky. It'd be dark in an hour. In winter, the sun set near to five pm here. How much longer did he have to wait? The roads were treacherous at the best of times, but after dark, they were downright dangerous if you didn't know what you were doing. He was wearing his full leather riding outfit; it was cold, and he intended to ride fast. Or if he came off, God forbid, they'd give him much-needed protection from a crash.

Where the hell was Lacey? He resisted the urge to pull out his phone and call her for the fiftieth time. She hadn't answered any of his calls so far, and it'd be no different this time. If she was able to, she would've called back by now. He gritted his teeth and drew in a deep breath. Letting anxiety overtake him wasn't going to help. He was going to look like one hell of a fool if he found her and it turned out everything she'd said in her note was true. That she'd chosen to continue her travels without saying goodbye to him. That she was actively avoiding him. He'd also get hauled over the coals by Charles, that was for sure. His job may even be on the line. Misappropriating police resources was not something he'd ever done before. And he hoped like hell he wasn't doing it now. But his gut feeling that Lacey was in danger was growing by the minute. And somehow Gabriel was involved. But how? And why?

His phone buzzed in his pocket and Nico had it out and to

his ear in one quick move.

"Hello, boss." It was Tyrell.

"Tell me you got her," Nico growled.

"We got her," Tyrell said, not hiding the triumph in his voice.

"Where?" Nico demanded.

"On the Murchison Highway. Looks like she's heading to Cradle Mountain or down to Strahan. But the second option is an awfully long way to go. If she's headed to Strahan, she won't get there till well after dark," Tyrell said.

Nico was already gearing up, pulling his helmet over his head, and pushing the start key on his bike. "Keep talking," Nico instructed. "I'm just switching over to my helmet mic. I'm going after her on my motorcycle. I want a cruiser in the vicinity. Ready to respond to my call."

"Right, boss. I'll also alert Strahan police, let them know a vehicle of interest might be heading in their direction."

"Thanks." Nico sat astride the motorcycle and kicked it off the stand, putting it into gear and taking off in a spurt of gravel down the driveway. He'd have to ride like a bat out of hell to catch up with Lacey. The turn off to Cradle Mountain was over an hour and a half ride away by car—but more like forty-five minutes with the way he planned to ride—and he had no idea what time she'd actually left his house. He was praying for later rather than sooner. It'd been an hour already since Dorothy had reported Smudge running around the streets. Was that around the same time Lacey had left his house? Or had she been gone for hours, and it was only then that Smudge escaped? He wished he knew.

Tyrell's voice sounded tinny inside his ear through the helmet earpiece. "It was Sally-Ann who found her. She came up with the idea. There're a couple of web cameras situated around the mountainous areas. Mostly used to predict the weather, and show if roads are passable. But you can also see traffic on certain roads. That's how we spotted her."

"She deserves five stars," Nico said. "How will we know if the van takes the turn to go to Cradle Mountain or continues onto Strahan?" he asked, opening the throttle now he was on the outskirts of the town and kicking his motorcycle into high gear.

"We're pulling up all web cams and CCTV in the vicinity. I'll let you know as soon as we do," Tyrell reported.

"Thanks. Talk to you soon." Nico hit the button on the side of his helmet to end the call and settled into riding like he'd never ridden before.

Tyrell called back half an hour later, just as Nico was beginning to worry. He was coming up to the turnoff to Cradle Mountain soon and needed a direction. Tyrell reported there were fewer cameras to choose from in that area, but the Kombi had finally been spotted on the road up to the mountain. The time stamp on the web cam when the Kombi had trundled past had been half an hour ago.

"Oh, and, boss," Tyrell said just as Nico was about to end the call.

"Yep."

"We found Dr. DuPont's car. It was parked in a little rest area around two blocks from your house. Partially concealed behind a copse of bushes."

"I knew it." Nico rang off without saying goodbye, increasing his speed, and ignoring the freezing wind creeping in down his neck and up his wrists through the small gap in his leathers. Gabe was involved.

The road was practically deserted as Nico roared up the inclines and around the sweeping curves. Low rolling hills, filled with agricultural land and pastures, gave way to steeper gradient and dense temperate rainforest as he crossed into the national park.

Where the hell was the van? Dave had given the vehicle a

clean bill of health after he'd fixed the fuel pump, but Nico was hoping something, anything, might break down on that old Kombi. He knew he was wishing for miracles, but right now, he'd take anything. The sun was almost touching the horizon behind him, and long, cold shadows reached across the road, almost like grasping fingers hoping to drag him off his motorcycle.

He came to the top of a tall ridgeline, noting the mountains proper appearing in the distance over the rise. As he hit the summit and then zoomed down the other side, he caught something out of the corner of his eye. There was a dirt road with a sign pointing to a lookout point above, but he was already winding his way down the other side of the rocky bluff, the open road in front, with not a vehicle in sight. Nico slowed and then came to a stop on the side of the road. Something tugged at the edges of his mind. A flash of something on the trees as he'd passed that small turn off. A color that didn't blend in with the dark-green trees of the forest, or the chocolate-brown of the damp earth.

A flash of tan and white.

Dotti.

Nico did a skidding U-turn and took off back up the road. Slowing as he came to the turnoff, he bumped and jerked through the potholes, all the time peering intently through his visor for that telltale color that'd give the Kombi van away. The lookout was a few hundred feet in from the road, following the ridgeline up and to the right. He broached the final rise, and the trail opened up into a clearing, with a spectacular view back over the land he'd just ridden through. Back toward the ocean and the setting sun. The edge of the lookout ended in an abrupt drop-off, several signs warning of the danger of the cliff. Two wooden benches were placed strategically to take in the vista below. It was spectacular, and Nico wondered why he'd never been here before; he'd passed by many times without stopping.

Nico put the motorcycle onto its stand and stepped off it, ripping his helmet from his head at the same time. It took him a few precious seconds to process the scene in front of him.

He'd been right; there was Dotti, her boxy body and tan-and-white paint job gleaming in the last of the sun's rays in the middle of the clearing. A parking area was off to the left, a small, white sedan parked up in the far left-hand corner. The sedan looked empty. The whole area was ringed in dense forest, effectively hiding the spot from the road.

But something was wrong.

His attention was pulled back to the van. It was rolling toward the edge. Gathering speed. Heading toward the gap between the two bench seats. What was happening? Was Lacey inside? Was she intentionally driving it over the edge of a cliff? His mind struggled to comprehend what was going on even as he ran toward the vehicle.

Then someone stepped out of the passenger side door, stumbled a few steps and then turned to watch the van as it picked up speed.

"Gabe?"

It was Gabriel. Nico's blood froze in his veins. Just like he'd suspected, Gabe had been involved in Lacey's disappearance. But where was Lacey?

Nico pulled out his gun and ran toward the doctor. "Don't move," he yelled. "Put your hands on your head and don't move."

Gabriel gave a startled jump and turned to face Nico who was still running, gun pointed at him. The van was only around twenty feet away from the edge now.

"Where's Lacey?" Nico screamed, skidding to a halt in front of the doctor.

"In there." Gabe pointed to Dotti.

Suddenly there was a muffled scream from inside the van.

Everything seemed to slow down then. Nico ran as hard as he could, not really sure what he was going to do, but wanting to stop the van somehow. Forgetting about Gabriel. Forgetting about everything. Lacey was in that vehicle. He ran. But just as he touched the rear window, the front wheels hit the crumbling edge, and the van flew in a graceful swan dive into the waiting branches of the trees below.

He skidded to a stop, teetering on the edge himself, arms waving to keep his balance.

"No!"

"No!" he screamed again into the wind as he watched the van plunge down the drop-off, breaking through the top branches of the trees that grew up the steep slope.

Then he saw something. A figure flung itself into the treetops even as the van crashed through the thick forest, leaving a trail of broken branches as it continued its nosedive. The Kombi smashed onto the rocks below and careened down the ravine, splintering through the thick undergrowth. Then it hit a large rock and rolled end over end, like a bouncing ping-pong ball down the slope, finally coming to a cracking halt, stopped by a huge trunk of an old pine tree. The booming sound echoed around the cliff face and down into the valley below.

Just as suddenly, everything went totally still and quiet.

Nico stood on the edge of the ravine, eyes fixed on the spot in the treetops just below. Had he seen what he thought he saw? Not letting despair overtake him, he drew in a deep breath and hoped. Hoped like hell.

"Lacey," he called out.

Nothing. There was no answer.

"Lacey," he screamed at the top of his lungs. "Are you there? Answer me."

A branch cracked somewhere below him.

Nico looked for a way down. The edge fell beneath him in

a sheer drop for around ten feet, but then the side of the ravine began to angle outward. It was over a forty-five degree slope. More like sixty degrees. But if he could get over this first lip, he could probably climb and scramble down there.

Nico turned, looking for something he could use. He had less than twenty minutes of daylight left, judging by the sun on the horizon.

It suddenly struck him that Gabe was nowhere to be seen. And the white sedan was missing. Not surprising. But Nico didn't have time to worry about that fucker right now.

Another branch cracked, followed by a small scream of fright.

His heart leapt into his mouth.

"Lacey," he called, cupping his hands around his mouth. "Is that you? Can you hear me?"

After endless seconds of straining to hear, he was rewarded with a faint, "Help! Help me. I'm stuck in a tree."

She was alive.

Lacey was alive.

"Lacey, it's me, Nico. I'm coming. I'm coming," he yelled, his voice cracking with emotion. Fuck. Who would've thought he could get choked up over the sound of a voice? But it was from the one woman who meant the most to him in the entire world. She was alive, and he was going to help her.

"Are you hurt?" Now he knew she was alive, he needed to ascertain what kind of condition she was in.

"Yes, but I don't know how bad," she called back, her voice drifting thinly over the distance. "I think my arm is broken."

Not good. But anything was better than dead; he could deal with a broken arm. He tucked his gun back into its holster and ran back to his motorcycle. He always carried an emergency first aid kit in the small space under his seat. And if he was lucky... Yes, there was a set of jumper leads too.

Would they be long enough for what he needed if he tied them together? Only one way to find out.

Jogging back to the cliff edge, he took out his phone and dialed Tyrell, nearly letting out a shout of joy when he saw he had reception. "I'm out at Blackpoint Lookout," he yelled into the phone as soon as his senior constable answered. "Send a car and an ambulance now. Make that two cars, we have an assailant on the loose."

"On it, boss." Tyrell was calm and efficient, which was exactly what Nico needed.

"Lacey has been hurt, but I don't know how badly. She's down in a ravine, and I'm going to try and reach her. Dr. Gabriel DuPont is a suspect in a kidnapping attempt. He's driving a small, white sedan. Put out an arrest warrant for him," Nico reported quickly, his words almost tangling on his tongue in his rush to get them out. "Do not let that fucker leave this island," he added with a snarl.

"Yes, sir. It'll take around half an hour for the first team to reach you." Tyrell didn't question Nico; he just did as he was bid. Nico wouldn't have answered, anyway; he was already pocketing his phone.

Just as he was about to run back to the edge, an idea occurred to him. Turning on his motorcycle engine, he rolled it forward until it was close to the edge and turned the headlight onto high beam, pointing it directly at the gash in the trees. He wasn't even sure if it was lighting up the area where Lacey was stuck, but it'd be dark soon and any light would be welcome.

He stared over the edge of the drop-off. It was a tad too far down to reach a point where the earth began to slope outward from where he was standing. His makeshift jumper-lead rope wouldn't reach. But around to the left, where the trees closed in and the clearing disappeared, the edge got lower. Within minutes, he'd tied his makeshift rope around a small but sturdy sapling growing close to the edge and used it to clamber down to a semi-flat spot where the ground was less steep. It didn't quite reach, and Nico was forced to jump the last few feet, landing awkwardly, and nearly tumbling down the precipitous, rocky slope. How he was ever going to get himself and Lacey back up there was a problem for later.

Using the shrubs to hang on to, he quickly slithered down the incline, until he reached the first line of trees, then worked his way along, drawing abreast of the path of carnage the flying van had left in its wake. Through the cracked branches and downed saplings, he could see the Kombi lodged up against the tree trunk around five-hundred feet farther down the ravine. It was crushed flat against the trunk, looking more like a pancake than a solid metal vehicle.

"Lacey, I'm here, where are you?" He peered up into the tree limbs. She'd said she was stuck up a tree, but which one? The light from his headlight barely reached this area, but it'd be better than nothing once the sun disappeared.

"Over here." Her voice was faint and Nico became worried. Was she about to pass out? She might fall if she did that. He shuffled along the steep slope, screwing his eyes into slits as he stared up into each tree he passed. Where was she?

"Lacey, can you keep talking, so I can find you?"

She croaked out an answer, and he followed the sound of her voice back up the hill. He must've missed her as he went past the first time. Finally, he stopped beneath the tree he thought her voice was coming from. How high up was she? The top of the tree seemed to have been shorn off. A victim of the flying Kombi van. He maneuvered around the tree trunk until he caught movement. There. He could just make out the pale oval of her face in the fading light. She was about sixty feet up the tree, around half the height of the remaining tree. It was a King Billy Pine, with branches fairly evenly spaced, hopefully making it relatively easy to climb.

Without thinking too much, he hauled himself into the lower branches. Sooner than he expected, he was level with Lacey. She was tucked into the crook of a larger limb, leaning against the trunk, one arm cradled against her side. The motorcycle headlight cast crazy shadows now he was up higher, and he was no longer sure if it was such a good idea.

"Hi, there," he breathed.

"Hi." She turned to him, huge eyes taking up much of her face.

He hardly recognized her. Lacey's face was covered in scratches, her clothing torn right off her body—her sweater hung in rags from her shoulders, and her jeans were ripped in a dozen places. He was horrified to think how many branches had scratched and clawed at her as she jumped out of the flying van. The tree may have caught her but it'd left its mark, almost like it'd bared its claws.

He kept all those thoughts hidden. She was going to survive. He'd make sure she survived this. Even with her face in tatters, she was still the most beautiful thing he'd ever seen.

"You're going to be fine," he soothed. "We'll get through this together. You just jumped out of a flying vehicle. Anything after that will be a piece of cake," he said, trying to lighten the mood.

She offered him a small smile, but he could see how much it cost her even to do that.

"Right." It was time to take charge. "I'm going to get you down, but let's do a quick assessment of your injuries first."

"My arm is definitely broken," she replied. Even from here, he could see that her forearm was at a slightly odd angle.

"I can splint that, immobilize it as much as we can." He had a triangle bandage in his first aid kit. And there were plenty of sticks around he could use as a splint. "Anything else."

"My leg hurts," she said through gritted teeth, indicating the front of her thigh, where a large shard of wood protruded from the middle of her limb.

"Oh, Jesus," he said before he could stop himself, grimacing at his lack of tact.

"It's okay. I know it's bad, and I know I look a mess," she replied pragmatically.

"Right this second, you look like a divine goddess," he replied, meaning it. "Strong and incredibly brave. You are always beautiful to me."

She made a grunting noise but didn't argue.

If he had to guess, the next fifteen minutes were probably the most physically agonizing time of Lacey's life. After he'd splinted her arm, strapping it securely to her chest with the triangle bandage, and removed the large piece of wood from her leg—she decided it'd hinder her climb down—and bandaged that tightly to stem blood flow, he decided there was little he could do for the myriad of other scratches covering her body. Excruciatingly slowly, he helped her down, branch by branch, sometimes supporting her whole weight from below until she could find a one-handed hold that suited. Using the sparse light from his motorcycle to see, Nico would find the perfect hold for Lacey, then wait on the next branch down and guide her good hand and feet until they were secure. He was extremely glad now that he'd thought of using his headlight. Without it, this task would've been impossible.

Perhaps he should've waited until the rest of the teams arrived. Until a skilled rescue unit was called. But that could take hours, and Nico just wanted Lacey safely down on the ground. Where he could finally cradle her in his arms and let go of the breath he'd been holding ever since her van flew over the edge of the ravine. And she wanted the same; otherwise, she would've refused to move. He was continuously amazed by how gutsy this woman was. How determined. With a core of steel.

At last, his feet were on the ground, and he grabbed her by the waist and lowered her gently to stand next to him.

"You did it," he breathed into her ear.

"Yes, we did it," she replied. "I couldn't have done that without you."

He settled her as gently as he could with her back to the King Billy, then removed his leather jacket and draped it around her shoulders before sitting beside her, waiting until her breathing became more measured. Until his breathing slowed down.

"Nico?"

"You don't need to talk anymore," he soothed. "You're safe now."

"Yes, but, there's something I need to tell you." She lifted her head, the lines around her eyes etched with pain. "There was someone else in my van when it went over the edge."

"What?" That was the last thing he'd been expecting.

"A man. Gabe put a drugged man into the driver's seat before he ran us over the edge. I think it might've been that young mechanic you told me about, Floyd?"

"Floyd Hamilton? He was in the van when it went over the edge?" Nico tried not to think about the flat-as-a-pancake van.

"I think it was him. At least that's what Gabriel implied." She stared at him for untold seconds as he tried to decide what to say. "He's dead, isn't he?"

"Most likely," he replied. "As soon as the team get here, I'll send someone down to check it out. But…"

"But no one could've survived that impact," she finished for him.

"It'd take a miracle," he conceded, suddenly realizing just how miraculous Lacey's survival was. He wanted to pull her into his arms and hold her forever. Never let her go. Let her know just how much he cared. How much he'd wanted this miracle. But she was too damaged, and he didn't want to hurt her.

Lacey seemed to feel the same sentiments as him, however, and she moved toward, him, wincing slightly as she readjusted her arm, so that she could lay her head against his shoulder.

"That's just awful." Her voice was small and fatigued, full of anguish. "How could Gabe do this? To me? To that poor young guy? Gabe is a monster."

He couldn't disagree. He just wished he'd seen it sooner.

Lacey sobbed quietly into the turtleneck of his woolen sweater. They sat for many long moments, Nico just feeling her skin beneath his palm where it rested at the back of her neck. Feeling her chest rise and fall as she breathed in and out. Reveling in the aliveness of her.

"And my van," she sobbed suddenly into his chest. "He killed Dotti, too."

"I know, baby," he crooned. "But you're still alive. And we can get you another Dotti." That was a promise he'd make sure to keep.

CHAPTER TWENTY-THREE

Lacey stared into the rain. It was funny, but raindrops and mist had almost become a comfort to her. Boat Harbour Beach draped in drizzle was fast becoming her favorite place. Tentatively, she crouched down and picked up a flat rock, testing the feel between her fingers. Smooth and round, a perfect skipping rock. But her right arm, her throwing arm, was in a cast so there would be no skipping stones today. Soon maybe.

She twirled in a big circle, taking in the gray clouds, the soft pastel beach sand, and the tall Norfolk Island Pine standing proud at the back of the sand dunes. This place felt like home.

Lacey had spent two nights in hospital after the kidnapping, where the doctors had pronounced that she was one lucky woman to have survived jumping out of a falling car with such relatively minor wounds. Until that stage, she hadn't thought of her wounds as minor, but in hindsight, they were probably right.

She'd been staying with Nico for the past two weeks, recuperating at his house, taking it easy while her wounds healed. Her broken radius was mending well according to the doctor, and while the cast covering her forearm from wrist to elbow was annoying, it didn't hamper her doing most everyday tasks. The wound in her leg had needed twenty-seven stitches, which'd been removed a few days ago, and that was also healing well. She was even encouraged to take gentle exercise.

It was actually the myriad of scratches all over her body, but especially on her face, that were the hardest to deal with, more than the broken bone or puncture wound. They'd scabbed over within a day or so, but every time she moved, the scabs broke open again and started to bleed. She looked like a victim of an explosion, as if she'd been cut by millions of pieces of flying glass and shrapnel. The first time she'd looked in the mirror, she'd hardly recognized herself. Then she hadn't wanted Nico to look at her, because she was so ugly. He'd merely stroked a gentle finger down the only part of her cheek that remained unscathed and reiterated that she was the most beautiful woman in the world, and a few small scratches wouldn't change that. She wasn't sure if she believed him, but the compassion in his eyes was enough to make her want to kiss him, even with her damaged lips.

Now, she'd taken to walking along the beach every afternoon. Smudge appreciated getting out even more than she did, and he was bounding up and down the wet sand, barking at a seagull. She almost wanted to join him, feeling some of his joy and exhilaration rub off on her. Most of the scratches were now becoming raised, pink scars, crisscrossing her body. She was feeling practically human again. Ready to face the world. Ready to make decisions that she'd been putting off for so long.

Ready to go back and face her parents.

She had to give them credit. Her mother and father had flown to Burnie to see Lacey in hospital as soon as they heard. Barry, especially, had been beside himself with worry, and he'd sat on the edge of her bed for almost an hour, just holding on to her foot, because that was the only part of her that didn't hurt.

But after the first half an hour of being solicitous, Elora had reverted to her normal narcissistic self. At first, flirting with the doctors, then when that didn't garner enough attention, telling everyone who'd listen that her daughter was lucky to be alive, and it was no thanks to the police that she'd survived. Within an hour, she was demanding an apology from Chief Inspector Shadbolt. Lacey had wanted to crawl under the covers and disappear, not wanting to deal with her mother's antics. But when Elora started to take her vitriol out on Nico, who was standing in the corridor outside her hospital room to give her and her parents' privacy, Lacey had had enough.

"Go home, Mother," she'd shouted. "You're making things worse. How dare you come in yell at my friends, making accusations about things you don't understand? For once, this is not about you. It's about me."

Nico had witnessed her mini meltdown, but instead of running away from her fucked-up family, he'd stood by her bedside and calmly faced down Elora's wrath, telling her that perhaps it would be best if she left. Elora was incandescent with rage and stormed out, vowing never to speak to her *impossible daughter* ever again. Lacey was almost relieved at her mother's words, but she knew it was all for show. Elora would sulk for a little while before deciding enough was enough, act as if nothing had happened, and want to resume her relationship with Lacey, but always surrounded by a slight aura of injured pride, as if everything had been Lacey's fault but she was too polite to mention it.

She knew she needed to face her mother, but only when she was physically strong enough. Barry had looked bereft, not following his wife as she stormed out the door, and Lacey felt a sudden stab of sorrow for what he had to deal with.

"I promise, I'll come and see you and Mum as soon as I can. Give me a couple of weeks," she'd pleaded. But in her heart, she knew things couldn't continue the way they were.

Her father had kissed her gently on the forehead, and said, "Always know that I love you." Then he left. Which broke Lacey's heart, because it was the first time he'd said those words aloud. Her father was truly caught between a rock and a hard place. He loved all his children very much, and currently, the best way he knew how to show that was to continue bringing in the money so they could live a financially stable life. And by keeping Elora happy, he kept them all happy. But the alternative—if he stood up to Elora, and perhaps even divorced her—would amount to launching World War III, and would perhaps tear the fabric of the family apart forever.

Matt had phoned the night she'd been admitted to hospital and said he was catching the first flight to Devonport, but she'd talked him out of it, saying she was all right and their parents were flying in. Suggesting that perhaps they all get together as a family soon instead. She was dying to see Matt and even Sammy, but there were things that needed to be said between them all that shouldn't be swept under the carpet any longer. Matt promised to come home when she was well enough to travel. And he also promised to help her find another Dotti when she was ready for that as well.

Sammy also talked to Lacey over the phone, using Barry's phone to chat once her parents had arrived, and for once, sounded conciliatory and even worried about her older sister. Elora had already told Lacey that Sammy had stayed at home to look after Raymond the poodle, to which Lacey merely rolled her eyes when her mother wasn't looking. Sammy never coped well with stressful situations…or hospitals.

Now, Lacey stared out to sea; the water was gray and turbulent this afternoon, a fresh breeze whipping up the whitecaps, and snarling her hair into tangles. It was too rough to skip stones anyway.

Her mind turned, as always, to Nico. In those first few hours in the aftermath of her brush with death, Nico hadn't left her side. It'd seemed to take forever for the rescue team to reach them. Lacey had remained huddled into Nico's arms the whole time, shivering from cold and shock, even Nico's strong embrace and his leather jacket wasn't enough to keep her warm. Nico had kept talking to her, stroking her hair, telling her everything would be okay. And she'd believed him. But it was still hard to reconcile that if she'd been a split second later in jumping out of the van, she'd most likely be part of that metal pancake that'd once been Dotti. Much like Floyd, whose body they had recovered the next day from the mangled wreck.

While she'd been wrapped in Nico's arms, she found a sudden urge to talk. To purge herself of those awful minutes as the van rolled closer to the edge. Talking also helped to keep the pain at bay, and so, through chattering teeth, she began her tale.

"When Gabriel drove up the road to the lookout, I had no idea where we were. But he'd already hinted at his plan to drive off a cliff and make it look like an accident. So I was really scared," she started hesitantly, talking through chattering teeth.

"That bastard," Nico had muttered.

"He had me tied up inside the van. But I knew there were sharp knives in one of the kitchen drawers. All I had to do was get to one." Lacey shivered harder as she remembered Gabe pulling to a stop in the clearing. From her position lying on the floor, all she could see was the sky above, which was turning gray as it got closer to sunset. "He turned off the engine and got out of the van. He went and stood near the edge. I don't know what he was doing. Maybe he was checking out the best spot to run the van over it. You know, looking for maximum height, maximum effect," she said sarcastically. "Maybe he was screwing up his courage to do the deed. Or just looking at the pretty sunset. I don't know. But in that time, I managed to wriggle up onto the couch, open the drawer with my teeth, and grab one of the knives in my mouth." Lacey had felt a little like a dog retrieving a stick. But this was no ordinary stick. This tiny paring knife was about to save her life.

"Just as I grabbed the knife, I saw Gabe through the front windscreen standing at the edge. He turned back toward the van, and I dropped the knife on the floor, and then flopped back on top of it. I went to work on the rope he'd tied around my wrists, not knowing how much time I had. A few minutes later, the driver's door opened and Gabe piled that young man Floyd into the seat. I wasn't sure what was going on, so I called out to Floyd, but he never answered. I think he might've been drugged, he was sort of lolling all over the place. Then Gabe went around and jumped into the passenger seat, and said, 'Let's do this thing.' I'd just started to cut my ankles free when Dotti began to move. He must've been steering her from the passenger seat." She stopped speaking, letting the memories wash over her.

"You're amazing," Nico had said then, staring at her with a newfound respect. "I mean, I always knew you were amazing, but that takes a certain kind of courage. A certain kind of determination to live. Not to just lie there and accept your fate."

"Hmm." Lacey wasn't so sure. The instinct to survive was a strong motivator, for anyone. "I was thinking a lot about Cindi," she admitted. "I wondered what it was like to die. And how that poor little girl had felt as her short life ebbed away. This might sound a bit crazy, but I suddenly saw Cindi in my mind. Whole and alive and laughing. Wearing a cute rainbow-colored shirt and a pink tutu, while she twirled around in circles. She was happy. Wherever she is now, she's finally happy." Lacey paused and gulped down a sob. "Seeing her like that gave me the strength I needed to keep cutting. To not give up."

"You're not crazy," he'd whispered into her face. "She helped you do what you needed to do."

"Maybe," Lacey conceded. She wasn't one for believing in spirits or ghosts or what have you. But Cindi had been very clear in her mind. "Anyway. The hardest part was getting the door to slide open," she continued. "By the time I reached the door handle, Gabriel was stepping out of the passenger seat. I knew I only had a second or so to get out before the van went over the edge. But the handle stuck. The door wouldn't open, and I screamed and screamed."

"I heard you," Nico said. "That's when I lost all hope. I knew you were in the van, and there was nothing I could do to stop it." There was utter anguish in his voice, and she understood how hard it must've been to watch Dotti head towards the cliff and feel powerless to stop her. His grip on her shoulders tightened. "I was so scared I was going to lose you."

Nico had left his motorcycle headlight on to give some light to the encroaching darkness. His face was cast in stark shadows as she lifted her head to stare into his eyes. She could see the naked truth written in his indigo eyes. That a part of him would've been destroyed by her death. She held him a little tighter.

"Everything seemed to happen in slow motion after that," Lacey continued. "The door jerked opened in my hand, and then the treetops came into view. I knew if I didn't jump, I'd surely die when Dotti hit the bottom, so I just hoped the branches would break my fall enough that I lived to tell the tale." Lacey could still remember the sensation of flying through the air like a bird for one short second before the branches ripped her skin to shreds as she plummeted between the foliage. "I thought the leaves would be softer than they were," she admitted.

"Well, they did catch you. And I still can't believe you survived that fall," Nico said into her hair.

She had been pretty lucky. It'd been the only option. But really... The whole idea was immensely far-fetched now she thought about it. Falling out of the sky. She pondered her survival for a few seconds. "Judo is all about learning to fall. In the beginning, that's the main thing they teach you. How to fall and not get hurt. Learning the throws comes last. Maybe that helped me. I don't know." She'd shrugged then, causing a stab of pain to shoot through her injured arm, and she clenched her teeth and leaned into Nico's solid, reassuring body.

When it became clear she'd finally run out of words, Nico had begun talking to fill the dark silence. He told her about his own mad dash up the mountain road, hoping against hope to find her. How Tyrell and Sally-Ann had found Dotti using web cams and CCTV cameras.

"I knew you'd come," she'd told him. Her faith in him may have wavered, but she knew he'd figure it out in the end.

And while Nico hadn't arrived in time to save her from going over the edge, he'd been the main voice in her head spurring her on. Telling her she didn't need a man to save her. She was strong enough to save herself. And if he hadn't figured out where she was going, and been there to help her out of the tree afterward, and called in the rescue team, she may still be stuck up there. In some ways, she owed him her life. In other ways, she was a little proud that she'd been able to save herself.

Nico had insisted she come back to his place after she was discharged from hospital, and she was more than happy to oblige. He'd been caring and attentive, staying at home for the first few days to be with her. He still had the ongoing investigation to deal with, and the phone had been ringing off the hook, a fleet of officers had paraded past his front door delivering documents, asking questions, talking logistics, while Nico directed everything from his living room, refusing to leave her alone. Even after she told him to go back to work, he denied her request. But on the third day, five full days after Gabe had abducted her, Senior Constable Tyrell appeared on the front porch. He'd had a call from an officer in the Strahan office. They'd found a man hiding in an abandoned shed on the edge of town who matched Gabriel DuPont's description. Where Gabe had been and how he'd managed to evade the island-wide search for so long was anybody's guess. But the bastard was now in custody, and he would be charged with kidnapping, the attempted murder of Lacey, and the murder of Floyd Hamilton. Nico confirmed Lacey's suspicion that Rania knew about Gabe's homosexuality, telling her about the journal entries, which were backed up by the young bakers apprentices' testimony.

Jayden had cracked easily under Sally-Ann's interrogation, revealing he'd gone to Rania's house to beg her not to tell anyone about what she'd seen because he knew how desperate Gabe was to keep his sexuality a secret. Rania had supposedly grudgingly agreed, but her word was clearly not enough, and it seemed Gabe hadn't believed she'd keep quiet forever. The fight Nico had witnessed that day in the parking lot had been when Gabe had found out about Jayden visiting Rania the day afterward. He'd been livid with rage, the apprentice had reported to Sally-Ann. Jayden was distraught when he learned that Gabe had been arrested, but not surprised. Perhaps, out of everyone who knew Gabe, Jayden had been the only one who'd seen into his confused mind down to the darkness that lay just below the surface. And

Nico was now working on the case to charge Gabriel with Rania's murder.

After Tyrell's call, Lacey was finally able to convince Nico to leave her side; he needed to be the one to bring Gabriel DuPont back to Burnie to be charged. Nico agreed and had returned much later that evening with a look of grim determination on his face. It must've been bittersweet for him. The doctor had been a good friend, and she knew it must still be hard to believe he was capable of murder. People never liked to suspect those closest to them had the ability to commit heinous deeds. The next day, Nico returned to work at the station full-time. But he always made sure to be home in time to cook dinner and spend time with her in the evenings. He was also there to take her to doctor's appointments, as well as back to see Imran twice since the accident.

Margie was more than happy to pop in every day to see how Lacey was faring. And she inevitably brought something home-cooked with her, be it cookies, cake, or a casserole. So Lacey and Nico were always well-fed.

It was good to reconnect with Herb and Margie, repair the wound that'd opened when Herb had been on Nico's suspect list. Margie at least, bore no grudge; she seemed to understand how conflicted Nico had been about the whole thing. It turned out that the older couple had decided to put their bicycles on the back of their car and drive to Queenstown to do one of the more challenging rides they'd been considering for a while on the Monday she'd been abducted. Herb had had enough of people staring at him and police questions. He needed to get away, and Lacey understood that. Herb talked about the steep hill climbs and long stretches of remote coastline, and how he'd felt some of his resentment at the situation he'd been put in drain away. Phone reception was patchy along their chosen route, and so

Herb never knew Nico had been frantically trying to get in touch. They'd stayed overnight and returned home to find their little community in absolute uproar. After Lacey heard their story, she'd been tempted to gently reprimand them for not telling Nico where they were going, and how it'd caused concern for their welfare. But she decided, in the end, there would be nothing gained from her admonishment, and so merely smiled at Herb and agreed that nature was a great healer.

Margie was sometimes overcome with emotion when she thought about how her own husband had been on top of the suspect list as a possible murderer. "Never in my life would I have suspected such a thing. I'm so proud of Herb. He stuck to his principles and kept that young woman's secret, even though his own freedom was at stake, just because she asked him to," Margie had said one day while making a pot of tea.

Lacey silently thought that Margie's morals were a little misplaced, but at least her allegiance to her husband remained staunch, and that was probably what mattered most.

Nico attended her every whim and comfort, making sure she was also mentally okay, treating her with kid gloves and organizing appointments with Imran. He was so sweet to her. Touching her gently, making sure she wasn't in pain, sitting and talking to her for hours by the fireside after dinner, about whether she might buy another Kombi van, and if she did what color it would be. About the best way to cultivate tomatoes in winter, and even just listening to her favorite music. The only thing they didn't talk about was what the future held. Together or apart. It felt so normal, and in those times, she could forget about what'd happened to her and what might lie ahead, cocooned inside a little bubble of Nico-induced warmth. But they were yet to return to the bedroom since she'd come home from the hospital. And as her scratches healed, and her arm began to itch inside her cast, Lacey felt her libido coming back, and she wanted him to stop tiptoeing around her. She was ready to make love, now she just had to convince him that he wouldn't hurt her with a tumble between the sheets.

Tonight would be the night she decided. She wouldn't allow him to take her hand and kiss her fingertips and then place them in his lap and change the subject. Tonight she would be the one to sit in his lap, kiss him deeply, and let him know exactly what she wanted. He was so worried that he'd hurt her, that she'd already suffered enough. But it was becoming a certain type of torture to have him so near, but yet to keep things platonic.

She'd had a lot of time to think about her and Nico over the past two weeks. They might not talk about a future together, but she was certainly thinking about it. When she first arrived in Boat Harbour Beach, she'd had an agenda. A part of her always realized she'd been running away from her problems. And from herself. She wasn't sure what she wanted from life, and so she'd put her life on hold so that she didn't have to make a decision. But then Rania had been murdered and Lacey had been dragged into the investigation. Being so closely involved with the crime scene and being around the team running the investigation, her passion for being a police officer, for being part of the force for good, had slowly reawakened. Then there was Nico. An extraordinary man, who'd hit her like a comet shooting from the sky. She hadn't been looking for a relationship, didn't think she deserved one, but it'd found her anyway. His indigo-blue eyes had taken her heart hostage.

They hadn't mentioned the L-word yet. But she knew she was in love with Nico. She didn't know if he felt the same way, however.

She could see the hazy shape of a future with Nico

evolving. If she took the job Shadbolt had offered her, she could stay in Tasmania. Stay and explore a relationship with Nico. But did he want that too?

"Here you are." She jumped at the sound of his voice as Nico appeared, walking over the sand toward her.

She brightened, pushing her damp hair out of her face. "You're home."

"Yes, Charles told me to go home early today. Something about a job well done." But his face darkened as he said the words and Lacey knew he didn't believe his boss's praise. He'd be beating himself up for not suspecting Gabriel from the start, for not keeping her under guard until they were sure they had the right man, for not getting to the lookout sooner, and for not being able to stop the van from plunging over the cliff. All vast miscalculations on his part and deserving of his condemnation. Nico deemed himself a failure, refusing to see the bright side of his actions. That he'd worked out where Lacey was, had thrown every resource into finding her, and had been there to rescue her in the end. Gabriel had now been charged with Rania's murder, although he was still pleading not guilty, and so the story of exactly why he'd done it and why he'd fled the scene, leaving her still alive, was yet to be unraveled. That made two murders he was responsible for. Added to the other charges of her kidnapping and attempted murder, it looked like Gabe was going to jail for a very long time. But one thing that still bugged Nico was the motivation behind Gabe's actions. Dr. DuPont still refused to talk about why it was so important nobody know he was a homosexual. Lacey had revealed the little she knew from her conversation with Gabe in the van, about how he needed to please his mother, how he needed to be perfect in her eyes. Perhaps Gabe would open up about his demons at a later date.

But for now… "It *was* a job well done," she said, turning to slip her good arm around his neck. "Neither of us picked Gabe as a suspect until it was almost too late. But he's behind bars now, and that's all that matters."

"I guess so." Nico let her lead him toward his house. "I've brought home takeaway tonight," he admitted. "Gabe's trial date has been set for June, with no bail granted until the trial. So it's a sort of celebration."

"Yes, let's celebrate," she agreed. But she had a different sort of celebration in mind.

* * *

After they'd eaten, Lacey tugged Nico by the hand, leading him toward his bedroom. She was so over all this waiting until she was one hundred percent healed. She wanted him now, and she knew her body better than anyone else. It was ready. She was ready to make love with Nico.

"I'm not sure about—" Lacey covered his mouth with hers to drown out his protests. Letting her kiss tell him the story. Setting him on fire with her urgency. Her tongue dipped into his mouth, tasting him, savoring him.

"God, I've missed this. I've missed you," he groaned into her mouth, hands roaming freely over her back, down her spine to cup her bottom and pull her up to meet his crotch, so she could feel the evidence of exactly how much he'd missed her.

"I've missed you too," she said, already tugging at the buttons on his shirt.

She let him undress her, helping him to pull her T-shirt over the cast on her arm. For a second, he hesitated when he caught sight of the many small, still-healing scars on her body,

"All I can feel at the moment is you. All I want is you," she said, drawing his gaze back toward her face. Which was also covered in scars, but she needed him to see her truth. "Nothing else matters. The only pain I'm feeling right now is the pain of not having you."

After that, he needed no more prompting. Soon they lay together in his bed, cocooned together under the blankets. She delighted in the feel of his skin beneath her fingers, relearning all the contours of his body she'd been sorely missing over the past two weeks. His hand slid over her hip, his mouth hot on hers as they lay side by side, staring into each other's eyes. Slowly, the heat between them built, getting hotter with every touch of a hand or lips on skin. Silently, he explored her, and a tremor ran through her as he kissed down her neck, down her collarbone, and over her breasts.

"Nico," she whispered. "Oh, God, Nico." His name was a devotion on her lips. A wish. Or a gratitude that he existed and was here with her now. He caressed her body so perfectly, like she was a musical instrument who only played for him. She forgot all her problems. Forgot why they were so wrong for each other and only remembered why they were so right.

I'm in love with you. The words whispered at the back of her mind.

When she couldn't take the building intensity anymore, she reached over and sheathed him with a condom without even asking, then nudged him with her knees until he hovered above her. Tilting her hips toward him, she invited him in, and they both gasped in unison as he thrust inside. Rocking together, it didn't take long for the crescendo to peak. She was so close...

She crested the wave, her deep moan as she arched her back into him, driving him over the edge until his own pleasure swamped him. He also let out a moan of unrestrained pleasure and then rested his forehead against hers, panting heavily.

I love you. The words were a mantra in her brain, drowning out every other thought. Their bodies fit perfectly together. Like two matching puzzle pieces. Like they were destined to be together.

"I love you."

The utterance hung in the air between them. Oh, shit. Had she just said that aloud? Had he heard her?

Nico lifted his head and his expression morphed from languid to guarded, and she had her answer. She'd said the words and now there was no taking them back. It was a point of no return, at least for her, and she didn't know where to go from here. Nico stared at her as if he were at a loss for something to say. She went completely still in his arms.

Shit. She was in love with him, but he was hesitating. Oh, God. Had she got this completely wrong?

"Forget I said that," she said as she tried to clamber out of bed.

But he caught her around the waist. "Wait, Lacey." He tried to kiss her to stop her frantic attempts to leave, but she was having none of it and pushed against him. He was stronger than her, however, and pinned her to the bed. "You can't just leave after saying...that!"

Oh, yes, she could. Just watch her. Again, she tried to get him off her, but with her arm in a cast and her leg suddenly throbbing, all the fight in her died and she went limp. Lying on her back, she stared up at him.

"I care about you, Lacey. Deeply. You're an amazing woman." He rolled off her carefully, as if she might leap out of bed now that she was free. But she remained where she was and he rested up on his elbow beside her.

"I know you care," she replied. Unless everything they'd just done had been a complete lie, then his body was telling her just how much he worshiped her. But it seemed his mind was having trouble keeping up.

"I also don't know where this is going," he said. And he

was right. Hadn't she thought exactly the same thing right before the abduction? Hadn't she been ready to leave him behind to continue her travels, then go home? But things had changed. She could see the potential for a future. But he'd shattered that illusion. "And I'm sorry that my heart isn't quite in step with yours," he added. His handsome face was cast in shadows, but it was enough for her to see the way the lines around his mouth drew down, showing his distress.

"I understand," she replied. "I'm not sad or ashamed I told you I love you. It's how I feel. Perhaps I shouldn't have sprung it on you so quickly, and I'm sorry for that. But I'm not trying to force you to say it against your will."

He brushed the hair gently away from her forehead. "You might be the best thing that ever happened to me, and I don't want to fuck it up. But…"

"I get it," she said, even though she really didn't. Would it be enough for her to know that she loved him, even if he didn't say it back? Should she stay and let him work through his reservations about her?

"Please let me go," she pleaded quietly, even though he was no longer holding her down.

He rolled to the side and lay on his back to stare at the ceiling.

"I think I just fucked this up," he whispered.

"No, you didn't," she said, easing her way out of the bed. "I did."

CHAPTER TWENTY-FOUR

"Lacey," a familiar voice called her name. She pretended to ignore it and wove her way deeper into the crowd of passengers thronging near the railing to get their last look at Devonport.

"Lacey. I need to talk to you." A large hand landed on her shoulder and she grimaced. It'd be so easy to throw the man behind her to the ground using the same judo technique she'd employed on that very first night she'd met him. The cast on her arm might hinder her, but she was pretty sure she could still do it. She ignored the urge but didn't turn around.

"Lacey, please." It was the anguish in his voice that finally did it. Tore a hole in the armor she'd erected around her heart. She turned slowly to meet Nico's gaze. But she really wasn't sure what else there was to say, so she just looked up into his face. His beautiful, scarred, imperfect, handsome face.

"Will you at least talk to me? Please don't leave like this."

She shrugged. She'd already made up her mind. She was going home. First to talk to her family, and then to restart her life. But not in Melbourne. She'd decided she needed to get away from her hometown, away from the controlling sphere of her mother.

It'd been three days since she'd said those fateful words.

Three days she'd spent cocooned in a hotel in Burnie, listening to her phone ring as Nico frantically tried to contact her but not returning his calls. She'd needed time to think. Needed time to sort through the whirlwind of emotions the past few weeks had elicited. Needed time to sort out her priorities. She was no longer the woman who'd bolted to Tasmania to escape her PTSD. That was something she couldn't escape from, she knew that now. Instead, she was learning to embrace it. Embrace what she'd once perceived as a weakness. Imran had taught her she might never return to the same person she was before she'd witnessed Cindi's murder, but she could still be a strong and resourceful person, who could contribute to society. It was time to stop running.

She'd also debated long and hard about what it meant to be in love. What love meant to her. And finally, she'd concluded that she couldn't be with Nico if he didn't love her. Nico cared for her deeply, that was obvious. And perhaps if she stayed, he'd come to love her eventually. But she needed more. She needed him to say the words *I love you*. She needed him to tell her that he felt the same heart-pumping ecstasy whenever he looked deep into her eyes. Felt the same familiar tenderness when their hands brushed together accidentally as they walked. Had the same aching hunger to have him bury himself deep inside her, and to stay that way forever.

Lacey wasn't sure why she needed to hear those special words. She'd pondered her and Nico's relationship long into the night. Nico was a good man—a great man, even. And most women would jump at the chance to have a man like him care for them, cherish them. Maybe if she was a different person, she might be able to see past his obvious issues around commitment to the potential of a life spent building that relationship into something steady and sure. But she wasn't that person. She had to hear those words to believe in the possibility that love was real. She could accept nothing less. Lacey was no expert on the psychology of love, but she understood that her difficult relationship with her mother had always colored every other human interaction she'd ever had. Her mother tainted everything she said and did with underlying emotional blackmail. Everything always came with a price in Lacey's life. That shield she'd erected around her heart to keep out her mother's barbs and emotional bombs also worked to keep everyone else at bay as well. For once, Lacey needed to hear those words out loud, to make her believe what Nico felt was real. He needed to love her enough to be prepared to knock a hole through her emotional wall.

"I'm listening," she said, taking a step away from him in an effort to reconstruct her mental fortification.

"Do we really have to do this out here? Wouldn't you like to find somewhere more private?" Nico asked, casting a wary gaze around. His long hair tumbled around his face in the strong wind, and he scraped an irritated hand through it to pull it away from his forehead. He looked tired. Tired and harried. Her fingers almost went to his face, to try to wipe away the sorrow resting between his brows.

"Nope," she replied, crossing her arms. Because she wasn't budging unless he gave her a damn good reason. She was already on the ferry. Unless he had something extraordinary to say to her, she was on her way home. A few people were turning curious gazes toward them.

"Fine." He took her elbow and drew her a little aside, closer to the metal wall of the main cabin and away from the bulk of the crowd. She allowed him to move her, but only because more people were flooding onto the main deck and they were jostling her for a position. She waited for him to speak.

"Charles told me you turned down the job offer," he said quietly.

"Yes, I did," she admitted, not meeting his gaze, staring out over the heads of the crowd toward the busy docks instead. It'd been a hard choice to make, but she knew she couldn't stay in Tasmania if Nico was here. Chief Inspector Shadbolt had been surprised by her decision, saying that if she ever changed her mind to come back and see him. But Nico didn't need to know that.

"I want you to stay." Her traitorous heart leapt at his words. "I want you to take the job at Burnie Police Station. I think you'd be great, and Burnie would be lucky to have you," he continued, taking a step closer. Her heart flopped over in her chest, feeling like a lead weight had settled there instead.

"Thank you, Nico," she replied as politely as she could. But she didn't want him to want her to stay for the job. Just because he felt guilty that he was the one driving her away from a perfectly good career. She couldn't stay and work with him in the same office every day if she knew her love wasn't returned. She needed more. And it seemed Nico wasn't ready, or wasn't prepared to give more. "But that's not enough."

He almost looked like he was in physical pain. His indigo eyes were dark and stormy when they finally locked with hers.

"Don't go, Lacey."

"We've already been over this," she sighed. She had a sleeper cabin booked for the trip across the Bass Strait and she was suddenly exhausted. The ferry sounded its horn, a sign it was about to leave. Nico needed to go if he didn't want to end up in Melbourne.

"I've been an idiot." He took her hands in his. They were cold, and she had a sudden urge to tuck them between hers to warm them up. To pull him in close and wrap her arms around his waist, just to feel his heartbeat beneath her cheek one last time. Because this was goodbye. She knew it now.

* * *

"It's okay." She stood on tiptoe to kiss Nico on the mouth. Such a sweet, gentle kiss. Full of forgiveness... And goodbye.

If his heart rate hadn't been skyrocketing before, it was now. The touch of her lips on his was all he'd been yearning for. The past three days had been absolute hell, hoping and praying she'd return his calls, turning up to work like nothing was wrong, pretending everything was okay to everybody who asked. He'd even fooled Sally-Ann. When inside he was a complete and utter mess, unable to function normally, because all he could think about was Lacey. If Charles hadn't told him that Lacey had been in to see him that morning and was planning to leave today, he'd still be sitting like a dozy dumbass in his office wondering when she was going to call him back. He'd run all the way up the docks and had to show his police badge to get up the gangway, then sprinted up the steps, searching every level of this damnable ferry to find her. He couldn't believe she was about to sail away forever and he nearly hadn't made it in time. He just wished they could go somewhere a little more private to have this conversation. But if she wouldn't budge, then he'd have to say it here, right in front of the whole goddamn world.

"I've been an idiot," he said again, drawing her nearer as some asshole jostled past them.

"I get it, Nico. I get why you can't love me. I'm broken. But that's okay."

What was she saying? That wasn't it, at all. That wasn't what he'd come to say. Corralling his thoughts, he bent his knees until his eyes were level with hers. Until she was looking at him. Really looking at him. She wasn't the problem; he was.

"No. You've got it wrong. I should've told you how I felt. But I let you walk away because I was afraid. You might think you're broken, but I'm the one who needs rescuing." He could deal with her problems; it was his own demons he was too scared to tackle.

"Why do you need rescuing?" she asked, suddenly going very still. "I'm not sure what you're trying to say."

There were so many reasons he wasn't worthy. But he needed to focus, tell it in a way that she'd understand. "I wasn't sure I knew what love was," he said, keeping his gaze locked on hers. Someone pushed past his shoulder, but he barely felt it. All that was important was right in front of him. He had to get Lacey to believe in him. "I had a difficult childhood, as you know. And I've never really let myself fall before. In love, that is. It's all been too hard. Like my heart wasn't built for love."

Lacey shook her head and opened her mouth as if to disagree, but he barreled on. He needed to get this out.

"When you walked out my front door the other day, I didn't understand what I felt for you. But these past three days, I now know I can't live without you."

"That's not the same—" she began to say gently, but he cut her off. It wasn't the same as being in love. Yes, he knew that. But he had more to tell her.

"It's so much more than that. We have a deep connection. I've never had such a strong connection, not with anyone else. I trust you implicitly. I love how we can just talk, how we understand what each other is thinking. I love your sharp mind, the way you instinctively drive right to the heart of a problem. And I would actively choose you to be with over anyone else in my life. I also never thought sex could be so satisfying, but at the same time so intense, like I might explode every time I touch you. I think about making love to you every minute of the day, but this is so much more than lust. And this all adds up to one thing." He took a deep breath. "I can say it now. In front of all these people. I love you."

"You do?" Lacey narrowed her eyes at him, seemingly unsure. She probably had every right to be dubious, after the way he'd treated her. But he meant every word. How did he convince her? Did she see it as too little, too late?

There was only one thing for it. Go big or go home.

He stepped back, dropping her hands and waving his own in the air. "Hello," he shouted at the crowd, using his loud, detective, authoritarian voice. "Hello, everyone, can I get your attention for a second." A few people at the front of the crowd turned around and eyed him curiously.

Oh, God, this was about the most painful thing he could ever do. He was a very private person and this was so far out of his comfort zone; he could be on Mars right now. Would Lacey appreciate exactly what he was doing?

"I just want to declare publicly, in front of everybody here, that…" More people turned around and their chatter died down as they listened to him. He drew a deep breath and took Lacey's hands again. She'd shrunk away from him when he'd started yelling, but now she had no choice but to look up into his face. "That I am in love with this stunning woman. I want you all to bear witness to how much I love her. And please help me to convince her to stay. Will you stay with me?" he asked, shifting his gaze from the audience to her. He stared down at her, willing her to answer, instead of gaping at him like a stranded fish.

A hush fell over the crowd as they waited for her answer along with him. It was only then that he wondered if this was perhaps the wrong way to go about it. Would she hate him for making her the center of attention? Would she turn him down anyway?

Lacey glanced nervously at the people by the railing, then licked her lips.

"C'mon, luv, give him an answer," a middle-aged man with a blue knit cap called out from the back of the crowd.

After frowning at the man in the knit cap, she pursed her lips and said, "I am going to see my family in Melbourne. I promised them I'd be there."

"So, you're still leaving then?" Nico's heart felt heavy, full of a million regrets. He'd failed to convince her.

"Yes. A promise is a promise," she said, but there was a strange twinkle in her eye. "But I guess they can wait a day or so, while I sort out my love life." A wicked grin lit up her face, that carefree grin he'd come to love so much.

He barely dared to ask. "Is that a yes? Does that mean you're staying?"

She nodded, and there were whoops of glee from a couple of ladies standing nearby. He picked her up and kissed her so deep and so long the rest of the crowd began to whistle and clap, saying things like, "Get a room, will ya?"

Putting her back on her feet, he steadied her as people flowed around them, heading inside out of the wind as the ship's horn sounded again.

"Oh, shit. We need to get off the boat," she said, half laughing, half in a panic.

"I think we're too late," Nico said, moving over to the railing and glancing down to where the dockworkers were casting off the lines.

"Looks like you might be coming to Melbourne with me," she giggled.

And that was okay with him. There was no other place he'd rather be than with her.

"I have a private cabin," she added, with a hint of a wicked grin, snuggling under his arm to stay warm as they watched the boat move purposely out to sea.

"Hmm." He turned her, so she was nestled against him, his body blocking most of the wind. "I think we should go and check that cabin out right now."

Pink scars were still visible on parts of her face, her jacket rolled up to reveal the cast still on her arm, a reminder of the trauma she'd endured. That they'd both endured.

"I love you, Lacey Carmichael. And I don't care who hears me."

"I love you, too. And I don't care who hears me either."

He kissed her then, with his back to the railing, the wind beating at his shoulders, and he was the happiest man alive.

CHAPTER TWENTY-FIVE

ONE MONTH LATER

Nico ended the call and put his cell phone on the kitchen table, then sat back in the chair, sipping his mug of coffee. It was Saturday, and he and Lacey had the whole afternoon to themselves, a certain kind of luxury in itself. Speak of the devil; he heard her footsteps coming down the hallway as she returned from the bathroom, followed by the ticktack of Smudge's claws on the wooden floor. That dog had become her shadow. And Nico didn't begrudge him one bit.

"It feels so good," Lacey practically sang the words as she appeared through the doorway, waving her arm in the air. "That thing was so itchy. You don't understand the pure bliss of being able to scratch an itch until you can't do it anymore."

He laughed and let his gaze follow her slender form across the room. They'd just returned from a trip into the new GP's office, where Gabe's replacement, Dr. Yvonne Marshall, had finally given Lacey the okay to have her cast removed. Yvonne was middle-aged, with two teenage girls and she'd been looking to take up a country practice just like this one. Nico thought she'd fit in well with the Burnie community, especially when she was prepared to open her surgery on

Saturday mornings. In part it was to help reduce the backlog of patients Gabriel had left behind. But it was also because Yvonne valued a holistic approach to medicine and had spent many minutes talking to Lacey about how she was coping with her mental scars, as well as her physical ones. Which meant she needed longer appointments and more time to fit everyone into her schedule. One thing Nico hoped was true about Dr. Marshall, was that she was a normal, wholesome mother, who had a great career as the new doctor in town and had absolutely no murderous intents. One psycho killer doctor in their town was more than enough.

Lacey had been ecstatic about having the cast removed, telling him all the way home in the Jeep how good it felt. She'd even said she felt so good she might be able to face a phone call to her parents tonight. This would be the first time she'd talked to them since she visited them a month ago. Nico had gone with her to Melbourne; he hadn't had any choice after he got stuck on the ferry. But the trip over, cocooned in Lacey's private cabin, had given them the time they needed to regroup; time for him to prove over and over again how much he loved her.

Lacey had decided to confront her family on her own, so Nico had stayed the night in a hotel, worrying about her the whole time as he paced back and forth, not even noticing the pretty lights of Melbourne CBD out his window. Lacey told him that she'd sat them all down, Barry, Elora, Matt, her brother, and Sammy, their younger sister, and told them all some hard truths about her PTSD and how badly it'd affected her. None of the family really understood what PTSD looked like, and so they were shocked to hear how dramatically her mental state had been impacted. Both her siblings had vowed to come and visit, to reconnect and rebuild their rocky relationships. The mother, on the other hand, had a different reaction. A steely aloofness, as if she were immune to Lacey's pain.

Then, Lacey had put in place some much-needed boundaries between herself and her mother. For once, it seemed that Elora didn't have much to say, apart from coldly stating that Lacey was no longer welcome at their family home. Nico was so proud of Lacey. That took a shitload of courage to let your family in on your fears, see the demons that lurked below the surface. But also to state what she needed and wanted from them, so she could get on with her life. Nico wasn't sure he'd be able to do it, especially not with a mother like Elora, whose only thought was about herself and her own comfort.

Nico had been shocked to find out Lacey's family was rich. Multi-millionaires, in fact. And Lacey had her own trust account on which she could retire comfortably tomorrow. But he was also proud to learn that she wanted to survive on her own. Not rely on her family money. There was a complicated tangle of emotions and beliefs all tied up with her family money that Nico had yet to explore. It seemed Lacey was almost ashamed of her wealth, wanted to leave her affluence behind, and live a simple, grateful life. Because money had never made her happy before. And he agreed with her.

They'd returned to Devonport on the next overnight ferry and both agreed that Lacey should move in with Nico. There was no reason not to; she'd been living with him anyway. And he hadn't regretted a single moment of having her there. Not now, not ever.

"I'll be able to do all sorts of things now that I couldn't do before, without the cast." She gave him a seductive sideways glance. "All sorts of things," she repeated with a sly grin.

"Great. Shall we go and explore those things right now?" Nico half stood, ready to take her up on her offer.

She laughed and came over to kiss him. He grabbed her by the waist, enjoying the fact that he could touch her whenever he wanted.

"Yes, we can," she said when he finally let her up for air. "But can I have a cup of coffee first? I'm parched."

"Sure." He sat down, feigning nonchalance, but had to readjust the uncomfortable bulge in his pants. The mere idea of having sex with Lacey set him aflame with desire every single time.

"I just got a call from the Strahan office while you were in the bathroom," he said as a means to distract himself from the way her ass looked so inviting in those jeans as she leaned across the countertop to grab a mug. "They finally found Floyd Hamilton's car." The little, white sedan belonging to Floyd had been found dumped and burnt out by a hiker on a trail leading out of Strahan early this morning.

"Where?" Lacey lifted her thoughtful, amber gaze from the coffee machine.

"Near Hogarth Falls." It was a well-frequented area close to the small town of Strahan, but the car had been driven a long way down a fire trail and hidden behind a large stand of King Billy Pines.

"Well, at least that answers that question." Lacey shrugged and turned to fill her coffee mug. It was one of the many pieces of the puzzle Nico was still trying to piece together about Gabriel's final days before they captured him. It was Floyd's car that he'd seen up in the lookout parking lot. The same car Gabriel had used to flee the scene, even as Nico watched Lacey's Kombi van fly over the cliff top. It seemed that after Gabe had found out about Floyd's stalking of Rania —possibly from Lacey's slip of the tongue after Sunday lunch —he decided to use the young man as a decoy. He'd somehow convinced the young mechanic to drive up and meet him at the lookout—Nico was still figuring out exactly what enticement Gabe had used; Gabe still refused to cooperate with police—and then drugged him and left him tied up in the trunk overnight. Planning to return with Lacey and the Kombi the next day.

Nico still couldn't believe he'd sat and had lunch with a murderer. Gabe must've waved them goodbye that Sunday afternoon after feeding them his roast lamb, then come up with this scheme as soon as they left. Contacted Floyd somehow—they could find no phone records between the two, so perhaps Gabe had spoken to him in person—and then jumped in his car and driven to the lookout to meet him. Then driven straight back and spent the rest of the night plotting the best way to abduct Lacey.

Gabe hadn't realized Lacey had survived the fall. And so when they'd first brought him in, he'd acted all sad and sorrowful that Lacey was dead. He'd concocted some bullshit story that he'd tried to stop the van from going over the edge. But Floyd had gone crazy and decided to take himself out in a blaze of glory, taking Lacey with him as a final fuck-you to Nico and the rest of the cops. Gabe had been in the passenger seat, trying to talk Floyd out of it, but decided to jump out when it became clear the young man wasn't listening. Gabe said he'd jumped in Floyd's car and driven away because he was terrified that he'd be implicated in the whole thing. And his fears had come true. Look at how the police were all pointing the finger at him. It was an ingenious story. But it'd never stand up in court. Gabe must know that. Nico wished Gabriel would finally admit defeat and confess. Confess not only to Floyd's murder and Lacey's attempted murder, but to killing Rania as well. Then her family might finally get some closure.

As it was, Nico was sure Gabe had stabbed Rania. They had Rania's journals as proof she'd seen him and Jayden together, which gave him motive. Nico had also gone over everything they knew about Rania's case with a fine-toothed comb and had found a clue in the coroner's report on Rania's death that he'd missed the first time around. Of the three drugs found in Rania's system, the coroner had commented on the use of adrenaline by the doctor. He said that adrenaline could be used in some cases to stimulate an increase in blood pressure, but recent research showed it should no longer be used in emergency cases, as this was documented to result in severe hypotension or lower blood pressure, the exact opposite result a doctor was looking for. Had Gabe known this and purposefully overdosed her on adrenaline? So instead of trying to save her, he was trying to finish the job he'd started? Nico had berated himself for not reading the report more carefully, relying on Tyrell to pass on the findings instead. But without a confession, this clue wasn't enough to convict Gabe, and they were still digging for that final bit of evidence that'd tie him unequivocally to the murder. Even though Nico was sure Gabe was responsible for Rania's murder, the specter of the Hobart serial killer still hung over the station. Some of his team were still clinging to the theory that while Gabe was responsible for Floyd's murder and Lacey's kidnapping, maybe Rania had been murdered by this mysterious killer.

Nico thought back to when the district commander had first told them about the serial killer all those weeks ago, and how he wished he could be the primary on the case, how it'd make his career if he ever caught one. Now, he wasn't so sure. He no longer needed the glory of bringing down a serial killer. Actually, it was almost the opposite. With Lacey in his life now, all he wanted was a happy existence and a solid career. One he could be proud of. But to have a serial killer in their midst would put them all in danger. A danger he could happily live without.

At least Karim was free now. He'd returned to Hobart with his family, a broken man, still searching for answers. Nico found it hard to feel sorry for Karim. He was still using cocaine—Nico had confirmed that through his connections in the drug trade. And he still couldn't forgive him for turning up at his door that night, trying to get to Lacey.

He looked up just as she brought her coffee over and planted herself in his lap, and he put away all thoughts of Karim and the sad possibilities of the wrong paths the Syrian man was sure to take from now on.

"Are you ready for Monday?" he asked, nibbling gently at her ear.

"Ready as I'll ever be," she replied, placing her mug on the table and swiveling on his lap so she straddled him. "I'm not scared, if that's what you're asking."

"Scared? You?" He made a grunting sound and kissed the tip of her nose.

Lacey was due to start her job in the force as a first class constable with the Burnie police on Monday, and he couldn't be prouder. She would start by walking the beat, just like all the other junior constables. Nico hadn't decided how he might be affected by seeing her at work every day yet. Trying not to treat her any differently to the other young cops.

But then again, everyone would know she was different. Know she was special to him. They'd just have to deal with it, he decided. Because Lacey was special.

"I hope you've been keeping those judo skills up to par," he joked.

"Oh, don't worry, I could still take you down any day of the week." She raised a playful eyebrow and ran a finger down his chest, tracing the ridges of his abs, and stopping to wander over his belt buckle. Slowly undoing the button of his trousers.

He smiled. Yes, she probably could. His tough little Amazon didn't let anything daunt her.

His computer dinged, and Nico leaned around Lacey, meaning to turn it off. But the name at the top of the email caught his eyes. It was an email from Patrick McTernan, the private investigator. He'd almost forgotten he'd hired this guy in all the clusterfuck of a mess they'd endured. After Lacey had been hurt and having to wrap up a murder investigation, he'd put it on the back burner.

"Do you mind if I just open this?" he asked as she continued to fumble with his belt buckle. She must've caught his sudden somber mood, because she bit her lip, then stepped up off his lap.

He opened the email and began reading.

"Fuck," Nico said softly. This wasn't the news he'd been hoping to receive.

"What?" Lacey looked up from where she was washing out their two mugs.

"Oh, fuck." Nico stopped reading and put his head in his hands.

"What is it?" Lacey came over, putting a hand on his shoulder.

"It's from the investigator I hired to look into my father's disappearance." He gestured at the computer screen.

"Yes. And?"

"He seems to think…" Nico looked up and began reading the email until he found the bit he wanted. "There is merit in the theory my father is still alive."

"Oh, wow." Lacey covered her mouth with her hand, beautiful amber eyes going wide.

"Here, read it for yourself." Nico pushed the computer over and stood, nearly knocking the chair over in his haste. He didn't need to read the words; they were burned into his memory like a brand. Pacing across the kitchen, he stopped at the window to stare out at the orchard beyond. Smudge seemed to catch his mood and pushed his wet nose into Nico's hand. He let his hand rest on the dog's head.

"It says that a man matching your father's description, but

going by the name of Reginald Smith, was living in Lorne for the past ten years," Lacey read out, the shock clear in her voice. "He's attached the photo Marco took. Have you seen it?" She leaned in to study the photo.

"Mmm? Yes," Nico confirmed. But he was only half listening. It was too much to take in. The man in the photo could definitely be his father. An older, slightly softer version, rounder at the edges. But it still sent chills down his spine.

"It also says the man caught the ferry to Tasmania two years ago. But that's where the trail goes cold."

And that was the scariest part of all. Not only was his father possibly still alive, but he might well be living on the same little island in the Indian Ocean as Nico. Was that merely a coincidence?

"Do you believe this guy?" Lacey stood and came over to Nico. "I mean, this could all be a big pile of horseshit." She wrapped her arms around his waist and laid her chin on his shoulder.

"I don't know," he replied. "It's certainly unsettling news. And I won't be telling my family any of this. Not yet. I intend to investigate this further myself." He certainly wouldn't show his mother that photo. It was like looking at a walking ghost, and it'd send her into a hysterical panic, he was sure. Catarina had phoned him several times in the past month to ask if he had news about his father, but he'd fobbed her off saying he hadn't heard anything, and he still firmly believed Serge was dead. Now what was he going to tell her?

"Okay. If you think that's best," Lacey agreed with him, but he could hear the uncertainty in her tone. He didn't care. He wasn't going to believe a damn word of McTernan's report until he'd thoroughly investigated it himself. The man went on to report there'd been no autopsy of the body in the car after the crash, and hence no definitive DNA evidence to prove it was Serge. Nico would investigate that claim as well.

Maybe he could get the body exhumed and have it tested... No, that was getting ahead of himself. Damn. Damn, double damn.

The last thing he needed now was the phantom of his dead father to come back and haunt him. He had everything he wanted. A great career, a comfy cottage to live in along some of the most glorious coastline in the world, and an amazing woman by his side.

Drawing in a deep, cleansing breath, he turned to kiss Lacey deeply, banishing the image of his father. He had much more important things to think about, and getting Lacey undressed and into his bed was top of his agenda right now. It was time to love his amazing woman. Everything else could wait.

Also by Suzanne Cass
NEW
Dark Tides Series
Mystery and Romance collide.
Into the Rain
Rain Washed

Stormcloud Station Series
(A Stargazer Spinoff Series)
Small Town Romantic Suspense
Clear Skies
Starlit Skies
Crystal Skies
Dawn Skies
Tangled Skies
Outback Skies

Stargazer Ranch Romance Series
Small Town Romantic Suspense
Combustion: Prequel Novella
Wildfire
Firelight
Snowbound: Christmas Novella
Snowfall
Cloudburst
Silverstorm

Island Bound Series
Mystery Romance (on an Island)
Books can be read as stand-alone
Bound by Truth
Bound by Silence
Bound by the Stars

Colors of the Earth Series
Small Town Romantic Suspense

Books can be read as stand-alone
Shadows in the Dust
Shadows in Deep Blue
Shadows of Red Earth

Romantic Suspense
Single Title
Island Redemption
Glass Clouds
Chasing Bullets

Love in the Mountains Novella Series
Small Town Short Romance
Novellas can be read as stand-alone
Rain on a Tin Roof
Lost and Found
Rescue his Heart

Please Leave a Review

The greatest gift you could ever give an author is to leave a review. You will be helping other people to discover this book and making a difference to me as an Independently Published Author. If you liked this book and want other people to read it too, please leave a review.

About the Author

Suzanne Cass is an Australian author who writes rural romance and romantic suspense abounding with passion and danger.

Her debut novel, Island Redemption, won the Romance Writers of Australia Emerald Award in 2016. Suzanne was also a finalist in the 2019 Romance Writers of Australia RUBY award.

She had always had a fascination with the tough resilience of people who live in our amazing red-dirt outback country. When not writing about the characters that inhabit her head, Suzanne can be found roaming the Perth beaches with her border collie, or encouraging from the sidelines as her two sons play sport.

Visit her website www.suzannecass.com or subscribe to her newsletter via: www.suzannecass.com/contact

Or you can stay in touch via my website
www.suzannecass.com

Facebook: www.facebook.com/suzannecassauthor/
Instagram: www.instagram.com/suzanne.cass/
Pintrest: www.pinterest.com.au/suzanne_cass/

Acknowledgements

A new series is always both exciting and nerve-wracking to write. And mysteries are especially tricky. I set this series in Tasmania because it's an extremely wild and extremely beautiful place, and I hope it stays that way for eons to come. Most of the places I've written about in this book do exist. But some of the places I have made up to suit my story. For example, the lookout near Cradle Mountain where Dotti is sent crashing over the edge doesn't exist except in my imagination.

Lacey has a difficult relationship with her mother, which shapes her whole personality through later life, and it even effects her connection with Nico. I spent a lot of time reading about people with narcissistic personality disorder and I think we may all know someone in our lives who is like this. And Nico has an emotionally absent father to deal with, an obstacle that also forms his views on life and love. Two complex characters who need each other to become a whole again.

There is a team of people who I couldn't do this without, beta readers (big thanks to Rebecca, Jennifer, and Ceara for their amazing feedback) and my ARC team, who are essential to an Indie Author like me, for their wonderful reviews. Big thanks to my editor, Nicole at Evermore Editing

To Gary, who doesn't read romance, but nevertheless is my greatest ambassador, and my two sons who are the light of my life.

And to you, the readers, it sounds so trite, but thank you for reading my books. I wish I could reach out and hug you all personally. You are the reason I keep writing.